D0937467

Matters of the Heart

A

Creole Love

Story

By
Mary M. Culver

East Baton Rouge Parish Library
Baton Rouge, Louisiana

This book is a work of fiction. All incidents and dialogue, and all characters, with the exception of some well-known historical figures, are products of the author's imagination, and are not to be construed as real. Where real-life historical figures appear, or battles and other historical incidents are portrayed, historical sources have been used for background, but the actual historical characters and historical events are shown in fictional form. In all other respects, any resemblance to persons living or dead is entirely coincidental, and errors in the portrayal of historical characters or historical events, are entirely the fault of the author.

Cover art by Anne Chase, book design by Molly Ebert

Published by Margaret Media, Inc.
Copyright © Mary M. Culver 2008

ISBN 978-0-9616377-8-1

All rights reserved. No part of this book may be reproduced or transmitted in any form or by any means—graphic, electronic or mechanical, including photo copying, recording, taping of information on storage and retrieval systems—without permission in writing from the publisher.

Printed in the United States of America
  by Sheridan Books, Chelsea, Michigan

Library of Congress Control Number 2008920903

Margaret Media, Inc.
618 Mississippi Street
Donaldsonville, LA 70346
(225) 473-9319

www.margaretmedia.com

Dedication

*To the Crescent City, may it revive as it has before,
and its unique blend of cultures vibrate again.*

Glossary: For readers unfamiliar with French terms, a short glossary
can be found at the end of the text.

Emile de Marigny stood stock-still in the middle of the dance floor, almost unaware of the couples swirling around him, the music barely penetrating to him. As the music came to a stop, he took up the slender fingers extended to him, and bent to kiss them. He bowed and then his eyes rose to meet hers.

He had watched her slender, lithe figure as she circled the dance floor in the arms of an elegantly dressed white man. It was a waltz, and he admired how easily, how smoothly she moved to the music. She was dressed in an ivory gown, which set off her own luminous ivory skin, and her shiny dark hair was piled high on her head, with just a few long curls allowed to fall beside her cheeks. As the music ended, her partner bowed to her, and tactfully withdrew, leaving her hand in hand with her latest admirer.

"You are... Nana,... aren't you?" he asked, still in a state of near shock, the words tumbling out awkwardly.

"Yes, Monsieur, but how do I know you? And why are you frozen comme ça,... in the middle of the dance floor?" Her beautiful dark eyes opened wide, as she smiled at him. He was a handsome young man, but his dark, wavy hair was standing almost on end, until he caught her glance and ran his hands through it, restoring it to some order. His dark eyes, almost black, were wide open as he looked at her, and from his accented English, she knew he must be a French Creole. His elegant evening clothes indicated he could afford the best.

"When I last saw you, my friend and I wondered if you would live," Emile answered. "I held you in my arms, but you were unconscious. Do you remember anything from the night of the fire?"

"No, but my mama told me the story. I have wondered these last weeks, as I recovered, if I would ever know the name of the man who saved me, who risked his own life in the fire to save mine. Do I have the honor of meeting that man tonight, or perhaps you know him? I'd like to know his name, so I can pray for him, and if possible I'd like to thank him in person."

Her voice was soft and melodious, so soft it was difficult to hear over the music again swirling around them. Emile was glad of an excuse to lean closer.

"Yes, Mademoiselle, I am that man, Emile de Marigny, and now, instead of standing here foolishly in the middle of this dance floor, may I ask you for a dance?"

He spoke awkwardly, but didn't seem to mind poking a little humor at himself, and as he smiled, she laughed softly in return. She already liked the frank honesty of this young man, who didn't seem to mind making fun even of himself.

Emile had not let go of her hand, and now he drew it closer, and his other arm reached around her small waist. He was sure she would assent, but he didn't want to take a chance. He wanted this dance more than anything else in the world. Still he made no effort to begin dancing; cocking his head a little, he smiled and waited for her consent.

Her eyes were dark, magical pools, and they shone at him with warmth and gratitude. Her face was beautiful in an exotic way, with very high cheekbones, and eyelids which seemed to curve in an oriental way.

"But of course, Monsieur Emile, not just one dance, but as many as you like would not be too many in exchange for a life saved.... A thousand or more dances, if you wish." And so they began that first dance together. Emile wasn't quite sure if she was teasing him or not, but he was sure he would collect all the dances she promised and perhaps much more. He realized he was smitten already, and his mind was churning with possibilities.

"Tonight, and many more nights, Monsieur, I will be here waiting for you to claim your dances," she offered, with a dazzling smile, which seemed to radiate to every nerve in his body. He felt like he was melting away.

Emile had remembered her from that night, but her eyes had been closed then, her long dark lashes alone had shown, but now he felt the full force of those beautiful, big, dark eyes upon him, and although he was a good dancer, especially proud of his ability to dance in fact, he suddenly felt as clumsy at dancing as he felt in trying to talk to this beauty. He took a few quick, short breaths, and began to feel more in control of himself. Still it was a shock. He had rescued the most strikingly beautiful girl in the whole ballroom, perhaps the most gorgeous woman he had ever laid eyes on in his entire life. A thousand dances, she said he could have! And before they took their first steps together, he knew he would be back to dance with her again, and again.

That night they danced together as long as the music continued. Conversation didn't seem necessary, their bodies moved to the music in a natural harmony. Emile felt as if he had been lifted to another plane of life, of pleasure,... and as he studied her face, he was sure she felt the same way. What was there to say? The music alone gave their bodies a chance to communicate on a deeper level. Spoken pleasantries would not add to what they were feeling. Later there would be time for conversation.

Time passed, but they were unaware of it, only aware of the sudden, and almost overwhelming sense of attraction, of magic flowing between them, perhaps so powerful since they both realized that her life was a part of their unspoken transaction; that because he had rescued her, this relationship had somehow started differently from all others.

The music stopped, and suddenly Emile remembered.

"Please come with me, I do want to claim all the dances you will give me, but tonight I came with a friend, and I have simply forgotten all about him! Come, let's get some punch, and find my friend before the next dance starts," and lifting her hand up to his lips again, he kissed it, then still holding on, he steered a way for them around the dance floor. Finally he saw John, heading for the punch bowl.

"Ah, there you are! Guess who I found?" Emile said, drawing Nana up closer. "This is the very same young lady whom I carried out of the burning building! Remember?"

"Yes, indeed. Mademoiselle, it is certainly good to see you with your eyes open, and so well recovered. We worried about you," John said, bowing to her. "Do I remember your mother calling you Nana?"

Emile looked nonplussed, and then burst out laughing. "I can't believe I forgot to ask your name. I know it's Nana, but Nana what exactly?"

All three of them laughed. "We didn't seem to have time for formalities yet, just for dancing! Yes, I am Nana, Nana de Lis, and I know Monsieur Emile's full name, but what is the name of your friend?"

Emile hurried to answer before John could. Somehow he didn't want to lose the initiative.

"He is John Morgan, and he's from New York City. This is his first trip to New Orleans. He was my roommate at West Point. We just graduated, and wanted to celebrate, so I invited him to come home with me, and get acquainted with New Orleans," Emile explained, but as the music started again, he smiled at Nana, and in a low voice meant only for her to hear, he added,

"But Nana, you don't need to remember his name, just remember mine!" They smiled at each other, and he drew her back onto the dance floor, holding her tightly to him.

She laughed softly. "You didn't even give me a chance to be courteous and ask him how he likes it here."

"That's true," Emile admitted, smiling triumphantly at her. "And so I'll answer for him, he *likes* it here!" Nana laughed, throwing her head back, revealing her beautiful swan neck, and letting her long curls tumble around her shoulders. And Emile smiled, and swung her as far across the room from John as he could. Out of the corner of his eye he could see John, still standing where they had left him, with a puzzled look on his face. Catching Emile's glance in his direction, he burst out laughing, and raised his glass of punch in a silent toast.

"I want to thank you for the beautiful lilies you sent to me at the hospital. It was you, wasn't it? And was it you who paid my hospital bill? That's what the sister told me," Nana asked softly.

"Yes, I confess to both charges, but I didn't know then that lilies were especially appropriate, because of your last name, de Lis - of the lilies," Emile replied.

"Lilies, especially the big white Easter lilies, they are my favorites, and roses too, especially yellow roses," she added.

"I'll have to remember that," he said, smiling at the thought of sending whole carriage loads of lilies and yellow roses to her.... Perhaps a carriage full of lilies one day, and another the next day, filled to the roof with yellow roses.

When the final dance ended, Emile asked, "May I come back and claim some more of my thousand dances at the next ball?"

"Mais oui, Monsieur Emile. I will save all my dances for you, if you wish."

"If I *wish*? Oh yes, that *is* a magical wish, and I do want *all* of them,... *every last one*!" he said firmly. "And how long must I have to wait for the next dance?"

"I will be here for Saturday's ball. That is only three days from now," she answered, her dark eyes sparkling as she laughed softly at him. "You are funny! So do you think you can wait until then, Monsieur?"

"Barely, it will be très difficile, but somehow I will survive,... on hope and anticipation! And please, since you acknowledge that I saved your life, can we forget the formalities? I would like you to call me Emile," he begged.

"Oh yes, pardon, I can begin that right away, Emile," she said. "But now I must go, my mother is waiting to escort me home. A bientôt, Emile."

Emile once again took that beautiful hand in his, and kissed it. "Au revoir," he said softly and with meaning, taking one last long look into those gorgeous dark eyes, before she was gone. He fully intended there to be more meetings between them, many more....

As they downed another cup of punch, John grinned at Emile. "I say, it looks like you saved her life, but lost your heart! Am I right?"

"Well, I would like to come back for the next dance this Saturday, and I admit I am bewitched. She is not only beautiful, but there seems to be much more to her. Already I think she could become important in my life....

"Now, John, are you ready to call it a night and head home, or would you rather spend a few hours at Madame Lucinda's Maison Bleu?"

Silently Emile was hoping that John would settle for a ride home, he had found the evening so perfect, he didn't want to lower the tone with the girls at Madame Lucinda's. Other nights, before this one, he would have willingly gone, but not tonight.

Perhaps sensing his friend's mood, John was willing to forego Maison Bleu's pleasures, so Emile whistled for Washington, who brought up the carriage from where he had been waiting half a block away.

The moon, a sliver of silver, traced thin crystalline patterns on the river's black surface, and flung slender shafts between the boughs of the live oaks which lined the drive, as they turned into Marengo. The Big House stood boldly drawn in the moonlight, its great white columns majestically surrounding the house, protective of all within it. But as Emile looked at his beloved Marengo, he realized the spell was broken; he knew with absolute certainty that he could not bring Nana here, to his home. But still he could see her, the magic could continue somehow, but in another, different world....

As Emile opened the door to the garçonnière, he said, "John, remember, we don't have to leap out of bed to any bugle calls tomorrow! Our summer has begun, so sleep as late as you like! And when we men sleep out here in our own separate tower, we don't have to worry about disturbing others, either when we come in late, or when we sleep late!"

"I guess there are some real advantages in having these exclusive quarters! Have a good night, Emile!" came the sleepy response.

Leaving John to take the bed on the first floor of the garçonnière, Emile slowly climbed up the narrow stairs to the second floor bedroom, and was in bed in mere moments. From the window he could still see that slender moon, and he could hear a whippoorwill call, and another answer, like a distant echo. He realized there would be limits upon his new relationship, but he knew he had found love for the first time, and he was not about to let go.... He would find a way, as many other men had done before him,... a world of love,... another world, a different world, one which could never be a part of his Marengo

*   *   *

It was nearly noon the next day when the two young men emerged from their garçonnière. Entering the dining room just in time for the midday meal, they found the black eyes of Monsieur Louis directed at both of them, with a glare. His wife, Madame Blanche, raised her face, turning her cheek to receive her son's morning kiss, and then extending a hand for his friend's more formal greeting - a kiss of the hand.

"Bonjour Mama, Papa, we are a little slow this morning, after a pleasant night in the city," Emile offered by way of explanation.

"Was the dinner dance nice?" his mother asked, pouring out two cups of coffee for them.

"Yes, very enjoyable," John answered, glancing significantly over his coffee cup at Emile, and deferring to him on whether he wished to bring up the rest of the evening.

"Pleasant, Mama, but the night was still young when we had escorted the young ladies and their chaperones home, so I took John on to another dance, and now we both know that the young woman and her mother, whom John and I rescued from the fire three weeks ago, have recovered. The young lady was at the dance last night, and John and I both recognized her. You may remember, we told you that the daughter was still unconscious when we took the two of them to Charity Hospital, so we wondered if she had lived. She has made a good recovery, and when we introduced ourselves, and told her where we had met before, she was quick to thank us for saving her life."

"That's good news. I have been praying for her ever since you told me the story of her rescue," Madame Blanche said. "Our laundresses did tell me that some of your clothes from that night are unsalvageable. They did the best they could, and managed to save some of them. But saving lives, well there is no comparison with the rescue of your clothes, so we forgive you! I'm just thankful that you both were unhurt, and no lives were lost."

"And that soot in my carriage, Washington has been able to scrub it out, so I don't have to replace the fine, new upholstery I had just put in it," Monsieur Louis muttered, then holding up a section of newspaper, he added,

"You gentlemen have been out so much lately that I don't recall if I showed you the *Picayune's* report on that fire. Somehow they did manage to get your names, and give you credit for the rescue. It's unconscionable that the firemen couldn't get there sooner! They said that when they started to the fire that night, they discovered that the new fire wagons they bought recently were too big to make it through some of the narrow streets, and they had to detour. They explained that's what caused the delay. I saved this clipping from the paper, so you could both have a look at it," Monsieur Louis said, handing it to John, who scanned it and handed it on to Emile, who read it through carefully, and the whole scene came back to him....

They had left the dinner and dance at the St. Louis Hotel, and dropped the young ladies and their chaperones off at their homes. Neither he nor John was ready to call it a night yet, so they were considering alternatives, either a visit to Madame Lucinda's Maison Bleu to spend an hour or two with the girls, or to find a card game to gamble on at one of the Bourbon Street establishments. Suddenly they both spotted a cloud of smoke beginning to billow up not far away from where they were driving in the carriage. Not hearing any clanging that might indicate that fire wagons were on their way, they decided to hurry on, and see if they could help.

It was a small yellow creole cottage, with two front doors. They jumped from the carriage, and ran up the steps. John began pounding on one door, and soon an elderly pair ran out, dressed only in their nightclothes. Emile banged on the other door, and when he got no answer, he turned to ask the couple,

"Does anyone live in this side?"

They both nodded, and the old woman said,

"Yes, dere's a motheh an' daughteh, an' dey waz home tonight. We waz all out hieh on de porch togetheh visitin' till it got dark."

John joined Emile, and together they kicked in the door. A cloud of smoke poured out at them, and they dashed in. Flames were licking at the sofa and climbing up the curtains in the front parlor, as they dove for the bedrooms in the back.

John was the first to emerge, carrying an elderly woman, who screamed at Emile,

"Git ma daughteh! She be in dat back bedroom. Please, mista, git ma Nana outa dere!"

She tried to get away from John, but he held her firmly, "My friend will do his best to get her out," he said, as he carried the twisting, struggling woman out of the house. Even when he put her down on the banquette, he had to keep an arm on her, to prevent her from running back into the house.

"Ma Nana be in dere.... We gotta git her out,..." she sobbed.

Emile opened the other bedroom door, and smoke rushed out at him, engulfing him; and already he was coughing. He groped about, and his hand found the wooden frame of a bed. He felt along the mattress until his hands felt an inert body. Quickly he took the body in his arms and bolted through the smoke. He tried not to let the air out of his lungs, and with his eyes closed against the smoke, he felt his way down the hallway to the front door. It was only when he got to the porch, and was able to breathe again, that he looked at what he held in his arms. It was a young woman, and her filmy nightgown left little to the imagination, as Emile quickly became aware. She had a slender, beautifully proportioned body. Her breasts nestled against his chest, her long limbs rested over his arms, her head was thrown back, revealing a neck - long like a swan; and her thick, dark hair fell down in a tide over his arm. Carefully he negotiated his way down the front steps. And once he reached level ground, he was able to get an even better look at the woman in his arms.

He breathed heavily. She was the most beautiful young woman he had ever seen, but there was no time for admiration. Her eyes were closed, and he was sure she was unconscious. He turned to John.

"Here, hold her a minute so I can get in the carriage, then hand her in to me. We need to get her to the hospital right away. She seems to still have a very feeble pulse beating, I can feel it in her wrist, and her neck. But who knows how long she was in there. She could have swallowed a lot of smoke."

John held her, and Emile jumped into the carriage and held out his arms. Carefully they eased her in. Her mother was right there, trying to scramble into the carriage, screaming all the while,

"Where you takin' ma daughteh? Git her te de hospital raight now, an' I go wid you."

"John, help that woman in. She must be her mother, so we have to take her along."

John took the woman's hand, and helped her in, then got in himself.

Washington, who had been watching the entire scene, saw that everyone was in the carriage, so he lashed the reins, and the horses took off for the hospital. He was able to pull right up to the door, and a medical steward in a white coat came out to help them. He took the woman from Emile's arms, and hurried off, with the mother scurrying behind him. Emile and John went inside more slowly, and were met by a nun.

"Gentlemen were you the ones who brought in the unconscious woman just now?" she asked. "And may I have your names, in case there is any investigation later? You both should at least merit mention for your heroism when the fire is reported in the *Picayune*."

Emile bowed slightly.

"Yes, ma Soeur, we brought the young woman in. I am Emile de Marigny from Marengo Plantation, and this is my good friend John Morton, who is here from New York, visiting me.

"We were just starting home, when we saw smoke, and followed it to find a house on fire. Since there were no signs of any firemen, we ran into the house, and brought out a mother and her daughter. I want to give you some money to help with the daughter's care, and if there is any left over, please will you see that some flowers are brought to her? Lilies perhaps. She didn't regain consciousness, so we brought her here, and her mother. What are the chances she will recover?" Emile asked, pulling a wad of bills out of his pocket, and handing all of it to the nun.

"Thank God you were there to help, and, Sir, your generosity is greatly appreciated. As for the child, it's difficult to say at this point what her chances are. We will see that someone is with her all night, and as long as is needed. We will do our very best, but of course, the outcome is in the hands of God. He may wish to keep her, only He will decide that...."

"But there is no need for you to stay. You have told us all we need to know. Again thank you both for your quick action. We will hope you have saved her life. Now, if you'll excuse me, I must go and help with her care. God bless you, gentlemen, and goodnight."

Emile and John headed back to the carriage. "I guess we've done all we can. Let's hope she comes to and is all right," John said, then he started scrutinizing his friend, and he burst out laughing.

"Emile, I'm sorry, I can't help laughing. I don't know whether you look more like a raccoon or a chimney sweep! You are soot from head to toe, except where the sweat has run down your face; there you've got white patches! I guess I look almost as bad," he added, trying to brush as much of the soot from his clothing as possible.

Washington was bending over, looking in the corners under his driver's seat.

"Don' eben hava towel or any rags forh yuh all te clean up wid," he said. "Is yuh ready te go home now?"

"Yes, I don't think anyone would want to kiss either of us, or even dance with us, the way we look now. Never would know we were the same fellows who set out earlier to have some fun!"

Emile grinned, as he tried to wipe his face off with his handkerchief.

So, looking like chimney sweeps, or filthy street urchins, who didn't belong in Monsieur Louis' fine carriage with its brocade upholstered seats, they set off for Marengo.

Once safely in the garçonnière, John said, "I guess the best thing to do is just drop all our smoky, sooty clothes in a pile on the floor, huh," starting the pile with his own clothing.

"There's sure to be some hollering and complaining around here when the laundresses see this mess tomorrow," Emile said, grinning and throwing his own clothes into the pile. "But when we explain, maybe they'll start treating us like heroes!"

Emile remembered every detail of that night, and how he had seen her, seen how beautiful she really was, and how, later at the ball, he had seen those eyes open at last. He took one more look at the newspaper article. They had the story right, but there was so much more to it, he thought. Perhaps even more than he could know, himself, at this time.

But then he came back to reality. He folded the article up, and put it in his pocket. Then he turned to his father. Who knows how long he had kept him waiting for an answer. And what might he be thinking? How much had his expressions given away, he wondered.

"Oui, that's pretty much the story, Papa, exactly as it happened. And if you don't want the article back, I might like to keep it for a while. You don't want it, do you?"

"No, you can have it. I must say, usually I can't find much truth in this newspaper, in fact in any newspapers. Haven't much faith in them reporters," Monsieur Louis grumbled. "I guess they have to get a story right once in a while, this one for instance. Now they can go back to their usual lies, and insinuations."

"Will you boys be here for dinner tonight? We thought John might like to try another of our local delicacies, so Louie plans to send some of the young boys out to catch crawfish, and I thought we might have them for dinner, if you'll be eating with us," Madame said, turning to Emile for confirmation.

"Yes, I thought that today we might do a little fishing, or take a ride down the levée. We do have plans for Saturday night in the city, but not tonight," Emile replied.

So that evening, John saw a large platter of steaming crawfish arrive from the kitchen.

"If they are too hot and spicy for you, just say so, and we'll find you something else. As for how to peel them, watch this," Monsieur Louis said, as he leaned closer so John could see how he peeled a few. "Of course, to be a true New Orleanian, you must suck the juice out of the heads, so at least try it, but we won't force you to adopt that local custom," and with that Monsieur Louis uttered a loud, sucking sound as he drained the juice from the crawfish he had just pulled apart. Then he looked up at John with a broad smile of pleasure, and everyone had to laugh.

"That's how!" he said, picking up another.

"They're like miniature red lobsters," Joan commented, awkwardly working the shell off one of his, and popping the first morsel into his mouth. "Spicy, yes, but very good. And not at all like eating big Maine lobster, entirely different, because of the spices, I guess. Delicious. Thanks for introducing me to them." He tried one hesitant suck, just to please his host, and then gave that up, but he continued to peel and eat the crawfish.

The next few days Emile and John spent at the de Marigny summer home in Mandeville, sailing on Lake Ponchartrain, and fishing from the family's dock.

*   *   *

Emile cast his fishing line out, then settled back down on the dock, pulled his hat down to shield his eyes from the sun, and said,

"John, you know the Quadroon Balls, like the one we attended the other night, they're a unique tradition here in New Orleans. Men from all over the world come here to attend them, and they say that our quadroons, or mixed-race women, are some of the most beautiful in the entire world, like the loveliest Hindu women, with their big, dark eyes, their pale, café au lait skin colors, and their lush black hair. Men come specially to dance with them, and sometimes they take these women on, and provide allowances and housing for them for a while, or even for a lifetime. Here that's called plaçage."

"Yes, I did notice the other night, that as a group, the women were strikingly beautiful. But I'm not sure I understand, when you say quadroon, do you mean that they are a quarter African?"

"Well that may have been the original meaning, but most of the time now, it just refers to people of mixed race. Mulattos, quadroons, octoroons,... we tend to loosely use the term quadroon to refer to all of them, and if they are culturally French, then we sometimes consider all of them Creoles. Some die-hards like to distinguish us French Creoles from the others, and occasionally you still hear us described as the 'ancienne population,' suggesting, I guess, that we French Creoles are basically pure, and not of mixed blood. How truthful and accurate that is, I couldn't say. There's been a good deal of interbreeding, although no one really talks about it, at least not in polite society...."

"So would Nana de Lis be considered a quadroon? It would be really difficult to distinguish her from someone of Spanish descent; her coloring could well be considered Hispanic. And do you plan to return to the ball tonight to see her, Emile?"

"If there isn't anything else you have in mind, John. After all you will be returning to New York in just a few days, so we'll do whatever you like. I certainly plan to meet up with Mademoiselle de Lis, whether it's tonight, or another night, I do know that. And, yes, she is a perfect example of our quadroon beauties, with her ivory skin, big, dark eyes, and lustrous dark hair, - and her curves, so fine! But, what would you like to do tonight?"

"I can't think of anything really. You have shown me all around New Orleans, so let's plan to attend tonight's Quadroon Ball. I know you don't want to miss out on a chance to dance with your new-found beauty, especially while she still feels in your debt, and is gracious enough to give all her dances to you! I'll even promise not to cut in on you!" John grinned at Emile.

Since the fish didn't seem to be biting, the two of them soon packed up their things, and headed back to Marengo to dress for their night in the city.

*   *   *

That evening they climbed the well-hollowed out stairs to the ballroom. As they entered, Emile's eyes were already searching across the room for Nana, but he had a few last minute words of advice for his friend.

"John, remember, if you dance more than one dance with some of these beauties, watch out for their mothers! They are lurking about, just waiting to pounce on any man who dances more than a dance or two with their daughters. Don't say yes to anything they propose to you, just enjoy the dancing!"

"Are you going to heed your own advice?" John asked, smiling at his friend.

"It may be too late for me! Mark my words, there will probably be a mother trailing me by the end of the evening! But, truthfully I have to admit, I may be ready to make a deal with her mama by then, we'll see!" And with that, Emile took off in search of Nana. When he found her, he bowed and kissed her hand. His other hand came from behind his back, holding a corsage of yellow roses, and he smiled awkwardly at her, like a little boy.

"May I?" he asked, reaching out to pin the roses on her. Nana nodded, so he pinned the corsage on her, delighting in the feel of her breasts beneath his fingers. He tried placing the roses on one side, and then the other, prolonging the enjoyment of touching her, and he recalled how her breasts had rested firmly against his chest when she was unconscious in his arms. The image made him feel dizzy. How long would it be before she would let him hold her again, and this time conscious and willing, he wondered?

"Thank you. They are beautiful, and you remembered yellow roses!" she said, her dark eyes watching the movement of his fingers. He couldn't quite read her expression.

"I've been counting the days," Emile said, and his lips brushed Nana's neck with a feathery light kiss. "The last few days seemed very long, until I could see you again."

"I found it long too, and was very pleased to see you arrive," she replied, arching her neck towards him, as if seeking another kiss, and Emile had to repress his strong desire to cover that swan neck with kisses. The music began again, and he swung her into the waltz, grateful for the opportunity the waltz gave for their bodies to be closer. Emile smiled slightly, as he remembered that his mother still considered the waltz to be much too scandalous to be permitted. As they reached the far end of the dance floor, he swung them into a turn, and as they pivoted, his leg brushed intentionally against the inside of one of her slender thighs. This beauty attracted him as no other had ever done, and he resolved to try and establish a relationship with her, one he hoped would far outlast the thousand dances she had promised him.

"Has your family always lived in our city?" he asked, longing to know more about her

"No, my grandparents came here from St. Domingue, to escape the revolution. And when they came, they were already free people. Neither my mother nor I have ever known slavery. *No one has ever owned me.*"

For a while they danced in silence. Her last words seemed to have thrown out a clear challenge. He looked intently into her dark eyes. Was she telling him she would resist entering a plaçage relationship, such as he had in mind? And if she was so determined to remain free from such an emotional dependency, why was she here, dancing at the very balls which were intended to lead to just such relationships? Was it pressure from her mother, or others in her family which brought her to the balls, somewhat against her own will? And did she feel the strong physical attraction for him, which he already felt for her, and could it overcome her apparent resistance to a relationship which she might see as restricting her freedom? He had to try. His dreams day and night all focused on her....

Emile's hand on her waist drew her closer to him. He knew he had to somehow convince her that he had never made such an offer of plaçage before, that his offer now was unique, and reflected his true feelings for her. His eyes met hers, and he hoped they would show his honesty, and that this was the only time he expected to make such an offer of committed love.

"Although I have known of these balls, I have never attended them before. Last time I came especially to introduce my friend to a New Orleans tradition, and I found you. Have you come often to these balls?"

"No, only a few, and just to please my mother," she responded guardedly.

"Does your mother come with you to these dances?" he asked.

"Yes, she would not let me come without a chaperone, and there are only the two of us."

"And so she is here tonight?" Emile asked.

"Yes, of course, but why so much interest in ma mère?" Nana knew, but she wanted to hear what her suitor had to say. She needed to hear his words, to judge his intent.

"Because I *need* you, and to continue to see you, I must seek her approval, n'est-ce pas?"

"Yes, that is the customary way.... I know I owe my life to you, Monsieur, but I am not sure I'm ready to give it over to you," came her soft reply. "I treasure my freedom. What you are suggesting, wouldn't I be agreeing to just another form of slavery?"

"Oh, mon Dieu, no! I want to look after you, to have the privilege of loving you, Nana. Can you not agree to that? I don't want to have to count the dances and leave, even after the thousand you've promised me! I want to be with you much longer than that...."

"My Mama knows you are the one who saved my life in the fire, and I told her that I had promised you a thousand dances, so she will not bother you, Monsieur, not for quite a while. Can't we just enjoy our time together for now? I am not sure I am ready to settle into any kind of exclusive arrangement just yet,... not with anyone; perhaps later, but we must get to know each other better before that can happen."

"Nana, ma chère. I am already sure, but I am willing to wait on your consent," Emile said, brushing her cheek with his lips. "I have dreamed of nothing but you ever since I had you in my arms that night when I carried you out of the fire."

She smiled at him. "You are very convincing, Monsieur. Perhaps it won't be very long before I can give you an answer, and perhaps it will be the one you desire. You must give me some time. You are asking me for a commitment I'm not sure I want to make. So many have had to struggle to win freedom. I feel some reluctance to give up even a little of mine, and even in the name of love.... Your people may find this difficult to understand...."

Emile nodded. "I think I can understand, and although I will find it hard to wait, I will, because you are so worth waiting for. I have never felt like this before, and I promise to give you my love, and to take care of you, always. And Nana, I can afford to give you so much. I am an only son, and my father has built up our fortune. You will not lack for anything. Have you heard of Marengo?"

"Oh yes, is that your home?" Nana asked, her eyes opening to their widest, which had Emile thoroughly bedazzled.

"Yes, Marengo is my home, and one day will be all mine," he responded, never taking his eyes off her. "I assure you, you will live well as long as I live. And if there is war, and I have to go, I will see you are provided for, even if something happens to me. I promise to make sure of that."

The music stopped. He took her hand in his. "Please call me Emile. I love hearing my name when you say it. And Nana, you are my first and only love. I want to love and care for you. Please don't keep me waiting very long,..." Emile said softly, and then he raised her hand and kissed it.

"I want to buy you a home, and provide for you. Your mother may live with you, if you wish, and I will come to you as often as I can. I can't consider that 'owning you,' but rather loving and caring for you. Can you not see it that way too?"

"But we don't know each other yet. My Mama wanted me to get educated, and to learn to speak properly, so she saved up the money and sent me to the Ursulines. They introduced me to beautiful music, taught me to play the piano, and to love books. Do you love those things too, Emile?"

"I do, I love the opera, and I too love books. I don't play the piano, but I would love to listen to you play. Do you have a piano now, or may I give you one?"

"Emile, that's too much too soon! No! My Mama has been trying to save enough for a piano, but that's difficult. She is a modiste, a fine dressmaker, not just a seamstress, and has many white ladies as her clients. She earns well, but we must live on what she makes. I do help her as much as I can, especially when she has many orders for the social season."

"The fire must have destroyed your home, did it not? Do you and your mother have another place now?" Emile inquired, wondering if Nana would give him an address so he could surprise her with a piano, and lots and lots of flowers.

"We are waiting for repairs on our little home. It was badly damaged in the fire, so we are staying with my mother's brother and his family. It's crowded, but we all get along."

"Why not let me provide you with a new home? I long to do that for you, if you will promise to be mine," Emile begged, as they started to dance again.

"I am honored by your proposal, but you must give me some time to think about it. If I were to agree, would you expect me to wait upon your arrival every day, or would I have the freedom to shop, to go to the theater, to walk with friends on the levée? I have heard that some women in plaçage are always hurrying home, even from Mass, to be there waiting for their protector, whether he comes or not. I don't think I could live like that, Emile...."

"I can promise now, that you would be free to do all those things, and that I would not expect you to be sitting around waiting for me. Usually I would come to see you on days we both agree on, although there might be times when I would come just on an impulse to be with you, but I would not be angry if you were out, only disappointed. I want to share my life with you. Please, Nana, let me love and care for you.... Is it too much to ask you to share your bed only with me, and with no other man? That's all I ask, for you to be mine alone, and I will look after you, and love you with all my heart."

"Are you married, Emile?" Nana asked, wondering what his answer would be, although she was already sure that whatever it would be, Emile would tell her the truth.

He shook his head, and smiled at her. "No, and I want only you, Nana."

"Surely there will come a time when your father will expect you to marry a nice, acceptable French Creole wife, won't there?" Nana watched him carefully for his response.

"Yes, that will happen, but that doesn't mean you will be forgotten, not at all. This commitment I long to make, it will be for life, your life and mine; and as I told you, if I am called to war as an officer, that I will see you are provided for, in case anything happened to me. I need you, Nana, and I hope that you will need me, once I can prove my love for you. My father assures me that the arranged marriage he hopes to make for me won't happen for several more years, and in any case, such an arranged marriage will not supplant a true love like the one I feel for you."

"The evening is almost over. Will you return for the next ball, Emile? If you do, and we can share the next ball, and perhaps another, together, I may be able to give you an answer. Give me a little more time. You are asking for a lifetime, you know...."

"Yes, I would love to hear you tell me right now that you agree, but I will wait, impatiently no doubt, but I will wait for your answer.... A short wait for a lifetime together, that's well worthwhile! Forgive my impatience, I just can't wait to love you!"

As the last waltz ended, Nana turned her cheek to Emile for a kiss, and although he started his kiss on her cheek, his lips soon found hers. She responded, and the kiss was long and passionate. When at last it ended, Nana's hands flew to her heart, as she caught her breath.

"Perhaps you won't have to wait very long for your answer, Emile," she said breathlessly, and his heart seemed to swell. He was confident she had enjoyed the kiss, and perhaps as much as he had.

"So I will be here for the next ball, Nana, and hoping for many more dances, many more kisses, and for a future together," he responded seriously, and he raised her hand to his lips, kissing first her open palm, then turning it over and kissing it on top, planting a kiss on each of her fingers as well. She gasped, and when their eyes met, they both smiled at each other simultaneously.

Only when he could no longer see her, did Emile turn and begin a search for John. When the two friends found each other, John laughed and said,

"You know, it's good you warned me about those mamas! You were right, and I had a couple of them at my heels after I danced a second dance with their beautiful daughters. I couldn't believe it, and if you hadn't warned me, I might have fallen into a trap. There's no way I could take one of those beauties back home with me! My father wouldn't even let me in the house, if I returned from here with a beautiful quadroon! Excuse me, but what is possible in New Orleans, would not be tolerated in New York, at least not by my family, and others I know.

"But how did the evening go for you, Emile? Still smitten?"

"Yes, more than ever. I am ready to support her, to send her flowers every day, to give her a piano, almost anything her heart desires. I promised her a little house of her own, where she and her mother could live. That little cottage they had was badly destroyed in the fire, and they are living with family while it's being rebuilt. She told me that her family have been free people of color for three generations, since before coming to New Orleans from St. Domingue. I find it difficult to understand, John, but she saw my proposition as just another kind of slavery. I wasn't expecting that, but she didn't refuse my offer, so I'm still hoping...."

"You know, it isn't hard to understand, her point about slavery. If her family has only known freedom for three generations, I can see that she might find an arrangement, like the one you are proposing, another form of slavery. I'm sorry, Emile, but I do see her point, can't you?"

"John, I'm in love with the woman, and I want to care for her, and love her. Is that slavery? I guess love could be seen as a form of slavery, as if two people are bound to each other, but that's the only resemblance I see. I would promise her a home, a piano and damn well anything she wants, in return for the right to love her and to expect her to love only me. Is that *really* slavery?"

"You have a point, but to one whose family had once been enslaved, it may look quite different than it does to you. Still I suspect you'll win out. I notice that she seems to enjoy your kisses more and more!" John grinned at his friend. "You must let me know how it all works out, so plan to write me now and then! Who knows but what we may be together again, serving in the military as second lieutenants! At least our West Point schooling gives us the advantage of starting out as officers, if there's a war, or if we are called up to fight Indians!"

The next morning after a round of Creole embraces and kisses on both cheeks, John boarded the train for his journey home. He waved from the window to Emile, standing alone on the platform, waving him off. It was likely that indeed they would meet again, in the service of their country, and in the meantime, he would be anxious to hear about his friend's romance.

But still he shook his head over it. How could a man manage both a mistress and a wife? He was sure that Emile, as the only child, would have to marry, and produce at least one legitimate heir for Marengo. A life with two women, both depending on him, sounded much too complicated.

*   *   *

While he waited out the days until the next ball, Emile decided that perhaps he should change his strategy. He resolved to merely remind Nana of his promises, and then to enjoy their time together and deepen their relationship. Perhaps he did sound too mercenary to her. John may have been right. For a family once enslaved, his offer may well have sounded like another form of slavery. He hadn't even thought of that, only of his love and desire for her, his need to care for her. Showing her the real depth of his feelings for her was the course to follow.

She and her mother were both sitting at a table when he arrived at the ball. He was pleased to see that she wasn't dancing with someone else, and wondered if this was indirect proof that she might accept a new relationship with him. He immediately went over to them, bowing first to her mother, and then bowing and kissing Nana's hand. Both of them smiled at him, but somehow he felt as if he and his net worth was being calculated by her mother, and for a moment he felt a sort of cold, damp sensation grip him, but he shrugged it off. Of course, she would want the best for her daughter. A wise woman in her position would certainly try to determine what his offer would mean, and how long it could last.

"Will you dance with me, Mademoiselle?" he asked Nana, and she smiled up at him, took his hand, and he felt her slide into his arms. His heart raced. There was an instant exchange of smiles, and he brushed her soft cheek with his lips. For some time they danced together in silence, a silence which seemed to rest on some sort of mutual understanding.

"Nana, this past week I have spent some time looking at houses, and even pianos. Can I take you and your mother to look at some of the houses? I need your opinion on which one you like the most," he finally said, and the hand he was holding as they danced, he drew up and gently kissed it, studying her expression as he did so.

"Please, chérie,..." he pleaded softly,... "and after a few dances tonight, do you think your mother would give her permission for me to take you for a carriage ride around the city? There's a full moon tonight, and a splendid sky full of stars...."

"My mother knows about your offer, and she seems to approve of you, so I guess she will agree to the ride."

Emile felt as if his heartbeat had speeded up, and his hands held her more tightly. After a few more dances, he said,

"Let's get some champagne for your mother, and ask her permission for our ride," and he beckoned to a waiter, and ordered a bottle of champagne. The waiter bowed, and soon followed them to the table where her mother waited, watching.

"It's such a beautiful moonlit night, I hope you will give your permission for Nana to come for a short carriage ride with me," Emile asked, as the waiter filled the old woman's glass and placed it before her. She took a sip, then put the glass down, and turned to Emile. She scrutinized him silently for some time, and then squinting coolly at him, she answered,

"Yes, Monsieur, she kin go wid yuh if she wants. I'ze gonna trust yuh wid ma daughteh. Jus' yuh bring her back safely beforh dis ball ends. Tonight it be a carriage ride *only*."

Emile leaned forward. "Has Nana told you that I want to care for her, if she will let me?" he asked. "I love her, and want to care for her, not just this week, or this year, but as long as I live. I also told her that, since I am an officer in the cavalry, I will make all the provisions necessary to provide for her if anything should happen to me."

"Yes, she tole me. It's raight generous of yuh, Monsieur, an' if Nana wishes te share life wid yuh, I won't oppose dat. It's up te her, Sir. She will give yuh an answer when she's ready. Now go forh dat ride, an' see yuh are back beforh dis ball ends. I be waitin' raight hieh." Again the old woman gave him a long, cold stare. "Only a little carriage ride, Sir, an' forh de sake of a future, I need te trust yuh. Is dat clear?"

"Yes, I understand, and I accept your limits tonight, because I do want there to be a future I can share with your daughter."

Emile poured out another glass of champagne for the old woman, then he took Nana by the hand, and together they left the ballroom. Emile slipped her arm under his, and held her tight, realizing that the well-grooved stairs must be treacherous for women with tiny, narrow heels. She came down slowly and carefully, but had to rely on him for help when she nearly slipped on the last three steps, and suddenly she was in his arms, more tightly than when they danced. For a moment he held her there, almost overcome, dizzy with desire, and he kissed her finely arched neck, and then her ear lobe before he helped her down the last steps.

He opened the door, and she followed him outside, taking the hand he extended to her. He whistled, and Washington pulled up. Before the old man could climb down and hold the carriage door open, Emile had helped Nana into the carriage himself, and then followed her in. As he leaned back to close the door, he couldn't help noticing the big eyes and full smile Washington was giving him.

"Will you take us slowly along the levée, then very slowly along Esplanade, and then *very, very* slowly along the lakefront," he ordered, smiling back at Washington.

"Yes, Sir, Massa Emile," Washington answered with a wink, before he scrambled back into the driver's seat, and they were off, the horses moving at a slow, stately walk.

Emile put his arm around Nana.

"Are you comfortable?" he asked, and when she smiled and nodded, he drew her close to him, and kissed her, softly and tenderly. Then for a while they simply watched as they passed through the Place d'Armes, and saw the slender towers of the Cathedral illuminated by the moonlight. There were many lights still glimmering from the windows of restaurants and bars in the French Quarter. The river was high, and where they could see it over the levées, the current seemed to boil in the moonlight. Ships were docked, as many as three or more tied together along the shore, bobbing and rocking in the current. Then they turned onto Esplanade, and could see mansions of two or three stories, surrounded by palms - coconut palms curving gracefully, the fronds of sago palms glistening in the moonlight and fountains spewing little rainbows up into the moonlit sky.

Emile took both her hands in one of his, and tenderly kissed each of them. He had withdrawn a ring from his pocket, and he slid it gently on the ring finger of her left hand. There was a large pearl, with smaller ones on either side. Nana apparently didn't see the ring, until Emile began to put it on her finger. She didn't resist, but smiled at him and then at the ring.

"Will you wear this for me?" he asked her, and she silently nodded her consent. He took her in his arms, and his kisses covered her face, her neck, her hands, and finally his lips sought hers. He thrilled at her response, and his hands caressed her bare shoulders, and slid down over the silky fabric of her ball gown, and cupped her breasts. Emile sensed that this was as far as he should go, and contented himself with kisses, and the feel of her breasts, her shoulders, and her tiny waist. He longed for more, but held himself back. Their kisses grew longer and more passionate, until even Nana was breathless. He heard her moan slightly.

"You must know I love you," he said softly. "But this is all I ask of you tonight. I fully intend to keep my promise to your mother. When you accept the home I want to give you, and the bed I will provide, then I hope you will share that home and that bed with me. Before that time, I will ask nothing more of you. Will you let me look after you, Nana? For a lifetime?"

"Yes, Emile, I will," she responded.

He could see, even in the darkened carriage, that her eyes were full of tears.

"Why are you crying, chérie?" he asked, giving her his handkerchief.

"Please love me, but don't take away my freedom," she said so softly he had to lean close to hear.

"I will try always to respect your freedom. I promise this will not be slavery for you, unless love itself is slavery, and if that's true, then *I am your slave*.... I love you, Nana, and I will not ever intentionally do anything to harm you, only to love you and care for you."

Her tears continued, and he respected them, simply holding her close, and trying to kiss the corners of her eyes, and kiss away the tear trails on her cheeks. Only partly could he understand their meaning. John may have been right, he thought, those who have always been free, probably couldn't understand, but he could respect her feelings. In fact he realized that only if he could do that, was there hope for the kind of lasting love he sought with her.

At the lakefront, he helped her out of the carriage. There was a breeze blowing, and he watched as it caught in her beautiful hair, and pulled it free. She was in a white satin ball gown, and Emile thought he would never forget how dazzling she was there in the moonlight, like his bride, with the lake all silver and black behind her. He embraced her, and they kissed. The arrangement, it seemed, was silently sealed.

The ride back was peaceful and quiet, as if all the tension underlying the decision had lifted. As the carriage drew up, people were slowly leaving. Emile helped her up the stairs, and they walked hand in hand to where her mother sat, watching their approach. A young man sat across from her, deep in conversation with her. He looked up, his eyes troubled, as he saw Emile with Nana, and he jumped to his feet.

"Here she is, your beautiful daughter, back safe and sound, Madame de Lis," Emile said, smiling as he seated Nana. Madame de Lis gestured to the young man, and said,

"Monsieur Emile, dis hieh iz our friend, Armand Saint Pierre. He plays hieh wid dis orchestra, an' he has a little orchestra of hiz own, all Creoles like we iz. Maybe someday yuh want te hire hiz orchestra forh a party at dat plantation of yuhrs?"

Armand bowed to Emile.

"It's a pleasure to meet you, Sir," he said. "I would welcome the chance for my orchestra to come play at Marengo someday."

"Perhaps we can talk about that sometime soon," Emile said, grasping Armand's outstretched hand. "But tonight, it's late, and the ball is ending." Then he turned to Madame de Lis and asked,

"May I take you both home?"

"Oui, Monsieur, s'il vous plaît," was Madame's succinct reply.

"And Monsieur Saint Pierre, is there someplace we can drop you off?" Emile asked politely, hoping that it wouldn't be with Nana and her mother.

"Thank you, but no, Sir. I have to stay for a short practice here with the orchestra. We need to prepare for our next ball. Goodnight to you, Monsieur. Goodnight ladies."

Emile helped the ladies up, and they went down to the carriage, where Washington ceremoniously held open the carriage door.

Emile was relieved. He didn't want to encourage the handsome young Creole as a competitor, by dropping him off with the ladies, and he did want to know where to send flowers,... and to know where to find Nana.

The mother gave directions, and finally they stopped before a green painted, frame house, and Emile helped them out, and up the stairs. He gave Nana a last kiss.

"Goodnight, chérie," he said, and waited until they were safely inside. The last he saw was her smile before the door closed, a smile which seemed to hold out promises for him.

"Make sure you know this address," he insisted as Washington closed the carriage door behind him. "I want to send flowers, and we will be coming back here."

"Yes'm, Massa Emile. Dat's sureh one beauteous girl, dat iz!"

And Emile felt that Washington had a new warmth and respect for him.

*　　　　　　　　*　　　　　　　　*

The next morning, after a croissant and coffee downed too hastily, Emile watched until his father had finished with his newspaper, and set out for his desk. Then he followed him, knocking respectfully at the half-opened door and waiting until he heard "Entrez." He entered, and carefully closed the door behind him.

"Father, there's something I want to talk to you about. I want to invest in some property in the city, and I wonder if you would mind parting with some money for that," Emile began, the croissant already turning into a hard lump in his stomach.

"What do you have in mind exactly?" his father asked, continuing to look at the pages of the big plantation account book open before him.

"A creole cottage, perhaps some sort of double, part of which I could rent out, and part I could keep to stay in myself, when I stay late in the city," Emile responded as calmly as possible. Perhaps he could convince his father of the value of a rental property, unless he saw through that, to the real reason for a house....

"Have you any particular house in mind?" his father asked, and without looking up, he turned to the next pages of the account book.

"Yes, I have narrowed it down to three, and whichever I can get the best deal on, it will be one of those three."

"Have you a specific tenant in mind?" This time his father's dark eyes were scowling at him, his thick, dark eyebrows knitting together in a frown. Emile swallowed hard before answering. He might as well be honest. Sooner or later the truth would come out.

"Yes, Papa, I have," he finally said. He felt a constriction narrowing his throat, and was surprised to hear his voice sound higher than usual.

"Aha, I see," his father replied, his eyes seeming to bore right through Emile's chest.

"Is this primarily a business investment, to turn a profit, or is it primarily a matter of the heart, of affection, Emile?" Emile was sure his father saw right to the core of things. There was no sense in trying to deceive him, that just wouldn't work.

"Affection, mon père," he said simply.

"This is your first such, er,... serious amorous adventure?" his father asked, his eyes back on the accounts.

"Yes, Sir, that's right, and I expect it will be the only one of its kind... for me."

"But you do understand that at some point I will make all the arrangements for a marriage with a French Creole of your own background and stature? Whatever this relationship is, it must not interfere with the marriage arrangements I will make for you as my sole heir. You understand that?" His father's dark eyes were sternly directed at his.

"Yes, Sir, I do." Emile swallowed hard, unable to refute what his father said.

"If I make a good arranged marriage for you, you must, of course, fulfill your role in that marriage, and if God sees fit, provide heirs for our Marengo. Is that clear?"

"Yes, Sir, entirely clear."

"So how much money are we talking about for this property?" his father's eyes returned to the ledger before him, and he slowly turned a page.

"About $15,000., mon père."

"Mon Dieu! That's a down payment for a veritable castle!"

"Well, I was hoping to purchase the place for cash, rather than carry a mortgage. That would mean it would be free and clear, if, as a soldier, anything should happen to me. And then there are furnishings, dishes, kitchen things, and so on, that I must provide...."

"Ah, mais oui, and with cash, you should be able to strike a good bargain for the house, and perhaps for some of the other things needed. I believe we can manage it. Just remember, I have laid some conditions down for my agreement, important limitations on your future. I must be confident of your agreement to the marriage I will later contract for you. That is essential. You must provide at least one legitimate male heir for our Marengo, and, of course, two heirs, both males, would be better yet. I must have your agreement on that."

"You do have my agreement, Papa. I understand. I will try my best to give you those heirs, but their gender,... that I cannot control, that is in the hands of le bon Dieu."

Monsieur Louis laughed dryly,

"Of course, I understand that. Your mother and I have not been too successful ourselves, since you are our one and only child. I simply demand that you do your marital duty when that time comes. And right now, I see no reason for rushing you into marriage, Emile. Young men like you should have a few years in which to enjoy themselves before they are expected to settle down. I do not plan to hurry you."

"I will keep my promise to you, Papa, and accept the marriage you will arrange for me," Emile said, thinking that it didn't sound to him like an unrewarding duty that his father was asking of him. It sounded rather like he was being assigned a pleasure,... that of keeping two women happy. But even if that had its appeal, he was relieved to know that there was no immediate pressure for him to marry; that he would have several years before it happened.

"Then I see no reason not to give you the cash now," his father concluded, turning to the paneled wall behind him, and reaching up with a key to open up one of the panels. Behind it, a metal safe appeared, and with a few quick turns of his hand, his father opened it, and pulled out a bundle of bills, all tied up with a string. Emile could see that there were at least a half dozen or more similar bundles, and several metal boxes in the safe. He knew that some of those boxes probably contained the de Marigny jewels, and other valuables.

Without opening up the bundle, his father handed it over to him.

"You can count it. There should be fifteen thousand there. That should take care of everything, house and contents, and perhaps some will be left over for other expenses. Let me know if you find any discrepancy," he said, returning to the account ledger, as if the interview was ended. Then he looked up once more at his son.

"Remember, this woman, regardless of her color and status, must never come here, to Marengo, nor can you expect me to include her or any offspring you may sire with her, as heirs to my lands and fortune. What you choose to do later, once Marengo is all yours, that, of course, I cannot control from the grave, but if you should produce suitable heirs from this arranged marriage I will contract for you, I hope you will have the good sense to leave our Marengo to them,... to keep it in our French Creole family, as it has always been," he said, and again his eyes returned to the ledger.

"Yes, mon père, I understand. Nana is a free woman however, a strikingly beautiful, fair-skinned Creole of color. So I do not have to buy her freedom."

Without looking up, his father dryly remarked,

"Eh bien, I guess that's a bargain for me, only a house to buy and its contents,... not a woman too."

"Merci, Papa."

Emile let himself out, and headed to his room to count the money. Tomorrow he would go to the city, and buy a house, and any furnishings which might be needed. He had trembled through the interview, but now his heart was singing. Quickly he pulled out a sheet of paper, and began to write,

> Ma chère Nana,
> Will you be able to come with me tomorrow or the day after, to help pick out your new home? Your mother may come too, if you would like her advice.

Washington, who brings you this note, will wait for your answer. Whichever day you like, we will stop for you around noon. Perhaps we can have luncheon together in the house you pick out as yours? I will bring a picnic basket and a fine bottle of wine!

My love always,
Your Emile

As soon as he sealed the envelope, he hurried down the stairs, and out the door, leaping out over the front steps of the Big House, and jogging to the stables. Washington was inside, currying down his father's favorite bay. He looked around, surprised at young Massa Emile's haste, and then he must have realized what it was about, and he smiled, a broad smile.

"Washington, can you drop everything right now, and take this note to the city? Do you remember how to find that house where we left the ladies off after the ball? I want you to go there, give this note to Mademoiselle de Lis, and wait for whatever answer she wants to send me. And now, right now, can you leave, and take care of this for me?"

"Yes Massa Emile. I 'members where dat place iz, an' I be ready te go dis verra minute, afta I put dis horse in hiz stall. I bring deh message back te yuh at de Big House soon as I can."

"And you will give me that answer at a time and place where neither of my parents will hear it, especially not my mother!" Emile added emphatically, following the old man as he put the bay back in his stall.

Washington's eyes twinkled, and he managed a slight grin, as he grabbed up a saddle, slung it up on old Ned, and tightened up the cinch strap.

"Yes, Massa Emile, I hear yuh!" he answered, as he finished up, and mounted the old gray.

As Emile walked back to the Big House, he saw Washington riding fast, headed out through the oak alley. He looked back, and Emile grinned and waved him on.

Now, whatever am I going to do with myself until I get her message, Emile thought, then he decided that as hot as it was already, a good nap might be in order, and yet, when he settled down on his bed, all he could do was picture Nana, and how he planned to celebrate with her once they found a big bed for their love nest. His daydreams brought a smile to his face, but he didn't find them conducive to sleep. Still they did fill the time beautifully. He imagined what it would be like to uncover all her beauty, taking off one garment at a time.

The sun was already dipping low over the horizon, its golden orb caught, so it seemed, in the needled arms of pines, the river alight with long gold and orange streaks, when Washington came slowly into the kitchen of the Big House and on, to the door of the family room. He knocked, and Emile, who had been restlessly waiting, sprang out to meet him.

"So what's my answer?" he asked, closing the family room door firmly behind him, and speaking softly to avoid any questions from his mother, who was in there knitting.

"She done said 'yes,' Massa," Washington said, a sly grin curving in the corners of his lips.

"Yes what? When? Tomorrow or the day after?" Emile demanded, trying to control his exasperation.

"Ah yes, she dun tole me 'tomorrow,' an' de time yuh said, dat's jus' fine wid her."

Emile nodded, grinning. "So, will you have a carriage and pair ready so we can leave early tomorrow morning? I have an errand to do before we pick up the ladies. I expect you to drive, of course. Around nine."

"Yes Sir, I sureh will have ebrythin' ready."

Emile gave him a conspiratorial grin, and slapped him on the back.

"You're a good man, Washington, and thanks!" he said. "And on your way out, will you tell them in the kitchen, that for tomorrow, I want a picnic basket with food for four, wine glasses, and a fine bottle of red wine. And Washington, I'm including food for you also in that four."

"Yes, thank yuh, Sir. I kin take care of alla dat."

*   *   *

Emile woke up early the next morning, with the sun, and the first notes of the mocking bird. He smiled as he stretched slowly; this was a day he couldn't believe had come about so much faster than he had expected. It was difficult even to remember what his life had been like before Nana, only that it had been boring and bland, with evenings spent with young ladies who flirted pleasantly enough with him, knowing he was the heir to that splendid plantation, Marengo, but compared to his beautiful Nana, well,... there simply was no comparison. And tonight or perhaps tomorrow night, they might spend together in the house he would give her. He decided that the first thing he would do in the city, would be to buy her the most glamorous, gorgeous negligée he could find, and already he was daydreaming about how he would ease it off her beautiful body.

He dressed carefully, wanting to look his best, and slicked down his black, wavy hair with a brush and water, combed his long sideburns into order, and studied his image in the mirror. Not bad, he thought, big, honest, dark eyes. Perhaps he would look more mature, more handsome if he grew a mustache, but he had tried that for a while, and found it simply wasn't thick enough yet to be impressive. He wished he was just a little taller, but he was afraid he had stopped growing, and would have to settle for his present five feet, and ten inches. He clipped a bit more off his left sideburn. It had seemed a trifle longer than the one on the right side of his face. Then he headed downstairs for breakfast.

His father was already reading the *Picayune* and sipping his coffee. He looked up, and gave his son a conspiratorial grin.

"You are up early this morning, and very nicely dressed too. You must be headed for the city."

"Yes, Papa, I hope to transact that business I told you about yesterday, concerning a piece of property."

"Piece of property! Ah yes, no doubt!" his father replied, laughing as he looked at his son.

"There's a possibility I won't be home for supper, and may stay in the city for a night or two, Papa. Will you let Mama know that, s'il vous plaît?"

"Yes, Emile, I will give her that message, and no more,..." his father said, and as Emile hurriedly finished up a croissant and his cup of coffee, his father looked him over as if he were noticing him for the first time in a long time, appraising his son, and then with a smile just lurking in the corners of his mouth, he said,

"Bonne chance, mon Emile, bonne chance! And do not forget what we agreed to. I will find you a good French Creole wife one of these days, a pretty one.... And in the meantime you will learn more about the ways of women, and how to please them, eh bien?"

"Merci, Papa, I remember what we agreed to, and I look forward to learning more about how to please a woman,... and I hope quite soon!" Emile smiled back, and wrapping his fingers around the big wad of money in his pocket, he set out to the kitchen for his picnic basket, and then to find Washington and be on their way.

*   *   *

First came a pack of dogs, racing out and barking, then children of every size and age came bursting out of the little green frame house as the carriage pulled up in front of it.

Emile walked up the shelled walkway to the house, and Nana's mother came out to meet him. This was not what he expected, and he was puzzled.

"Don't yuh pay no 'ttention te alla dat!" she said, waving towards the children and the dogs, both of which seemed to be trailing at his heels. "Dey belong te ma son, and ma odeh daughteh, Nana's oldeh sisteh, Mignon. Nana, she be comin', jus' takes her a while te decide what she be goin' te wear. You'll have te get used te dat, Monsieur!"

Emile felt a great sense of relief. He and his father often experienced such delays as his mother prepared to go out with them. The master bed, oversized as it was, could still be covered with piles of discarded outfits before she was dressed and ready. For one or two horrible moments he had wondered if Nana had experienced a change of heart, and was sending her mother out to tell him to leave, and that everything was over between them.

He leaned against a pillar of the porch, ran his hand through his hair to settle it down after the ride, and then felt again for the money in his pocket.

Nana emerged, "I'm sorry. Did Mama tell you I am sometimes late, and not to be disturbed, that I really was coming?"

"Sometimes?" her mother scoffed, but she did manage a slight smile for her daughter.

"You look perfectly lovely," Emile said, smiling and taking Nana's arm in his.

She was dressed in a tight-fitting, pale silvery blue jacket and matching full skirt, and a little edging of white ruffles showed at her neck. He noticed that she held a parasol of the same silvery blue shade, and over her arm was a navy blue purse, and her feet were clad in soft, navy blue kid slippers. He could just see their tiny leather straps over her ankles, as her skirt flounced up, and he longed to touch those straps and pretty ankles. She wore a little silver blue hat, with a fake stuffed swallow perched on it, its wings partly raised for flight, and a pale blue veil just covered the front of her hair and a little of her forehead. He thought she was dazzling, and she greeted him with a full smile, as he kissed first her hand, and then her cheek.

"You are simply beautiful, Nana!" he said, standing back a little to get the full effect, and then he helped her into the carriage, where her mother had already settled.

"Well, you know we Creoles are not allowed to wear bonnets or hats, only tignons that we must wrap around our heads, so I am taking a chance, but Mama and I just finished making this hat, and it goes so well with my dress."

"I seriously doubt anyone will bother you about that hat, as long as you are with me, and it is very attractive. When you are with me, I hope you will not wear a tignon. Somehow that seems demeaning. But now of other things. Are you ready to pick out your house today?" Emile asked, as soon as he had joined her in the carriage, sitting down on the seat beside her. He sat so close that he could feel the softly rounded shape of her hip against his.

"I am to pick out the house? I thought you would pick one out," she said, surprised by his offer.

"No, I will help only if you ask. This is your big decision for today, and perhaps it will be followed by an even bigger decision later on," Emile responded.

"I am ready to negotiate, and to pay for one house today, the one you will pick it out! I came earlier this week, and narrowed things down to three that I think you will like, now the rest is up to you, chérie!"

A small man with snowy white hair met them at the first house, and accompanied them as they examined the three houses. When they had seen all three, Nana asked to return to the second house. She quickly moved ahead, and opened the front door herself, and went into the living room. She turned all around, smiling as she turned toward Emile.

"You really mean for me to make the choice?" she asked softly.

"Yes, chérie, I want you to decide. It's to be *your* house," Emile assured her.

"Then this is the one. It's perfect, Emile. I am so happy!" she said, spinning around on her heels exuberantly, then into his arms. The agent conveniently had picked this time to retreat to the kitchen, and Nana's Mama seemed to have disappeared upstairs.

"Then let me settle things with the agent, and it will be yours!" Emile said, giving her a quick kiss on the lips and heading out to the kitchen.

Soon he returned. "It is all yours, Nana, except you and I must sign a few papers, and then we will have a picnic lunch wherever you would like, on the lakefront, in a park, or here in your new house. I already have bought a dining room set, and a big bed, and linens for it, and a few towels. I hope you will approve of my choices. Then after lunch, I will take you to select what you want for the kitchen, some china and silver, pans, and so on, and also the furniture you would like for your living room, and a comfortable sofa, chairs and an armoire for the bedroom. We will also get some things for your mother's bedroom."

"A sofa for the bedroom? Do we need that? Why not just one for the living room?" Nana asked.

"Oh yes, we *must* have a sofa for the bedroom," Emile said emphatically, smiling at Nana. Then very softly, so only she could hear, he whispered, "Variety is especially important in the bedroom!" and laughed when he saw her blush. "And of course, we must have two sofas for the living room too," he added, giving her another smile, the meaning of which wasn't hard for her to understand.

"So many sofas, Emile?" she commented very softly, and he threw back his head and laughed.

"And I assure you, chérie, we will make use of all of them!" he replied with a teasing little smile, and she had to laugh, even if she also blushed. He gently touched her cheek where the blush was rising. He saw it rising in other tempting places, but he restrained himself from touching, and settled just on looking, which made Nana blush even more.

The dining room set, the beds and other items Emile had already ordered, arrived just in time to use the new table and chairs for their picnic lunch.

"How did that happen so fast?" Nana asked Emile.

"I sent Washington to tell them which house to deliver to, and to tell them we needed the dining room table and chairs right away, and the beds by tonight!" Emile said. "Do you like my choices? If not, we can send them back, and you can pick out new ones. I am hoping that you like what I selected. We can use the table and chairs right now for our picnic lunch, since you have decided you want to have it in your new home. I hope we will agree on our bed too, otherwise it will be tomorrow before another one can be delivered, I'm afraid. And I would not like to start our new relationship on a hard floor...."

Emile pretended to be sad at the thought of sending back the bed, and Nana blushed again, and gave him a kiss.

"You could have picked out everything, Emile. Your taste is perfect, so let's keep the dining room set, and use it now," Nana said, beginning to unpack the picnic basket.

"And the bed?" Emile asked, coming up behind her, putting his arms around her, his hands on her breasts, and resting his chin on her shoulder.

"How about our bed, chérie? I hope you approve of it too. Do you?"

"Oh yes, Emile, I've never slept in such a beautiful, big bed before."

"Well, it needs to be big, Nana, if you plan to share it with me," he whispered, continuing to hold her tightly to him.

"Right now I want to take care of your appetite for food," she said, arching an eyebrow at him, and slipping out of his grasp.

"And later on, my other hunger?" he asked, and even though he was smiling, she saw that his eyes were passionate as he looked at her. "Only you can satisfy that...."

"Yes, but be patient with me, Emile, I have never shared a bed with any man,..." she explained shyly. "That's one reason this has been a big decision for me. "

"Ma chérie, I will always have patience with you," he assured her, his dark eyes looking at her so tenderly. "And all the more reason not to send the bed back. I want your first true experience of love to be the best it can be.... But for now, we'll start with lunch!"

Nana called upstairs to her mother, "Mama, lunch is ready, will you come eat with us now?"

"No, chile. Yuh go raight ahead an' eat, I git around te eatin' lateh. Raight now Washington iz still finishin' puttin' up de bed, and den I'ze gonna make it up forh yuh, wid all doz nice new covehs an' all."

Emile thought Nana's mama was showing excellent tact. He really wanted to share this first meal in the new house just with Nana. He found the wine goblets he had ordered put in the lunch basket, and a bottle of red wine, and poured out a glass for Nana and one for himself. He lifted his glass,

"To you, chérie, and to your new house. May it be the scene of much love and happiness."

She touched her glass to his, and said simply,

"Thank you, Emile. I grow more in love with you each day, and I pray it will last for both of us...."

Again they touched their glasses together, their eyes meeting over the rims, and seeming full of unspoken promises.

Later, they went to select more furniture, china, silver, and kitchen necessities. It took quite a while, far longer than Emile expected and at every store they visited, but finally it was arranged that everything would be delivered the next day. Then Emile stopped at Antoine's, and selected dinner, which Washington would pick up before he started home with the carriage.

Mama de Lis asked to be dropped off at her brother's house.

"You will not stay and have dinner with us, Mama?" Nana asked.

"No, but I'll come visit yuh tomorrow sometime," she said, then she turned to Emile,

"It's a lovely house. Yuh're raight generous te ma daughteh. Thank yuh."

"It's my pleasure entirely, to care for her," he responded before she hurried away into the house.

"Now Washington will take you to your new home," Emile said, squeezing Nana's hand in his.

"You will come in too, won't you?" Nana asked him, as they reached the doorstep.

"If that's what you want, chérie. I will be happy if invited, but it's your house, and it's your decision."

"Yes, Emile, that is what I want," she replied, and the look in her dark eyes was almost more than he could handle.

"Then I will come in with you," he said, kissing her as gently and tenderly as he could.

When they walked up the steps to the little house, Emile handed Nana the key. As she bent over the lock, he couldn't resist admiring her curves and embracing her waist. She turned the key, and the door opened, and Nana faced him again, smiling and waving the key to her new house. She took his hand and they crossed the threshold together, kissing tenderly as soon as Emile could close the door behind him.

"I don't know what to say, Emile, except thank you, and that's not nearly enough," Nana murmured, her lips feathering his neck with kisses.

"You, my darling, make it more than enough," he whispered between kisses.

Washington arrived with their dinner, and when he had said goodnight, and started on his way back to Marengo, Emile made sure all the doors were locked for the night.

Antoine's had even included candles, and Emile fished out a pair of crystal candle holders from the picnic basket, lit the candles and placed them on the new table.

"I asked them to put candles in, so we could have our first dinner together by candlelight," he said, stroking her dark hair, as the light of the candles played in it.

He pulled out her chair for her, and they settled down to dinner. Afterwards he took the lighted candles, and led the way.

"Since we still have no living room furniture, I guess there's only one place where we can settle down," he said smiling at her, and he started up the stairs to the big master bedroom, holding her by the hand. At the top of the stairs, he stopped and turned to her.

"You are ready for this, Nana? Is this what you want?" he asked, their faces both illuminated by the candles he held up between them. "I told you I would not take away your freedom.... You must consent before I take another step."

Her face, her body so beautiful in the candlelight, as he waited for her answer....

"Yes, Emile, this is what I want, to spend the night with you in the home you have just given me, and to hope we will have many more nights here together."

Emile put the candles down, each on a little bedside table, and he drew Nana into his arms.

"I have one more present for you, Nana," and he picked up a box from the bed, and handed it to her to open. The ribbon and paper came off quickly, and she pulled out a beautiful, white silk negligée.

"Oh, Emile, how lovely! And tonight I will wear it just for you!"

"I was hoping you would," he responded softly. "May I help you?" he asked, and she nodded. He thought he had never seen anything as beautiful as her face, her eyes, her smile in the candlelight, and she came to him, and let him undress her, and dress her in the negligée. Although passion pulsed through him, and he longed to cover every new curve he saw with kisses, he restrained himself. She was still too shy about her body. Undressing her more slowly and passionately would have to come later....

"Oh, mon Dieu!" he exclaimed, his hands feeling the softness of the silk over the curves of her body.

Then she helped him undress, and both of them touched each other's bodies slowly and self-consciously.... And the beauty of it all was caught in the flickering candlelight.

"May I pick you up, Nana?" he asked, and when she whispered a "yes," he did so, and carried her to the bed. He spilled the silk from her shoulders and her breasts, and knelt above her, touching her gently, and kisses followed his touch, until he was sure she was ready.

"You told me this will be the first time you have been with a man?" he asked.

She nodded silently, one of her slender hands resting on his bare chest.

"There may be a little pain at first then, but it shouldn't last. I will be as gentle as I can be, and you must tell me, my sweet, if you want me to stop, at any time, please."

"I will not want to stop, Emile," she answered, and her hands reached to fondle his body, as he caressed hers. Her eyes closed, and her breathing was as fast as his. Her fingers caught in the dark hair covering his chest, spurring him on.

"Nana, may I?" he asked, and when she reached for his shoulders, and pulled him to her, he knew she wanted him as much as he wanted her, and he lowered his body on hers, and they came together. She held him tightly to her, joining her movements to his, until their bodies tensed together. For some indefinable moments they clung to each other, carried in a tide of pleasure together. The candlelight caught their bodies in soft splendor.

"Emile, I do love you," she said tenderly, and his fingers loosened and moved gently around her, as if in affirmation, touching her breasts and hips, and then they grew still, curled around her hips, and both of them slept.

In the morning when she woke, one of his arms was still around her, and she smiled at his tousled hair, his body beside her, and snuggled closer. To sleep together was another joy.

Later they awoke together. She was still curved in the shelter of his arms.

He smiled and gave her a tiny, effortless kiss on the shoulder nearest his face.

"I am not the first woman for you, am I?" she asked softly. "You don't have to answer if you don't want to, Emile, but you did seem to know exactly what to do, and I was glad of that, since I'm so inexperienced!"

"No you aren't the first woman, but you are the first woman with whom I am also in love, and that is what matters, chérie."

"Yes, that is what matters. No other love before me?"

"No, you are absolutely my first love."

"This is a wonderful, special bed already," she said, turning a little and looking over the bed, and the rest of her bedroom. "I didn't even notice last night, that you already had curtains up in the windows."

"I bought some, and your mother must have seen them and hung them up. You wouldn't want the entire neighborhood watching, would you? I guess she agreed on our privacy. Maybe Washington helped her, when he came upstairs to set up the bed and mattress. So we can even play in the sunlight this morning, without being watched,..." he added. They smiled at each other, and his hands reached for her, touching her everywhere.

"Yes, we should celebrate our first morning together, just like we celebrated our first night together," she said, turning her body to face his. Her dazzling smile urged him on.

"I am hungry for you again," he said, kissing her breasts, her long swan neck, her lips, and drawing her to him. He was ready, but he deliberately held back, until he was sure she was ready. Her breath came in short, soft gasps, and the long dark lashes covered her eyes. Her beautiful, long neck arched below him.

"Oh ma Nana," he cried out hoarsely, and came to her. "Please, love, show me you love me,... and tell me now, can you?"

"Emile, I do love you,..." her answer came, a soft whisper, and her hands reached for his hips, and pulled him to her.

Their embrace held them together, their bodies joined tensely, then slowly they came back to reality; their room, the bed they shared together, the sunlight spreading over them, her body a soft golden ivory....

"You love me now?" he asked, smiling tenderly at her.

"Yes, Emile, I am all yours," she answered, her lips forming a kiss on his shoulder.

"Perhaps I should get you a servant, a slave," he murmured. "It would be such a pleasure to have someone bring us coffee and croissants here and now."

Nana startled under him, and he noticed her look of alarm.

"Is something wrong, chérie? You don't want to go back to that old green house so soon, I hope?"

"Oh, no, not that. But promise me you will never give me a slave,... ever, Emile"

"I want to give you someone to help you dress, do your hair for you and bring me the coffee I am longing for in the mornings. If I buy a slave, I will free her, will that satisfy you, Nana?" He suddenly realized how strongly she felt about slavery, and he kissed her profusely in his regret.

The glory of the morning seemed shattered by his thoughtlessness.

"I'm so sorry," he said. "What I said was thoughtless, please forgive me," and he gave her more kisses, then he sat up and fished the negligée up from the floor where it had been flung the night before.

"I believe your mama has arrived and made coffee. It smells wonderful! I will go downstairs and get some coffee for us, if you will promise to have it right here in bed with me, and wearing your new negligée," he said playfully teasing. He looked down and was relieved to see that once more she had a smile for him. He pulled up his pants, slipped on his shoes, and headed downstairs.

Soon he returned with a tray, and handed her a cup of coffee.

"It seems strange, doesn't it, I don't even know if you like your coffee with cream or sugar, or both," he said, holding out cream and sugar for her.

"Café au lait, with sugar and with you," she said softly, smiling up at him, gorgeous and radiant in the silk negligée. Apparently she was willing to forgive his terrible slip. He settled beside her.

"I brought this tin of biscuits from the picnic basket. I didn't think to have croissants or brioche for this morning, but perhaps you will have a biscuit or two. They are English shortbread biscuits, and very good."

"Hmm, they are delicious. Thank you, Emile."

"More coffee, chérie?" he asked, and when she nodded, he filled her cup again.

When they had finished, he put everything back on the tray.

"I will go downstairs to shave and wash up," he said, picking up the tray. "There's water and a basin here, and our new towels, so you can wash up right here. Then we should dress to go finish our shopping, and buy furniture. Would you like me to come back up, and help you dress, or will my presence only slow things down?" he asked, grinning at her. She laughed, and languidly stretched, the negligée falling open, and giving Emile a sudden, rapid heartbeat.

"Your presence would likely slow things down," she said, smiling primly up at him. "And I am a little shy about washing up with you hanging around watching. Later on, perhaps, but not yet," her eyes pleaded. "I have never shown my body to a man before...."

"Some day I would greatly enjoy giving you a bath, or even being allowed to join you in the bath. That can be a really wonderful experience for us both, but today I will honor your request for privacy. Just call me if you change your mind, Nana!" He picked up the tray, and grinned back at her from the doorway, then she heard him on the stairs, humming something.

Her mother had been right. I will just have to adjust to her slower pace, he thought, as he washed and shaved. He threw on a shirt, and gave some attention to his hair. A cravat came next, and he was knotting it, when Mama De Lis appeared.

She gave him a curious look. "Iz it a good mornin', Monsieur?" she asked, frowning slightly, her little dark eyes brimming with curiosity.

"Oh yes, a wonderful morning, thank you! But I could use a little help now, if you please. Can you speed up the dressing going on upstairs? We need to go finish up our purchases for the house this morning, but it might be noon before we can even leave."

Mama de Lis nodded understandingly. "Dis child, she always been one slow dresseh, but I see what I kin do. Have yuh tried givin' her a little coffee? I already made some a while ago. Coffee usually helps"

"Yes, we have had coffee and a few biscuits. I guess it's the decision-making about what to wear that takes so much time and effort. But, of course, we only have what was on our backs yesterday, so it shouldn't take very long this morning, should it?"

"Dere ain't no tellin', Monsieur. But I dun brought her anudeh dress forh today; lateh when yuh come back, I git Washington te help me bring oveh her things, if dat's what yuh want...."

"Yes, that's exactly what I want. I hope she will move in completely, and of course, you may too. That downstairs bedroom is for you."

"I'll jus' be in an' out, Sir. All ma sewin' is spread out in a room at de odeh house, so it's easier te work dere, and often I works late into de night. On nights when yuh can't be hieh, den I'll come,... keep ma baby from bein' lonely. Also I helps her wid her clothes, so I kin do dat den."

"Every time I have seen her she is beautifully dressed. Do you both make her clothes?"

"Yes, Sir. My ladies buy der patterns straight from Paris, an' when Nana likes 'em, we make up gowns forh her too, jus' different colors, so dey don' look too alike. But now, let me go see jus' what I kin do upstairs, an' take her dis dress I dun brought."

Soon a vision in muted taffeta plaid came down the stairs, plaid which changed shades with the lights and shadows, and a little hat to match, with green bows holding the short veil in place.

"Will I do?" Nana asked, smiling and turning around for him to see.

Emile whistled through his teeth, and smiled in approval.

"Eh bien! You are spectacular, ma chère! And I know that if I had stayed to help you, neither of us would be downstairs yet and ready to go!"

Outside he could see Washington waiting with the carriage, so after a quick kiss he took her by the arm.

"Mama, are you coming too?" Nana called out to her mother upstairs.

"No, chérie, I stay hieh an' unpack some a yuhr things. Lateh, when yuh come back hieh, I'll git Washington te help, an' bring de rest oveh. I knows da two of yuh will pick out alla whatja need, jus' fine...."

When they arrived at their first stop, a furniture store, Washington came around and quietly said to Emile,

"Massa Emile, I needs te tell yuh, dey ain't gonna wait on yuh if yuh both go in dere togetheh. Miss Nana knows dat, so yuh go in, do some talkin' an' den I brings her in, and stands wid yuh so dey kin think she maybe a maid, or maybe ma daughteh. Dat way it works betteh."

"All right. I never thought of that. No wonder it took so long to get waited on yesterday. I had no idea why," Emile said, frowning a bit as he helped Nana out of the carriage. She reached up and touched the frown lines between his eyebrows with a finger.

"You go ahead in, and Washington will bring me in,..." she said, pursing her lips up as if to blow him a kiss. "That way there won't be any trouble...."

So Emile cooperated, although he felt some anger at the thought that he couldn't just bring Nana in with him, on his arm. How could anyone deny entrance to such a vision of loveliness, he wondered. He was just beginning to realize that the caste system which he had been well aware of since childhood, which separated black slaves from their white owners, except when they had played together as little children, also seemed to apply to those whose color fell in between, even if they were officially free. There was so much he had to learn, if he was to protect his lovely Nana from embarrassment and pain.

Inside, a salesman came up immediately, and began showing him the sofas and chairs they had in stock. Then Washington came in, with Nana on his arm, and they simply joined him. No word of explanation was offered, nor was any asked for. Quietly Emile consulted with Nana, and soon everything was arranged, with delivery set for the next morning.

They followed the same procedure when shopping for kitchen utensils, silver, china and more linens. Emile went along with the game, because the last thing he wanted was to see Nana's feelings hurt, but inwardly he boiled at the restrictions.

"Can you think of anything more we need to buy today?" he finally asked her.

"No, Emile, nothing but groceries, and I suspect my Mama has taken care of that for a few days. Before we left, she told me she had found a nice little row of stores only about a block away from our house, stores run by our own free Creoles, people she knows."

"*Your* house, my darling, remember?" he said, smiling.

"*Ours*," she insisted, smiling back, as he took her hand and kissed it.

"Then are we ready to go home?" he asked, and she nodded happily.

Sure enough, as soon as he opened the door for her, and followed her in, he could smell some wonderful odors coming from the kitchen. He walked in, and found Mama de Lis busily rolling out fresh biscuits to go with the chicken and rice she already had cooking on the stove.

"Ma daughteh, she still needs te learn a lot about cookin' an' kitchen stuff," she said, dusting the flour off her hands, and grinning at Emile.

"I didn't expect her to know all that, and I already asked her this morning if she would let me provide her with a maid and a cook," Emile replied. "I want her to be the lady of this house, not to have to work for her keep."

"Well, lateh yuh kin git her a maid or cook, but forh now I come an' take care of alla dat," Mama de Lis responded.

"Then you must eat with us when you can, and let me pay you something for your efforts," Emile insisted.

"We talk about dat lateh, raight now I don' wan' mah dinneh te burn, or dis nice little house eideh! None a us wants anudeh fire! God already dun make us walk tru de fire, surely dat's enough of a trial.... Eben in de Bible, He don' make people walk tru fire morh dan once."

Emile took that as a hint, and went to take off his jacket, and ask Nana if she would have a glass of claret or port with him. He had remembered to stick a bottle of each in the picnic basket.

"My dear, will you take a glass of port or claret with me? Your mother seems to have dinner well under control. I don't expect your mother to do all the cooking, so later perhaps we should talk about getting a maid, and a cook."

He noticed that while he had been in the kitchen, Nana had taken off her town dress and hat, and was in a creamy, simple muslin dress, ornamented only with a wide, bright blue ribbon sash, high under her breasts, and long sleeves, gathered with blue ribbon at her wrists. He thought she looked utterly delicious. But then nothing he had seen her in, made her look anything but that, he realized.

He poured out three glasses of claret, putting one glass down in the kitchen for Mama de Lis.

"This is for the cook, so don't use it on the chicken. If you think the chicken needs claret, take some more. This glass is for you, not the chicken!" Emile said, trying to look stern, but not succeeding. His dark eyebrows came together like his father's, but not as convincingly. Already he could see that Madame de Lis had gotten over her initial doubts, and had a genuine smile for him.

"Jus' one little glass forh me, but I make dis chicken real drunk, den he taste much betteh!" she answered, taking the bottle and sloshing a cup or more of claret into the chicken gravy.

Emile had to chuckle as he headed through the dining room.

"Washington is bringing in some of the china and the silver we bought today. The rest will be delivered tomorrow," he added, noticing that the table was already covered with a tablecloth and napkins.

"Why only two places set?" he asked. "Mama de Lis, I hope you will join us tonight, especially since you have cooked such a wonderful meal." Without another word, he looked about and found china and silver, and set a third place at the table for her. From where she stood in the kitchen, Madame de Lis could see what he was doing, and Emile noticed her lips turn up in a smile of appreciation.

Nana also had a smile for him, when he handed her a glass of claret.

"Thank you for including my Mama," she said softly.

As Washington brought in boxes of silver and china, and some more linens, Emile asked him,

"Will you have some of Mama de Lis' fine chicken here? She has agreed to eat with us tonight, so will you stay for some chicken?"

"No, Sir. I eat back in de kitchen at de Big House."

"You are welcome, Washington, if you decide to stay. And thanks for all your help today. I think you prevented some bad moments by telling me how to handle things at the stores. The day before, there were long delays, but I had no idea why. I'm embarrassed to say I had no idea about such things. So thank you, and I'm sure Nana thanks you too."

Yes, Sir," the old man said, bowing. "Any time I can, I means te help,..." he said, and he cast a long, approving look at Nana, before leaving. "Will yuh be needin' me in de mornin', Massa Emile?" he asked on his way out the back door.

"Maybe you should come for a while. There could be a few more things we'll think of, and need the carriage to get. Not too early, around noon perhaps...."

"Yes, Sir, I be hieh den," Washington said, and was on his way.

When everything was ready, Mama de Lis brought in the dishes, and set them on the table.

"Dis china, it's verra pretty," she said, admiring the table, as Emile lit the candles.

"It should be, your daughter picked it out," he answered, turning and winking at Nana. He pulled out a chair for Nana, and intended to do the same for her mother, but by the time he had pushed Nana's chair in, her mother had seated herself. But she did look pleased as she saw him hurry to assist her.

Emile dished up chicken, rice and peas for each of them, and they passed the gravy to each other. For a few minutes there was an awkward silence, which Emile tried to fill with a short blessing in French. Then he smiled, flipped open his napkin, and began on what was a delicious dinner. Out of the corner of his eyes, he watched Nana and her mother, noticing that both of them had perfect table manners, manners that even his Mama Blanche would have approved of, he thought; but the thought brought a stab of pain, as he realized that the women of his two worlds would never meet. He knew he needed to ask a lot of questions to be better prepared for other expeditions to restaurants and stores, but he shoved all that out of his mind. Such matters as that, he thought he would prefer to discuss with Mama de Lis alone, at some future time. He knew he had to prepare himself, or inevitably there would be slights and embarrassments for Nana, and at all costs he wanted to avoid bringing anything like that to the one he loved.

Between the candles, at the center of the table, he had placed a big vase of white lilies, and they were luminous ivory in the candlelight.

Nana looked up, first at the lilies, and then at him.

"Such beautiful lilies," she said, "Thank you, Emile. Is there nothing you have forgotten?"

"I hope not, but I'm sure there is, and gradually we will take care of whatever I have forgotten. If either of you think of things, you must tell me," he added, refilling their wine glasses. "And since I knew we would be busy today with shopping and settling in, I bought some French pastries for dessert, from Maurice's, which I think is the best bakery in New Orleans." Emile had a difficult time not saying that was his family's opinion, and switching it to just his own. With time he thought he would get more accustomed to dealing with this curious gulf in his life. He certainly would have to think ahead before he spoke, and make whatever changes he needed to. He didn't want to hurt Nana inadvertently. This was an aspect of their life together that he hadn't anticipated at all, and already in their first twenty-four hours together he had become more and more aware of the need for caution on his part. He had much to learn if he was to make this love blossom and grow, as he so wanted it to.

The pastries were a huge success, and then he moved three chairs from the dining room into the living room, where he was sent with his coffee and cognac, while the table was cleared. Nana soon joined him, and he poured a cognac for her.

"My mother shooed me out of the kitchen. I wanted to help her with the dishes, but she wouldn't let me," she said apologetically.

"I guess the next thing we need, is to find someone to take on the cooking, cleaning, and laundry," Emile said. "I certainly don't expect your mother to take on all that, and I don't want you to. Perhaps we can ask your Mama for suggestions. She may be able to recommend someone. I want to pamper you, as well as love you, Nana, chérie."

Later Nana's mother appeared in the kitchen doorway, and announced she was going home. She came and gave her daughter a long embrace and kiss, then Emile accompanied her to the back door, and handed her a key. He said,

"Tomorrow afternoon I must make an appearance at Marengo, so will you come here and keep Nana company? Here is your key. I will be back in a few days. I hate to leave at all, but I must. I hope you understand."

"Yes, Monsieur. Years back, I waz in de same kinda situation as my Nana iz now. Plaçage, I know what dat be like. No matter how yuh both feel, dere be long periods of loneliness ahead forh her. I know all about dat, an' I will be raight hieh te help her."

"I hope they won't be long periods. I will do everything I can to be here with her, but I do thank you for coming when she needs you. Just in the last two days I have learned how much more I need to know, to protect her from the slights and hurts of the world. I need your warnings. You may see things I won't see at first, so help me learn my way around all the prejudice, all the unwritten rules I don't know. Please help me to shield her. I don't want to bring her pain," Emile said softly, as he saw her out. Her gaze back at him softened.

"I'll do ma best, Sir, I sureh will,... an' I know yuh mean no harm te come te Nana. Sometimes it jus' gonna be hard te stop de pain.... It's not yuh, but der be a lotta meanness out dere in dis world...."

Emile returned and sat down next to Nana.

"It will be wonderful to have some living room furniture tomorrow, and I think that large Persian carpet will look perfect in here, and the other one you picked out for the bedroom too. Gradually things do begin to make your little house look like a home."

"Our home, Emile, and thank you for all of it. It will soon be very cozy."

He took their empty cognac glasses and the bottle in his arm, and held out a hand to her.

"Are you ready to go up to bed?" he asked.

"Yes, especially if you are staying for the night, Emile, are you?"

"I am, if you want me to, chérie," he said.

"Oh yes, Emile, please. I do want you to... very much."

"Then, my love, I will stay with you. There will be nights I can't be with you, and days also. I know they will be very long ones, when I have to be away, but your Mama has promised me that she will come, so you won't be alone. These are problems we will have to adjust to. I'd much prefer to stay here with you all the time, but we both know that can't happen. My mother knows nothing about us, and I guess it will have to stay that way. My father knows just that I have found love, and he understands, but still he needs me to help, especially as cane harvest and processing gets underway. The busiest times come in November and December. At Marengo then, we work around the clock until all the cane is harvested, and processed. My papa is too old to do all the supervision; he expects me to take over, and learn by supervising, so those will be months in which I won't be able to come to you very often.

"Please, Nana, don't give up the rest of your life. Meet your friends, entertain them here in your home, and go out. We will work out a schedule soon, so you'll know when I will come. I will never expect you to just stay here, locked up and waiting for me. This little house I have given you must not be a prison for you. I want to play a big part in your life, but I don't want you to sacrifice your life for me. Do you understand, chérie?"

"Yes, Emile, I know I will be lonely when you can't be with me, but I think I understand. You have to be in two different worlds, and I dread it when you have to marry. I don't know how I will be able to share you, but at least your marriage won't be right away. But now, when must you leave me? Tomorrow or the next day? Tell me now, so I can get used to the idea. Don't shock me at the last minute, please...."

He held her hand, but was unable to meet her eyes.

"My father does not demand an arranged marriage for several more years, but tomorrow afternoon I must make an appearance at home. I will only be gone a few days, and I will be dreaming of you the entire time. So will you allow me to share your bed tonight?"

"Yes, and love me hard, to make up for when you are gone the next few days," she said, drawing him to the bed with her. "I guess we never could have had a two week sort of honeymoon together, but it will be very difficult to part with you tomorrow. Now that we've been together these two wonderful nights, the nights apart will be so lonely...."

"Ma chérie, I will be just as lonely, thrashing about in my bed, thinking of you, and wanting to be with you," he said, and began to help her undress.

The talk about inevitable separation had roused him, with the realization that he would be without her for several nights, and Emile found it difficult to hold back, and wait for her. He tried to be as gentle as possible, and his touch and his kisses sought out all the places he knew would please her. Soon her hands were pulling him to her, and he came, almost bursting with passion.

"Come, come with me now, my darling," he cried out, and resonating to the passion of his call, she quivered in his arms, joining him in a rush of such intensity that afterwards they both lay together, contented but completely spent. She held him to her for a long time, wondering how she would ever be able to let go, and spend those nights without him. He opened his eyes, and saw her tears,

"Chérie, please don't cry. I can't bear to see you cry," and again he began to try to kiss her tears away. "You love me, don't you? Just as I love you? Isn't it better to be together this way, even if we have to be apart at times? Dancing together at the balls would never have been enough, would it? And I wouldn't be able to bear it if you were living with another man...."

"No, I know that, it's just that I am dreading the times we have to be apart, Emile. Why must the world be so cruel and force us to separate?"

"Perhaps, if the separations are too much to bear, I could take you to France. There people are much more tolerant, and we could live together, married. But we would have to give up our life here. Unfortunately we will never be accepted here in New Orleans society, as a couple. We both know that is sadly true. Perhaps your people would accept us, but mine would not, and I do owe a debt to my family, and to the business we run....

"I hope we can learn to share our love and to be together as much as possible. But if we have to flee to Paris, then that's what we'll do. However, before we reach a decision like that, I hope we can try things here for a while, and just see if we can manage. If we go to France, it will probably be as a penniless couple, since I know my father would disinherit me. When I asked him for some money for this house and its contents, he made me swear that I would accept the arranged marriage he will contract for me, and try to give him one or two male heirs for Marengo. If you bear my only son, perhaps our son could inherit Marengo, but only after my father's death. There are cases in which exactly that has happened. But let's forget the future for now, and just enjoy our time together."

He stayed in her arms, kissing her shoulder and neck, holding her until he felt her relax, and her gentle breathing told him she was asleep.

The next morning he brought her biscuits and coffee, and settled in the bed with her. After a biscuit, he leaned over for a kiss.

"I know there will come a day when we'll start having breakfast downstairs, but for now, this is sort of special, eating here together in our special bed!"

Nana managed a smile, but he noticed that she was somewhat subdued, as if already thinking of the parting ahead.

"We have a lovely new hip bath now, and your Mama is here, and already heating some water for your bath. I'll bring it up. I'd love to help you bathe, or we could enjoy a bath together," Emile said, smiling at the thought.

"I am not quite ready for that," she murmured. "A bath would be lovely, but I am very shy, so sharing it with you, that will have to wait for another day, someday in the future."

"I can live with that, as long as I can look forward to it someday, can I?"

"Yes, when I am more used to being around a man, it could happen, and then perhaps we can both enjoy it," she responded shyly, unable to look him in the face.

"All right, it sounds as if you would like a bath, even if it is alone, so I'll go get the water." He leaned over and fingered her breasts as he kissed her. She took hold of him, and the kiss became longer, more passionate.

"I don't know how I will force myself to leave you later," he said, pulling away, throwing on his pants, and shoes, and heading for the stairs.

"Hot water will be up very soon," he called out, and she listened to his footsteps on the stairs.

"Oh, God help me," she whispered out loud. "Will love always come with so much sadness? I don't know how I will bear his absences...."

Madame de Lis arrived just in time to comfort her daughter. After a quick lunch, together they cleared the dining room table, and scrubbed it down. Then they laid out some fabric, and pinned pattern pieces on it. Her mother knew the time of the first departure was imminent, and she wanted to have Nana busy with something, to help cut the sting.

Emile came into the kitchen, and picked up the empty picnic basket.

"I will try to bring back some nice wines, a bottle of cognac, and perhaps some champagne for us to celebrate my second coming," he said, trying to smile as if nothing significant was about to happen. He came to Nana, put his arms around her, and gave her a somewhat perfunctory kiss. She was hurt; he seemed distracted, as if he had already made the break to his other world.... A world she knew she would be unlikely to ever enter with him.

"I promise, chérie, I'll be back as soon as I can, probably in a couple days. In the meantime, do enjoy yourself with your friends. Invite them in to see your new home, and go out too. You will feel so much better if you do that, and I am trusting your mother to see that you do. A bientôt, stay well, my darling."

When the front door closed behind him, and she saw him climb into the carriage, and set off, she burst into tears.

"You didn't tell me it would be this hard, Mama. I'm not sure I can bear living like this."

Her mother took her in her arms. "If dis turns out te be too hard forh yuh, den we'll jus' hafta find yuh a fine, free Creole man of color, one who kin stay wid yuh alla de time. I knows yuh dun wanna eben think about dat raight now, but maybe lateh...."

"No, Mama, don't even say such things. Emile and I love each other, and look how much he has done for me already? He did say this morning, that if the separations were too difficult, he would take me to live in Paris, where we could live together openly, and even marry."

Madame de Lis nodded in a preoccupied sort of way. "Dat's good, baby," she said, and frowned and turned away, hoping her daughter wouldn't read her expression. Dey all do say dat, at de beginnin', but den dey don't go,... she thought to herself.

Nana found the first day and night without Emile to be almost unbearable, but with each day that passed, she found things got a little easier. Her mother kept her busy with the dressmaking, and she had also brought a hat form, which they covered, and began to decorate, making their own artificial flowers for it. Nana didn't feel ready to invite friends to her love nest, but she was willing to go for some walks with them, and visit in their homes. They chatted and laughed together, but suddenly a silence would drop over them. Nana didn't even want to talk about her new relationship, although she knew that they were all aware of it. They were tactfully silent, and waited for her explanations, but she made none.

Three long days passed very slowly, and then just as the twilight was setting in, she heard a knock at the door, and she ran to open it. Emile stood on the doorstep, smiling, and she flung herself on him. After a long embrace and kisses, he asked, "May I come in your house?" and she took him by the hand, and led him in.

"Have you missed me?" he asked, holding her tightly to him, and kissing her.

"I can't even begin to tell you how much," she answered. "But come see, the furniture and rugs have come, and we've got things pretty much in place. Perhaps you will have some other ideas about placement," she said, taking him by the hand into the living room. "What do you think?" she asked, bouncing about with pride and joy over her new things.

"It looks wonderful. I can't think of any changes at all. Now did you have that sofa put in the bedroom, and did you blush deeply when you told the movers where to put it?" He chuckled.

"Yes, I know I blushed, and one of the movers looked at me and smiled, which made it even worse! But come see upstairs, you may want to place the sofa however you have in mind. I have, as I told you, no experience with things like you are planning,..." she said.

He thought she blushed delightfully as she spoke, and he had to give her a kiss.

"Then I guess we just have to make a trip upstairs right now," he said, taking her by the hand, and heading up the stairs.

"Very nice," he said, smiling approvingly. "Now all that remains is to try and see if the placement is right," he added, and taking her up in his arms, he put her full-length on the sofa.

"Well, the fit is right. Now for the final experiment," he said, beginning to unbutton her dress. Nana began laughing, but she didn't resist, as the rest of her clothing ended up on the floor. Emile knelt beside the sofa, and began to kiss her.

"I've had some very long, lonely days and nights to think about this, so now I'm going to kiss you, from your little toes to the very top of your head," he said, and he began kissing her toes, then working up her body with kisses. As he did so, he slowly loosened his own clothes, until they were both nude. She moaned with the pleasure of his kisses, and soon he joined her on the sofa, kneeling over her, and pressing her legs apart.

"So how's the sofa?" he asked breathlessly. "Will it do?"

"Oh yes, Emile, it's perfect," she said softly. "Please,... there is room for you to lie on top of me,... please...."

A half an hour later, he lazily asked "So do you think this sofa is a good fit? Shall we keep it, darling, or do you want to send it back, and try another? We can keep trying until we find just the right one," he answered, grinning at the thought of what opportunities that presented to him, and kissing her.

"Keep it, Emile! It couldn't be any better!" she purred, laughing up at him.

"Oh, I'm disappointed. I was looking forward to trying out lots and lots of sofas with you!"

He was rewarded with a giggle, and a little slap on his cheek.

By this time it had turned completely dark outside, so he got up, pulled on his pants and shoes, and went downstairs. Her mother had evidently left, so he locked the doors, and came back upstairs.

"Now for a little cognac," he said. "Will you have it over there, or in bed?"

"Over here, I think," she said, smiling as he handed her the cognac.

She was desperate to ask him how long he could stay this time, but thrust it out of her mind. It might be better not to know, and have that sadden their hours together. She already knew that she would probably always have to restrain herself from asking that question, as long as their relationship lasted. It would be the sadness which would always be, like a gray rain cloud, hovering over her,... like her tears, always there, waiting to be shed....

*   *   *

When Emile had finally come home after several days and nights spent in the city, he found both his parents sitting together in the family parlor. He found their intent look at him very disconcerting.

His mother took his hand, and he gave her a kiss on the cheek.

"Your father told me you were tending to some business for him in the city. Did it go well? And have you had dinner, mon chèr? We have just finished ours, but I'm sure we can find something for you, if you haven't eaten." She smoothed her graying hair back with her fingers, tidying the parts which fell over her forehead back over her ears, and tucking a few loose strands back into her chignon. Emile had long recognized this as a characteristic gesture of hers, especially when there was something bothering her, or something she was uncertain about. He smiled at her, noticing out of the corner of his eye, that his father was smiling conspiratorially, and winking at him.

"Yes, Mama, it was a real estate transaction, and it went very well. With Papa's help, now I have a place to stay when I am late in the city, and don't feel like taking the long ride home. It's nothing special, just a little house, but over time it will be cheaper than staying at the St. Louis Hotel, and it does give me more freedom to stay later at parties I am enjoying."

"I seem to remember that your father once had such a piece of property, and used to spend some nights there in the city, instead of taking the long ride home," his mother remarked.

To Emile her answer seemed very straightforward, and he was unable to read anything into it.

"That's true, but I finally sold the property, and ended that deal," his father said, giving Emile a meaningful look.

"Ah yes," Emile answered vaguely, wondering if there was any hidden message in what both of them had said, and whether both of them knew it, or only his father.

"And as for dinner, no, I haven't eaten, so it would be very welcome."

Madame Blanche rang the little bell that sat on her worktable, and immediately Peter answered it, appearing in the doorway, and bowing.

"My son has just arrived home from the city. Can you fix him some dinner please, Peter?"

"Yes'm. I fix it directly. Massa Emile, would yeh like it in hieh, or in de dinin' room?"

"In here would be just fine, Peter. Thanks." Emile sat down and stretched out his legs. They were stiff from the long carriage drive.

His father looked over at him, rubbing his fingers over his long, drooping gray mustache. Finally he spoke,

"Emile, I will be needing you to go back to the city in a few days. In fact I'm counting on you to conduct most of my business there, with my factor, and others,... our banking business. It's wonderful to have you take all that on for me. I really don't much relish trips to the city any more, but I know you do, and you'd be bored if you spent most of your time out here, with us old folks."

"Glad to do it for you, Sir," Emile responded, grateful for the cover his father seemed to be providing for him, but amazed. Maybe in his youth, he had also had a similar sort of romance. The picture of his father in such a situation seemed suddenly amusing. He had never even considered the idea before! But surely that would explain why suddenly he had fallen in with the entire scheme. What an interesting idea, someday he hoped he'd learn if he was right, and he wondered if he would ever learn exactly what his mother knew.

The tray with dinner arrived, and he dove in. There was a shrimp and okra gumbo, warm French bread, and a large slice of apple pie for dessert.

Later, after he lay alone in his bed, he thought of Nana, and wondered if she was as lonely as he was. He realized that he had suddenly acquired a new role. While here at home his role remained the same, the dutiful son, now nearly grown up, but still under the implicit control of his parents, whereas with Nana and her mother, he had several new roles, as the head of a household, a lover, and soon perhaps a new father. He was a provider now, even if the money for the venture was all from his father. He hoped that his father would forget about the arranged marriage, at least for several more years, but he did realize that he had committed to accept one eventually,... perhaps in four or five years.

Fortunately Emile heard little more about the possible arranged marriage, and he was free to pursue his deepening relationship with Nana. Soon, in fact, she was able to tell him that she was expecting.

"You don't need to treat me as if I am a fragile piece of china, and will shatter in your arms," Nana assured him, laughing at his solicitude. Still, it would be her first child, and she was nervous about childbirth. Her mother had promised to be with her, and that gave her more confidence. In their community of free Creoles of color, Madame de Lis was well-known as an experienced midwife.

For Emile and Nana, their life together brought them great joy. He could hardly bear the days and nights he had to return to Marengo, and they had to be apart. The only thing he found disturbing was the fact that he couldn't take Nana with him to so many things he was eager to share with her, and their relationship often seemed to have to be contained within the four walls of their little house. Felicity Street, he thought, it was the right name, but somehow the barriers presented to them both by society left them largely to themselves, unable to share experiences at the theater, the symphony, and the opera. While Emile was unable to share his world with Nana, she was also reluctant to bring in her Creole friends, but gradually she did, beginning with Armand St. Pierre and his band of musicians, then adding a few of her girlfriends. They accepted Emile and so they began to develop a circle of friends, among Nana's people, the free people of color, and their little home on Felicity Street became alive with music, voices and laughter.

*   *   *

For Emile and Nana, the months passed happily, and one day, when Emile was at home at Marengo, Washington came to him,

"Mama de Lis says yuh betteh come quick, if yuh want te be dere when de baby's born!"

"Oh, mon Dieu! Really? Bring the carriage around, Washington, I'll be right there!" And after throwing a few clothes in a bag, Emile hurried to the family parlor. He found his Papa there, at his desk, working on the plantation ledgers.

"Papa, I have to hurry to the city, I think it's my first child coming, so please think up an explanation for my absence. I will be gone several days, so come up with some kind of tedious business deal you need me to stay in the city and negotiate, one which will take at least several days, maybe a week, please...."

"Bien. I can do that. Bonne chance, Emile!" his father replied, looking up at his son with one of his very rare smiles. "Now, hurry off, I'll take care of things here!"

Emile smiled back at him, and was out the door, down the steps of the Big House, and into the carriage faster than ever before.

"Let's go, Washington!" he yelled. "There's no time to lose!"

When they arrived at Felicity Street, he quietly opened the door, after knocking and getting no reply. Evidently Mama de Lis was upstairs with Nana. He took the stairs two at a time.

"Am I here in time?" he asked, sticking his head hesitantly around the door to the bedroom, a bit nervous about what he might see. He could see Nana in bed, and her mother bending over her.

"Yuh be in time, forh sureh. First babies, dey take der own sweet time!" Madame de Lis muttered, without turning around to him.

"May I come in?" Emile asked, a bit uncertain about what the role of a prospective father might be, under the circumstances.

"Yeah. It could be a while yet," Mama de Lis said. "Come hold her hand," she ordered, and Emile sprang to do just that. He kissed Nana's hand stretched out to him, then planted another kiss on her forehead, then another on her cheek.

"So, chérie, how are things going?" he asked softly.

"Very slowly, Emile. This started to get painful yesterday, and still is.... Maybe now that you're here, our baby will hurry up and come," she answered, then gasped.

Emile noticed a little bowl of water, and a washcloth on the bedside table, and he moistened the cloth, and gently wiped Nana's forehead, which was glistening with perspiration.

Her big dark eyes seemed to focus on him. "Thank you," she whispered, and then he saw her eyes widen, and she let out a moan.

"Oh, Mama, will it be over soon?" she sobbed.

"Yes, ma baby, I see de little head raight now. When de next pain hits yuh, give a big, big push."

Emile could hardly bear to see Nana in such pain. He kissed her hand again, and prayed it would soon be over. An hour passed, very slowly, he thought, marked by Nana's moans and heavy breathing. Finally she screamed, a long, high scream, and Mama de Lis shouted,

"Dat's it, honey chile. Yuh done it, hieh's yuhr daughteh," and Emile saw a small, pink creature, tiny legs and arms flaying out, before Madame de Lis wrapped her in a towel, and handed her to Nana.

"All that effort, and you're such a little thing," Nana crooned softly, hugging the baby to her, and kissing the top of its head.

"Emile, take your first look at your little Nanette," she said, smiling at him.

"Oh Dieu merci, that's over. Why must the arrival of new life be so painful?" he said, kissing Nana's forehead, and getting a look at the rosy face of his firstborn.

"You surely gave your mama a hard time," he said softly, kissing the little hand which was waving toward him.

"Now, Nana, feed dat chile beforh she starts a'yowlin'," Mama de Lis ordered, and taking hold of the little bundle, she pushed back the towel, and helped the baby find Nana's breast. Soon all three of them laughed when they heard the noisy sucking.

*   *   *

It was harder than ever before for Emile to stay away. He had to spend some time at Marengo, but increasingly he needed to be with Nana, and their baby daughter. Even though he couldn't be there every day, he was able to mark his daughter's progress, her first smiles, when she first crawled, then walked her first tottering steps, and finally to hear her first words. His love for Nana grew even deeper, now that they had a child to share. Emile basked in the pride and wonder of fatherhood. It was one of the happiest periods of his life, just as all his days with Nana had been. But it was even better, now that their little daughter had arrived. Before he would go to Felicity Street, he had to stop not only for presents for Nana, but now for presents for their little Nanette as well, stuffed animals, frilly little dresses, and baby books. And, of course, always presents for her mother, usually glistening ones!

But one morning at Marengo, as Emile chafed to leave for the city, he and his father were having coffee, and the old man emerged from behind his newspaper with some shocking and unwelcome news.

"Emile, the news doesn't sound good. It looks as if we are about to get into that war with Mexico. How likely are you to be called up?"

"Right away probably, Papa, if it does come to war. Our Army is small, and every West Point graduate will be needed to help provide officers," Emile replied, stirring sugar into his second cup of coffee. "I haven't really followed the news recently. What leads you to that conclusion?"

"Well, there seems to be constant arguments over California, and over most of the border. War looks inevitable; it seems to be just a question of when, not if. And as I've read about all this, I thought about your 'property' in the city. Although I don't want to have any direct contact, at the same time I will help you with an advance of money to take care of things, if you do have to go serve your country. That I will do as soon as you hear you have to go, and during your absence, I will send Washington into town weekly to see what else might be needed. I will do whatever is necessary, but I will do it all through Washington."

"Papa, I will be very grateful for your help, and so will everybody involved."

"Son, do things go well there for you? Is the 'property' all you expected?" His father had a slight smile as he used the word 'property.'

"Much more so, couldn't be better! The 'property' couldn't be any finer! And actually, as you know, we have a little daughter now! She is adorable! And she has just begun to talk!"

Again his father gave him a tight, little smile, then said,

"There is one more thing, however, that we need to discuss. If you must go fight the Mexicans, I want you married before you go, and preferably your nice French Creole bride pregnant with an heir for Marengo. I hadn't planned to have to arrange all this so soon, but rather to give you several more years of freedom. Now however, we must arrange a suitable marriage, and preferably with your legal wife pregnant before you leave for war."

"I see your point, Papa, but you must know how very reluctant I am to engage in a marriage at this time."

"I do, but the arrangements may take a while to complete, so I think I must begin on it right away. I'm sorry to push this matter on you so soon, but it's the war, and the fear of something happening to you, without assuring the future of our beautiful Marengo. You may not be enthusiastic about wedding at this time, my son, but I'm sure you can see the reasons for taking care of this before you are called into service. And this was my condition, if you remember, when earlier you asked for my financial help."

"Mon Dieu, I am totally unenthusiastic about marriage now! But I made you a promise, so if it must be, then I must agree to it. Just find me a pretty and congenial young lady, one who doesn't seem very demanding. Suddenly my life seems to be getting almost beyond managing.... I *love that property*, Papa, truly. But I swore I would accept the marriage you would arrange for me, and I will, but not with enthusiasm.... Actually with sadness and regret, but I know I must keep my promise to you."

Emile's father nodded, and continued to look at him. Finally he said,

"Now that we have agreed on the necessity of your marriage before you have to leave for Mexico, I want you to accompany me to the opera tomorrow night. A number of fine French Creole girls will be making their social coming out, and among them is the one I have thought would make you a good wife, and be a good mistress for Marengo. On our way, we will make a stop to pick up a bouquet I have ordered, and during the intermission, as is customary, you will visit this young lady in her family's box, and present her with the flowers. If you approve of my selection, your mother and I will invite the family to Marengo for Sunday dinner, and while I pursue the negotiations with her father, you may escort the young lady around Marengo, and use that time to become better acquainted with her."

"Yes, Papa, as you wish," Emile answered dutifully, and the eyes he turned on his father were spiritless, even sad. "You know how I feel about a marriage now...."

"Yes, and but for the war, I would have allowed you a few more years before insisting on marriage, but the war has changed all that. The young lady I have selected for you is from a fine but impoverished French Creole family. The father has a well-known weakness for gambling, and I know he can't afford to turn down my excellent offer for his daughter. Because of the rush, I will ask no dowry, and of course we don't need it, and I doubt they can afford one. Her name is Marie Therese Massenet. Make the best of this, my son. It need not interfere greatly with your other relationship, you know,... just as long as you live up to your duties as a husband."

*   *   *

The next evening Emile dressed for the opera with considerable reluctance. His valet, Tom, seemed to sense his master's mood, and was quietly comforting.

"Tonight I go to meet the woman my father has picked out for me to marry," Emile said softly.

"Massa, dis may seem too soon forh yuh, but yuhr papa, he gonna pick yuh a good woman, a dat yuh kin be sureh," Tom responded, moving in front of Emile to tie his cravat.

"It's come too suddenly,... I am not ready for a wife yet, but I have promised, and my father insists on the marriage before I am called up. With graduation from West Point, I'll be called up fast, even before a war is official, and my father wants me to try to present him with a possible heir. He is thinking more of Marengo's future, and not of mine." Emile's voice was angry and bitter.

"Dat may be, Massa, but he wants te be sureh about de future of dis hieh fine place, an' all its people," came the soft reply.

"Well, no matter how I feel, I'm to meet this woman he has in mind tonight at the opera. Everything seems to have already been decided without me!"

"So dis be a big night forh yuh," Tom responded calmly, as he eyed his young master, and concluded that he had done all he could for his appearance. No woman could be displeased with dis young man, and wid a future as mistress of dis fine place, he concluded to himself silently, as he smiled, and opened the door for his young master. He also had to admit that he felt sorry for him, but that was the penalty of being the heir to Marengo.

The drive to the city was a silent one. Emile had nothing to say to his father, nothing would do him any good, now that his father had made his decision.

Once they reached their box, he put the flowers down beside his seat, wishing that he could pick them apart, and throw each rose petal and stalk down on the audience below. As the orchestra began to tune up, about twenty young women rose to their feet, smiling and waving in response to the applause and the loud shouts of approval, in both English and French.

"If you look to the box three boxes away from ours, on the right, you will see your future bride," his father said, not even looking up from his perusal of the night's program.

"I think you will agree with me, that I have picked you out a very pretty bride," he added, looking first at the young lady in question, and then at his son.

Emile didn't want to look, but he had to. Apparently she would share his life and his bed, and there was nothing he could say which would make a difference. He tried to appear casual as he looked over at her. Unlike most of the other girls standing and waving, she was not in pale pink or blue, but in a rich, dark green gown, which showed off her figure beautifully. Although she was quite petite, she was very well-formed, with a tiny waist, full breasts, and a lovely profile. As he gazed at her politely but coolly, she turned and gave him a full smile. Apparently she was informed of the discussions regarding their future. And before his eyes, there arose another woman's face, that of his Nana, and he shook and turned away from the girl who smiled at him. He would have to go through with it, he knew, but it would be difficult to treat this young woman as his wife.

When the first intermission came, his father gruffly reminded him,

"Emile, it's time for you to present yourself," so he took the flowers and dutifully but angrily stalked off to make the required call.

Marie Therese was surrounded by young men, each bearing flowers, but the moment she saw him, she brushed the others aside, and stepped towards him.

"You are Emile de Marigny?" she asked softly, accepting the pink roses he mutely handed to her. "I look forward to Sunday when we can become better acquainted, and you can show me around your beautiful Marengo. Your father and mother have graciously extended an invitation to my family. So we will be joining you for Sunday dinner."

Emile was surprised to hear that the invitation had already been extended. He thought he had understood that it would be made only after he gave his approval to this woman this very night at the opera. Things seemed to be moving too fast, and to be out of his control. Still he did find her quite pretty, so he bowed over her hand, and played along with the game. He didn't see any other alternative left for him, unless it was poverty with Nana in Paris, and that would surely mean the loss of Marengo, a consequence he was not yet ready to face.

"Yes, Mademoiselle, I too look forward to Sunday, and I will be glad to show you around Marengo, a place I love deeply, as I hope you will also," Emile answered. He couldn't bring himself to say anything more, so he bowed as he kissed her hand, noticing how small it was, and what pretty fingers she had. He held her hand for a few moments, studying it, and the deep green eyes she turned upon him.

"Do you play the piano, Mademoiselle? You have such artistic hands," he asked, thinking of how those hands might also play upon him, and a flush of warmth rose within him, in spite of his efforts to remain calm, even cool. He squeezed her little hand slightly before letting go.

"Yes, I do play the piano, but not very well yet," she answered. "If you enjoy listening, I will try much harder," she said, and her promise seemed to convey more than just trying harder at the piano.

"Is that a promise, to try hard?" he asked, smiling a little, and wondering how she would respond to his double entendre.

"Yes, to try hard to please,..." she answered softly, turning the effect of her deep green eyes fully upon him.

"Then I look forward to that," Emile answered, meeting her gaze with his dark eyes; then bowing again, he left the box. The orchestra was beginning the introduction to the second act, and he was very relieved to be rescued by the start of the music.

When he returned to the de Marigny box, his father looked up at him.

"So,... have I picked well for you?" he asked.

Emile waited to answer. A silence was about all that was left to him, since he knew he had no grounds on which to base a refusal, a refusal which in all likelihood would be rejected outright. "She is pretty,... very petite, and she has a nice smile, and tremendous green eyes," he said, and with that, father and son pretended to become absorbed in the second act of *The Magic Flute*.

As the Opéra finally came to an end, Emile couldn't resist another long glance at the woman he would marry, and their eyes met. It seemed to him that those deep green eyes were full of promise, and he nodded and smiled back, swallowing hard as an image of his Nana rose before his eyes. It would be difficult, he knew, but somehow he would have to manage the situation. He would have to satisfy both women, but suddenly he found himself looking forward to that challenge. If this marriage had to be, then that would be his challenge.

On the ride home, both men were silent, and Emile entertained himself by imaging how this bride of his would look when finally he would see all of her on their wedding night.

When his valet Tom appeared to help him undress, Emile answered his unspoken question.

"She is pretty, petite, and with big, dark green eyes," he volunteered.

Tom knew better than to ask any questions, but he also knew that his young master was not entirely displeased with his father's choice.

Before he fell asleep, Emile imagined a Sunday walk with Mademoiselle Massenet, and with what pride he would show her his Marengo. Would he be able to entice her to walk down the other side of the levée with him, and under the willows? There, if she agreed, they might be able to become a bit better acquainted, and he fell asleep with a smile on his face.

*   *   *

Saturday passed very slowly. Emile ordered that his horse Rudi be saddled up, and he took a long ride all around the plantation, admiring the high growth of the cane, and then riding by the quarters, amused at the children playing about there, and acknowledging waves and smiles. Many adults had apparently finished their work for the day, and were either busy in their own little garden plots, or relaxing in rockers on their porches. He knew that some of their people were angry and resentful, but most of them seemed to accept their lot, and their master. He hoped that when he was the master, he would be able to do better than that. He had long planned that one of his first acts when he took over the management of Marengo would be to tear down the stocks. His father sometimes had recalcitrant slaves put in the stocks for a day or two, but he didn't approve, and removal of the stocks would be a positive gesture. He also intended to see that rewards would be given for good or improved performance, something his father had never bothered with, except for the usual small rewards given to adults at Christmas time. And if the plantation finances would permit, he planned also to improve the diet of his slaves, and make it more varied. Surely all that would be possible.

What improvements would he make to cane production and processing? He would add vacuum pans, and as soon as he could afford it, he wanted to lay railroad tracks from the fields to the sugar house, then on to the dock, and add automatic conveyor belts to carry the cane from the shed where it was loaded, on into the grinder. These improvements he knew would greatly improve and speed up the entire process, and there would still be plenty of work for his slaves. Sugar production was a long ways from becoming more automatic than that.

Marengo was his future.... How could he even consider leaving it for Paris?

Then as he neared the levée, from which he could see the small patch of willows that bowed and shone in the sunlight reflected from the river, his thoughts again turned to the next day, and he began to anticipate whatever degree of closeness his prospective little bride would allow him. The willows clustered thickly by the river, and would provide cover for whatever experiments he chose to make. At least he might be able to determine if this wife he was to take was a hot-spirited lady, or if he would have to bed a cold fish, one who, after giving him two sons, might demand a separate bedroom and a separate life. Unfortunately, the decision that he was to wed her had already been made without him. Whatever she was, she would be his. Tomorrow perhaps he might be able to determine her nature, if she would give him a chance. He frowned as he rode back to the stables.

Late the next morning the Massenet family arrived, and were escorted into the formal salon, with its long crystal chandeliers, its marble fireplace, topped by the marble and gold Louis XIV clock - the reason given by his mother for stopping Emile as a child, from jumping and running about in that room,... "that you will damage the clock!" Emile had never liked the formal salon, first because of the restraints laid upon him as a child, and also because its elegant brocade furniture was simply not comfortable,... slick and slippery for both children and adults, and not at all comfortable. Perhaps when he was the master of Marengo, he would have all that brocade furniture reupholstered or replaced.

After greeting Mademoiselle Massenet and her mother with kisses on their hands, and bowing to her father, a short, white-haired French Creole, whose hands were in the air even to emphasize his first words of greeting, Emile escorted his intended bride to a sofa, and after she was seated, he joined her, sitting close to her. She put a little hand down on the small space of brocade left between them. Emile wasn't sure if this was a protective, defensive move, aimed to block him from moving closer, or whether it was an enticement, encouraging him to take her hand in his. He decided on the latter, and as he took her hand up in his own, he quickly moved closer to her. His move was greeted by a smile, and he thought he detected a twinkle in those fascinating, deep green eyes.

Fortunately the habit of giving compliments was well-ingrained in Emile, so he began his reluctant courtship.

"You look very beautiful again today, as you did the other night at the opera. That deep green gown distinguished you from all the other girls being presented, in their pale pinks and blues. I liked that, and today, again you wear green, only a softer shade, just right for daytime, and perfect, with your beautiful green eyes."

"Merci bien," she responded. "It is such a lovely day, will there be time, perhaps after lunch, for you to show me around your beautiful Marengo?"

"I had planned on that. I believe we are to have some wine now, and then dinner, but after dinner, I will show you around. Is there anything special you would like to see?"

"I saw your gorgeous oak alley as we arrived. I can't imagine anything more beautiful than it, but perhaps you will show me the gardens. I have heard that Marengo is famous for its flower gardens."

"I will look forward to that very much," Emile answered, handing her a glass of white wine from the silver tray held out before them by Tom. His eyes flicked up, and caught a quick wink in Tom's eyes, a wink which seemed to be signaling his approval of the bride-to-be.

As Emile handed her the glass of wine, his fingertips just brushed hers, and he lifted his own glass in salutation to her.

"To you, Mademoiselle, and to our future here," he said, and felt a strong feeling of pleasure course through him as their eyes again met. He sighed guiltily, as he fought it.

"Tell me, do you prefer to be called Therese, or Marie Therese? It seems rather strange to have to ask that. We are still virtually strangers, but soon it appears, we will be much closer," Emile continued. Physically he found her very attractive, but he was still astonished that here they were, about to be affianced, and yet they knew so little of each other. It seemed like a bizarre way to arrange for a lifetime together. Wasn't the attraction of love a better way? A relationship based on mutual attraction and love, as his was with Nana? Surely.... He was brought swiftly back to reality as he heard his little, prospective mate begin to answer his question, a question he had quite forgotten he had asked.

"Yes, please call me Marie Therese, and may I call you Emile?" she responded, taking a sip of her wine. "It does look as if our fathers may reach an agreement on our future today, so we should begin to learn more about each other right away. I know you have finished up at West Point, but aside from military matters, what are you interested in?"

"Of course I am interested in the best possible management of Marengo, whatever are the latest inventions which improve the cultivation and processing of sugar, but I also love music, and I enjoy a good novel now and then, and I love opera and the theater. Now, of course, I have a new and absorbing interest,..." he answered, looking at her with some amusement.

"And what is your new, absorbing interest?" she asked softly.

"I look forward to exploring a new life of marriage, and learning how to please you, when you become my wife."

Marie Therese blushed, and Emile was fascinated, watching her cheeks flare up, and the blush spread down her chest, as far as he could see. She looked at him, momentarily speechless. "My pleasure as your wife?..." she finally murmured.

"Yes, although I realize that some men care only for their own pleasure in the marriage bed, I can't see how that can possibly be as successful as mutual satisfaction. I do intend to see that your needs are met, as well as mine, chérie. And since our parents most likely will agree on our betrothal today, I will give you just a little taste of pleasure today, but not as great as that which I hope to give you on our wedding night. Today we will try to find out how well-suited we may be to each other emotionally,... and learn if we can be compatible...."

Emile watched as a flush spread from her cheeks down her neck, and to her breasts, and he was longing to hear her response, but just then Tom appeared in the doorway to announce that dinner was ready, so Emile escorted Marie Therese into the dining room, his hand firmly resting on her little waist.

"More of that later," he whispered in her tiny, petal-like ear, as he seated her next to him at the table, and he couldn't help noticing that she was still blushing.

Feeling much better now that he realized that his father had not saddled him with either an ugly or an unintelligent mate, Emile ate heartily, but he noticed with some amusement that Marie Therese watched his table manners, and his appetite, but simply pushed her food around on her plate, seemingly unable to eat very much. He didn't think that she was distressed by thoughts of the coming engagement and marriage, so perhaps her loss of appetite for food might be a good indication of her level of emotion,... a good signal, he thought, looking forward more and more to their tour of Marengo. The only question was whether she would allow him to lead her over the levée and on, into that lovely, secluded spot under the willows.

At last his mother inquired if anyone would like more coffee, and Emile knew that even if their parents decided to remain at the table, it would not be viewed as impolite if he took Marie Therese on the proposed tour. He quickly put his napkin on the table, and asked if they might be excused, and when he received four nods accompanied by smiles, he pulled out her chair, and extended his hand for hers. She took it willingly, and let him lead her outside, and down the front steps.

"Since you mentioned flower gardens, we will visit them first, since some of our finest surround the house," he said, taking her along the south side of the house, where beds of daffodils, tulips, hyacinth and roses were all in bloom.

"How beautiful!" she said, and he picked an especially beautiful rose for her, carefully avoiding the yellow roses Nana loved so much, and settling on a bright fuchsia one.

"My mother, and grandmother have both supervised the planting of flowers, and you will find that, no matter the season, there will be color and beauty in our gardens. Perhaps you will also be willing to continue to look after our flowers," Emile said, holding the rose up to her cheeks, and admiring the reflection of its color in hers. Then carefully pulling the few thorns off, he handed it to her.

"There," he said, "and for you I have removed all the thorns, as I hope to be able to do in our life together."

"Thank you, Emile," she said, smiling and tucking the rose into a buttonhole at the top of her pale green bodice, where Emile thought it looked as if it had never left the garden. As he studied the placement of the rose, his eyes also followed the shadowed hollow between her breasts, as far as her dress would allow, and he noticed a slight flush rise not only on her cheeks, but on her neck and breasts. He rather enjoyed the signs of her sensitivity, but decided it was time to proceed on with the tour. He took her hand, drawing her away from the garden, and starting down the long lawn to the levée.

"Emile, I like the sentiment you express. As for me, I will try hard never to provide any thorns for you. That is my hope."

His hand trembled at her waist, and he drew her close. Her lips responded gently to the tenderness of their first kiss. Then he lowered his head, and kissed her bare skin, just above where the rose was placed. In response, he was pleased to hear a little exhaled breath.

He straightened up and smiled down at her.

"A good beginning?" he asked, and she shyly nodded.

"But besides our growing relationship, this walk is to show you what you will be mistress of, so let me point out to you the houses over there where our sugar engineer, our overseer, and our doctor stay. The doctor comes weekly to take care of the health needs of our workers, and of any of us in the Big House who need his attention, and we do have a small clinic and hospital in which a few of our older women serve as nurses. We also have built a chapel; you will see it next on our right. We use it, and our slaves use it too. Some come to our services, but later on

Sundays a minister of their own preaches. You can hear the singing now. It's worth a visit just to hear the singing, but we can do that later on, not today. Their minister is one of our slaves. It's better that way, since often ministers coming in can be full of rebellious fire. This way we have some idea of what is being preached, and now and again my father or I stop by just to check that the message isn't inflammatory."

"How many slaves do you have here? And do you have any trouble with them?"

"Well, the acreage is nearly 20,000, so we need a large labor force. I think we have well over 375 slaves, but of course, some are either too old and infirm to do much work, and about 50 to 75 are children. Our elderly men teach the youngsters to fish and trap, supervise their collection of firewood, help with the poultry and livestock, or weed in the gardens; while the elderly women help either with the cooking, the sewing, the laundry, or the nursery. We do provide a supper in a communal dining room, so slaves don't have to come in from a long day's work and prepare their own dinner. Breakfast and lunch are carried out to those in the fields, usually by some of the older children. You can see the slave kitchen and dining room now, on our right, and just behind it, the other long building, that's the nursery. Back of the cottages we just passed, for the doctor, and overseer, you can just see the stables, and beyond them are the barn, the chicken yard, and the fields for the cattle. We raise our own cattle and hogs, and we do have a smoke house also back there, to smoke meat, fish, and any game we shoot.

"As for trouble with the slaves, we don't have much, even though I think my father is often too harsh in his punishments. I plan to take down the stocks when I become master, and to try to win our people's cooperation through more use of rewards, like time off, or money, or credit at our little store. You can see the store over there, near the hospital. We keep it well-stocked with things our people want, cotton and silk fabrics, ribbons, kerchiefs, toys, tobacco, various preserves, even shoes and boots, and we do extend credit to them, so they can work off the cost of what they buy from us. The store stays busy, especially right before Christmas.

"I guess we are very fortunate there is so little trouble with our people. But right now we have a family we think has run away. Unfortunately it's our blacksmith, and his wife and son. My father recently punished the wife for getting in a fight with another woman in the quarters. She has a difficult temperament, and this isn't the first time she has gotten into fights, so my father put her in the stocks for a day and night, and yesterday, soon after she was released, they couldn't be found. Her husband is a good blacksmith, and if they aren't found, we'll have to replace him. She was a field hand, so perhaps we'll also buy another field hand or two. I'll have to go to the slave auction soon. I do conduct most all of our business that must be done in New Orleans, since, as my father has grown older, he doesn't enjoy trips to the city any more. The slave patrols will hunt for the runaways, but by now they may be far away, and that might be just as well, since she did encourage dissension. Even if they are found, I think my father wants to sell them. He will try to sell them as a family, however, since we don't like to break up families if we can avoid it."

"Do you often sell your slaves?" Marie Therese asked, looking a bit worried.

"No, I can only think of one other case in all the years I remember, and that was a single man who was also a troublemaker. As conditions go in the Deep South, I think our people are not dissatisfied. We try to treat them well, and I will try to do even better, when I take over.

"Last on our right are the slave quarters. Each family has its own little house, with two rooms, and a loft, a fireplace, and a front porch. As you can see from here, the houses are set up off the ground, and we have shelled walkways, both to offset flooding. And behind each house is a garden, and in some cases, also a chicken yard and shed. We buy any produce that our slaves don't want for their own use. But I must admit, stealing is something of a problem. We buy hens one day, and they disappear that same night, and sometimes we end up buying them again! Everything of ours must be locked up at night, especially the chickens, turkeys, and smokehouse, and our overseer, my father and I have the only sets of keys,... but still things disappear!

"Can you think of any more questions now? If not, then let me take you to the levée."

Emile steered Marie Therese to the levée, his hand firmly on her waist, then he helped her up to the crest.

"There's our dock. We do enjoy traveling, and we send off our sugar, and other products. We have a permanent arrangement with Captain Winston Rutherford of the *Southern Belle*. He has a fine, new paddle wheeler, and stops here most weeks, bringing us mail, guests, and things we have ordered, and in turn picking up our produce either to take it to the city, or north to Saint Louis. All the years I went to West Point, I traveled with him. Perhaps one day we can take a cruise together. He has an orchestra for dancing, and the food aboard is excellent. The cabins are very nice, and I have seen the honeymoon suite and it is especially attractive. In the future, do you think you would like to take a trip with me on the *Southern Belle*?"

"Emile, it does sound very inviting," Marie Therese replied, smiling and blushing.

Emile was so touched by her blush that he leaned down and gave her another kiss. She responded so well that momentarily he felt dizzy. He smiled, gratified by her response, and immediately thought of his planned visit to the willows. He took her by the hand, and helped her down the levée. For a few minutes they just stood hand in hand, watching the river.

"The river has so many faces," Marie Therese observed. "Today it is a vivid blue, just like the sky, and it seems to have its own fleet of little white clouds...."

Emile nodded in appreciation, then for a while they just stood silently watching. Only a short distance away, a great white heron fished, the plumes on his head ruffling up in the breeze. He watched them and then returned to his fishing, and soon they saw him flip a fish into the air, and close his beak on it. A lump slowly descended down his long neck.

Finally Emile broke the silence.

"I'm sure you know that it isn't safe to swim in the river. Even a good, strong swimmer is unlikely to come out alive," he said.

"Yes, I know, and I am not much of a swimmer," she replied, looking a bit fearfully at the swirling, fast-moving current.

"We'll just have to teach you to swim, since often in the summer we go to our house in Mandeville. It's cooler there, right on the Lake, and we do enjoy swimming and sailing there. Until you can swim, I would be very uneasy taking you out on our sailboat, " Emile answered, and holding her hand, he led her down to the willows.

"Here we can't be seen easily, and we can see anyone approaching before they can see us," he explained. "It's time to get a bit better acquainted, and find out if we can be compatible," he added, drawing her close. "May I?" he asked, but even before she could answer, his lips closed on hers, and what was at first a tender, gentle kiss, became passionate. His hand sought her breasts, and cupped them, then one hand reached down beneath her bodice, and gently he caressed her nipple into hardness. She gasped, but seemed to enjoy his touch, and made no effort to stop him. Then he picked her up, and carried her to a spot well-hidden beneath the willows. Marie Therese couldn't help wondering if he had taken other women to this spot before he took her there. But she pushed that thought out of her mind. He set her down, and took his jacket off and placed it on top of the long grasses. Then he took her up again in his arms and gently put her down on his jacket, bedded down amid the tall grasses.

"Don't be afraid. I promise I will not take you until we are man and wife officially," he said, and stretched out beside her, kissing her again, his tongue exploring into her mouth, his hands reaching up beyond her stockings, and caressing the soft skin of her thighs. His fingers probed further, and she moaned as he reached between her legs, and gently pressed within her. He continued to kiss her, and his hand continued his tender but continuous pressure, until she tensed, and turned her body into his hand. She broke from his kiss, her breath coming in quick gasps. It was clear to Emile that this was all new to her, that no man had touched her like this, so privately, before he had. He was more than satisfied by her reactions. Momentarily he stopped the movement of his hand, and looked at her.

"May I continue to pleasure you, chérie? Tell me, do you enjoy this? I promise this is as far as I will go today, just pleasuring you this way. May I continue?"

"Oh yes, please," she gasped, and her eyes closed, and her entire body quivered, then went tense. Her gasps turned into soft moans, and she stilled. He knew he had brought her pleasure, perhaps it was even the first time a man had touched her like that. He had to know.

"Am I the first man to bring you pleasure like that?" he softly asked.

"Yes, Emile, you are the first," came her whispered response.

"And did it pleasure you, chérie? I think and hope it did," he answered, his own body already hard against hers.

"Yes, I never knew I could feel like this," she exclaimed. "But show me, Emile, I want to bring pleasure to you now," she said, and her little hand reached down and opened his trousers, and felt for him. He exclaimed both from surprise that she would take the initiative this way, and even more from the pleasurable agony of her touch.

"You really mean to do this? I mean,... short of the final meeting of our bodies?" he asked, studying her green eyes, pressing closer to her, and kissing her fervently. Her hand began to gently move. He had already been stimulated by her swift, strong release, and he was hard, and very ready.

"You need to tell me what works, and makes you feel good. I have never done this before," she whispered. "Does this feel good, Emile? Tell me...."

"Oh, mon Dieu, yes, yes,..." he responded, and his entire body tightened. He moaned, and she felt moisture in her hand, and suddenly he relaxed. For a few minutes they remained silent, holding each other, then his head came up off her shoulder, and he grinned at her, a wide, relaxed grin, and she knew she had succeeded. He moved slightly, and from a pocket, brought out a handkerchief, and wiped the moisture from her hand, and threw the handkerchief into the river. For a few moments they watched it move away, puffed up with air, like a little sailboat, until it disappeared, submerged by the current.

"Later, when we are married, that is what will make babies for us, when I put it into you instead of the river!" he said, grinning again. Marie Therese threw back her head and laughed. At least it appeared that Emile would be shockingly honest with her! She had known nothing of what happened between a man and a woman, and in less than an hour he had begun to teach her. He smiled at her again, and in an off-handed sort of admission, he said,

"I guess we got a little ahead of ourselves. Still there's nothing wrong about finding out how each of us reacts to pleasure. And now we know we both can enjoy married pleasures. But I think I should have asked you first, before we lay down in the willows, if you agree to marry me. Do you?"

"Yes, Emile, I will marry you, if you want me," came her soft response. "Do you?"

"It's true, I must confess, when my father set out to convince me that he wanted me to marry before I would be called up to serve in the military, I resisted. I didn't feel I was ready to marry yet, but now I can't pass up the opportunity to marry you. I'm afraid if I wait until I return from military service, you might be already married, and I would regret that very much. My father wants at least a pregnancy before I leave, so the possibility of an heir to Marengo could exist, if something happened to me. Can you accept that?"

"Yes, I understand your father's very logical reasoning, but more than that, I believe I can learn to love you, Emile. Do you think you can learn to love me?" Marie Therese had heard rumors that this heir to Marengo played around in the city, and that he might have a mistress. Although she didn't want to ask him outright about all that, she did want him to make a commitment to her now, before they married.

For a moment or so there was silence, as she waited tensely for his reply. He looked away, and scuffed his boot into the tall grass at their feet. Finally he looked at her and answered.

"Right now, I can tell you that I don't want to lose you, so yes, I want to marry you. Is that enough to content you, at least for now?" Emile said, kissing her playfully.

Marie Therese realized that he hadn't actually said that he could learn to love her, or that he would remain only hers, but at least he had said he wanted to marry her. That might have to be enough to satisfy her now. How could she ask for more? After all they had just met. In time she hoped that he would be able to say he loved her, and that theirs could grow into more than just an arranged marriage, into a loving commitment to each other.

He helped her up, brushing the grass off her clothing, and she did the same for him. His fingers proprietarily arranged her short dark curls back in place, fluffing out those in the back, which had been straightened from lying in the grass. To Marie Therese it seemed as if he had already taken possession of her, as if she had become his property, and she wasn't entirely sure that she liked that. She wanted a relationship, a marriage in which she would have some standing too, not just become a man's property. A little fear nestled in her heart, but she knew she couldn't question her father's decision, his mind had already been made up; for him there was much to be gained financially from this arrangement. Her wishes would not be considered. The deal would be made by now, she was sure. Perhaps it would be all right. Emile seemed to be a gentle and considerate man, at least so far, during their very brief courtship. All she could do was hope she was seeing his true nature, and that there was not another, more difficult side to him, which would come out after their vows were said. She would just have to trust her initial impressions, and so far they were good; he had been courteous, considerate, and seemingly honest with her, and he had already shown that he cared about her and her needs, even if he might never come to love her. She thought they would be able to make a go of it, this marriage, and perhaps in time she would even be able to get him to love her, and to tell her he did. She was willing to try....

"I guess it is time we made our appearance, and find out what our parents have decided," Emile said, smiling at her. "And then we can tell them what we have decided."

He helped her up to the top of the levée. Holding hands, they slid down the slippery grass on other side, laughing together, and then walked back across the long lawn to the Big House. They found the adults sitting just where they had left them, in the dining room, with wine glasses and coffee cups. His father, pulling at the ends of his mustache, gave them a long, solemn look, and said,

"I see you two are holding hands. Can you both live with an engagement now? How about you, Emile? Are you agreeable to this marriage?"

"Yes, Papa, I believe I can marry Marie Therese."

Then Monsieur Massenet looked up at his daughter, and asked,

"Marie Therese, my child, can you agree to this marriage, and to an engagement beginning today?"

"Yes, Papa, I agree."

"Then, if both of you agree, let me fetch the traditional de Marigny engagement ring," Monsieur de Marigny said, and went into the family parlor, where they could hear him working the combination of a lock. In minutes he was back, and handed a little box to Emile.

"You are the appropriate one to put this on your fiancée's finger," he said to his son.

Emile opened the box, and picking up the ring, he held it up for Marie Therese to see. There was a very large center diamond, with two smaller ones nestling on either side. Then Emile took her left hand in his. "May I give this to you?" he asked softly, and when she nodded, he slipped it on her finger, and took her hand up and kissed it.

"What a beautiful ring! Has it been in the family a long time?" she asked, admiring it.

"It's been the de Marigny engagement ring for at least three generations," Monsieur Louis said. "And to make it available for you, I have just given another ring to my wife! That's also been a family tradition. We de Marignys couldn't ask our wives to give this ring up without providing them with a beautiful replacement."

Emile could see as he watched his fiancée's expression that she was on the verge of tears, but he hesitated to ask their meaning. One day when they were alone, he knew he would ask. It did appear to Emile that neither of them were overly enthusiastic over the life-long commitment which had been forced on them.

*   *   *

As the clouds of war loomed closer, so did the arranged marriage. The engagement to Marie Therese Massenet was announced in the *Picayune* before Emile had a chance to tell Nana about it.

He arrived early one morning at the house on Felicity Street, and Nana holding their little Nanette in her arms, met him at the door, with kisses. Then she saw his expression.

"What is it, Emile? You haven't fallen out of love with me, have you?" she asked, her eyes filling up, one hand flying up to her cheek.

"Oh no, ma chérie. Never that. But may I come into your little house, please? There's some news I have to share with you."

"Of course, come in, Emile. Just let me run upstairs and put Nanette down for her nap."

He sat down on the sofa in the living room, and when she returned, she sat down close beside him.

"Yes, news?" she asked apprehensively, studying his face for any clues.

"It looks like our country will soon be at war with Mexico, and if that happens, I will be immediately called up, and will have to go," he said, thinking one blow at a time was more than enough.

"Oh, how terrible. I will worry about you every day you are gone, Emile. But I'll be right here, waiting for your return. We can handle that, even if the separation will be so very hard."

"My father has promised me that if I have to go, he will see that you are well-provided for. He will give me some money which I will leave with you, if I must go. He asked me to tell you that although he will not be in direct contact with you, he will send Washington in every week to see what you might need, and he will provide for you while I am gone. You can trust him on that. He won't forget you. And don't be at all hesitant to ask him for anything you need. He wants to help.... But, my darling, there is more...."

"What more is there?" Nana asked, anxiously.

"Remember when I told you that before he gave me the money to buy this house...."

"What? He wants the house back? I will give it back to him," she interrupted.

"No, chérie, this is your house as long as you live. It's the promise he required from me then, that I would accept the marriage he would arrange for me, and try to provide an heir for Marengo. That's come up again now, since he wants it all resolved before I leave. So you will see a formal engagement announcement in the *Picayune,* and depending on when I am called up, there must be a wedding before I leave. I am so very sorry, please understand, I regret this more than I can say. If it weren't for the war, we might have had three or four more years together before I would be forced to marry, but war has changed everything. If I were not to survive, there must be an heir to Marengo. My father demands that of me. I have no choice in the matter. I have given him my word in exchange for his help with this house."

"You do still love me, don't you, Emile? I love you very much. Somehow we'll manage. Please don't forget me." The tears were coming fast, and he took out his handkerchief and gently tried to blot them dry.

"Yes, I love you, ma chérie. Nothing has changed between us. I love you every bit as much as ever, and if you will still have me, I will not give you up. You are my true love, my first love, and as I told you, no arranged marriage can change my love for you. What makes me very sad is that I won't be able to spend as much time with you after the marriage, but if you will trust me, and if you still love me, I will never forsake you."

Nana threw herself into his arms, and he could feel her sobs. There was so little he could say to comfort her.

"I do love you, Nana, only you. Please remember that, regardless of what happens. I can't refuse my father, you know that. Everything my father has done for us, the money for this house and everything in it, and his future intention to see that you are looked after while I am gone; all that is based on my promise to accept this marriage he is arranging. Please understand, I would much rather be with you, my darling, you are my one true love."

"It has all come too soon, Emile. I was hoping we would be able to see each other and be together for several more years before a marriage was forced on you. But I love you, and I will always be here for you, no matter what."

Nana smiled up at him through her tears, as he dabbed them away with his handkerchief.

"Now for some better news. I am going to stay with you two nights, and then I must go. The engagement will be in the papers, if it isn't already, and the wedding is set for two weeks from now, but sooner if my military orders come and force the date to be pushed up. Please, ma chérie, remember it's you I love, no matter what. And in the next weeks, I will try my best to come and spend some time with you, whenever I can."

This time it was Nana who took him by the hand, and led him upstairs. She clung to him passionately, until finally he picked her up and gently laid her on the bed.

"Do you want me to bed you, chérie?" he asked, sadly.

She simply held out her arms to him.

"I need to hear you tell me so, Nana. Can you?"

"Yes, Emile, please come to me. I can hardly live without you...."

So he flung off his clothing, and then he undressed her, and their bodies met in a frenzy of longing. He could feel her sobs even as they reached the pinnacle of their passion. She cried out, and then was still in his arms. He found even in the warm relaxation, the aftermath of their love, that he began clenching his teeth in frustration. What could he do? He had given some thought to escaping with her to France, but he knew even with the money his father would give him to help tide Nana over while he was gone in the military, that would not be enough to cover more than just the voyage to France. After that they would be penniless. He was afraid to ask her what she thought of the idea of such an escape, afraid she might favor France....

He held her until she fell asleep in his arms, her cheeks still wet with tears.

The next day he wanted to get her out of the house, to do something special together. He remembered that there was an opera scheduled for that evening. He felt sure he could sneak her into the family box. He knew his parents weren't planning on attending, and it might divert Nana from all that lay ahead.

She woke when the baby cried just a single cry, changed her, and brought her to bed to nurse her. Emile turned to watch. Nothing could have been more beautiful to see than his Nana nourishing their baby daughter. Soon the baby had gone back to sleep, a sweet little smile of satisfaction curled on her tiny, pink lips. Nana turned her beautiful dark eyes, eyes like a doe, on him, and he kissed her, and then brought her coffee and biscuits. They sat up in bed, and as he finished up his coffee, and started to pour them each another cup, he asked,

"Nana, do you think your mama could care for our Nanette tonight?" And when she nodded, he asked, "Then how about a trip to the opera tonight? My family has a box, and won't be coming in, so I'm sure we can slip in and use it."

"That sounds lovely, Emile. I would enjoy that, as long as the opera isn't too long. Since it will be our last night together for a while, I want to have as much time as possible with you, my darling."

"Well, we can always leave the opera early, if it seems to be running long. Let's plan on it then. Of course, if what to wear poses such a dilemma for you, we might end up skipping the opera entirely, especially if I help you dress...." he chuckled at the thought, and she smiled back at him.

"I'll really try to hurry, just for you, Emile!"

"Oh, I don't mind, we can just spend all night dressing and undressing you, and skip the opera entirely. I could live with that! " he replied, grinning at her.

When Mama de Lis arrived that afternoon with groceries and began to make dinner for them, Emile wandered out into the kitchen, leaving Nana sewing in the living room. She was finishing up a dress she hoped to have ready to wear that night.

"Madame de Lis, I am thinking of taking Nana to the opera tonight, as a distraction from some sad news I had to tell her. My family has a box, but won't be using it tonight, so I thought we might. Would you be able to look after our Nanette this evening?"

"Sad news? First tell me 'bout dat," she asked, as she shook out cornmeal to dip the fish into. Then she straightened up, and faced him, her little dark eyes fixed on him, her forehead lined, her eyebrows drawn closer. He could easily see that her feelings about him and his place in her daughter's life had become more negative. He shrugged, and his arms flew out in a gesture of frustration.

"I'm very sorry about this, but it's out of my control. First, the newspapers say that we are about to go to war with Mexico, and if that's so, I will be called up right away. Then, because my father is anxious for another heir for our plantation, if something should happen to me, he has arranged a French Creole marriage for me, and it will be very soon. Without this war, I had expected several years would pass before he would force me to marry, but the war has speeded everything up. I had to tell Nana. I also told her that no arranged marriage would stop my love for her, but that I wouldn't be able to spend as much time with her as I had hoped and planned on, before all this came up. This news has brought lots of tears, and I thought maybe going out this evening to the opera might help distract her. What do you think?"

Madame de Lis returned to spreading out the cornmeal. It appeared that she didn't want to look at him.

"Sir, it be dangerous te try te go in togetheh, te de opera. Yuh git stopped, an' den she be eben sadder, if dat happens."

"Does she have an evening cape with a hood? That might work...." Emile continued to press the idea.

"Yeah, she haf one, but, Sir, I dun think dis hieh's a good plan. Too dangerous, too hurtful if yuh git stopped...."

"Maybe with the hood, it could work. I already mentioned going, and she seemed to be enthusiastic about it, so it's difficult to back out now. I wouldn't want her to think I'm embarrassed to be seen with her,... that's so far from the truth."

Emile wasn't picking up on all the clues Mama de Lis was giving him, so after dinner, he got on his evening clothes, and sat down on the bed, watching his beautiful Nana nurse their daughter, and then get dressed. He wished he had thought to stop and buy her some more jewelry. Perhaps tomorrow before he left....

"Your mother says you have an evening cloak with a hood, and suggested you wear it," he said when she was finally ready. She quickly retrieved a dark blue velvet cloak from their armoire. Looking in at their clothes all hung together there, she turned back to him,

"Please leave a few of your things there, Emile. It will help me believe that you will be coming back to me."

He rose to help her with her cloak. "Mon Dieu, of course, if you wish, chérie. All of them if that will help!"

As they walked out to the carriage, Emile ebulliently said to Washington,

"Tonight will you please take us to the French Opéra, and come back for us in a couple of hours. I'm taking my lady to enjoy some music...."

"Duz yuh think dat won't cause trouble, dat yuh won't be stopped at de doorh?" Washington said, giving Emile a very doubtful, gloomy look.

"I don't think that will happen. We are going to sit in the shadows in the box my family owns. They're not planning on coming tonight, that I know, so I don't foresee any problems."

Washington let them off just outside the French Opéra, but then he decided to stick around, just in case. He circled the block, then came back to take a spot less than a half block from the building. He drew up the horses, and just waited.

Emile checked to see that Nana was well-concealed in her hooded cloak, and then he escorted her into the building. They went up the stairs in a crowd of others, and then he took her arm and headed in the direction of the de Marigny box. Just outside it, an usher started to open the door to the box, but then he closed it again in front of them.

"Monsieur, I know you have every right to use your family's box, but you cannot bring that woman in with you. I'm sorry, but those are the rules the House has set." He stood firmly planted before the door, his hands behind his back. "Creoles of color, no matter who they are with, must sit either in the second balcony, or in the special section we reserve for them close to the stage, on the main floor.... No place else is open to them, unless Sir, you want to rent one of our few latticed boxes for the season. I'm sorry, but those are the only options."

"But why is that?" Emile asked, in an icy tone. "How can you deny us entrance to my family's box?"

"I must simply refuse the woman entry. You, Monsieur, can go in alone if you wish, and I will be glad to escort your friend to either of the sections we reserve for Creoles of color, if she wishes to sit there, or you can pay for one of our few latticed boxes...."

Emile snorted derisively. "A latticed box, how very convenient! Then he tried to calm down, and in a soft, gentle tone, he said,

"Nana, those alternatives just won't do. I want to be with you. So, shall we find something else to do tonight, perhaps a ball, my sweet?"

She nodded silently, and they left, to the cacophony of the orchestra tuning up.

When they reached the street, Emile drew her aside, into the shadows, away from the brightly lit Opéra House.

"I'm so sorry, ma chérie. Your mother tried to warn me, and Washington too. We are both free, and this is a land which is supposed to guarantee our freedom, our freedom to associate. After all, it isn't as if I am accompanied by one of my slaves! Why should we not be allowed into my family's box? No one else is involved, just us.... I did think that with your hood on, no one would challenge us. And why should they, anyway? But here we are, all dressed up and ready to celebrate. Would you like to go to the Quadroon Ball? There is one tonight, I believe...."

Her lower lip was quivering, and he could see she was very close to tears.

"Emile, if you don't mind, I think I'd rather go home, and spend our last evening together at our little house,..." she said softly, and he heard a sob as she finished speaking. He noticed that Washington had pulled up right beside them, and with a very long, sad face, was holding the carriage door open for them.

When they were both in the carriage, Emile put his arms around Nana, and drew her to him. "I am so very sorry," he said, kissing her over and over. "I will never make such a mistake again. I wanted to bring you joy, not sorrow, Nana, my darling. Please forgive me for my stupid ignorance. Who has the right to enforce such unreasonable rules?"

When they got back to the house on Felicity Street, Emile was relieved to see that as soon as they arrived, Madame de Lis was preparing to leave. She waved goodbye, and Emile was glad he didn't have to explain why they were back so soon. He dismissed Washington to go home, and followed Nana in. She had already gone upstairs, so he grabbed up wine glasses and a bottle of champagne, and slowly followed her upstairs. She checked on Nanette, who was sleeping quietly, then sat down on the sofa, in her beautiful plum-colored evening dress.

"I'm going to set off a champagne cork," he warned her, directing the cork well away from her. It popped out, and speeded across the room, landing on his pillow on the bed.

"I guess there could be some meaning behind where that fool thing landed," Emile said, hoping to get at least a smile from Nana. She managed a weak smile.

"Here, have some of this fizzy stuff," he said, handing her a full glass of champagne.

Then, he put the bottle on his bedside table, and bringing his own full glass, he joined her on the sofa, and brushed a feathery kiss on her cheek.

"To my beautiful, true love, to you, Nana, and all the love and happiness we share, and will continue to share," he said softly, bringing his glass to clink on hers. They both drank, and he could tell that some of the tension he had seen in her was beginning to drop out of her shoulders, her back, and from those beautiful eyes. She managed a brighter smile for him, over the brim of her glass, and he soothed her shoulders, gently rubbing them. Then she turned fully toward him, her beautiful, big, dark eyes focused on him, with a look of such tenderness, it brought tears to his eyes, and he felt even worse about the pain and insult his naive ignorance had brought upon her.

"And to you, Emile, the man I will always love," she said softly, and drank to him.

After two glasses of champagne each, Emile noticed that the atmosphere had decidedly eased. He kissed Nana's cheek, and said,

"Now, if I may be permitted to unbutton all those little buttons down your back, I will carry you to our bed, and then, if you wish, I will pour out some more champagne."

She turned so he could reach the buttons, and he began to work on them, kissing her back, as more and more of it was revealed to him. Finally he eased her arms out of the gown, and his hands reached for her breasts. His breath was hot on her shoulders.

"Turn back to me, ma chérie, please," he asked, and she did, and he saw that her eyes were at last dry again. He took her by both hands and drew her to her feet, as he got up. Then he just held her, as the gown rustled to the ground around her feet, followed quickly by her petticoats, and her lacy chemise.

Holding his hand, she stood naked before him, proud of her body.

"Tu es magnifique!" he said softly, kissing her shoulders, and her breasts. Then he picked her up as gently as he could, looking down at her lovingly, and carried her to the bed, where he soon joined her.

"Can I pour you some more champagne?" he asked.

"No, I have had enough for now. Perhaps later."

He kissed her long neck, and the shoulder nearest him, and laid his head in the curve of her neck. "Can you forgive me for this evening's mistake?" he asked. "There is so much I need to learn, so I don't bring you unhappiness, which is the last thing I want to do, Nana."

"I understand, and I forgive you. It might have worked, and then we'd have had wonderful operatic memories to share. Perhaps it will be easier if you try out your ideas first on my Mama. She once was in a position similar to mine now, and she knows better than both of us what can be done and what can't. I didn't want to disappoint you by raising doubts."

"Only now am I beginning to realize that she may have tried to warn me off earlier this evening, but I just didn't hear, I guess. I will listen much more carefully in the future, both to what she tells me, and to what Washington tells me. He is very loyal to me, and he adores you, so he will tell me any truth, to avoid having you hurt."

Emile began to caress her slowly and very gently, until finally she rolled over closer to him, helping him out of his clothing.

"Can we be slow tonight?" she asked softly. "I know this may be our last night together for some time, from what you have told me."

"We can take all night, chérie, if that would please you," came his answer, and he continued to gently play with her as long as he could. As much as he wanted her, he was proud that he was able to restrain himself for several hours. Finally he could stand it no longer, and he began to kiss her with more force and passion.

"Can I take you now?" he cried out. "Please, Nana, let me know all of you, all your love. I can't live without you, Nana, really,... please believe me. I will never forsake you, or leave you, my love...."

"Emile, come to me, now. I love you, only you, and I always will," she whispered.

His touch became more forceful, more violent in his passion, but she had expected that, and was ready to join with him.

"Love me, love me now, Emile. I am all yours,..." she said, and they met each other in agony and pleasure so powerful that it was hard to tell the difference.

"You will come back, won't you?" she begged at last, when they lay intertwined and pleasurably exhausted.

"Oh yes, ma chérie, I will be back, and even when I am not with you, my heart will always be with you," he said, and she heard a sob come from him. "Never do I want to be away from you. Some circumstances I cannot change, but I will be with you as much as possible, whenever I can, I swear to you, my darling."

Nana woke to the sounds of the first birds singing, welcoming the dawn, and she watched the sky change from dark gray to lighter gray, and then the sun broke into the room, spreading its rays until the room, and their bed were ablaze in gold. She turned to Emile, and woke him with her kisses.

"Emile, I have some special news for you. I believe I am pregnant again. I hope you are ready for another child in seven months or so."

"That's wonderful news to wake up to, ma chérie," he whispered, smiling and giving her a long, tender kiss. "I wouldn't want our Nanette to be an only child, as I was. It's a lonely childhood. I'm happy to hear that we are going to give her some company!"

"Love me once more before you have to leave," she whispered, and he did, in the golden light of a full sunrise.

*　　　　　　　*　　　　　　　*

A breakdown of the diplomatic negotiations between the United States and Mexico foreshadowed the inevitability of war, and forced a change of dates for the de Marigny marriage. The big formal wedding, which had been planned for the Cathedral, had to be cancelled, and a smaller affair was quickly scheduled for the little, country church in Mandeville. A reception would be held at Mon Plaiser, the de Marignys' Mandeville house, and afterwards the newlyweds would spend a few days together there, with a staff provided from Marengo to look after them. Emile de Marigny had already received his orders to report for duty, so the honeymoon would be very short, only a few days, and not long enough for that leisurely voyage that Emile had looked forward to, on the *Southern Belle*. That would have to be postponed.

It was painful, Emile found, to smile at his pretty little bride coming to him down the aisle. When she stood beside him, she had to reach out and take his hand. It was not offered.

But as he stood beside her, painfully making the responses he did not want to make, he did have to acknowledge that his father had, at least, picked him a pretty little Creole, with an inviting smile, and a softness of nature, which he hoped would also be true of her body, when he finally got to discover all of it later that night. The small taste he had already had, under the willows at Marengo, had only served to whet his appetite for more.

Marie Therese smiled up at him as she repeated her vows after the priest, and after a nuptial mass, they led the way out of the church, followed by their five bridesmaids and five groomsmen. Only a short carriage ride away was Mon Plaiser, the de Marigny home on the lakefront. There both families and the bridal party lined up to receive their guests. The house was beautifully situated across the street from Lake Ponchartrain itself, and after all the guests had finally departed, the young couple walked under the live oaks, and along a pale path of moonlight to the Lake. The Lake lay placid, like a great silver mirror, stretching out before them, and a full moon surrounded by a bevy of stars greeted them. Emile embraced her, and kissed her in the shadows of the live oaks, then finally he took his bride's tiny hand, and led her back to the house. He poured out a glass of champagne for each of them, painfully remembering his last glass of champagne with Nana, and he knew he would need several more glasses tonight to go through with what he had to. She was pretty, in a tiny, very feminine way, and he knew he had to make her first full experience of love one she would remember. Although he looked forward to it, as any man would, when presented with a sweet, little virgin wife, he also dreaded it, and he had to remind himself not to take out his own frustrations on her. She was not to blame for his dilemma,... a dilemma he hoped he could keep her from knowing....

The big front bedroom was flickering with candlelight. Silently he unbuttoned her wedding dress, and helped her out of it. Underneath she had several layers of frothy lace-trimmed petticoats, and he began to rouse as he let them slip down. He pulled down her chemise, baring her to the waist. He had to admire her tiny but well-proportioned body, and took the time to finger her breasts. It was just a sort of investigative, possessive touch, not really a caress. He hadn't yet awakened to more than a sensual interest, no spark of passion had ignited him. Then there was lacy underclothing, and he drew it off, and escorted her to their marriage bed. He sensed that she was embarrassed by her nakedness before him, since he was still fully clothed. He began to undress, and saw her eyes open wide, as he flung aside his clothing. Clearly this was her first view of a naked adult male, and one who had at last become fully aroused. Then he flung the covers back, and climbed in beside her. She tried to cover herself with the sheet, but he pulled it away, and she quivered under his gaze. They lay naked beside one another.

"Now that we are husband and wife, I want to see all of you," he said coolly. He raised himself on one elbow, and looked, his hand moving possessively over her, touching her nipples, then roaming down her hips, and her inner thighs; exploring, not yet caressing. Her eyes seemed frightened by this almost impersonal investigation. The planes of his face seemed hard and severe, not loving, as she had expected.

Despite his resentment and anger over an arranged marriage he was not ready for, suddenly Emile realized that his demand to see her naked, must seem embarrassing, or even brutal to her, and he tried to atone. Briefly his frustration and anger had gotten the better of him, so silently he repeated to himself his vow not to take his own frustrations out on her. This was her first night as a married woman, and he owed it to her to make it something she would remember with joy not embarrassment, perhaps even with passion, but not with fear. He sighed softly, and resolved to do better....

"I take it you have never seen a man completely naked before, nor have been totally undressed by a man, and subject to his gaze?" he asked, trying to keep his voice gentle.

"No, Emile, but we have said our vows, and now I am yours," she said softly, as if agreeing to whatever demands he might place on her.

"I will be gentle with you, Marie Therese, and you must tell me to stop if you feel too much pain. Our joining may be painful a time or two, but soon that will end, and I hope you will come to enjoy the act of being my wife."

A spark was coming alive in him, his heart was beating faster. He managed a gentle touch of her breasts, and ran his hands caressingly over her hips and thighs. Without the sheet, he could see how pale her skin was, white marble, without the ivory glow he was used to.

He began to kiss her, first on the mouth softly, then on her neck, and her breasts, and worked his way down between her thighs, pushing her legs gently apart, and kissing the moist, warm place between them. He heard her gasp, so he continued, until her breathing was coming fast, then he eased his body on hers, and his hands worked over her breasts, while he kissed her neck, her ear lobes, and finally honed in again on her lips, this time harder and more passionately. He forced her lips open, and his tongue explored her mouth, until he looked down to see if she was ready. Her eyes, which had been closed, had opened, and suddenly he noticed what deep green pools were there, and their beautiful, fathomless depths spurred him on.

"May I?" he asked softly, poised above her, placing most of his weight on his hands.

Her head twisted back and forth spasmodically from his touch, never had a man touched her so intimately, or taken her to such heights of pleasure, and she whispered, "Yes, Emile, yes please, I am yours...."

"Remember, you must tell me if it is too painful, and I will stop," he said, and as gently as he could, he entered her. He glanced at her eyes, and seeing no signs of pain, he began to move slowly at first, then faster, and she began to move with him. He could not stop himself now, even knowing it was not Nana, and soon the pleasure overwhelmed him, and he had a dim sense that she had responded to him, that he had made her a woman and his wife, and it had been pleasurable for her. It was over, at least for this first night. He had done what he had promised his father, and he had to admit he had enjoyed it. He would have to try hard and often enough to hope he could leave her pregnant before he had to set off for Mexico. He smiled in the dark, knowing that would not be a chore.

"Did you experience something new?" he asked her.

"Oh yes, Emile, it was wonderful," she answered softly, and even after his somewhat brutal denial of her desire to be covered, he had to believe her. He had indeed given her pleasure on their first night together. And gently, as if in atonement for his earlier cruel exposure, he pulled the sheet up over her, tucking her in as one would a child, and pressing down on her soft lips with a last kiss. Then he moved away from her, and tried to settle down for the night, but a sense of guilt hardened the lines of his jaws. He had not intended to be harsh or cruel, but somehow he had been, as if punishing her for his anger at having to marry. He would have to try not to inflict his own anger and guilt on her or her body. And he admitted to himself, that he could manage two women in his life, and that he could enjoy them both, even if he loved only one of them, and with a passion he doubted he would ever be able to replicate. But this little new bride,... he would enjoy bedding her, he couldn't deny that, but it would be primarily out of a sense of duty.

*   *   *

The evening before Emile had to leave, he took his new little bride to the opera. Perhaps it would be the last opera of his life, so he found it ironically amusing that it was *Tannhäuser*, with its theme of passionate love, and also its juxtapositioning of two different women, Elizabeth, like his new little wife, and Venus, like his own great love, Nana, much as it was in Tannhäuser's own troubled love story. He hoped the woman beside him didn't sense his painful identification with the hero. He comforted himself with the awareness that his wife didn't know enough of his own love story to see his identification, or to sense his own agony.

He pulled his chair over close to Marie Therese, and put his arm around her.

When the lights came back on, and the curtains swished closed for the first intermission, they both stood up and stretched. Looking down over the audience on the main floor, Emile became startled when he saw, in the section reserved for the Creoles of color, Armand and Nana, and both of them were looking up at him. He wondered if they could see Marie Therese, who had sat back down on her chair, which was in the shadows. He saw Armand wave up at him, and he waved back.

"Who is that, Emile?" Marie Therese asked.

For a moment he was speechless. So she had seen the wave. Had she also seen his Nana?

"It's a friend of mine who sometimes plays in an orchestra we have hired for dances. He's a talented violinist." Emile hoped his voice sounded as casual as he wanted it to be.

"And the lovely woman next to him, the beautiful Creole of color, is that his wife?" Marie Therese inquired.

"No, she isn't married. She plays the piano with the orchestra," he answered, his heart beating very fast, so very fast that if his little wife had put her palm on his chest, she would have sensed his secret then and there.

"You know her too?" Marie Therese continued her questions, and Emile wondered if she had any inkling of whom she was observing.

"Yes, all three of us are friends," he said a bit curtly. "Let me go down to the lobby and get some champagne for us," he added, and without waiting for an answer, he was gone.

Something about Emile's curt responses, and his seeming retreat from the box piqued her curiosity, so Marie Therese got to her feet again, and looked down, exchanging glances with the couple. They were Creoles of color, the man a little darker than the woman. The woman was strikingly beautiful, a pale ivory like a Spanish woman, and with the same sort of dark eyes, and luxuriant dark hair. Both women looked at each other for a long time. Could that possibly be the mistress people had told her that Emile had taken? The two women continued to look at each other in a way which seemed to indicate that they each had some idea of who the other one was in the life of their man. Finally Marie Therese couldn't stand it any longer, and she retreated to her seat in the shadows, but she continued to watch the couple, knowing that they could no longer see her. If indeed this is Emile's mistress, how, she wondered, could she ever compete with such beauty? And surely she must be a more experienced lover....

Suddenly she noticed her Emile. He walked down the aisle, and presented the couple with glasses of champagne. She saw them talk briefly, and the young Creole beauty directed an openly loving gaze to Emile. He kissed her hand, and held it as they continued to talk, then he finally bowed and left them. Marie Therese's heartbeat quickened. That must be the woman he loved.

Soon he returned to their box, bringing two glasses of champagne with him, and presenting one to her. She still held in her mind the picture of that Creole of color interacting with Emile. Oh God Almighty, why did it have to become apparent to her so soon? They had barely begun their married life, and already she was sure she had seen the other woman in her husband's life.

Emile leaned over and gave her a gentle kiss, but she was so distracted that she barely noticed it, and hardly responded. Then he settled down to watch the remainder of the opera as if nothing whatever had occurred. For Marie Therese, the rest of the opera passed very slowly, she wasn't aware of any of it, the music swept by her unnoticed, and she could feel the tears slowly moving down her cheeks.

"Is something wrong, chérie?" her husband asked, noticing her tears.

"It must be the music, I'm sorry," she replied, her throat so full she could barely whisper. "It's very moving."

He gave her another long look. Could she have possibly figured out who that was, and what his relationship was with that beautiful Creole of color? Surely it was most unlikely. Perhaps he shouldn't have given Armand and Nana those season tickets, but all he wanted to do was make Nana happy with the gift of music while he was gone, and since he couldn't be with her, he had persuaded Armand to accompany her. Now, although he didn't know how it could have happened, somehow he was sure that both women had recognized each other's importance in his life. Nana had seen his wife and Marie Therese had seen his beloved.

Such intense interest shown, and now the tears.... His wife evidently had some idea of the role Nana played in his life. But if Marie Therese had any sense of his relationship with Nana, would she bring it up with him? If she chose to remain silent, things might work out. He would simply have to wait and see,... and be much more careful about attending events where both women might be present. He smiled slightly as he considered what the mathematical chances were of both couples attending the opera on the very same night. Not a very high percentage, but what kind of damage had occurred, he wondered. Women could be so acutely sensitive, especially when it concerned matters of the heart. But even if she had sensed Nana's role in his life, perhaps Marie Therese would never question him, and they would be able to live together for years without any discussion of what she had seen, or what she might fear. That was the way dutiful wives were supposed to handle such situations, and Emile hoped that would be true in their case. He didn't want to be drawn into a web of lies; he was prepared to fulfill his marital duties, even with enjoyment, but he knew he could not renounce Nana. Not now, not ever....

*   *   *

Nana had grieved so badly when Emile had last left her, that her mother thought it was time to try almost anything to improve her daughter's mood, so one morning she took her to Mass at the Cathedral, where Père Antoine put his hands on Nana's head and gave her a special blessing. "It is good to see you here again, my child," he said, and his gentle kindness drew a tremulous smile from her. If plaçage meant she could no longer receive the Blessed Sacrament, she could at least receive a blessing from saintly old Père Antoine. He would not judge her for her lifestyle, nor could she see such a love as she had for Emile as sinful....

Afterwards her mother led the way to a little wooden house on Saint Ann Street. Nana had no idea where they were going, or who they were about to visit. She was fairly certain that they didn't have any relatives or friends that lived on Saint Ann Street. But she just followed along dutifully, as her mother led the way through a gate into a fenced yard, and up the shelled walk to the door. Her mother rang a little bell, and they waited for a while on the doorstep. Then suddenly the door opened, and a heavily veiled, very well-dressed white lady brushed out past them. At the door stood a tall, slender Creole of color. She had a long face, with a sharp aquiline nose, high cheekbones and a high forehead, and Nana felt as if her eyes burrowed right through her. She wore big, dangling gold hoop earrings, and both her arms were covered with heavy, gold bangle bracelets. Her dark hair was brushed straight back from her face, and covered with a tignon that drew up into seven points, and glittered with gold pins, and small, colorful jewels. She held her head high, her chin thrust forward, and she stared at them imperiously, her hands on her hips, with fingers covered with rings.

"Yuh want te see me?" she asked, pushing up the bangles on one arm.

"Yes, Madame, I bring ma daughteh, she has need a yuhr help," Nana's mother replied very politely, her eyes downcast as if she was afraid of meeting the woman's eyes directly. Nana marveled. Seldom had she ever seen her mother back down like that before another woman.

"Come in," came the woman's quick response, and they followed her into a room which had a white linen-covered altar at one end, with statues of St. Peter, St. Anthony, and St. John the Baptist, and in the center of the altar, surrounded by many small candles, was a figure of Mary holding the Baby Jesus in her arms. The woman knelt, crossed herself, and her rosary moved through her fingers. Nana and her mother knelt too, just behind her, working their rosaries.

Finally the woman rose, and taking Nana by the hand, she led them into another room. Here there was another altar with the figure of a large black doll on it, white candles around it, and a large box sat on the floor on a white cloth, with blue and pink candles placed at each corner of the cloth. The woman knelt again, at one end of the white cloth, and beckoned for them to take their positions on two of the other sides. They remained silent, and on their knees for sometime. Nana heard something rustling inside the white box, and saw the sides of the box protrude out a little. It frightened her, as did the entire atmosphere in this second room.

Somehow it seemed very different from the more traditional Christian altar in the first room. She rubbed at the goose bumps forming on her arms. This must be magic, voodoo magic, she realized, and shivered a little, although the room was quite warm.

"I am Marie Laveau, an' I see dat yuhr Mama has brought yuh te me. No doubt yuh've heard of me."

Nana nodded silently.

"Iz dere a man who causes yuh te come te me?" the woman finally spoke, turning to Nana.

"Yes, I am en placée, Madame. We love each other very much, and he comes often to see me. He has given me a home, and much more, but he is an officer, and must leave soon to go fight in the war. Because of this, the arranged marriage his father is forcing him to make, has been pushed up, and I will see less of him, even when he is here. I'm afraid this marriage may cause me to lose him, and I am afraid for him in the war.... Please can you help?"

"Stay hieh an' continue te pray. I will make yuh up two special little bags. One will have a red ribbon on it, dis yuh must put under hiz pillow when he comes te yuh. It will hold 'em in love wid yuh. The other little bag will have a blue ribbon on it, an' dat one yuh should put in hiz pocket beforh he leaves, it will keep 'em from dying in de war, an' make 'em come back te yuh. He won't be able te resist.

"But I need a little piece of yuhr hair te put in de red-ribboned bag, so kin I snip some off? I will take it from underneath where it won't show. All raight?" and she picked up her scissors, and when Nana nodded, she cut off a small lock from the back, close to Nana's neck, so close in fact that Nana shivered at a prick of the scissors.

"Forh dis I dun need yuhr blood, Mademoiselle, so relax," Madame Laveau said, laughing, and Nana tried to smile. Madame stood over her, her arms akimbo, as she scrutinized the Creole beauty kneeling there before her.

"I certainly don't need te make yuh morh beautiful, or morh encitin'," she said, smiling coolly as she studied the young woman. "Yuh iz alla dat already!" she added, stroking Nana's hair with her long, bejeweled fingers.

"What is yuhr name, chile?" she finally asked.

"I am Nana de Lis." The reply came softly, respectfully, but not submissively, the voodooienne noticed, then she added "Yuh are pregnant too, are yuh not? It iz hiz child yuh carry. Do yuh want te know if it be a boy or a girl, an' if it will be born, an' yuh an' de child both recover well from de birthin'? I have de power te see alla dat, an' tell yuh, yuh know. Just a touch of yuhr head gives me much knowledge about yuh."

"Oh, yes, can you please? I hadn't even told my Mama that I was pregnant. How did you know, Madame?" Nana asked in astonishment.

"I see de child's little aura showin', a strong little light around yuhr belly, but let me go make up de potions forh yuh," and with that she left the room.

"Yuh are pregnant agin, Nana? Are yuh sureh?" her mother asked excitedly.

"Yes, it's very early, but I'm sure."

Madame Laveau returned, with a cloth bag in one hand, which she handed over to Nana.

"In hieh are de gris-gris I made up forh yuh. Remember, de bag wid de red ribbon will keep 'em in love wid yuh, an' yuh must put it under hiz pillow when he sleeps wid yuh, de bag wid de blue ribbon iz forh hiz safety durin' de war, an' yuh must make sureh he has it wid him alla de time he iz gone, in hiz pocket, de pocket nearest hiz heart. Now let me test forh yuhr child," she said.

"Dis little bottle is full of holy watah, an' by de way de bottle moves, when I hold it oveh yuhr stomach, we'll know if yuh carry a boy or a girl." She lowered the bottle on a string over Nana's stomach, and immediately it began to move, going faster and faster.

Marie Laveau laughed. "Jus' look at how fast it moves! Yuh carry a verra active, healthy boy, Mademoiselle. And all will go well wid de delivery, forh both of yuh."

Madame de Lis deposited a few coins on the white linen square, and on the way out, in the first room, she and Nana both lit candles, and expressed their thanks to Madame Marie Laveau.

"Madame, may I ask what was in that big white box in the other room, the box which seemed to move a little?" Nana asked, her curiosity getting the better of her.

"Dat's de Great Zombi. He'z my snake companion, an' he comes out forh special, big voodoo celebrations. I didn't really need 'em today, jus' te answer yuhr questions. Anyway, come back, if I kin help yuh some morh," she said, as she closed the door after them.

"Mama, if the number of candles we have lit this morning, both here and at the Cathedral, will help, then Emile's love for me should be simply flaming," Nana said, carefully carrying home the cloth bag. And she did remember, and put the little bag with the red ribbon under Emile's pillow.

*   *   *

The next morning the *Picayune* had a drawing and an article on the de Marigny wedding, and much as Madame de Lis wanted to hide them from Nana, she knew it would be better for her to see them, and to know it had finally taken place. She knew that the news would help her daughter to understand why she would not see her lover for a while, even if it hurt her. Such was always the pain of plaçage relationships; Mama de Lis well knew that from her own experience when she was young and in love. So when Nana came down for coffee, wrapped in Emile's big, blue velvet robe, she saw the paper lying on the table, picked it up, and opened it out. In front of her was the de Marigny wedding article.

"It's happened," was all she said, and then she put the paper down, and drank two cups of coffee nonstop. Finally she picked the paper up again, "I have to see what she looks like. I believe when Armand took me to the opera the other night, we saw her in the de Marigny box with Emile. She was very pretty, and she and I looked at each other, and I think she sensed that I play a role in Emile's life, but of course, I didn't realize then that they were already married, but still I did feel she was the bride his father forced him to agree to," Nana said, and began to scrutinize the drawing very carefully.

"At the opera Emile brought us champagne, and right there in the theatre he kissed my hand, and I'm sure she saw how long he held it. And my expression must have given me away, but I couldn't help it. I love Emile, and I'm sure it showed."

Nana continued to examine the drawing. "He's smiling," she said in a sad tone.

"Well, yuh didn't 'pect 'em te be cryin' forh yuh raight den, didja?... Comin' out of de church wid dat bride on hiz arm?" her Mama answered, trying to get even a little smile from her daughter, but she was unsuccessful.

"She's pretty, don't you think, Mama? Prettier than me? She is mighty petite too, she barely comes up to his shoulder. Men like petite," she added in a somewhat resentful tone.

"Dat piture dere, dat's jus' a drawin' somebody did, so 'course dey gonna make her look good, but no way iz she prettier dan yuh, Nana. He will do what he hafta do, and since he be a man, he gonna enjoy doin' dat, but it won't be long beforh he be darkenin' dis door agin," her Mama said as she sat down and began to stir her coffee with a heavy hand.

"Dat's jus' one morh a doz arranged marriages. He dun tole yuh hiz papa forced it on 'em. But don' yuh doubt dat he'z in love wid yuh, powerfully in love wid yuh, baby, an' dat's what matters.

"Now, honey chile, whatja want me te make yuh forh breakfast? Yuh gotta eat, chile, an' keep dat chin of yuhrs up, an' look yuhr best. He be comin' lookin' forh hiz baby doll 'forh too long, yuh'll see."

"Please, Mama, I'm just not hungry," Nana said, continuing to study the sketch of the de Marigny wedding.

"Yuh might as well figure on eatin' or I'ze gonna spoon it down yuhr throat, one big spoonful afta anudeh. Yuh need te eat te look beautiful. He be back hieh any day now, yuh jus' wait an' see! He'z got a passion forh yuh, honey, an' eben if he duz enjoy hisself wid dat somebody new hiz Papa find forh 'em, it's jus' not de same thing as what he's got wid yuh. Yuh'll see. So iz yuh gonna eat, or duz I hafta spoon it down yuhr pretty little throat forh yuh? I'm thinkin' an egg an' ham, or pancakes. Which yuh want? Yea I know yuh don' want anythin', but yuh might as well pick yuhr torture! One or de odeh, which it gonna be?"

"Mama, I'm not a child any more, and I'm not hungry either!" Nana protested.

"Den it be eggs, 'cause dey iz easier forh me te push down yuhr throat!" her Mama said, and she went to the kitchen and started breaking eggs, and beating them up vigorously.

Nana took up the paper again. "Let's see, when did the wedding happen?" She found the date, and started counting on her fingers.

"It was ten days ago, so you may be right, Mama. He might be coming any time now. But if he keeps me waiting two or three more weeks, I will begin to wonder if he still does love me. "

Mama de Lis hurried out of the kitchen with some scrambled eggs and ham for Nana.

"So iz yuh gonna eat dis, jus' te please me, an' so yuh kin look yuhr best, or iz I gonna hafta force dese eggs down yuhr throat?"

"I'll eat them, just for you, Mama," Nana said, smiling a little and picking up her fork to attack the eggs. She knew when there was no sense in arguing.

"Eat 'em forh 'em, darlin', cause he be around hieh any day now. I knows dat forh sureh. He iz downright addicted te yuh, yuh'ze hiz darlin' baby, an' he ain't about te forgit yuh. I think he *always* be comin' around hieh, dat's what I think. Yuh got hiz heart, an' he's like a fish dat's been caught. He ain't able te break free. Yuh got 'em, hook, line an' sinkeh, ma baby doll. An' yuh already tole 'em yuh'z pregnant agin, didn't yuh?"

"Yes, he knows, and he seemed very excited about it. Still I'm so afraid that maybe he'll be contented with her, his new little plaything, and will gradually stop coming to me."

"No, baby. I dun't think he iz eber gonna git oveh yuh, an' dat's a fact. He be a'comin' around forh years an' years, yuh'll see. He may be a man, an' Lawd knows, dey kin be downraight terrible, doz men, but dis one, he loves yuh, truly he duz, an' yuh always gonna haf hiz heart, eben if he grows te love dat odeh little woman he got now, yuh iz still gonna be hiz first, an' best love, alla hiz life long. And dat's de truth, de Lawd's own truth! And dat's what dat conjure woman Laveau dun tried te tell yuh too.... An' besides dat, yuh dun already give 'em hiz first chile, an' now, very likely hiz second one too. Dat's gotta count forh somethin'! He be 'round any day now, you'll see."

Old Mama de Lis was right. A few nights later, there was a knock on the door.

"I git it, baby, so yuh won' be disappointed, if it's not de raight man dere."

She opened the door, and it was the right man, smiling at her.

"Am I allowed in?" he asked, looking a bit anxious.

"Yuh sureh iz. She'ze been lookin' forh yuh, an' mopin' around dis place wid one big, sad hounddawg look, jus' awaitin' forh yuh. An'..." Mama dropped her voice very low and soft so only Emile could hear her,

"I dun brought her de weddin' notice in de papeh, so she could begin te git used te de idea, an' yuh wouldn't hafta spend alla de night explainin' te her. She knows, so don' say much about it. She still don' handle it real good.... But come on in dis house. She be upstairs, so yuh kin go on up dere an' surprise her raight now...."

It didn't take any persuading. Emile ran up the stairs two at a time. He poked his face around the lintel.

"Will you permit me in, Mademoiselle Nana?" he asked, but before she could do more than smile at him, he was across the room and burying her in his arms.

"Oh, mon Dieu, how I have missed you, Nana! I couldn't let another night pass without seeing you. Everyone thinks I am staying in town tonight for business, but you and I know, *you* are the most important business I could ever have, and I am here to spend the night with you, if you will still have me. Will you, chérie?"

"Oh Emile, will I have you? I have yearned for you every day and every night. This big bed is so empty and lonely without you. Please come and fill up the empty place."

That was all the invitation he needed. He tore his clothes off, spilling them all over, on his way to the bed.

"Ummmm," was all he could say, as he took her in his arms, and held her as tightly as he could. She clung to him with all her strength, and her lips eagerly sought his. Her eagerness spurred him on, filling him with a powerful tide of passion, and he knew she would not make him wait long. Finally he lifted himself above her, and their eyes met before hers closed.

"Oh, Emile, I love you so,..." she murmured, and her hips rose to meet him.

It was the most powerful experience he had ever known, and when, at last, they were both spent, he lay on top of her, her beautiful, high breasts pressed tightly against his chest. Her hands moved slowly, languidly down his waist and hips. He kissed her eyelids and her long neck, as sleep reached out for both of them.

The next morning he awoke to find her big, dark eyes on him. He kissed her and for a while they lay together, her body curved against his. A perfect fit, he thought.

"I've been trying hard not to ask how you like her,..." Nana said. "But I can't seem to help it.... I saw you together the other night at the opera. She's pretty, and very petite...."

"She's all right. I can live with her, and as you know, my father wants her pregnant before I leave, so I have to work on that, but darling, she *is not you*, and I have only one passion, and it's you, ma chérie. All of me is yours, and will always be, as long as you want me, and I'm alive...."

"Emile, don't say things like that,... as long as you're alive. You have to go fight, and I will worry about you the whole time you're gone. Please don't think like that, ever! All the money I would spend on clothes and things for this little house, I'll be spending on candles. I will be lighting them every day until you return safely. In fact I already started; I lit three yesterday morning at the Cathedral, and several more during the rest of the day."

He reached for his pillow to puff it up under his head, and his hand encountered something.

"What's this, chérie?" he said, pulling a little mesh bag out from under his pillow, and holding it up. "It's not one of those Cathedral candles you just mentioned, I can see that!"

Nana smiled. "I was so sad this week, knowing what was going on in your life, that my Mama made me come with her to see Marie Laveau. Do you know who she is, Emile?"

"I've heard the name, of course. So what is this little bag supposed to do to me? Make me more virile when I'm with you? I didn't think you found me lacking in that way! Or is it to discourage me from bedding anyone but you? To make me impotent when I should perform as a husband with my new, little wife? Which is it, chère?"

His voice had a sharp, almost disapproving tone, she thought, and she was relieved to see that in spite of his tone, he was still smiling as he studied the little bag.

"Oh no, none of those, but she did promise me that it would mean you would always love me, and come back safely to me," Nana said, retrieving the little bag from his hand, and kissing his hand.

"But you don't need that! I've already told you so many times that you are my first and only love. I will always love you, Nana, and will come to you as long as you'll let me. You don't need love potions or herbal concoctions from that voodoo queen. You already own me, totally!"

"I hope so, Emile, because I am all yours, and I never want to live without you."

She turned her dark eyes full on him, and her smile arched invitingly. "This little bag, it's,... what do you call it? ... insurance! And I have another one too, one you must stick in your pocket, and keep with you all the time you are gone. She told me it would keep you from being killed, and bring you back safely to me. You must promise me that you won't forget to keep it in your pocket. She said to put it in your vest pocket, near your heart. It could help.... I will give it to you later, before you go. Can you stay another night?"

"Yes, everyone at home thinks I am in town to finish up business for my Papa. He knows, and surprisingly is providing me with reasons I must stay in town overnight. It amuses me; he helps come up with excuses so I can spend nights with you, but at the very same time he forces me into this arranged marriage! And it surely would be an irony if you have given me two children before anything comes from that arranged marriage!"

"I guess you will be gone when this baby comes. If it's a boy, will you agree to call him Lucien? And if it's a girl, I'd like to call her Helene."

"Anything you say, Nana, my darling. I am just sad that I probably won't be here when this great event happens, but your Mama will come and stay with you while I'm gone, won't she?"

"Yes, I'm sure she will. I wanted you to be the first to know, but she was with me when Marie Laveau, without my saying anything, asked me if I knew I was pregnant. Mama just looked at me with perfect astonishment. She hadn't guessed it herself, and that's amazing. She's usually the first to figure such things out. Sometimes with my married sister, Mignon, Mama knew even before Mignon did! When it's a pregnancy, she is uncanny."

"Did you think to ask that Laveau woman whether it will be a boy or a girl?"

"Yes, and she says this time it will be a boy. She took a bottle of holy water, and dangled it by a string over my stomach, and it moved very fast. She laughed, and told me that it's a boy, and from the way the bottle was moving, that he's very vigorous and healthy, and will be born at full term."

"I'm not a big believer in that woman's powers, but she does have a fifty/fifty chance on this boy/girl prediction, doesn't she?" Emile grinned, and Nana had to laugh.

"Yes, but I've heard she's made many, much more difficult predictions than this one!"

"Well, if her little bags of whatever make you feel better, then I will go along with it, just for you, Nana. I think I hear your mother bustling around downstairs, and making us some breakfast, so let's get up. We have a whole day to spend together, and you can decide exactly how you would like to spend it."

Emile dressed quickly and headed downstairs. Nana stretched luxuriously, and before she even stuck a toe out of bed, she leaned over and put the gris-gris back under Emile's pillow. There was no reason to take any chances, she thought. And Emile didn't seem threatened by it, once she had explained.

Later that morning, with Emile pushing Nanette's baby carriage, they walked along the levée, looking at all the ships docked along it. It was a beautiful day, with a clear, deep blue sky, and the river reflecting it. And there was a nice breeze, not cool, but pleasant, warm and dry. Nanette, sitting up in her carriage, squealed at the seagulls wheeling overhead, and smiled and pointed at all the brilliant beds of flowers in bloom, and bowing to the wind in the Place d'Armes

They stopped and had café au lait and beignets, sharing sips and little pieces of beignet with Nanette, who giggled and asked for more.

Finally she had enough, and when they resumed their walk, Emile and Nana stopped to kiss the powdered sugar off each other's lips.

"Beignets make for such nice, sweet kisses," Emile said, smiling and enjoying the last of the sugar from Nana's lips, kissing and then licking to get all of it. Nana smiled at him as they sauntered down to the French Market. There was a steady hum of voices punctuated with laughter, and the calls of roosters, the oinking and squealing of pigs, and the braying of mules. Nanette was all eyes and ears, and tried to imitate the animal sounds. Emile joined in, braying like a mule, and soon all three of them were laughing. He saw a stall with jewelry displayed, and he stopped to let Nana examine it, hoping she would give him an idea of what he could buy for her.

"What do you like most, ma chérie?" he asked, fingering a pair of pearl earrings, and a gold chain necklace with a large pearl teardrop on it.

"Would you wear these and think of me when I am gone?" he held the necklace up to her lovely, long neck. "I would love to imagine you wearing these, and thinking of me," he added, fishing out the money to pay for them. Then he led her to a nearby bench, and fastened the necklace around her neck. He handed her the earrings.

"I'll let you put these on yourself, then I'll kiss them into place," and he did. Later, he held up a frilly little bonnet, and Nana nodded and smiled, so he got it for Nanette, and they stopped to put it on her. All three of them laughed at the new bonnet, and Nanette sucked on the ends of the ribbons tied in a bow under her chin.

"Nana, I have a special surprise for you, which should arrive tomorrow," Emile said, smiling and squinting at her through the sunshine. She touched the side of his eyelids with her slender fingers.

"I know you are thinking hard when you squint up your eyes like that, or else it means you have been up to some mischief. It isn't just the sun, although it took me a while to figure that out. It must be mischief this time! Do I really have to wait for tomorrow to find out what it is? So, what have you been up to?" she asked, her fingers smoothing down his dark, wavy hair, her chin tilted up to him, a smile twinkling in her dark eyes and on her lips.

"Only tomorrow will tell," he said, giving her a quick kiss on the cheek. "You will just have to stand the suspense till then!"

They had a perfect day and night together. And the next morning, as they were just finishing the last of their breakfast coffee slowly and leisurely, there was a sudden, loud rapping at the door.

"I know what that is, and I'll get it," Emile said, hurrying to open the door.

"Bring it right in," he said, and three men struggled to bring in a fine piano, and a bench to go with it. "Put it over here," Emile said, smiling at Nana, and pointing to the wall which formed the side of the staircase.

"Nana, if you want it somewhere else, tell me now while these strong men are here to move it wherever you want," he added. "I've got better things to do today than move this piano around!" he said, grinning at her. "Will this do, Mademoiselle?"

"Oh, yes, Emile, what a wonderful surprise! I've always wanted a piano. Thank you!" and she flung herself into his arms, covering his face with kisses.

"But you haven't seen it all. Open up the piano bench," he ordered, and she did.

"It's full of music, books of music!" she cried, searching through them, and finally pulling out one which was titled *Compositions by Mozart*. He pulled out the bench, and she sat right down, and began fingering out the first page. Then she stood up, and turned to hug him again.

"So does this surprise make you happy, ma chérie?" he asked.

"Oh, very happy, Emile. Thank you so much." She settled back on the bench, and began to work out the first piece, and he sat down in the nearest wing chair, and tried to read the newspaper, but found that only a line or two would make sense, and then he would have to watch her again, her lovely profile, her chin lifted slightly, her long, dark curls falling down around her face, as she leaned forward, studying the music, her slender fingers hesitating over the keys. He knew his gift would be a success, and her delight and happiness only increased his own. He hoped it would help to fill up the time while he was gone, and his heart became heavy at the thought of leaving her.

As the day drifted into sunset, he became afraid of how she would handle their last night together. He was reluctant to tell her that in only one more day he would have to leave to join the cavalry unit to which he had just been assigned. Perhaps it would be best to only tell her as he was actually leaving. That might make the pain of parting shorter, and allow them to share one last wonderful night together, perhaps without tears.

But the tears came, all the same, and the best he could do was try to kiss them away. She clung to him, her dark eyes seeming to try to memorize his features and his body.... And when they became one, it was in a frenzy of passion and sadness. When they finished, and he tried to pull his body off of her, she held him, her nails digging into his shoulders, and he was helpless to stop her tears. He stayed on top of her, trying not to move, until he was sure she was asleep, and then, his movements slow and gentle, he lay down beside her. His thoughts would not let go of him, and he lay there awake in the darkness, wondering how he could balance the needs of both his women, when he returned to a life in which he would have to plan on dividing his time between them. While a part of him was filled with male bravado; he couldn't deny it, he knew he could satisfy them both. Still another part of him worried about how he would maintain his own emotional balance, sharing his feelings between them. There was no question about his love for Nana, but somehow he would have to save a little feeling back for Marie Therese. She was also his responsibility now, and he had to be fair to her.

Emile woke to the cool, gray light of the beginning dawn. He reached for Nana, but the bed was empty beside him. He looked up, and saw her standing at the window, her long fingers holding the curtains back, her body pale ivory under the transparent negligée. He yearned for her, and held out his arms. "Nana" was all he had to say, and she was there, in his arms, the silky negligée yielding to his touch, as he reached for her breasts.

The light in the room was gradually increasing, and he was glad of that, he wanted to see her, and to remember her just as he saw her now. She knelt between his knees, and slowly lowered her ivory body to join his. He responded eagerly, with a rush of feeling, and when, finally, consciousness of the world returned, that world had moved into the full light of a bright and dazzling dawn. He stroked a long, dark lock of her hair.

"I love you, Nana, just remember that" he said softly, kissing the lock before he let it fall from his hand. Their eyes met as he gently arranged her long, dark hair around her face, and down onto her breasts.

He knew that the leave-taking should be short, so he gave her another kiss, and got up. He washed, aware that her eyes were on him the whole time. Then he dressed, and ran a brush through his unruly hair.

"I will bring up some coffee," he said, and she heard him on the stairs. Soon he was back, setting the tray down on her bedside table. He fixed her coffee, proud that he now knew exactly how much sugar and cream to add, and handed it to her.

"How did you not see the little box on the tray, beside your coffee cup?" he finally asked, smiling with anticipation. "It's for you, ma chère. Please open it now!"

She opened the box, and sighed with pleasure. "Oh, Emile, how gorgeous!"

He took the sapphire ring out of the box, and slid it on her finger. "Please remember me whenever you look at your ring, and remember how very much I love you, Nana. You mean everything to me," he said softly, and accepted her kiss of thanks. There was a silence, as she turned the ring this way and that, catching the rays of the morning sun, and watching the sapphire blaze into light; brilliant shafts of blue spun out of it, and across the room. She turned to Emile, and softly said,

"Thank you, my darling. I will always wear this ring and with it on my finger, I will think of you,... always."

"I will write whenever I can, and tell you how to reach me," he said finally, putting down his empty cup. "I don't want you to come down to the door to see me off, that would be too painful for both of us. I want to remember you here, in our bed, just as you are right now."

She reached out to her bedside table, and picked up the second little mesh bag, this one tied with a blue ribbon.

"This is supposed to carry you safely through the war, and back to me," she said. He bent over, and let her put the little bag in his vest pocket. Her dark eyes met his, and slowly she withdrew her hand, and patted him right over his heart.

"Don't forget to change the gris-gris over to your uniform pocket," she said, bravely trying to smile. "Please take good care of yourself; don't be too daring and courageous. Nothing foolhardy! And promise me you won't forget to carry this little bit of luck with you all the time you are gone. Darling, just do it for me...."

He bent over her, and gave her one last, quick, gentle kiss.

"Just for you, Nana, I'll remember it every day. Take care of yourself and our little one. When I return, I hope you'll be able to play lots of new pieces for me on the piano. I love you, Nana, never for one moment doubt it, and I will do my best to come back to you," he said, and then he left her.

*   *   *

Emile had to face a second leave-taking, this time from his wife, his parents, and Marengo. After returning from the city, he mounted his favorite horse, and silently, alone, he rode around the plantation, taking in all its beauties - the live oak alley, the magnolias full of waxy blooms, and the graceful willows by the river's edge. The river itself, a constant through his entire life, and now, as calm as it could ever be, its surface full of starkly white clouds, which elongated as they sailed on the current. He turned back, away from the river, and smiled as he looked up at the Big House. It was home, warm feelings, and the memories of his childhood. Its great white columns, towers of strength, would help to give him strength as he remembered it all, perhaps in the midst of artillery fire, or in the silent, parched nights on a Mexican desert. Marengo was a part of him, as it would always be, and one day he would be its master....

Marie Therese watched him from the window of their bedroom. Why did he not invite her to accompany him on that last ride, she wondered sadly. When he drew closer to the Big House, she moved back and let the curtain fall into place. She didn't want him to see her there, watching. She couldn't untangle her feelings, so how could she explain them to him?

There was a final, quiet dinner, with champagne, and there were Creole embraces and kisses shared with both his parents, then it was time to go upstairs and spend a last night with his little Marie Therese. He planned to leave very early in the morning, when only his father would be up. That way this departure would be less tearful.

Emile put his arm around Marie Therese's tiny waist as they went up the stairs together, and once in their bedroom, he helped her undress. Their bedcovers had already been turned down, so he picked her up and gently placed her down on her side of the bed. He smiled at her, as she pulled the sheet up around her, remembering how nervous he had made her that first night when he refused to let her cover herself. Perhaps that had been cruel, a reflection of his frustration and anger at being so quickly shunted into the marriage. This time he did not object, and soon he joined her.

"There are a few things I must tell you," he began, resting on his elbow, and looking over at her.

She silently wondered if that would include any explanation of where he had been the last two nights. Before their marriage, she had heard rumors that he had a beautiful mistress, a free Creole of color, and she was hurt, that although he would spend his last night with her, he had left her alone the past two nights. They had only been able to spend a few days together on a honeymoon, and after that he had been gone to the city overnight many times. She would not mention any of this, but she hoped that he was about to tell her that the unexplained absences would end when he returned. And was it the beautiful Creole of color she had seen at the opera, the one who had given Emile such a look of love, and whose hand he had so slowly kissed? The looks she and that woman had exchanged, seemed to indicate that they both sensed each other's roles in Emile's life.

Also she knew he had given a will to his father to be placed in the family safe, but he had not offered to show it to her, or to explain its terms. Perhaps part of it dealt with that beautiful Creole. Perhaps he already had children from her, and had to provide for them in the will.

There were times when she felt that her presence at Marengo was intrusive. To the family and to her husband, she felt she was still a stranger, or perhaps merely a contract,... indemnified to meet their goal of an heir; a cruel distortion of all the fairy tales she had read as a child,... tales which told of the arrival of a fairy prince, of romantic love, and of the magical birth of a son, with prince and princess expected to rule the kingdom in lasting happiness. But Emile was speaking to her, and she needed to refocus and hear what he was saying.

"I will be joining the 2nd Dragoons under General Zachary Taylor. All I know now is that his forces are assembling at Fort Jessup, here in Louisiana, and are to construct a camp near the Rio Grande, there to await further orders. It will be a long trek on horseback, and then probably a long wait in the heat, before we see any action, unless the Mexicans choose to attack us before we can settle in. When I know more, I'll send word home as to how I can be reached, so you'll be able to write me, and I will write you when I can. Just as we are troubled here with yellow fever, that will be true there, and I expect we will be on the march quickly, since the General will want to achieve a victory before the yellow fever season poses as severe a threat to his troops as the Mexicans will. If I am right about this, there won't be much time for letter-writing, but I'll do my best."

"Emile, promise me, that you will take care of yourself, I'd rather have you come back whole, than hear that you had won a medal for bravery, especially if that courageous act leaves you badly wounded, or dead and buried in some godforsaken corner of Mexico."

"I will remember that advice," he said, smiling slightly, and then his arms reached for her, caressing her wordlessly, in ways that seemed to her almost methodical, rather than loving. His kisses ranged over her body, and gradually she rose to a level of passion which trembled on the verge of tearfulness. Their love showed no abandon, and she longed to hear him utter words of love, but they still hadn't come. She felt hurried to the point of climax, but reached it, and tumbled into a pleasurable release with him. He lay on her, his weight almost oppressive. Finally his even breathing and the totally relaxed feel of his body told her he was asleep, and she eased out from under him, and turning her back on him, she curled up on her side of the bed, leaving a space between them. *Can I learn to share him? Will I truly be able to trust him someday,* she wondered. *Will the evasions and abrupt silences come to an end? There* seemed to be so much of his life he was unwilling to share with her.... It was a long time before she could fall asleep....

In the grayness of the breaking dawn, she felt him begin to move about, and finally he got up, and in the half-light she saw him dressing. He was resplendent, strikingly handsome in his dark blue uniform, with its golden epaulets. He kissed her hand, grabbed up his bag and his military shako.

"Can I see you in your shako?" she asked, so he put his bag down, settled his shako on his head, put the chin strap in place, and struck a pose as if at attention, grinning jauntily at her.

"I hope your colonel keeps you too busy for you to get around any ladies, you look entirely too handsome in that uniform!" she said, smiling at him.

"Is there anything we should tell my father? I'll stop for coffee with him, and I know he will ask. He is anxiously awaiting word of the possibility of an heir for Marengo."

"It's too soon to be sure. I guess you can tell him there is a possibility, but that I'll have to tell him in a month or so. I'm sorry I can't really tell you for certain now, before you leave. All I can say now, is that it *might* be true. Take care, Emile, and let me hear from you when you can. You will be in my thoughts and prayers."

She saw him stop and take something small from the pocket of the suit he wore the day before, and put it in his breast pocket, but it was too dark to see what it was. She reached for a little package on her bedside table and handed it to him. "Open it now," she said.

He pulled out a small gold cross on a golden chain. "Please wear it, Emile, and let it remind you of me, and keep you safe," she said softly.

He nodded, and put the cross on. "I'll remember that, and remember you," he said. He blew her a last kiss, picked up his bag, and the door closed behind him. She heard his brisk footsteps on the stairs.

Was this to be all, the last sound of his footsteps that she would ever hear? Marie Therese wiped away her tears, and lay awake in the gray darkness until the sun rose.

"Please God, bring him back safe and sound," she prayed. Then she rang her bell. It would be a good morning to have breakfast in bed. That, she knew, was Madame Blanche's routine, and it might well become her own. She had no desire to face Monsieur Louis and his questions. Emile would surely have stopped for a cup of coffee with his father, and told him all there was to say at this time. Another month or two, and Monsieur Louis would be asking her what hope there was, and perhaps by then she would be able to give him a more positive answer. Even in his farewell, Emile hadn't really told her he loved her; was she only valued for producing Marengo's heir, she wondered again sadly. Perhaps when he returned, they could find their way to real love. She would hope and pray for that, as well as for his survival....

*   *   *

After Emile's departure, with each week with no word from him, Madame de Lis became increasingly worried by her daughter's state of mind. The best part of her days was spent either practicing at the piano, or helping her mother with the sewing for her white patrons. The rest of the time was increasingly spent in sleeping, or simply moping, and it was difficult to persuade her to eat a proper diet.

In despair, Madame de Lis decided to enlist some of Nana's friends to help get her out of the house and among people. Antoinette Lefon and Lucille Chauvin both took Nana out with them, and were finally allowed to visit the little house on Felicity Street. For the first time in a long while there was laughter in the little house, and the sound of voices singing along with the piano. Nana still offered them no explanation for the house and its expensive contents, and they politely asked no questions. Still they all knew that she had managed to snag the wealthy young heir of Marengo into becoming her lover and protector, and they recognized that good fortune had indeed come her way, bringing a house, its lavish contents, and fabulous jewelry. None of them had failed to spot that large sapphire blazing from her finger or the diamonds or pearls she also wore from time to time.

And then there was beautiful little Nanette, with her dark curls, her green eyes, and her fair skin. She could easily follow in the footsteps of her mama, her grandmama, and her great grandmama, into a plaçage relationship which would give her love and security. All of them knew that such relationships could provide better for women of color than anything else could, and all of them hoped one day to establish similar relationships. They might crave a young man of their own color, their own kind; but they knew such a man, while he could provide love, was unlikely to be able to provide security, nor would such a man be likely to help conceive children with even lighter skins than their own,... children who might pass on without notice, into a world closed to their parents and grandparents; a white-skinned world, in which few, if any, doors would remain closed to them.

All her friends were planning on attending the voodoo ceremonies which traditionally took place on St. John's Eve, where Bayou St. John joins Lake Ponchartrain. They would take some picnic baskets, and a few bottles of wine, and spend the evening there. When Nana grew tired of their attempts to persuade her to attend, she finally agreed, and along with Madame de Lis playing the role of their chaperone, they all piled into one of the starred street cars available to the gens de couleur, and which ran to and from the Lake on that special evening. The mules, their long ears popping from holes cut in their decorative straw hats, plodded along through the heat, and everyone was singing and laughing, until they reached the selected spot by the Lake, and all climbed out. Before it was time to light candles and start dancing, they spread their picnic out on a big, red and white checked tablecloth under the trees, and lit into it, finishing up with two bottles of red wine.

Soon the drums began to be heard, and people gathered to dance. The last rays of the sunset were vanishing from amid the trees, when Nana and her friends went down to the waterfront. Some large boulders jutted up along the edge of the Lake, placed there to help protect the levées in storms, and they carefully climbed out onto them, and began to wash their arms and legs off. Not only did the water feel cooling, and helped to get rid of any stickiness from their picnic, but it was considered a necessary, preliminary ritual before the ceremonies that night. Nana didn't particularly care about the ceremonial aspects of ritual washing, but she was finding it very comforting and cooling. Her friends were ready to join the dancing, and when they asked her, she declined, electing to stay quietly by the waterfront.

She watched the pastel colors of the sunset receding from the still mirror of the Lake, and felt peaceful, although she did pray for Emile's safety, and daydreamed about him. In fact, she was still daydreaming of their last night together, and of how they would celebrate the night of his return, when she felt a pair of strong arms grip her around the waist, and lift her from her rock back to the shore.

She tried to turn within the embrace of the arms, which held her tightly, and faced a tall, dark man, with bright red and yellow painted lines along the tattoos on his face. He wore a long scarlet jacket, richly trimmed with much gold braid, and blue pants with a line of gold braid down their sides. He was grimacing at her in a way which made her fearful.

"What a pretty lady!" he exclaimed. "An' all by yuhrself, too."

"Please, Monsieur, let me go," Nana begged, trying to twist and release herself from his strong grip.

"Not so fast, pretty thing. First I want te know yuhr name, an' den yuh must promise te dance wid me, an' den te stay all night wid me," he said, and the sensual overtones of his voice and his request made Nana even more afraid. He held her with one hand, and with the other, she saw, he was loosening his trousers, until they dropped, revealing only a bright blue loincloth. Nana gasped in panic, as she saw he was completely aroused.

"I belong to another man," she sobbed, "so I am not free to do your bidding...."

"But I dun see anyone comin' te yuhr rescue, so let me enjoy myself wid yuh, a dance or two, an den a night togetheh hieh, raight on de grass," he persisted, leering at her, and holding her with such strength that she knew she could only evade him with subterfuge.

"All right, just a dance or two, but then you must promise to let me go," she conceded, trying to ignore the rest of what he had asked for.

She forced herself to relax within his arms, hoping that might induce him to ease his grip on her, but it didn't work. In fact he pulled her closer, holding her tight to him, and she could feel his male arousal. In growing hysteria, she began to turn and wrestle against him.

She looked over his shoulder to see if any of her friends or her mother was near enough to help her, but she saw no one she knew.

Suddenly the man started to carry her to where the dancers were moving, their shadows growing longer in the light of flaming torches. The drums were beating out a compelling rhythm, faster and faster, and she saw the dancers' bodies moving to keep up with the drums. Her attacker fumbled with one hand at her skirt, roughly pulling skirt and petticoats out of his way. Then he reached below his loin cloth, and prepared to rape her. She knew he would have her; there wasn't a moment to lose. She struggled frantically in his arms, and cried out "Oh no! Please, put me down, right now! Stop, please stop!" and in total desperation, she began to cry, giant sobs breaking from her.

Suddenly the grip of the big man was broken, and he collapsed on the ground, carrying Nana down with him. She felt gentle hands lift her to her feet, and she looked up into the face of a light-skinned Creole man, not nearly as big as her attacker. It was her violinist friend, Armand Saint Pierre.

"Oh, thank you! I was trying hard to get away from him, but he wasn't listening, just continuing to attack me. Oh, mon Dieu, you rescued me just in time!" Then Nana stopped to catch her breath. "He was already telling me what he wanted to do with me the rest of the night, and I couldn't seem to get away! You aren't as big or strong as he is, so how in the world did you manage to get me away from him?"

Armand laughed. "I'll answer your questions, but first let's put some distance between him and us, since the effect of bashing him over the head could wear off any time," and he took her hand, and they fled to the fringe of trees on the other side of the circle of dancers.

"Now to answer your questions. How did I get him to let go of you? I gave him a good whack on the head with a tree limb! Size isn't all that matters, sometimes it's just having the right weapon at the right time, and I think that's what happened. Now, aren't you Nana de Lis whom I met briefly when I played in the orchestra at the Quadroon Balls, and do you have friends here tonight, to whom I may safely escort you? I hope you remember me, Armand Saint Pierre. Our mutual friend, Monsieur Emile de Marigny asked me to accompany you to the opera, while he is in Mexico, and we went together, just once, recently. Do you remember? And I'm the one who told you that I'm studying music with

Edmond Dédé, the violinist and composer. Perhaps you have heard of him, have you, Mademoiselle?"

He still held her hand, but Nana was not finding that presented any problems.

"Oh yes, I have heard of him, and what a wonderful career you have chosen, Monsieur Armand. I am envious of you, I love music, and I do play the piano a little, but to make a career in music.... Why that must be wonderful! And yes, I am Nana de Lis, and indeed I do remember going to the opera with you. I am still a bit incoherent because of my narrow escape, but please accept my thanks for your very timely intervention."

"Do you know into whose grasp you had fallen?" he asked, and pointed to the circle of dancers. Standing high above everyone, on a platform in the very middle of all the dancers, was the big man whom they had left lying on the grass by the lake. He had shed his scarlet jacket, and wore only his blue loincloth. His tall, lean body was covered with painted tattoos. Nana shivered, and turned away from the sight.

"What a shame, he made such a quick recovery!" Nana exclaimed. "I hope he doesn't see me. I don't want to have anything to do with him the rest of this night, or any other time! No, I don't have any idea who he is, but I do know the woman who is walking towards him. Just look at how the dancers are all moving out of her way, clearing a path for her. That's Marie Laveau, isn't it? She walks like a queen! But who is he? He must be important too, so who is he?"

"Yes indeed, that is the famous Marie Laveau, and the man towering in the middle of the dancers, that's Dr. John, the witchdoctor. If he had hold of you just a little longer, he might have put a spell on you, and forced you to drink some sort of bad-tasting potion, and you might have been in his hands for the rest of your life!"

Nana didn't know whether to laugh or take her rescuer seriously. She looked up at him, and decided it was safe to smile. He didn't seem to be taking all he had said to her very seriously, although she found the implications very frightening.

"Well, whatever power he has, I am very glad you rescued me from his clutches. He repelled me with his talk, and I didn't feel at all safe as long as he had ahold of me. As for my friends, they said they wanted to go dance. I was enjoying sitting on a rock at the edge of the Lake. I found it so peaceful there by the Lake that I didn't want to leave. Besides, I wasn't at all sure, I wanted to get caught up in that dancing.... I'm frightened of voodoo, but my friends persuaded me that it would be a nice outing, and I let them talk me into coming."

Dimly, over Armand's shoulder, she saw her mother, talking with some other women not far away.

"I see my Mama now. She may be worrying about me, so let me take you over and reintroduce you to her. It's been quite a while since you met her at the Quadroon Ball."

Armand was still holding her hand, so she gently pulled him along until they reached her mother. Madame de Lis saw them approaching, and she was giving Armand a very careful appraisal. Evidently what she saw, pleased her, and with a broad smile, she came forward to greet them.

"Mama, this is Armand Saint Pierre. Remember he came over to talk with you at the last Quadroon Ball we attended? He is a musician studying with Edmond Dédé, the violinist, and before Emile left, he bought some season tickets, and asked Armand to escort me to the opera. Well, it's Armand who just rescued me from the arms of a dreadful man,..." Nana began.

Armand took Madame de Lis hand, and kissed it. "Actually I arrived just in time. The 'dreadful' Dr. John was about to slip off with your daughter! It looks as if he is so absorbed in the dancing, and with Marie Laveau, that he may have forgotten about your daughter, at least for now."

"Mama, could we tell the others that we are going home? I am afraid to stay here, afraid that vicious man will see me, and try to get me in his clutches again. Please...."

"I'm sorry that you are leaving so soon, but I do think it's the wisest course," Armand agreed.

"Let me go find our friends an' let 'em know we be leavin'," Mama de Lis said, "Jus' yuh stay raight hieh, Nana, so I know 'xactly where yuh be."

"And I will stay with you until I see you safely on the streetcar, and on your way back to town," Armand added, watching as Madame de Lis moved away.

"May I call on you some afternoon or evening, Mademoiselle? I can bring a few of my musical friends, and we'll bring our instruments and enjoy some music together."

"Yes, that sounds very nice indeed. We are at home most evenings, so please come when you can. I do have a piano, and with some practice, perhaps I will be able to accompany you."

Armand had been holding her hand all the time. Now he raised it up, and studied the big sapphire ring on the third finger of her left hand.

"Does this ring have some special meaning?" he asked, quietly watching Nana's eyes.

"Yes, but I am not married. Emile gave it to me, the same man who gave us the season tickets to the opera. He is away, serving with the dragoons in Mexico. I do miss him very much, but he is now a married man. Before his father insisted on an arranged marriage, Emile spoke of taking me with him to France, where we could have gotten married...."

"Ah, I'm sorry for him, but glad for me, since I am already quite anxious to develop a friendship with you, Nana."

She blushed, as she realized he had used her first name for the first time.

Madame de Lis returned, sparing Nana from any further questions, but Armand walked them to a waiting streetcar, and stayed to wave them off.

"I will be calling on you, and I'll bring a couple of the members of my little orchestra, and we'll make it a musical evening," he said to Nana, just as the streetcar began to move away.

He waved and smiled at them, and Nana waved back.

"Nana, chile, dat's one fine-lookin' Creole, an' wid such nice gentlemanly manners too," her mother said approvingly, after the streetcar had moved away, out of his hearing.

"Mama, I am grateful to him for getting me out of a very difficult situation. I felt like that Dr. John was trying to kidnap me, and that he had the worst of motives. I was completely helpless since he was too strong for me to get out of his arms, then Armand saved me. I am very grateful to him, Mama, but I still belong to Emile, and I hope he still loves me. You may see Armand as a nice, Creole man, unattached, and a likely prospect for a husband, but although I like him, it can never move beyond friendship. I will enjoy music with him and his friends, but that's all!"

"But jus' yuh think, Nana, he could be a husband who'd be wid yuh ebry night, not jus' a lover yuh gotta share wid hiz wife. Emile, he loves yuh, but, chile, he haz anudeh woman now, hiz wife, an' yuh gonna hafta live forh jus' doz few nights he kin spend wid yuh, an' de rest of de time yuh gonna be alone an' miserable. 'Member, I knows how dat iz, an' I jus' don' want dat forh ma chile. Dis man, he be good forh yuh, he already wants yuh, an' he be loyal; I sees dat in 'em already. He can earn yuh a good livin' too, wid hiz music. Don' make up yuhr mind aginst it so quick. He could be de best thing dat eber happen te yuh.... So jus' give it a chance, baby."

"Please, Mama,... no more...."

The rest of the trip was passed in silence, except for the clip-clop of the mules pulling the streetcar. Even when they got home, and her Mama invited her to have a cup of tea, they drank in silence. But when Nana went up, and climbed into bed, she again realized how empty the bed was, and she knew her mother was right; it would be empty most nights, even when Emile did come home. She loved him, she knew that, but was she prepared to spend so much of her life in loneliness? She didn't have an answer, and she cried herself to sleep.

During the day she was busy, helping her Mama clean the little house, practicing on the piano, and laying out patterns and sewing, but the nights continued to be lonely. A few days passed, and one evening there came a knock at the door, and Nana could hear laughing male voices outside.

Her mother answered the door, and in came Armand, accompanied by two friends, all three of them carrying somewhat battered musical instrument cases.

"I hope this is a good time for music," he said, smiling and kissing Nana's hand.

"Any time is a good time for music," Nana said, smiling back. "Please come in, everyone. May we fix you a cup of coffee, and a few biscuits?"

They agreed, so Nana laid the tablecloth on the dining room table, folded and set out some napkins, and opened up a tin of biscuits, and put some on a plate. Her heart seemed to turn over when she realized these were the biscuits Emile had brought her. And she remembered how they had sat up together in their bed and nibbled biscuits and drank coffee together. She didn't allow herself to stop and realize exactly why she felt guilty, she just recognized the feeling, and tried to push it aside. Soon the coffee was made, and they all helped themselves, and then settled in the living room.

"I hope you have fully recovered from that nasty encounter with Dr. John the other night," Armand said. "I told my friends a little about that, especially since it gave me a chance to claim I was your knight to the rescue!"

"Yes, I've put that incident behind me, but I must admit I never want to meet up with that man again, especially if I'm alone! I don't think he can be trusted, and I don't think I'll ever be going to him for gris-gris!" Nana answered, rolling her dark eyes, but smiling. Then she added,

"But when you finish your coffee, you must come see all the books of music I found in the piano bench. The piano and all the music were gifts, and I am still finding new music, and being happily surprised."

Armand looked long at her, his dark eyes clearly showing that he understood where the music and the piano must have come from. Was Nana telling him this as a reminder that she was not available, or was it just an expression of her surprise and delight over all the new music? It was too soon to tell whether he was being warned off, or not. For the time being, it would be friendship, he decided, although he definitely wanted the relationship to go beyond friendship, if and when that was possible. Her beauty, her warm vivacity, her love of music.... Already he knew he was attracted, more attracted than he had ever been before. This was a lady he was prepared to wait for,... if that's what it took....

A violin, a cello, and a flute emerged from the music cases, and together with the piano, they were able to create some fine music.

The time passed, and suddenly Armand realized that it was nearing midnight.

"Unfortunately we must go. All of us have day jobs," he said, smiling at his friends.

"Oh, do you play with some band, or orchestra?" Nana asked.

"Only occasionally. Sometimes we fill in when the regular musicians are sick, as I do with the group which plays for the Quadroon Balls. As regular jobs, we all work days in the same factory, making cigars. But that's all right. The faster the fingers go, the more cigars we make, and the more money we earn! Besides the dexterity helps us as musicians," he added cheerfully, and they all laughed.

"Please do come again soon. It's been a wonderful evening," Nana said, as Armand took her hand in his, and kissed it, his lips firm but gentle on her hand.

Armand looked around at his friends. "I believe I speak for all of us, we will look forward to another musical evening here. This street is well-named Felicity Street; this was a very pleasant evening."

Nana flinched at his comment. She had other emotional associations with the street's name. There was no reason she should feel guilty, and yet she did. The little house on Felicity Street had brought her much happiness, and she owed it all to her beloved,... her Emile. These were just friends, all united in their love of making music together,... surely Emile wouldn't see anything more than that, and yet she couldn't excise a slight feeling of betrayal from her heart.

Mama de Lis had enjoyed the musical evening, but even more she had enjoyed seeing her beloved Nana smiling and relaxed, totally enjoying herself. That trip to the Lake, while it didn't result in their attendance at any voodoo rituals, since they had left so early, had brought this fine young man to their house, and perhaps he might rescue her Nana again, this time from what could only be long-term unhappiness in an unequal relationship. She liked Emile, and she was sure he loved her daughter, but for Nana, a long-term relationship with Emile could bring more pain and sorrow than love, she felt sure of that. But she also knew that if she showed even the slightest preference for Armand Saint Pierre as the man in her daughter's life, that could doom his chances; so she kept her feelings to herself, and just prayed that time would give the relationship a chance to bloom from friendship and their mutual love of music, into an enduring love and perhaps even into marriage.

            *   *   *

When Marie Therese had come to Marengo as a new little bride, she brought with her only one slave, her beloved Mammy. Her parents had asked her what she would most like added to her trousseau, since they could not afford a dowry, and she had said "Only Mammy;" and so they came together, just the two of them, to this beautiful place, both of them as strangers. Mammy had easily become accepted as one of the house servants at the Big House, her warm, extrovert sense of humor had helped to smooth things over, and win her many new friends among Marengo's people, but her little mistress had not made as good an adjustment.

Marie Therese had sensed from the start that Emile seemed merely dutiful as a husband, and before she could even get to know him, he had received his orders to report for duty. This would not be peacetime duty, for certain war loomed ahead. And though he had made love to her that last night they were together, his farewell kiss the next morning was, she thought, perfunctory, and he had left without saying the words she longed to hear from him,... without telling her he loved her. She wept, not primarily out of sadness over his departure, though she knew she would worry about him, but because of the void she felt in their relationship. She had hoped for better than this in her marriage, and had daydreamed so many dreams, which now she doubted would ever come true. Still she told herself firmly that she must at least give things time. Perhaps when he returned from the war, it would be different. They could make a fresh start. She would not give up hope. In fact she vowed to do everything in her power to help him come to love her.

Emile's parents were politely formal with her, and his father seemed to be unable to resist his daily glance at her midsection, although he did refrain from asking her any embarrassing questions about whether she was or was not pregnant. She felt sure that as authoritarian as he was, he had insisted on an arranged marriage for his son before he left, to secure, if possible, the inheritance of Marengo. She did not feel any warm emotion directed to her from either of his parents, but perhaps that would change after she delivered a fine, healthy grandson. Even though Emile had been frequently absent from their bed, on his mysterious one or two night stays in the city, which his father and he explained had to do with plantation business; at least when Emile was around, - with the exception of that brief touch of cruelty on their wedding night, he had been unfailingly polite and considerate, but now that he was gone, she felt more of a stranger than ever.

One morning when Mammy arrived with coffee and croissants, she found her little mistress in tears, still in bed, surrounded by a collection of scrunched up wet handkerchiefs.

"Ma precious baby, yuh mustna cry yuhr little eyes out. Things iz bound te get betteh, yuh gonna see dat real soon," she said soothingly.

"But what if he doesn't come back, what if he dies in that hellish country? Then what becomes of me?"

"Mistress, if yuh not be pregnant, yuh could get dat Catolic ordeh, an' go back home, an' take back yuhr own name. Den yuh could start all oveh, maybe eben git anuder husband."

"An annulment, is that what you mean? How could I tell my priest that I never got bedded as a bride, when I know that would be a lie?" was the sobbing response. "And besides, I think I might be pregnant,... so what then?"

"Den yuh gotta stay hieh, I guess, but I stay wid yuh, an' yuh be feelin' betteh in a few months. Dos first months, de ladies cry a lot, an' feel sad, but dat passes. Yuh be yuhrself agin real soon. Have yuh tole de ole man an' hiz missus yet? Jus' dat news might make 'em a lot nicer te yuh, so tell 'em today, an' let's us jus' see how dey be te yuh afta dey hear de good news. A gran'son, dat's gonna please 'em a whole lot! So finish up dat coffee an' dem rolls, an' tell me whatja want to wear forh dis important 'nouncement day, huh?"

Marie Therese scrambled to the edge of her big matrimonial bed, and reached for her slippers with her little feet.

"I'm just not hungry, Mammy, and if I eat, you'll probably have to run for a bucket before what I eat comes back up. I feel exactly like that!"

Again the tears came to her eyes, and she dabbed at them with another clean handkerchief Mammy handed her.

"Oh, Lawsey, *dat iz one sureh sign yuh gotta baby in de front pocket!* An' dat sickness, it pass pretty soon. Den yuh be wantin' te eat ebrythin' in sight, frog legs, crawfish, jus' about ebrythin', yuh'll see!"

"Mammy, pleeeaa...sse stop talking about food, especially frog legs.... Oh, dear, fetch me a bucket or that washing bowl over there on the dresser, I need it now,... *right now*," and Marie Therese held a towel up to her mouth as retching sounds began.

Mammy had to admit, "yuhr little face almos' as green as dos eyes of yuhr'n," but she did produce the bowl just in time. Three wrenching coughs, and her mistress lay back down in bed, her face white, her breathing coming hard.

"I hope this isn't going to last eight more months.... It won't, will it, Mammy? If it does, I'll be dead before this baby is big enough to even be born."

"I knows it be mostly de boy babies dat make forh dese bad mornin's, so dat should make yuh feel betteh, jus' aknowin' dat, eh? An' in a month or two, yuh be oveh dis." Mammy took a wet washcloth to her mistress's face, then gently patted it dry.

"Yuh res' dere a bit, den when yuh gits te feelin' betteh, I get yuh dressed up real nice, an' yuh go down an' tell 'em de good news."

"Good news? Eight more months of this? But maybe Master Louis and Madame Blanche will stop being such cold fish to me. Oh God, please bring Emile back soon, please hear my prayer! At least when he's here, it's not quite so lonely, even if he is gone a lot to the city"

"I hear yuh," Mammy said, soothingly trying to agree, even though already she had her own suspicions of what took dat man te de city so often. She seen a little box on hiz dresser, an' since no one waz around, she had peeked inside de box to see 'xactly what her little Missus was gonna git. It was a gold ring, wid a single, real big sapphire. A couple days passed, an' nothing morh happened, an' den dat little box jus' disappeared, it did, an' on a day when de young Massa Emile was goin' te de city. An' dat mornin' beforh he left, she noticed he waz in a specially good humor, just a'smilin' an' a'hummin' as he went out de big front doorh. Mammy had her suspicions, an' she hoped dat whatever dis "she baggage" he waz playin' around wid in de city, would git tired of him when he couldn't come so often no morh, an' she'd present 'em wid hiz walkin' papers. She hoped dat her little Missus' pregnancy would have a steadyin' influence on dat man, an' she wouldn't hafta tell her precious darlin' one word about her suspicions. Of course, if things got too lonely, an' dose old folks stayed so icy te her, a charge of adultery might move a priest, an' her little lady could go home, pregnant or not. De pregnancy wouldn't matter much, if dis man could be proved te be regularly sportin' about wid hiz "fancy girl" in de city. She'd watch for every clue that could help her little Missus, so maybe she could shed dis man,... sluff 'em off, jus' like a useless, ole snakeskin.

An hour later, Mammy helped her Missus put on her new, pale green dress, with the pretty white lace collar and cuffs, and Marie Therese went downstairs to speak with her in-laws. She knocked on the door to the family room, and a bass voice boomed out "Entrez," so she opened the door and went in. Both Monsieur Louis and Madame Blanche were there, he was at his desk, with his horn-rimmed glasses on the edge of his nose, and his ledger book out in front of him. Madame Blanche, in one of her usual black taffeta dresses, was sitting in a russet wing chair, by the window, her fingers busy with her tatting.

"Monsieur, Madame, I'm sorry I'm late and missed breakfast, but I'm having trouble eating these days, especially in the morning," Marie Therese began, nervously twisting her fingers together in front of her.

At her words about having trouble eating, especially in the morning, her father-in-law quickly looked up at her, and studied every inch of the petite woman standing in front of him. Madame Blanche's fingers stopped, and her eyes also came to rest on Marie Therese.

"Sit down, child," she said, and Marie Therese felt that already the tone of her voice sounded milder, perhaps even a little warmer. "So, might you be expecting?" she asked.

"Yes, I was hoping I could tell Emile before he had to leave, but I wasn't quite sure then," she answered. "Today again I felt nauseous, and when Mammy brought me croissants and coffee, I got sick as soon as I took two bites. Perhaps, if all goes well, I will give you a baby grandchild in eight months or so."

"Grandson, I hope," came the gruff reply from Monsieur Louis, and he adjusted his spectacles and his eyes returned to his ledger.

"I guess I will have to stop making lace, and concentrate on baby things," Madame Blanche said, her fingers busy again. "Do you knit or crochet, my child?" she asked.

"No, but I'd be glad if you would teach me," Marie Therese said, managing a smile in the direction of her mother-in-law.

"Bien, we shall start today. But first come with me, and we will select some patterns and material, and get our sewing ladies busy. They can make up some little flannel covers, and all sorts of other things you will need, and after we get them started, I will begin teaching you how to knit." And for the first time since the child had arrived at Marengo, her mother-in-law put her arm around her daughter-in-law's waist, as they left the room together.

Mammy, who was bustling down the stairs with the tray full of breakfast dishes, saw the two of them, and her lips twitched into a broad smile as she headed into the pantry. Perhaps de ole lady could warm up, afta all, although she had doubts dat Monsieur Louis could. She had him figured out as too tight an' constipated te yield te anybody! She wasn't sureh he could eben manage a smile, unless he dun won de lottery, a big, big one, an' didn't have te share it wid nobody else! Maybe den he'd smile, if he ain't entirely forgot how te smile!

*   *   *

It was a long, hot and dusty ride from Louisiana's Fort Jessup to San Antonio. There the cavalry were allowed a few days for their horses to recuperate, and then they were off once more, over drier, hotter, dustier country; the flat, desolate openness broken only by tall cacti, mesquite, and here and there dense thickets of chaparral,... none of which made good firewood for their campsites. Emile and his friend John Morgan met up in San Antonio, and rode together as the troops headed for the Rio Grande. At night they had to reconnoiter not only for Mexican soldiers, and gangs of banditos, but for rattlers, scorpions, tarantulas, and other such inhabitants of the desert which might invade their tents. The new tents they received looked very nice, but somehow someone had forgotten to make them waterproof, and their bivouacs were either unbearably hot, or dark thunderclouds blew up, and the rains poured down, through the tents, soaking them to the skin. Nights could be cold, and with the rains, almost unbearable. Emile thought the daytime heat, the humidity, and the rains were even worse than in summers in south Louisiana. And seldom in Louisiana had he experienced nights as bone-chilling, and wet.

At last they came in sight of the Rio Grande.

"What's so grand about that?" Emile asked, grinning at John. "It's muddy and ugly, and not nearly as grand as our Mississippi River."

Soldiers were testing its depth, falling in, still dressed in their uniforms, to seek relief from the heat, and it was clear that at its deepest, even short soldiers had their heads well above water. Then suddenly, as they halted their horses by the bank, they saw an unbelievable sight, for wartime. A whole bevy of young women approached the river on the Mexican side, threw off all their clothes, and went naked into the river. The American soldiers watching, breathed a collective sigh of pleasure at the sight, and about forty of them flung themselves into the river and began swimming towards the Mexican women. Briefly the two groups met, with shrieks and laughter from the women, and loud, macho shouts and exclamations from the American soldiers. Language differences did not seem to be presenting any barriers.

Emile burst out laughing. "Our introduction to Mexico! War should always begin like this!"

John grinned back at him, "If this is some sort of omen, this war might be more enjoyable than most wars! And it could start here with Mexican-American bambinos! Maybe some lovemaking and interbreeding are the solution to wars! Nobody would have the time or spirit for making war, if things could begin like this!"

But soon they heard shots sound from the other side of the river. Some Mexican soldiers appeared, armed, and with their guns at the ready, to protect their senoritas.

"I guess they don't appreciate our fellers getting in with their girls. But it was nice of them to fire warning shots at least, and not just start picking our soldiers off," John said.

"Maybe those shots are also omens, and the Mexicans really can't aim any better than that!" Emile suggested. "Still our men have decided to leave the girls alone," he added, watching as the American soldiers headed hastily for the safety of the north bank of the river. But even with the gunfire, most of them were still laughing, and shouting back at the girls.

"It must feel awfully good to be wet and cool for a few minutes. I'm sorry I didn't take the opportunity for that at least. I'm tired of being wet through with hot sweat, so even that muddy water looks appealing," John remarked, looking enviously at the dripping soldiers.

That night, just back from the river, the Americans made bivouac, and after making a careful check for dangerous critters, and stomping on a few scorpions and enormous, hairy tarantulas, John and Emile settled down, wrapping themselves completely up in their blankets in order to protect themselves from the ferocious Mexican mosquitoes.

"I got your wedding announcement, Emile, so I suppose you are a married man by now," John began.

"Yes, there was no way my father was going to let me leave for duty without going through an arranged marriage. He hopes I have left my little bride already pregnant, so that there might be an heir for our plantation, if I don't make it back." Emile's voice sounded bitter, John thought.

"So did you get to pick your bride from among some promising French Creole prospects?" he asked.

"Oh no, with us, it's like dynastic marriages. The right names, the right dowries, and sometimes adjacent plantations, so they can be brought together through marriages. My father arranged everything. I just had to show up for the official engagement and for the marriage vows, and then do my duty, and hope I fathered a male child. That's all there was to it!" And this time Emile's tone seemed even more bitter, more resentful.

"So do you fancy the girl your father picked for you?" John asked after a brief silence.

"She is pretty enough, petite, nice body, big green eyes, but I'd be lying if I said I was in love with her. My heart belongs to someone else, someone you met when you came to visit me, remember?"

"Nana, the girl you rescued from the fire?"

"Yes, John, that very one. As part of the deal of the arranged marriage, my consolation prize was that my father gave me the money for a house in the city, and all the trimmings,... furniture, silver, china, everything.... So I was able to give my Nana a fine home, and even a piano as a parting gift, just before I left."

"Did your father know what all his money was going to be used for?" John asked, and he heard Emile laugh, a laugh that sounded very cynical.

"Of course he did! It was like he bought me off! I had to swear to accept the nice, French Creole girl he picked out for me, go through with the marriage, and try to get her pregnant before I left; and for agreeing to all that, I could spend the money he gave me on my beautiful Nana. He knew, and said not a word about it. In fact he conspired with me, thinking up good reasons that I had to stay in the city overnight, on his business! It made me wonder for the first time, if he had once been in a similar situation! I have no proof, of course, but I suspect it might have been true, although I see no signs that he still continues in such a relationship."

"So how do you manage, Emile?"

"Surprisingly well, John. I wondered if I could keep up the pace with both my women, but I have found I can. Of course one is merely a matter of duty, the other a matter of love."

"Well, I am still a bachelor. I've enjoyed myself very much in New York society, and my summers on the coast, but recently I think I've met the woman I want to marry, and when this is all safely over, I hope to go back and propose to her. My parents know her, and I told them my plans just before I left, and they are in complete agreement with my choice; so I don't see any complications, if the lovely lady will have me, and she has led me to believe she will. I spoke to her before leaving, and she will wait for me, she says. So I may soon be joining the married ranks too."

John wanted to continue on, but he could hear that Emile's breathing had changed, and he knew that his tent mate had fallen asleep.

*   *   *

This war with Mexico was the first real war the United States would fight on foreign soil. It was a proving ground not only for a nation which was a relative newcomer in the game played by recognized international powers, but also for new weapons, and for a new, well-trained officers corps graduating from West Point. Many of those who would be generals on both sides in the Civil War would have their first baptism under fire in the war with Mexico. The war also would help to polish the political profiles of would-be and actual American Presidents.

Southerners saw in expansion, new hopes for a stronger South in Congress, and even possibly for an extension of slavery into additional new states that might enter the Union. Large parts of Texas were deemed to be just right for the production of cotton.

A newly popular slogan on many lips, the cry of Manifest Destiny offered a rationale. Americans saw destiny as marking out their nation to control from the Atlantic to the Pacific.

Was there even a belief about nations which were the fittest - surviving, and expanding, at the expense of those less powerful, and less effective politically? American political circles and newspapers were full of such ideas, although they had not yet been formulated into a precise theory.

Mexico, since achieving its own independence from Spain, had tottered from one revolution to the next. In contrast, a strong, self-confident America was expanding, seeking logical frontiers, but was blocked in that expansion by Mexico. Wasn't it clear which was the fittest? Which nation saw its future as one of confident expansion? Which people were prodded to achieve, to succeed, and which were described as indolent, and less motivated? Americans knew the answer, and American history from its very beginning offered plentiful illustrations to support such arguments.

Once Texas had been a part of the Spanish, later Mexican lands, and when the Republic of Texas joined the Union, a definitive southern frontier had to be established. Mexican politicians were infuriated by the loss of Texas, and anxious to reclaim it. Would both nations ever agree to the new status of Texas, or to a recognizable boundary between them without war? And furthermore, blocking American expansion, there were still two great Mexican territorial units, the first being the California Territory, and the second the Territory of New Mexico - which contained the future states of New Mexico, Arizona, Utah, Nevada, and the western part of Colorado.

American attempts to solve outstanding issues with Mexico peaceably, and even to buy the territories the United States wanted, were greeted with anger, and taken by Mexicans as a national affront made by her rich, insolent Yankee neighbor. At the order of President Polk, American forces under General Zachary Taylor had edged their way into the land between the Nueces River and the Rio Grande, land which Mexican leaders and even a fair number of Americans considered Mexican territory. General Taylor was also instructed not to challenge Mexican forces with any offensive moves, while Commissioner John Slidell was still in Mexico City, attempting to secure the desired border peacefully, offering ever higher prices for California, and the Territory of New Mexico, and seeking Mexican recognition of the new status of Texas as a member of the Union.

In the throes of yet another revolutionary change of government, neither the soon to be outgoing President of Mexico, nor General Mariano Paredes, now assuming power with blistering anti-American rhetoric, desired a meeting with Slidell. So John Slidell, after waiting patiently for weeks to consult with the Mexican authorities, finally left for home, saying of the Mexicans, "we can never get along with them until we have given them a good drubbing."

Although the presence near the Rio Grande of a considerable American force was explained as necessary to protect Texas, that purpose could clearly be achieved without encroaching on land hitherto regarded as Mexican. General Zachary Taylor was to remain on the defensive, but he was also instructed that if Mexican forces mounted any offensive challenge to him, or if Mexico declared war, he could himself then take the offensive. Informed Americans were sure it was only a matter of time before something of that sort would happen.

Old Zach's infantry and artillerymen had a smooth journey by ship from New Orleans first to St. Joseph's Island, when sandbars prevented them from landing at Corpus Christi, and then they basked in sun and sea for months, as gradually all of them were moved to the mainland. An enormous city of white tents sprang up on the long, wide stretch of white beach outside Corpus Christi, and with the exception of sand fleas, continuous drill in the heat, and poor food, for the infantry it was almost like a free seaside vacation.

The mounted dragoons were not so lucky. They had to make the long journey overland from Fort Jessup, Louisiana, to eventually join the forces already at Corpus Christi. Despite the strict discipline imposed by then Colonel David Twiggs, - known more affectionately by his troopers as "Old Davey, the Bengal Tiger," and all his imaginative, eloquent cursing, the arrival of the 2nd Dragoons brought about more carousing and more brawling. Sanitation, never apparently much of a concern to General Taylor, became even worse the longer the army was in one spot, and along with the inevitable cases of dysentery and diarrhea, the first cases of yellow fever made their appearance. And the tents continued to leak. The General was anxious to move on. When they reached higher elevations, it was known that the danger of "yellow jack" would diminish.

News of the failure of the Slidell mission prompted an order in early January, calling on General Taylor to move his forces to the banks of the Rio Grande. The portly, bull-necked, white-haired figure of the "Bengal Tiger," with his 2nd Dragoons, led the marching columns, followed by the new light artillery of Major Samuel Ringgold. Other units would follow them, the 1st, 2nd and 3rd Brigades, each on successive days; altogether an army of 3,554, accompanied by over 300 wagons. Skirmishers prowled far out in front and along the sides of the parallel columns of men, keeping their eyes peeled for any signs of a Mexican army.

They passed through beautiful country, the prairie painted with the colors of many spring flowers,... lupin, wild primroses, phlox and fireplant. And herds of wild pigs, wild cattle, and antelope watched the columns with fearless curiosity, and provided fine additions to the soldiers' diet, as did also the wild turkeys, geese and ducks.

Although the troops were miserable in their wool uniforms during the day, they were more than welcome in the cold nights. Most nights they slept on the ground, with their weapons beside them, without tents, blankets or other amenities. They found it difficult to believe that such scorching days could be followed by such cold nights, and cursed the climate of that wretched land.

Young Lieutenants Morgan and de Marigny were impressed as they looked back at the army, weapons glistening in the sun, the men marching in good order, after their long months of drill at Corpus Christi. It had become an army worthy of the name, disciplined and enthusiastic, toughened up for what lay ahead. They saw the fastest moving jack rabbits they had ever seen, whole packs of them moving so rapidly it was hard to shoot them, even when whole columns of men were trying! And another young Lieutenant then known as Sam Grant, later to be better known as Ulysses S. Grant, started out with a Mexican wild mustang, which had never known a saddle or man on his back before the first day of the march. The far-ranging battle of mustang and rider kept the men laughing. As Grant would write later of himself and his mount:

> The first day there were frequent disagreements between us as to which way we should go, and sometimes whether we should go at all. At no time during the day could I choose exactly the part of the column I would march with; but after that I had as tractable a horse as any with the army.

Emile laughed, and pointed out to John, "Here they come again! The mustang bucking and kicking, and Grant, like a flea, clinging on for dear life!"

"Too bad we can't figure out how many more miles those two have covered than the rest of us cavalry on our trained mounts. For every ten miles we cover, they must have bucked their way through at least twenty, or maybe thirty!"

Occasionally as the dragoons stopped at water holes and ponds to let their horses drink and rest, they would encounter Mexican cavalry, and those who could communicate, did so very politely, and then watched the Mexicans until they disappeared over the horizon. So far, this as yet undeclared war was still a polite affair, though no longer as exuberantly romantic as the first day's encounter with the Mexican senoritas in the Rio Grande!

The biggest excitement on the march was a wide-ranging brush fire, set by Mexicans off in the distance, and the Americans had to ride through it, worrying about their own boxes of cartridges, and their caissons of artillery ammunition exploding.

A Mexican officer under a white flag galloped up as the Americans approached the Aroyo Colorado, and informed General Taylor that General Francisco Mejia, the commander at Matamoros, would consider their crossing of the Aroyo as an act of war, and would respond accordingly.

Engineers were called up to cut the fifteen to twenty foot high river banks down, so the wagon train could pass, and General Taylor warned the Mexican officer, that "if a single man of yours shows his face after my men enter the river, I will open fire on him." American troops roared their approval of "Old Rough and Ready's" reply.

Soon the 1st Brigade was ordered into the water, and carefully they proceeded, holding their cartridge boxes and muskets up high. It was the military textbook classic time for an attack. Those who watched, held their breath, expecting the Mexicans to open fire as soon as the Americans filled the river, but the crossing was not contested, and bands played "Yankee Doodle" throughout the entire process, until all the American forces had reached the other side.

Settling in beside the Rio Grande, with Mexican forces on the other side, and the town of Matamoros gleaming white in the sunlight, the bands of both sides opened up. The American bands played "Yankee Doodle," "The Star-Spangled Banner," and "Hail Columbia," but the consensus, even among the Americans, was that the Spanish bands played more "voluptuous" music, and even classical music, with repertoires far more extensive than that of the American bands! Nearly every evening there were free concerts, and for the benefit of those citizens of Matamoros who came out to listen and observe, American and Mexican forces passed on parade, with their colors flying, bands playing, and for a while those were the only challenges offered.

Other than concerts and parades, during most of the daylight hours the Americans, under the direction of their engineers, worked on the construction of a large five-sided fort, first called Fort Texas, later renamed Fort Brown, in honor of its commander, Major James Brown, who died of wounds suffered there. Once the fort was nearly finished, its walls of thick, dried mud and what lumber could be found, more soldiers were ordered to help drag heavy siege guns into place there.

By this point those who were homesick, sick, or tired of all the work in the heat, and dreading the start of real hostilities, were receiving printed material in English from the other side, urging Catholics to give up their "unholy cause," that it was "sinful to fight against other Catholics and their Church," and printed handbills offering two hundred acres of Mexican land to a private, and more acres to officers, and men with lengthy military service. Taylor's army was about 24 percent Irish and other foreigners, and about 10 percent German, and in the early days by the Rio Grande, over a hundred men deserted, swimming across the river. While some continued to desert, their numbers dwindled rapidly after "Old Rough and Ready" ordered his pickets along the river to fire on any of his soldiers who were seen swimming away.

After nearly a month of competition in parades and music, suddenly on April 25th, 1846, word reached General Zachary Taylor that a Mexican cavalry force of about sixteen hundred troopers had crossed the Rio Grande upstream, and was bearing down upon his American army. The General immediately ordered out a force of some sixty-three dragoons to investigate. One wounded dragoon arrived back in a cart, with apologies from the Mexican commander, that they had no hospital facilities to provide for him. Taylor learned that most of his dragoons had been "cut to pieces," and about seventeen were captured and would be treated as prisoners of war. The Mexicans had taken the first hostile action, and war had begun.

"Old Rough and Ready" called for reinforcements to be sent quickly from Louisiana and Texas, and notified the War Department in Washington that "...hostilities may now be considered as commenced." He then set out to secure his supply base on the coast, leaving five hundred men to hold Fort Texas.

This march back to the coast was not like the triumphal march inland taken so recently; men were to sleep on the ground, fully dressed and with their arms beside them, and there were to be no fires, either for cooking or for warmth,... nothing that could alert the enemy.

General Taylor's parting words to the garrison left at Fort Texas were: "Hold on as long as you can," and "use your ammunition sparingly." The men hurried to finish the last wall of the fort, and just in time. Soon they heard Mexican bands playing, saw soldiers forming up, bells began to clang, and priests in vestments came out of Matamoros to bless the troops, and anoint the Mexican cannons with holy water. A heavy bombardment soon began, a "shower of iron," which was to last for six days, but which surprisingly took few casualties. Mexican infantry and cavalry surrounded the Fort, but were unable to take it, and surrender terms were rejected, so the siege continued.

When reinforcements arrived from New Orleans, General Taylor became confident, that with these additional troops, Port Isabel would be able to defend itself, and orders were given to return to lift the siege of Fort Texas. So the army began its march from the coast back to Fort Texas.

When Emile and John lay down at night on the ground, they could feel the pulsation of guns, and knew that the Fort, still at some distance from them, was under heavy fire. And the next day as the columns rode on through the dry ravines and deserts, they came upon a large Mexican army spread out in battle formation, across the road ahead. As General Taylor ordered his own forces into their battle lines, the Mexicans watched, while their bands played. Nothing was undertaken to impede the American forces as they swung into position, and placed their artillery. The Mexicans outnumbered the Americans by at least two to one, and perhaps much more. With the sunlight obstructing his vision, Emile was still sure that the Mexican forces must consist of somewhere between five to six thousand, and he knew that their own forces numbered between seventeen hundred to perhaps slightly more than two thousand. Still he couldn't see very many artillery pieces on the Mexican side; perhaps a dozen or so, while he knew his own side had at least twenty. He had watched the artillery units practice while at Corpus Christi, and he knew the men were amazingly fast at positioning, loading, firing, and preparing to refire. That entire process could be accomplished while the Mexicans were still initially placing their guns.

Emile and John hurried their men into position. Colonel Twigg's 2nd Dragoons, and the Fifth Infantry were on the far right, but in a critical position astride the contested road. Next to them they saw the new light, maneuverable artillery of Major Samuel Ringgold, and beyond them other infantry forces, and two other artillery units.

"I'd rather charge than wait under fire," John shouted to Emile, as a heavy barrage opened up from the Mexican guns.

"It's not so bad," Emile shouted back, grinning at his friend, as they watched the cannon balls land well in front of them, then bounce slowly through the tall grasses, allowing plenty of time for men and horses to get out of their path.

"Maybe they'll never find the range!" John shouted back, grinning and pointing to the cannon balls slowly rolling towards their horses' feet. "They seem to specialize more in making noise, than in taking careful aim!"

In contrast, the American artillery was creating devastatingly wide paths of disaster in the Mexican ranks.

"I guess we gotta respect those poor fellows for standing and not running. Our guns are cutting them to pieces," John shouted.

A Mexican cavalry attack headed across the field at them, but before it reached them, Ringgold's guns had advanced to a position from which they could enfilade the approaching cavalry, and so many Mexicans were knocked from their saddles, that the drive quickly ended in a hasty and disorderly retreat. All those not yet in action could see that the unwieldy, heavy Mexican guns could not even get positioned quickly, nor were they quick to fire, or even very accurate in their aim. In contrast, the new "flying artillery" designed by Major Ringgold was clearly a key to the success of the Americans at Palo Alto. It could be swung into position rapidly, and moved again easily if need be. Its crews were speedy after their many rehearsals before going into action, and their guns were aimed with deadly precision.

The entire American right wing pressed forward, fierce fighting occurring between the lines. Mexican cavalry made an attempt to turn the American left flank, but again another artillery unit moved out and stopped that advance. The dragoons were called out, riding down fleeing

Mexican infantry, and aiding the hard-fighting American infantry in routing them. But finally the exhilaration of pursuit was replaced by deadening exhaustion.

Darkness came, and the fighting ended. Taylor's forces now held the land on which the Mexicans had stood at dawn. Americans picked up the Mexican wounded as well as their own, surgeons worked by torchlight completing the most urgent amputations, and soon wagons full of wounded were sent off in the night to Port Isabel. Their moans and cries preceded them, and lingered in the ears of those on the battlefield, who now labored with picks and shovels to bury the dead of both armies. When that was done, the men were ordered to sleep in position on the battlefield, with their arms at the ready.

For the American Regular Army, the battle at Palo Alto on May 8th, 1846, had been the first real battle since the Battle of New Orleans in 1815. They had opened the road before them, and driven a much larger Mexican army into disorderly flight. It was agreed, both then and later, that a large part of the American success rested on the new, more maneuverable guns invented by Major Samuel Ringgold, who mortally wounded on the field, would die at Port Isabel, unconscious and unaware of the critically important role his guns had played.

The next morning the Americans were on the move, anxious to get to the relief of Fort Texas. In the distance they could clearly hear the guns which were continually pounding the Fort. Advance parties tried to make their way through dense chaparral, watching out for any Mexican forces. The road was cut by deep ravines, and on either side of it, the chaparral formed an almost impenetrable barrier. Units became separated from each other, and in one of these ravines, the Resaca de la Palma, they could see a large Mexican force spread out ahead, awaiting them. Since it was late in the afternoon, the Mexican commander, General Arista, had apparently concluded that his men were safe from attack for that day, so the mules of their pack train and artillery caissons had been unloaded and unhitched, so they could graze, and the men relaxed, smoked their cigars, and began to light campfires and prepare an early dinner.

Scratched and bleeding, and with their uniforms torn from the sharp chaparral, the Americans kept on creeping up through the thickets along the roadside. Their guns advanced, and a fierce artillery duel began. Emile and John ordered their dragoons to charge the enemy gun emplacements, but they were unable to hold them, until the 8th and part of the 5th Infantry joined them. Then the enemy guns were captured, and turned against the fleeing Mexicans. Unaware of what was happening to his forces, General Arista was still in his tent, composing a message extolling what he considered his "victory" of the previous day, when suddenly he was urged to join in the flight, leaving his tent and all its contents to fall into American hands. As the Americans pursued the Mexicans, a loud yell of triumph came from them, frightening the fleeing Mexicans even more, and causing some of them to prefer their chances with the river rather than with their pursuers, a choice which led to several hundred deaths by drowning.

Lieutenant Emile de Marigny was, at one point, ordered to report to General Taylor, and to urge him to move back out of enemy fire. When he rode up, he smiled as he saw "Old Rough and Ready" sitting astride "Old Whitey" in his usual relaxed fashion, with one leg slung up around the pommel of his saddle.

"General Taylor Sir, Colonel Twiggs respectfully asks you to consider moving back out of the line of fire," Emile said very politely, after saluting.

The General looked at the young lieutenant before him, and his eyes began to twinkle.

"Tell your Colonel, I was just considering moving a bit closer, so the balls will fall behind us." And he smiled broadly at the young man. "That will be all, Lieutenant. You may thank your Colonel for his considerate suggestion."

The results of this American victory could be measured in part by the spoils taken: A Mexican general, a colonel and a lieutenant colonel, and many other men captured, eight of their twelve artillery pieces, nearly four hundred stands of small arms, and 155,600 rounds of ammunition, hundreds of mules, wagons, and forty sacks of food supplies. Another measure would be the loss of only three American officers and thirty-six men out of a force of about two thousand, with wounded numbering twelve officers and seventy-one men. Mexican losses were large, but could only be estimated to be over a thousand. General Taylor professed himself to be proud of his men, and commended them on their "coolness" their "readiness to fight," and their "brilliant impetuosity," all of which showed the "best qualities of the American fighting man," and their "honor to serve their country."

That night in Matamoros no bands could be heard, no parades were seen, no church bells clanged in victory, and strangely, not even a dog barked in the night. The streets were dark and deserted.

Immediately upon receiving news of the two victories, the griping began in Washington. Many complained that General Taylor should have immediately marched into Matamoros and taken the city, imprisoning all the Mexican troops found there.

General Taylor knew that his troops were exhausted, that the Mexicans still greatly outnumbered his forces, that he needed to reprovision his men, and that the pontoon bridges he had requested from Washington months earlier, had never arrived. They would have greatly facilitated his army's passage over to Matamoros. Furthermore, his two victories had occurred even before the Congress had approved the War Resolution, or passed the legislation to supply his army, or called up more volunteers, other than those he had already directly requested from the governors of Texas and Louisiana.

On May 18th, with his troops rested and resupplied, General Taylor took Matamoros unopposed, not a shot being fired. But many of the Mexican troops he took prisoner, chose not to honor the generous parole granted them by General Taylor, and would show up to fight again. Mexican patriotism, it seemed, was stronger than the promise given in exchange for parole.

A naval blockade of Mexico's eastern seaboard ports was now ordered, and likewise a blockade of San Francisco, and other Mexican ports on the Pacific. Also U.S. forces were sent overland to aid in a takeover of Mexico's California Territory and her New Mexican Territory. America, it seemed, was going to win the territories it had sought through negotiations before the war. Mexico had refused to consider such deals, and would soon be without both the territories, and the money once offered for them. In addition, now there was the loss of life in the war, and the national humiliation not only of losing the war, but soon, even of the capture of their national capital, Mexico City.

*   *   *

No letters had been received either in New Orleans or at Marengo from Emile de Marigny, and the level of tension rose, especially when news of the fighting reached the city, and when a formal declaration of war was finally issued in Washington.

For Marie Therese, life had become a little happier with the softening attitude of Madame Blanche. Their relationship had warmed as Madame taught her little daughter-in-law how to knit and crochet, and as they sat together making things for the baby. The house servants had also warmed to the little newcomer, largely through her unfailing politeness, her smiles of appreciation for whatever they did for her, and through the praise they heard her Mammy constantly heaping on her. The ice was not broken with Monsieur Louis, not even cracked, but perhaps even that unyielding autocrat would melt a little if the child Marie Therese was carrying turned out to be the grandson he wanted.

She faithfully wrote to Emile, telling him all the news of Marengo, and of the growing relationship between her and his mother. She sent her letters, several each week, off to the city whenever anyone was heading that way, but she did wonder if any of them would reach her husband, since she knew the army was moving about rapidly from place to place. The war could be over before any of her letters reached him, she thought, and hoped that might turn out to be true. In the meantime, her fingers were worn from constant use of her rosary, her intercessions and prayers dedicated to the protection and safety of her husband, and the safe delivery of a healthy baby boy.

For Nana, the days and nights were also long, and the bed so empty beside her. Her mother helped her with the sewing of her maternity wardrobe, but so far she was still wearing her normal clothing, and no one would notice the increase in inches around her waist. It had been so very tiny beforehand, that now it seemed simply normal in size. She was glad of that, since she really didn't want to have to discuss her condition with her new musical circle, especially not with Armand.

She spent several hours a day at her piano, and had mastered quite a few of the piano parts needed to play with the other musicians. Her faltering had ceased, and she played with much more confidence and ability. They all complimented her on her progress, especially Armand.

Although she had previously paid little attention to the news, she now studied the newspaper daily, always hoping to find something which might assure her of Emile's safety. The last night they had spent together was in early April, she had marked the date on a calendar, and crossed off so many days since then. It was now the beginning of July. Finally there was a letter from him, the envelope soiled and wrinkled, as if it had been carried through heavy rains, and she opened it up carefully, since the paper was limp and could easily come apart in her hands. She spread it gently out on the dining room table. It had gotten wet clear through, and was hard to read. It was a very short message:

Ma chérie,
This can't be long, because the army will soon be underway. Everyone else around me is using this short break to sleep, but I just have to tell you how much I miss you, and long to be with you.

I love you more than I can possibly express. Please take good care of yourself, our Nanette, and our baby. The moment I am back, I will be with you, my darling. Until then, this letter must deliver my hugs and kisses, a poor substitute I know, but it will have to do for now!

Give our daughter hugs and kisses from me! And for you, I send an unending stream of kisses!
Your own Emile

Nana read the letter over and over, then kissed Emile's signature, and put it under her pillow. It would stay there, she resolved, until the next letter came, or Emile himself arrived home.

Twice or three times a week she tried to get a letter off to him, and she thought about keeping a diary to share with him when he returned, but she wondered how he would react to her musical evenings. She looked at the first page with nothing written on it, and she decided to put the diary away. She would use it later to record all the wonderful things their baby did in his first few years of life.

One Sunday afternoon Armand came to visit, and this time he was alone. He invited Nana to take a stroll with him through the Quarter, and along the levée. Momentarily she hesitated, but her mother encouraged her.

"Little walk, dat be good forh yuh, baby," she said, so Nana grabbed up a light shawl, and they set off. They stopped and Armand bought coffee and beignets, and they found a bench on the levée, overlooking the river, and settled there. He told Nana of the latest operatic scores he had been learning, and the audition he had recently had, which won him the chance to play with the French Opéra Orchestra. They talked about some of the compositions in Nana's collection of music books, those she was working on, and ones they hoped to play together at their next musical evening. Then they sat silently, companionably, and watched the slow movement of ships on the river, some high in the water and empty of cargo, some loaded to their decks and wallowing low in the water. A seagull landed not far from them, and walked importantly in their direction. Nana smiled, and broke off a piece of her beignet and threw it to him. Soon they were both busy trying to keep up with the bird's insatiable appetite. Finally they finished up their coffee, threw the last pieces of beignet to the gull, and Armand took Nana's hand to help her to her feet. He continued to hold it, and his dark brown eyes met hers.

"You know, Nana, I want to be with you every day. Do you feel this way too?" he began slowly, watching her expression carefully.

"Armand, I do enjoy your visits, and miss you on the days you can't come,..." she admitted.

"Would you consider it too soon for an engagement? I want to marry you, chère. I want to make you my wife, to give you my name, to look after you, and to have a family together."

Nana fingered the sapphire ring Emile had given her, then she looked up at Armand.

"But I am pregnant with his child," she said very softly.

"I still want you, and I can give that child a name, and help raise it. Please consider what I am saying. I won't ask you to give me an answer now, but promise me you will at least think about it. He cannot marry you, or probably even give this baby his name legally, but I can, and I love you very dearly."

Tears brimmed in Nana's eyes, and she was silent, still fingering her ring.

"I have grown very fond of you, Armand, and I am honored by what you say. Please understand I don't feel I can give you an answer until Émile comes home, and I can learn what his feelings are for me. I have loved him, and he has loved me. I still love him, and this is his child I carry, and you already know our little daughter, Nanette.... I can't make any decisions now. And I don't know if I can even ask you to wait for an answer. It would be wrong to tie up your life. It could be two or three years until he returns, but I owe him that, he asked me to wait for him, and I promised I would...."

Armand nodded, and took Nana's hand in his.

"I expected you to say that. I admire you for the loyalty of your love, and I can be content to wait. I promise not to press you hard for an answer, just let me be around you, and look after you. That will be enough for now? Can we agree on that?" he asked, kissing her hand.

"I guess I can accept your companionship, and the protection you give me when we walk out, or go places together. But I can't make you any promises. I do still love him, Armand.... I can't promise you that after two or three years I will feel free.... And this does seem too much to ask of you...."

"Let that be my decision. I will treasure every minute we share, and I will respect you, Nana. I ask nothing more than just to be with you,..." he said, and she had to turn away from those wonderful, sincere dark eyes.

They walked through the golden afternoon sunlight, and Nana allowed him to hold her hand. At her door, he seemed willing to accept it, when she did not invite him in. He knew she had been moved by his proposal, and needed time to think things out. Pressing her now, or asking too much of her time and attention would only be counterproductive, but as he walked home through the sunshine, he knew he had said what he wanted to,... and what he had to say, if he was to be honest with her. Expressing his feelings for her honestly, that was all he could do, except hope. He knew she was fond of him, but that she didn't love him; still he was confident that, given time, he could persuade her to let him look after her for the rest of her life, and that he would accept her children as if they were his very own. He felt sure that with Emile's return, the long, unavoidable absences would prove too painful, and that Nana sooner or later would have to end the pain and suffering. Perhaps after that, someday she would be able to care for someone else. He was sure, that with time she could learn to love him, and for that he was willing to wait.

Nana closed the door quietly behind her, and stood there, just leaning on it. She wasn't ready to talk about what had just happened, or even to think about it. Her emotions were too stirred up. But her mother was sitting in the dining room, and her dark eyes were narrowed and fixed on her.

"So, did it happen?" her mother asked, trying to remain expressionless so as not to bring on a negative response.

"What, Mama?" Nana asked, with a sigh, taking off her shawl and hanging it up.

"I jus' know he waz gonna ask yuh somethin' important. I could feel it in de air."

"I guess I'd better tell you, or you will just keep worrying at me about it. Yes, Armand told me he loved me, and that he wanted me to marry him. I told him I was pregnant, and he said he would treat the child as if it was his, and give it his name. Then I told him that I felt I couldn't give him any answer until Emile came home, and I could see how he felt about me. Mama, I love Emile, and I carry his child. And there's our darling little Nanette, his daughter.... I can't just throw everything aside. Perhaps Emile no longer loves me, although his letter said he did, and perhaps when he gets home, he won't be able to see me; his wife may take up all his time and attention. But until I know one way or another, I can't even consider giving Armand the response he wants to hear, and I don't think I have the right to make him wait what might be years, until I know one way or the other...."

"Baby, he be willin' te wait. Dat's one loyal, lovin' man. Don't yuh turn 'em loose. Dat's not what he wants. Someday yuh may be free te go te him, dat's what he's a'hopin' forh, an' he don' mind de waitin' as long as he thinks he's gotta chance...."

"Armand is a good man, and in a way, I'm afraid that if I see a lot of him, I could fall in love with him, and that wouldn't be fair to Emile. He went to serve his country; I have to wait for him to come home. I owe him that,... I promised him that."

Nana suddenly buried her face in her hands, and wept. Her mama tried to soothe her, stroking her shoulders, and offering her tea, but all she got was a shake of the head, and then Nana silently headed upstairs. When she saw that big empty bed, the tears started up again. She buried her head in the pillows, pulling Emile's pillow tight to her. He had only been gone since April, and already she was having trouble picturing him clearly in her mind. What did that mean, she wondered disconsolately. And would he ever come back to her?

*   *   *

The Second Dragoons received new orders. They were ordered to march to Tampico, and to wait there to be transferred to Lobos Island, where they would join a large force landing to take the city of Vera Cruz, and then heading for Mexico City itself. It was a daunting operation, but the authorities in Washington had evidently decided that even with General Taylor's resounding victories in the north, Mexico would not negotiate. The only way to win the war would be to take Mexico City, and dictate the terms of surrender there. Some Americans were even beginning to talk excitedly about simply absorbing Mexico, all of it; but others opposed such dreams, the population was so poor, so backward, how would America deal with such a people? There was no history of democratic government or democratic institutions. Taking on Mexico would be like being saddled with a very sick relative, who was close to death, and even if revived, would always be bedridden and needing care,... a bottomless pit for Americans' tax dollars.

Sometimes it seemed to both America's two top commanders in the war that Washington was concocting every kind of delay and obstacle, as if to sour any presidential ambitions that either Zachary Taylor, or Winfield Scott might be harboring. The great amphibious landing and march to Mexico's capital would not be given over to "Old Rough and Ready," despite his victories in northern Mexico, nor did President Polk want it to be placed in the hands of General Winfield Scott; but congressional leaders and his cabinet pushed him finally to give the command to Scott, perhaps with the hope that the venture itself would somehow diminish the presidential chances of "Old Fuss and Feathers." There were so many chances for failure in such an ambitious campaign,... enough to shatter presidential ambitions rather than enhance them.

Of the 20,000 or more men Scott asked for, he would start out with only 9,000; of the specially designed surfboats he ordered, less than half arrived in time; and of the wagons required to haul supplies with them on the long march to Mexico City, he initially received less than half, all of which would have to be assembled at the beachhead, having been shipped in pieces to save space. Then there was the matter of timing. General Scott knew that his invasion needed to commence as early in 1847 as possible, if he were to avoid having yellow fever take as many or even more of his men than would be taken down by Mexican guns. But between delays in receiving troops and supplies, and the vagaries of weather, what was initially planned to start in January, actually got underway on March 9th.

And before action could begin, a preliminary reconnaissance was made by Commodore Conner and General Scott aboard a captured steamer, the *Petrita*. Both had their top staff with them, such later luminaries as Robert E. Lee, Joseph Johnston, P.G.T. Beauregard, George McClellan, George G. Meade, and others. A few shells were lobbed at the vessel from shore batteries, some fell short and then some fell long. If the Mexicans had managed to adjust their aim in time, the course of not only this campaign, but of the American Civil War might have been changed. But the little ship quickly moved out of range, and with it went a chance to reshape history.

The hazardous honor of hitting the beaches first was bestowed upon General Worth's 1st Brigade, and around dawn on March 9th, the men began climbing into the surfboats. The decks and rigging of the supporting U.S. warships were crowded with observers, shouting encouragement, and brass bands provided music for the operation.

Holding their cartridge boxes and guns over their heads, men plunged from the surfboats into the shallows, and once ashore, ran to their colors - flags set up on the beach; and once assembled, began to charge up into the sand hills beyond the beach. It was expected that Mexican forces would challenge the landings, and inflict heavy casualties in the water and on the beach. It was widely rumored that the enemy was hiding behind the sand dunes, waiting. But nothing happened, and in a matter of less than six hours the full complement of troops, and the supplies needed for the first several days, had landed without incident. The Mexicans had lost their best chance of putting a damper on the arrival of the Americans.

The 2nd Dragoons, minus many of their horses, were landed in a later wave to hit the beach, and as soon as enough of their horses were also on dry land, they were assigned to patrol the sand dunes, and to alert General Scott if they encountered any Mexican forces. As the infantry and artillery took positions, totally encircling Vera Cruz, the Dragoons were to continue their patrols, and ward off any Mexican units attempting to break through to the city. American supplies continued to reach the beach, but besieged Vera Cruz was reported to have less than a week's supply of food. Heavy guns from the navy were needed to crack the thick walls of the city and its fort, and six were put ashore, each dragged several miles into place by two hundred men. The guns sank into the loose sand, and even had to be maneuvered over a lagoon, but at last on March 24th a full barrage opened up, flattening walls and ceilings in the city, knocking out the bastions of Fort San Juan de Ulua, and blasting open a fifty foot wide hole in the city's wall.

For the infantry and cavalry there was little to do but wait, while the artillery did its job. Some shells came their way, but as Emile and John and others soon discovered, most of their suffering came from the sand fleas, jiggers, and other insect pests; and the only way they could get a decent night's sleep, was to smear the grease from their fatty pork rations all over their bodies, and wrap themselves as tightly as possible in blankets or bags.

So effective was the bombardment, that no massive assault with bayonets was needed, and U.S. casualties for the entire operation, from the landing to the surrender of Vera Cruz on March 27th, were thirteen killed, and about fifty-seven wounded. A few cases of yellow fever were reported in the city, and since the cause of this frightful disease was not yet known, General Scott was remarkably lucky. The American garrison he had to leave in the city, he ordered placed in the waterfront area of the city, where stiff breezes blew away the mosquitoes, not yet identified as the transmitters of "el vomito."

It was past time to move on, into higher, healthier elevations, where Santa Anna was waiting, blocking the National Road near the town of Cerro Gordo. Dragoons reconnoitered to determine the enemy's positions, and military engineers, under the leadership of Robert E. Lee, P.G.T. Beauregard, and George McClellan found a narrow mule path which could be widened to bring American forces up behind the main Mexican positions. With considerable effort and manpower, they were able to maneuver artillery pieces by ropes up and down the rough terrain until they were on a high hill behind the Mexicans. A direct assault from the left frontally on the Mexicans was poorly led by General Pillow, and was unsuccessful, resulting in many casualties; but the artillery fire from front and rear caught the Mexicans in a heavy crossfire, and although both sides fired incessantly for three hours, American charges finally won out, with fierce hand-to-hand fighting with bayonets, swords, and the butts of guns all coming into play as both sides contended at the Mexican breastworks.

After five hours, it was over; the Mexicans had fled, been captured, wounded or killed. About three thousand were taken prisoner, over twelve hundred killed or wounded, and Santa Anna himself had fled, leaving his false leg, his elegant carriage, a good deal of money, his silver dinner set, and all his official papers behind. A few lucky American officers sat down to the dinner he left behind, enjoyed his wines, and topped it all off with some of his fine cigars.

General Scott reported to Washington that American casualties amounted to 431, and the reputations of the West Point military engineers, Lee, Beauregard and McClellan were made. With so many prisoners, General Scott ordered that they be disarmed, and paroled, but some were to disregard their parole, and be met again outside Mexico City.

Other towns were taken with little or no opposition, but a force of two to three thousand cavalry stood waiting, under General Antonio Lopez de Santa Anna himself. Emile and John ordered their men to the saddle, and prepared to charge, when the Mexicans veered off, avoiding an encounter, after taking only a few rounds of artillery fire.

In August of 1847, American forces topped the last high mountain ridges and saw the Valley of Mexico spread out below them, and many grew silent, and shook their heads. Mexico City gleamed in the distance, its many church spires and domes visible, its thick, strong walls yet to be scaled or breached, its eight long causeways, all fortified, yet to be taken. The enormity of the task ahead was daunting. General Santa Anna had been busy collecting more forces to meet them, and everyone knew they would fight fiercely in the final defense of their capital.

Back in the States, the tide of public opinion was beginning to run against the war, as casualties mounted, few though they were, and as hopes for a negotiated peace were again spurned by the Mexicans. Even the army turned surly, volunteer terms of service expired, and not wanting to chance an epidemic of yellow fever among those waiting to return home, General Scott ordered the transports loaded quickly, once volunteers had returned to the lowlands around Vera Cruz. Those who remained grumbled, since they had not been paid for months, which may well have been a factor in the increased marauding some volunteer bands inflicted on Mexican civilians. Discipline had to be tightened, with some of those caught stealing and carousing, receiving twenty or more lashes. And officers, even including their top commander, General Scott, became increasingly disillusioned, and believed that the Polk administration was not committed to providing them with the necessary supplies, or additional troops needed to win the war.

Emile de Marigny and John Morgan had both received their captaincies, and John, shot in the foot at Cerro Gordo, was shipped home. Emile was able to send off messages to his family and to Nana, that John would mail in the States.

*   *   *

At Marengo a letter from Emile was greeted with much relief. It provided evidence that so far he was alive and unharmed. Monsieur unsealed it and read it first silently, then he read it aloud to both ladies, and handed it over to Marie Therese, who took it up to her bedroom to read and reread.

Dear Family,

My friend John has taken a shot in his foot, and is being sent home. He has promised me he will mail this letter to you from wherever he disembarks in the States. So, perhaps with luck, you will receive this one!

In early March we made a totally successful landing south of Vera Cruz, and took the city with a heavy bombardment so the expected bayonet assault was mercifully not needed.

The Second Dragoons, in which John and I serve, were assigned to patrol the outer perimeter of our lines, and prevent any attempts by Mexican forces to break through to the city.

For us that was an easy assignment. We rarely encountered any Mexican cavalry, and when we did, they rode away without challenging us.

But things changed after that. When we went inland we helped blaze a trail through thickly forested hills and ravines, around the Mexican forces defending their National Highway, and when they discovered us behind them, the fighting got very fierce. It was during that battle yesterday at Cerro Gordo on April 18th, that my friend John Morton was wounded.

All of us are tired, hungry, and ready to come home. We can't believe that the Mexicans are still refusing to negotiate terms, so the worst of the fighting lies ahead, as we move on to attack Mexico City itself. If and when it is taken, that should force a surrender, and soon after, I guess we will all be coming home.

Until then, continue to pray for us, and that success comes to us quickly. My love to all of you, and my prayers especially for Marie Therese, and our child, whom I presume has been born by now. If I

am a father, do I have a son or a daughter? I'm sure you have written
me, but so far no letters have reached me.

My love to all,
Emile

Strange, Marie Therese thought, that Emile doesn't know he has a
fine, healthy son, whom his father chose to name after one of the war's
heroes, the Creoles' own, Captain Pierre Gustave Toutant Beauregard.
She had sent him several letters telling him of the birth of their son,
and his progress, but clearly the letters had not reached him. She said
a silent prayer of relief at the news that perhaps her husband would
soon be coming home, but she dedicated several rounds of her rosary to
preserving him safely from harm in the last dangerous stage of the war,
the attack on Mexico's capital. She also prayed that their own relationship
would deepen into real love with his return home. They were married,
but they were still strangers to each other.

*   *   *

In New Orleans another letter brought relief and joy.

Nana opened it, kissing Emile's signature at the bottom. The letter
was short, but at least she knew he was alive, unhurt, and still loved her.

Ma chérie,

I won't trouble you with the details of this terrible war, except
to tell you that your beloved is now a Captain, my new rank having
been awarded for bravery in action at Cerro Gordo.

Both sides fought fiercely, and my friend John took a shot in
his foot there. He has been sent home, and has promised to mail
this letter to you when he gets to the States - that way I think you
are more likely to get it. John's wound is not very serious, except
that his days of marching are over, and even putting his foot in the
stirrup is very painful. Later, at the worst, he might have a limp.

Some of our heaviest fighting lies ahead. We will have to take
Mexico City, since so far the Mexicans refuse to surrender or even
to negotiate an end to this war. Keep me in your prayers.

Do we have a child? And was Mme. Laveau right that it would be a boy this time? Perhaps you have written me, but so far I have received no letters from home. If I come home soon, maybe your letters will finally catch up with me - back in New Orleans!

Do some serious practicing! I will be looking forward to hearing some fine music, and filling up that big bed, if you still want me there.

I love you as ever, dream of you, and yearn to be with you. Take good care of yourself, Nanette, and our baby Lucien or Helene. I rather think it might be a Lucien this time! Whether it's Lucien or Helene, enclosed are hugs and kisses for our children from their Papa! And many, many more for you!

My love as always,
Your own Emile

Nana read it over several times, and the tears came to her eyes. She would light more candles at the Cathedral, and pray hard every day for his safety, and for his return very soon. Perhaps she only had weeks to cross off on her calendar, rather than months. And how he will love his Lucien, she thought, looking over at the cradle near the bed, in which their son was sleeping soundly, his little thumb tucked in his mouth. Although Nanette and Lucien kept her very busy, she would have to find more time to practice. She wanted to please Emile with all the pieces she had learned, and in every other way.... She lived for him and for their little ones.

*　　　　　*　　　　　*

For the hard campaign to take Mexico City, counting the reinforcements which had arrived during the summer, General Scott had about 11,000 combat-ready soldiers. Out of his grand total of about 13,000, nearly 2,200 were sick and unfit for duty. Mexico City had around 200,000 inhabitants, a large number of whom could be counted on to aid in the city's defense; and General Santa Anna had rebuilt his army to a strength of about 30,000, although he was now reaching the bottom of the barrel, forcibly seizing conscripts and convicts.

Most of the approaches to the city were well-fortified, and assaulting them would mean heavy casualties. Scott learned from his scouts that perhaps the best route of attack would be through the village of San Agustin, but a heavily fortified hacienda blocked the road north of San Agustin. On one side of the hacienda was impassable marsh, and on the other was an ancient lava field, rutted, ridged, and fissured. Captain Robert E. Lee led a small group out to see if there was any possible way to get through the pedregal, or old, hardened lava field. Mexicans hiding in the fissures and behind the rocks and ridges fired on the band, so they withdrew. The engineers had already decided that the surface was strong enough to support the movement over it of mounted men, and artillery. Under Captain Lee's direction, a road was chopped out of the hard lava surface, and artillery was already being moved out onto it, when Mexican artillery fire became too heavy and the Americans were forced to pull back. It appeared that General Santa Anna had arrived with a large force and was to the north of the Americans, with another Mexican force under a rival Mexican General Valencia to the south. Possibly the fierce competition between the two Mexican Generals, Santa Anna and Valencia, helped to save the Americans from being squeezed between the forces of the two, or perhaps it was Santa Anna's lack of enthusiasm for fighting a major battle on the pedregal, but whichever it was, the Americans were miraculously spared.

In the meantime, American reconnaissance had discovered a ravine which was behind the forces of General Valencia, and could be the path to a surprise attack on Valencia, who was to be distracted by a diversionary attack to his front. A heavy rain turned all trails into slippery mud, and it was broad daylight before they reached the outskirts of the Mexican camp. Still evidently they had not been detected, and as they attacked from the front, the second attack began from the rear, and within twenty minutes that Mexican Army was fleeing from the scene, their own guns captured and turned against them. Santa Anna's troops to the north began to withdraw; even though they could see the flight of Valencia's men, with many of them falling prisoners to the Americans, but still they did not intervene. General Scott, when informed by Beauregard of the successful charge of his infantry, wondered why he had dragged so many artillery pieces all the way from the coast, saying,

"I am an idiot to bring artillery so far, and at such expense, when I have such soldiers."

General Santa Anna withdrew to Churubusco, to which the remnants of Valencia's army also retreated, and the Americans followed, to be subjected to heavy artillery fire, and musket fire from troops fighting with sheer desperation to hold this last main stronghold before Mexico City. American forces were hit by horrible crossfire, coming from cornfields, ditches, hedgerows, the fortified church and convent of San Mateo, and a heavily manned and fortified bridge over the Churubusco River. The thick walls of San Mateo were fiercely defended not only by the men within, but by guns embanked just outside the walls, and by artillery across the river. American forces made a costly frontal attack, and a flank attack on San Mateo, while other troops attacked directly on the armed bridge, and two other attacks were launched by brigades crossing the river high above, and way below the bridge. Mexican forces on the other side of the bridge greatly outnumbered the American infantry, and Mexican lancers at first faced no American cavalry, until Captain Lee reported to General Scott, and then he ordered a squadron of dragoons and another rifle company to go north of the bridgehead.

Sent with his dragoons to the north side of the Churubusco River, Emile found the fighting intense, the most intense he had yet experienced. He took a shot to his right arm, and another to his right shoulder, and as he was struggling to stay in the saddle, his horse was hit, and went down, taking him down also. His right arm and leg were caught under his horse, as it writhed and finally fell still. Although it was terribly painful being pinned under his dead horse, the body did shield Emile from further injury as the fighting continued all around him. He lost consciousness, and only much later, when he felt someone trying to pull him free from under his horse, did he briefly regain his senses. The pain was so intense as others struggled to free him, that again he lost consciousness, only to come to now and again in an open wagon, thrown to and fro against other wounded men, as they were taken back to the coast.

At Vera Cruz the bloody bandages on his arm and shoulder were removed, and surgeons prepared to extract the bullets. There was nothing to dull the pain, only a stiff brandy, and then a leather piece was shoved in his mouth.

"Bite down on that, Captain," the surgeon told him, and began probing around his shoulder, and then his arm, finally extracting the two bullets. Mercifully Emile became unaware of what was happening to him, and only revived when his shoulder and arm had been washed down, and new bandages were being placed on his wounds.

"Doesn't look like you will be doing any more shooting in this campaign, Captain. Did you take your wounds at Churubusco?" the surgeon asked.

Emile nodded.

"We got our heaviest casualties from that fight," the surgeon said, as he finished up the bandaging. "We will keep you here only a day or two, and then put you on a ship headed to New Orleans," he added. "We have several hospitals there to look after you men."

Emile managed a weak smile. "I won't need a hospital there, New Orleans is my home," he said, before he passed out again.

It was only on the ship headed homeward, that Emile began to be fully conscious for longer periods. For several days he practiced simply sitting up on the edge of his bunk, and finally he felt strong enough to leave the fetid-smelling ward below deck, and make his way up to the deck. He filled his lungs with the fresh sea air, and got his first look at the heavy rolls of luminous green which met the ship, and the brilliant sunlight. The world was still there, and he was still in it, he thought gratefully. And from that first trip to the deck on, he tried to spend as much time as he could in the invigorating, stiff wind, surrounded by the ever-changing blue and green moods of sea and sky. Only when his legs got weak, and his right shoulder and arm got to throbbing, did he finally return below deck, to the smells and groans of wounded men.

It was almost sunset when the ship finally tied up in New Orleans, but Emile had come on deck much earlier, spotting familiar landmarks along the Mississippi with growing exhilaration, and then finally seeing his city, all rose and gold in the setting sun. The joy of still being alive, and of returning home, and seeing New Orleans again, was almost more than he could bear, and he found himself swallowing hard, and brushing tears from his cheeks. He could easily see the spires of the Saint Louis Cathedral, gloriously rosy in the sunset, and he fingered the little gold cross at his neck, and said a silent prayer of thanksgiving. He was alive and he was home.

Since no one yet knew he was home, and there would be no carriage waiting to take him to Marengo, he could rush to Nana first. He might even be able to spend a week with her, he thought. So strong was his anticipation, that the walk he had intended to make around the Place d'Armes, and along the levée, filling himself with the joy of his city,... even that would have to wait until after he spent a night with Nana. He realized that since his baggage had never caught up with him before he left Vera Cruz, he should at least stop in the city and buy a change of clothes. He hailed a carriage, and went down on Royal Street, and bought some clothing and other necessities. As thin as he was, he knew that nothing he had worn before, would still fit. He thought about changing right there in the store, but decided against it. While he had waited in the tent city at Vera Cruz for transport home, they had given him a new uniform, with fine gold epaulets, so he would make his first appearance in it.

With his own errands completed, Emile stopped at a jewelry store, and after examining a lot of different necklaces, earrings, and rings, he picked a lovely gold necklace with garnets and diamonds of graduated sizes, matching drop earrings of garnets and diamonds, and a gold ring also set with garnets and diamonds. He could already see the necklace on Nana's glorious ivory skin, and he would slip the ring on one of her long, slender fingers. His anticipation was so great, he could hardly stand waiting while his gift was wrapped. He hailed a carriage, but the short ride to Felicity Street seemed longer than ever. At last he paid off the driver, and stepped out right in front of the little house. The windows were open, the transparent curtains stirring in the breeze, and sounds not just of a piano, as he expected, but of a small orchestra came to him.

He knocked, and his heart knocked hard too, as he waited. Madame de Lis answered the door. Her eyes opened wide, and she greeted him with a big smile.

"Well, ain't yuh de big surprise! Welcome back!" she said, and quietly he slipped in.

His Nana, wearing a pale yellow dress, was seated at the piano, her long skirt spread out around her, her full sleeves moving as her hands worked over the keys. Her hair was down, most of it fastened back with a pale yellow ribbon, but a few long curls clustered around her face. Her eyes turned towards the door, and suddenly she was on her feet, and racing into his arms.

"Oh, Emile, at last you are home!" she cried, only to be silenced by his long, passionate kisses. They were oblivious to everyone, although the music had stopped.

Her hands had reached for his shoulders, and suddenly she drew back. His jacket had just been thrown over his shoulders, since it was difficult to get it on over the bandages.

"Oh, mon Dieu, what has happened to you, Emile?" she asked softly, her fingers lightly touching the bandage on his shoulder, and then the one on his lower arm.

"You have been wounded, my darling? I hope my hands didn't bring you more pain there,... I didn't see the bandages till now. Is it bad?"

"I am recovering. I took two bullets, but they were taken out, and the wounds are healing well. Soon I'll be as good as new, chérie, so don't worry. In the meantime, being right-handed, I have to humbly ask for help in the simplest of tasks!"

Once their embrace ended, Emile became conscious that there were others around them.

"Have you gotten your very own orchestra, Nana?" he asked, laughing. "I heard the music welcoming me the minute I got out of the carriage."

"The four of us play together when we get the chance. And I apologize; let me introduce you, Emile. Perhaps you remember Armand Saint Pierre, and these are fellow members of his little orchestra. With the cello, is Marcel Beauchamp, and our flutist is André Boisblanc, and I am their dreadful accompanist, and how they stand that, I just don't know!"

There was a murmur of disagreement, as the three returned Emile's bow.

"Oh no, Mademoiselle, you are much too modest! You have become a fine accompanist for us," Armand exclaimed as they began to pack up their instruments. It was clear to all that Nana and her returning officer needed some time alone.

"Gentlemen, it's been a very long time since I heard anything but military brass bands, so do stay. I would enjoy listening," Emile said. Giving Nana another kiss, he reluctantly loosened his hold on her, and took a seat in one of the wing chairs. He couldn't take his eyes off his beautiful Nana, and he sighed with joy, as he finally relaxed. None of his dreams could compare with this reality.

"For a brave Captain, yes indeed, we will be glad to play some pieces!" Marcel replied, and they began to consult with Nana as to what to play. Madame de Lis came with a glass of claret for Emile.

"As I 'members, yuh always did like de claret, so I brought yuh some. Ebrybody hieh had der suppeh a little while ago. So kin I fix a plate forh yuh, Sir?" she asked, and he nodded, accepting the claret from her with a smile.

"Yes, thank you. I have been on a steady diet of hardtack and salt pork, so I would welcome anything but that!" Emile answered, and soon she was back with a plate of chicken, little fresh peas, and rice smothered with gravy. Emile dove right in. Then came real, dark roasted New Orleans coffee, and a piece of sweet potato pie. When he finished up the last bite of pie, he settled back to enjoy his coffee and claret with music.

The group played for about an hour more, then they said goodnight. Mama de Lis made herself scarce, and finally Emile and Nana were alone. She rose from the piano bench, and he came to meet her.

"Oh, ma chérie," was all he managed to say, his voice breaking, and he held out his arm for her, embracing her as best he could. They kissed tenderly and gently at first, both of them near tears, then hard and passionately. Emile held her tight to him, wanting to feel her body against his. Finally Nana looked up at him, and they smiled at each other through their tears.

"Oh, thank God, you are home," Nana whispered. "And you have a special surprise...."

"So did we make a son, you and I? And is he my surprise?" he asked.

"Yes, Emile darling. He is asleep upstairs in our room. Come see," she said, taking him by his left hand, and putting a finger to her mouth, they tiptoed up the stairs together.

"He has outgrown his cradle already, so we had to get a crib. Several of the musicians you just met, made one for him," Nana said softly, drawing the little sheet back, so Emile could see his son, from his dark curly hair to his tiny toes.

"Lucien?" she whispered, smiling at Emile, and seeking his approval of the name.

"Yes, Lucien," he answered softly, smiling, and giving another kiss to Lucien's mother.

"He usually sleeps through the night, but if he should wake, I'll feed him and he will settle back down until morning. Like the birds, he tends to wake up and greet the sunrise, but you can sleep longer, Emile. I'm sure you need some rest now. You will stay, won't you?" Nana's eyes pleaded.

"Yes, I was hoping you would ask me to," he said. "May I, Nana?"

"Oh, yes, Emile, I was praying you would. Have you been to Marengo yet?"

"Not yet. I have been dreaming of you, Nana, and hoping that nothing has changed between us, and that I could spend some time with you now. My family doesn't yet know I'm back.... The ship only arrived at sunset, and I hurried here. Everything and everyone else can wait! It's you, I've been dreaming of, my darling,... all the time I've been gone. And it was my memories of you that carried me through the fighting. Is it too early for us to warm that big bed?"

"No, sweetheart, it's not too early. Please come," Nana replied, her big dark eyes beckoning, her hands drawing him to the bed. He lay down, and she pulled off his boots for him, and gently helped him shed his jacket and shirt.

"May I?" she asked, reaching for his belt, and the buttons of his trousers.

"Please," he said, his eyes meeting hers, then watching her fingers. Between them there was no shyness or embarrassment over nakedness.

Their bodies knew each other well, and gloried in each other. Soon he lay proudly nude before her.

With his one good arm and hand, he helped her out of her gown, her chemise, and undid the buttons of her petticoats. She threw everything off, and stood before him nude, as beautiful as ever, not even a stretch mark to show she had borne him a second child. He rose to meet her, and his left hand fondled her everywhere, his right hand gently holding her hip close to his. Her hands rested gently on his chest, her fingers moving from one nipple to the other. He bent and kissed her nipples, excited as always by the firming of her dark areolas. The softness of her skin as their bodies touched, the curves he knew every inch of, roused him, but he knew, even as long as they had been apart, he must wait for her, so he lay down, pulling her gently after him, until they lay together side by side. He continued his progression of kisses, until her hands gripped him, and she moved on top of him. Their eyes met, and their lips, and gently she eased down on him.

"Oh, Nana," he cried out. "I thought I'd die; that I might never be with you again. This is too perfect to be true,... I love you so." And he let her set the rhythm for both of them.

"Emile, love me, please," she whispered softly, and with a hoarse cry, he did, and he felt her body quiver, as she came with him.

He held her to him all night long, lovingly aware of her body, and her soft breathing on his neck. Perhaps there had been no happier night than this one, in his entire life. He thought it was even better than the first night he had known her, since this time everything was enhanced by his close brush with death, and by the realization that he might not live to experience another night like this. He had sensed all that as he lay on the field of battle, guns firing, swords and lances clashing, his body helplessly wedged under his horse, his arm and shoulder seething with pain, his blood leaving his body in a continuing stream of red, steadily draining him of life. When mercifully unconsciousness came, he had only been able to wonder if he would ever wake to another day of life,... another kiss, another night like this.

He must have drifted off to sleep, but he woke to the sounds of their son, a little cough, a sneeze, and then a loud, imperative cry. Nana quickly picked him up, changed him, and then brought him to their bed. She laid him between them, and offered him her nipple. Emile watched, overcome with emotion. No Madonna and Child painting could rival this, he thought, and he wasn't embarrassed when Nana saw his tears. There was no shame in his tears, they were tears of pure joy. He was overwhelmed, so grateful he had been allowed to live to know he had a son, and to watch his son feed at Nana's breast.

Lucien worked hard at both breasts, then fell into a totally relaxed sleep on the second breast. Nana stroked his cheek, but that didn't encourage even one more swallow. She smiled at Emile.

"He's finished," she whispered, gently detaching him from her breast, and laying him down between them both. Then they all fell back asleep, peacefully, for several more hours.

When Emile awoke again, he opened his eyes to find two sets of eyes gazing at him. Nana smiled, as he took her hand and kissed it, then he turned to their son, who lay between them, meeting another set of dark eyes which regarded him solemnly. His tiny fingers were curled possessively around his mother's fingers, and his little feet began kicking strongly at his father's chest.

As Emile thought how much he wanted to kiss Nana, to begin this first day back together with lots of kisses, and perhaps more, suddenly he realized, this little being had first priority over those breasts he loved to caress, and that his very position, there between them, might be symbolic. They had created him, but he would demand his own place in the world.

Emile watched as those lovely breasts disappeared into a negligee, and Nana came around to his side of the bed, and gathered him into her arms, and kissed him lingeringly. Then she took the bandages off his arm and shoulder, and washed both wounds gently, patting them dry with a towel.

"They are both quite deep. Still very painful?" she asked, frowning a little.

"Sometimes, especially when I get tired. But they are improving every day," Emile said.

Nana dressed both wounds with some salve, and gently put new bandages on. Then she asked,

"Do you want your uniform today, chèr?"

"No, it's a relief to finally be out of it! I bought a new shirt and some trousers, socks and underwear yesterday. All my belongings that I took with me to Mexico seem to have mysteriously vanished after I was wounded. I threw the bag down on our upstairs sofa last night."

Nana nodded, and smiled, "Ah yes, *our* sofa!" she said, smiling mischievously at him. She got the bag and opened it, and unbuttoned the shirt and pants for him. Then she poured a basin full of water, and came to Emile with soap, a washcloth, towel, and the basin.

"Would you like me to help you wash?" she asked, and when he nodded, she began gently to wash and rinse his face, his hands, and his chest. As her hands moved over his chest, Emile had to lift up and kiss her. He was longing for more, but knew he would have to wait until a more appropriate time when his son was not so intent on watching.

"Does he smile, this Lucien of ours?" he asked.

"Oh, yes. He'll have a smile for you as soon as he has gotten used to you."

Then she turned to the baby, and smiling and half-teasingly she said, in a high, lilting tone,

"Lucien, this is your Papa. I've told you about him, and here he is, safe and sound."

The baby's dark eyes regarded his mother for a long time, then turned their solemn gaze on his father.

Emile laughed. "He hasn't decided about me yet!" Then, musing over the interchange between mother and son, he added,

"Do all mothers always speak to their babies with that special high tone of voice?"

Nana laughed back at him. "I guess so, Emile, to babies and to pet dogs and cats too."

"And at what point do mothers stop using that special tone?" Emile asked, taking Nana's hand in his, and fondling and kissing it.

"I don't exactly know, but at some point they do stop, perhaps I won't know until I reach that point with Lucien! I guess when we start helping him realize he is a little boy, and not a baby anymore,... probably when he's around three or four. After all, I do still talk to our Nanette like that...."

Nana laughed. "Funny, I hadn't even stopped to think about how I speak to him! It just seemed to happen like that from the moment he was born...."

"And your Mama, does she talk like that to Lucien?" Emile continued.

"Oh, even worse! Her voice is higher, and she uses more baby talk with him. Just wait, you'll see. She absolutely dotes on him, and spoils him rotten!"

Nana took up Lucien, changed him, and put a little pale blue shirt on him. He wrestled with his mother, fighting the shirt which came down over his head, and resisting his mother's efforts to put his arms through the sleeves. Emile laughed proudly, seeing how feisty this little son of his was. Nana spared an amused look at Emile, as she finally worked the little hands down and through the sleeves.

"There! He surely has a will of his own, and already likes to resist! Especially whenever I try to put clothing on over his head. As warm as it is, I don't dress him up much, unless I plan to take him out. And if the weather is fine, I try to take him out for a little while every day. He seems fascinated looking at other people and places, and he usually sleeps better after an outing."

"Do you have a baby carriage for him?" Emile asked.

"No, I had to return the one I borrowed for Nanette back to my sister," Nana replied. "With her new little daughter, she needed it back, and he is getting too big for the basket I've been putting him in."

"Well, then I think we should plan on getting a baby carriage today!" Emile responded, smiling at Nana as he started getting dressed. She put Lucien down in the middle of their bed, where he could watch them.

"He would put up a big fuss if I put him back in his crib now," Nana said, smiling proudly at their little son, and coming to help Emile with his shirt buttons.

"I'd love to hold him, but I think I'd better do that when I'm sitting or lying down. My arm is weak still, and I'm afraid if I try to carry him when I'm standing or walking, he could wiggle free. I see how strong he is, for such a little fellow!"

"After he's had his cereal, and you've had some breakfast, that might be a good time for you to sit in one of the chairs in the living room, and enjoy some time with him. He's usually less feisty, and more relaxed after he's eaten, and you will be able to manage him much better there, with the support of the chair. I promise I'll be right there to help, and if everything goes well, then I can play some music for you both," Nana said, taking up Lucien. As they went downstairs, Lucien looked over his mother's shoulder, still gravely studying this strange, new man who had just appeared in his world.

Nana put Lucien in his highchair, and her Mama brought out a little dish of cereal, and a wooden mug full of milk.

"So how iz ma baby dis mornin'?" she asked, giving Lucien a big, noisy kiss on his forehead, and he chortled, kicked out his little toes, and smiled, a big, wide smile.

"Look at ma little man jus' a'smilin' forh hiz Gran'mama. How about dat!" Grandma de Lis said, putting both hands on her hips. "Has ma baby had a smile forh hiz Papa yet?" she asked.

"No, Mama. He's still studying his Papa, but soon he'll have a smile for him, won't you, my little boy?" Nana said, speaking first to her Mama, then turning with a big smile to Lucien. Then she gave Emile a kiss on his cheek, as if to console him.

"Once he gets used to you holding him, and sees you smiling at him, he will have a smile for you too, Emile! Remember, he only just met you this morning!"

After they had finished breakfast, Emile went and sat down in one of the upholstered wing chairs in the living room. Nana arranged a pillow under his arm, and then gently put Lucien down in his father's arms.

"Does that feel all right, Emile?" she asked.

"Yes, and what a feel it is, to have my firstborn son in my arms," he said, and Nana could see that Emile's eyes were brimming with tears. She hoped Lucien wouldn't see, or he might begin crying, and that wouldn't be such a good start for father and son together! Fortunately Lucien was too contented to cry, after his warm cereal, and with a comforting pair of arms around him.

Nana settled on the piano bench. Nanette, who had just emerged in her nightgown, ran joyfully to welcome her father back.

"Papa, you're back! I love you!" she shouted excitedly, and gave him moist kisses.

"Why what a big girl you've become!" he exclaimed, kissing her back, and Nana noticed that his eyes had begun to fill up again.

Nanette bounced over to her mother, and they share a morning hug and kisses.

"Did you wake up hungry?" Nana asked, still hugging her daughter to her.

"Uh-huh!" came the response, from a Nanette buried in her mother's chest.

"Then go to Grandma in the kitchen, chérie. She will fix you a nice breakfast," and Nanette nodded, and ran off to the kitchen.

"How does our Nanette take to her little brother?" Emile asked.

"She is very good with him. We got her a baby doll, and she plays mama to it, just as she sees me do with Lucien. So far, no jealousy at all, and she's very gentle with him."

"That's good news. I'll have to be sure to give her as much attention as I do Lucien," Emile replied, smiling down at the son in his arms.

"Thank you, Emile. She will love that. Now I'll play a lullaby for you and Lucien, a new one just printed, by a German composer called Brahms."

And by the time she finished, both father and son had been lulled to sleep. She stayed with them, playing soft melodies. Then after a while, she took Lucien gently out of his father's arms. She stood, holding their son, and looking down at his sleeping father. She would leave Emile to sleep too. She could see he had come back exhausted, thin, and in some pain. She would treat him like a baby too, at least until he had regained some of his natural vitality. She offered up a silent prayer of thanks, that he was safely home. Her heart was so full.... Gently she ran a finger through his wavy hair, and pressed a soft, little kiss on his forehead, before heading very quietly up the stairs. She would dress Nanette, and take her outside after her breakfast, so father and son could both sleep.

Later that day, after the children's afternoon nap, Nana settled Lucien in his basket, and they went to look at baby carriages. Without saying a word, Nana let Emile go into the store first, and after he had gotten a salesperson engaged for a while, then she followed him in. Emile turned to consult her, allowing Nana to make the selection, and then he nodded, smiled, and paid for it. He pushed it with his one good hand, until they were outside, where Nana put Lucien in it, with his blanket, and little stuffed toy dog.

"I don't think you should try to push him yet, Emile. You should let your arm heal up some more before you do that," Nana said, taking over with the carriage.

"Is there somewhere special you would like to go, Emile?"

"Yes, I was in such a hurry to see you and to meet our baby, that I didn't stop to enjoy New Orleans yesterday, so today, let's go to the Place d'Armes, and stroll a little down around the French Market."

"Yes, let's, but you must promise to tell me when you begin to be tired, or your arm begins to hurt, all right?" Nana said, smiling fondly at him. He nodded, still unable to take his eyes off her, or to have the words to respond. His eyes filled up with tears. His return seemed still so miraculous, like a return to life, to love, to all he was afraid he might never see again.

They made a slow circuit around the Square, with Nana making a quick dive into the Cathedral, taking Nanette with her.

"I need to light a candle, Emile, in thanks for your safe return," she said, leaving him momentarily with the carriage and his son. Emile bent over, and tried smiling and then whistling to Lucien. He noticed that when he rounded up his mouth to whistle, Lucien tried to round up his little lips too, and Emile laughed at the sight, and drew his first smile from his son.

"Thank you, Lucien; I was beginning to wonder how long I would have to wait for my first smile! Too bad your mother wasn't here for that,... and it was just us men!"

"Us men... what?" came Nana's laughing voice.

"Oh, I was just thanking my son for giving me a smile, and telling him it was a pity his mother wasn't here to see it too." Emile said, chuckling, and giving Nana a kiss on her cheek.

"Ah ha, did you see that? He smiled for me again, and this time his Mama was right here to see it!" Emile said, smiling back at his son, and then at Nana and Nanette.

"I can't quite believe that I am really home, here with you. It's still somewhat overwhelming. There were times when I wondered if I would ever return here safely," he said, and as his eyes teared up, so did Nana's. They walked silently for a while, Emile taking in all the familiar sights of his city, and Nanette jumping along, holding his hand. She, at least, was not silent, pointing out flowers, people walking their dogs, and the carriage mules, with their colorful straw bonnets. Finally Nana spoke teasingly to Emile,

"I guess your next introduction to fatherhood can be feeding your son, and seeing just how long it takes him to spit spinach or cereal all over you! He has wonderful aim, you'll see! "

And that night Emile did indeed get his baptism - of mashed green beans and potato. The initiation into fatherhood was proceeding quickly.

Mama de Lis laughed heartily. "Now we jus' gotta talk yuh into changin' a nappie. Dat lil cannon he got, he aims it real good, dat he doz! He already got both hiz mama an' hiz gran'mama, now hiz papa oughta git hiz turn!"

"Oh, Mama, we can spare Emile from that experience! He's just come home and he's been dealing with real cannons firing. Besides, he's only had one day to adjust to fatherhood," Nana said, laughing at both her Mama and Emile.

Emile was relieved that his son was so cooperative about going to sleep at night, and sleeping through the night. His Papa and Mama were able to share their nights without interruption. Lucien didn't wake until the first mocking bird began to sing, but then he joined in, first with soft questioning sounds, then more vociferously. His mother responded quickly, and Emile continued to enjoy watching as those breasts he loved were offered to his son. As he watched, and listened to his son smacking gustily, he realized that even with all its later trials, there was still something beatific about parenting, and about these two little miracles he and Nana had created.

*   *   *

Emile had said nothing about going to Marengo, and Nana didn't want to raise the subject, but she knew the time would come when he would have to let his family know he was back. One day, during their daily afternoon stroll, with Lucien in the baby carriage, and Nanette holding her Papa's hand, they were slowly ambling along Royal Street, when a carriage slowed down as it passed them, and Emile was face to face with his father. Neither of them shouted anything to each other then, but Nana knew that her second honeymoon with Emile would soon come to an end.

That night they made love passionately, both aware that this might be the last time for quite a while. He put Nana on top of him, urging her on, until both of them spun into pleasure together, reeling into a shower of stars. When at last they lay breathing hard, and still embracing each other, Emile fondled Nana's breast, and said softly,

"I was hoping I could stay much longer with you, and these days together have seemed so natural, as we have enjoyed being a family, but Nana, now that my father has seen me, and there's no doubt in my mind that he recognized me, I will have to make an appearance at Marengo. You know that, chérie, but I also promise you that I will be back, just as soon as I think I can slip away. I love you, I need you, and I don't want what we share to end, ever...."

"Yes, Emile, you must let them know you are safely home. I'm sure they have been praying for you, and lighting candles for you, just as I have been. I understand, but I'm sad that our wonderful time together has to end.... Please, darling, don't let it be too long before you come back to me."

"I'd be here all the time, if I could, but I do promise, you won't have to wait long for my return. Whether my father helps provide me with business excuses or not, I will find a way to come back to you as soon as I can."

And in the morning, Emile nervously drank three cups of coffee, and refused any other breakfast suggestions.

"You know, Emile, you are very thin, and it will take a while for you to get your strength back, so promise me you will try to eat, and take care of yourself," Nana said, as he held her tight in a last embrace. Nanette was holding onto her Papa's leg, and she held up her arms to him. Emile picked her up, and hugged her and kissed her on both cheeks.

Nana was astonished to see Washington waiting outside with the carriage.

"Did you tell him to come?" she asked Emile.

"No, but when my father saw me yesterday, I felt sure he would order the carriage to come for me this morning, and sure enough, there it is! I don't want to leave you, Nana, but I must. Just remember, I will be back as soon as I can," he said, giving Nanette and Nana both several more kisses. Nanette was beginning to cry as he handed her over to her mother, then he opened the front door, and strode off to the carriage, climbed in, and was off.

Nana hoped he would turn back once more and blow them some kisses, or even just wave from the carriage, but he didn't look back. Perhaps looking back was just too difficult emotionally, she thought, and instantly forgave him.

Emile was so emotionally upset, both by his leave-taking, and by what lay ahead of him, that he couldn't even sleep away the long drive to Marengo. Surely his father would not have told his mother and his wife that he had spotted Emile in the Quarter with a beautiful young woman, a little girl dancing along holding his hand, and a baby carriage? And evidently he hadn't sent any special message to him by way of Washington, who had merely given him a silent nod, as he opened the carriage door for him. He hoped he wouldn't have to explain, but could say that he had only just arrived in New Orleans on a hospital ship. Surely that would be enough. There would be too much excitement, too much embracing and kissing. And no one would think to ask him exactly when his ship had docked, nor was he about to explain that he had been in New Orleans for nearly a week.

As the carriage turned into the gates, and down the long alley of live oaks, Emile was soothed by the wonder of being home, by the tranquility of the oaks all festooned with gently stirring Spanish moss, and by the beauty of the gardens and the rolling lawn leading down to the river. The river itself was one broad stretch of gold, shimmering in the sunlight. Emile sighed at the beauty of it all, and again tears came to his eyes.

Washington opened the carriage door for him, and as he slowly got down, clumsy with the wounds on his right arm, the old man said,

"Hieh yuh be, young Massa, home agin," his eyes expressionless, not giving a hint of what he might have thought of picking Emile up from Felicity Street, and not from the docks.

Emile stretched his legs, and looked up at the Big House. Why did his life have to be so complicated? This was his home, his beloved home, but the woman he loved could not be here with him. And now he had to be convincing.... He was off the ship, and home again, at last.

As he stood there, his little wife came running to meet him, as pretty as could be, with a smile just for him. She was a picture in turquoise, with lacy petticoats flouncing up around her, and her dark curls flying around her forehead and cheeks, as she ran to him. He embraced her, then held her out admiringly, noticing that her green eyes were filling up with tears. He had to struggle to hold back his own tears of joy.

"What a lovely picture you are, greeting me!" he said softly, giving her several kisses in succession, which he found were warmly returned. Then, putting his arm around her tiny waist, they walked together up the steps to the verandah, where his Mama and Papa awaited him.

"Dieu merci, you are safely home at last," his Mama murmured, and he felt the tears on her cheeks, when he kissed her. Over her shoulder he looked at his Papa, who gave him a wink, and Emile knew that his secret was safe. Apparently this was to be another male conspiracy.

He shared a Creole embrace with his father, and then they all entered the house together.

"Dare I ask? Am I a father, and if so, of a boy or a girl? I'm sure you wrote me, but what with all our moving about, and then my being wounded, your letters never reached me."

"You have given us a grandson," his Papa announced benevolently, putting an arm around his son's shoulder and even managing a slight smile of approval.

"Yes, Emile, and your father thought it best we go ahead and have him christened, since we weren't certain when you would get home, so we did," Marie Therese told him, adding,

"I'm sure you know that if anything had happened and our baby had died before he was christened, the Church says he could have gone to hell, or at least to purgatory...." Her green eyes were big and anxious as she looked at him, hoping that they had done the right thing, since he hadn't been around to be consulted.

"And I picked a good name for the little fellow. We named him after our fine Creole hero, Pierre Gustave Toutant Beauregard. I felt sure you would agree with that, Emile," his father explained, adding, "And my good friend, Pierre Gustave Beauregard even agreed to be parrain for our little Pierre. He was home briefly, so he was able to come for the baptism, and do his part!"

"So where is our little Pierre Gustave?" Emile inquired. "Not here to greet his father returning wounded from the war?"

"He is fast asleep, it's his afternoon nap time. He'd have greeted you with angry wails if we had gotten him up too soon," Marie Therese exclaimed. "As soon as he wakes, Mammy will bring him to see you. It was my decision to let him sleep. I didn't think you'd want to meet your son for the very first time, when he was throwing a temper tantrum! As you'll soon see, he is quite the decisive little fellow, and doesn't hesitate to make his needs known!"

Madame Blanche was lightly fingering the bandages on Emile's arm and shoulder.

"What happened to you, Emile? Is this serious?"

"Well, Mama, it was when it happened! I took two bullet wounds, one in my shoulder and one in my lower arm, and sprained my wrist when my horse went down. I had just been shot, and was trying hard to stay in the saddle, when my horse was shot and killed, and I ended up on the ground, partly under him. It was just as well I was unconscious, since there was no way I could get myself out from under my horse, and my wounds were very painful. That happened at Churubusco, one of our worst battles; cavalry and infantry from both sides were all mixed up together, shooting at close range, slashing about with sabers and lances, and even hitting people with their gun butts. That's what it was like when I lost consciousness. I have no idea how long the battle lasted.

"The first thing I remembered after that was being in great pain, as several medical stewards were trying to get me out from under my dead horse. I only remember waking up now and then on the jolting wagon ride back to Vera Cruz, being jostled against other wounded men, and then later when the surgeons worked on me. A surgeon took two bullets out of my arm, poured some alcohol in the wounds, then stitched me up, and had me put in a hospital tent with lots of other wounded men. They were anxious to get us out of there, both because they needed the space for the next wounded to come in, and also because yellow fever is very bad in the coastal lowlands; so within a week I was on a hospital ship, which just brought me here, to New Orleans. The surgeons wanted me to go to one of the army hospitals, but I told them my home was here, so they didn't insist on the hospital, and released me.

"So here I am, a bit the worse for my experience in Mexico, but things are healing well, and one day, they tell me, I should have full use of my arm back again. I will need help cleaning and dressing my arm, and I was told not to lift anything heavy, which might reopen the wounds. Then, in a couple weeks our own Dr. Rideau can take the stitches out.

"I don't suppose you have any recent news of how the war is going? Churubusco, where I was wounded, was expected to be the last big battle before our forces converged on Mexico City. It appears that the only way we'll bring an end to this war, is to capture Mexico City, and dictate surrender terms from there. Have you heard? Has that happened yet?" Emile turned to his father.

"No, I haven't read about that. So far the *Picayune* has just reported on the very battle in which you were wounded, nothing more. It seems to take forever to get the news from there. When it was General Taylor's actions in the north, that news got to us quicker, through Texas, but as soon as General Scott moved inland, the news from that front has come to us very slowly." His Papa brought him the last newspaper, and poured him a good, stiff brandy.

He took a sip and savored it, as his mother spoke,

"Emile, we will be having dinner very soon now, and afterwards you would benefit from a good nap this afternoon. You look very tired, chèr, and I imagine your wounds give you some pain. In fact, I think you would benefit from afternoon naps for a couple of weeks, until you regain your strength." His mother gave him a worried look, as she rang her little hand bell to call someone from the kitchen and inquire when dinner would be ready. Tom appeared, and smiled at the sight of Emile.

"Good te see yuh back, Massa Emile," then he turned for a short conversation with Madame Blanche, who, when they finished, turned to her son, and said,

"By the time you have finished your drink, Emile, I believe dinner will be announced."

After a fine Marengo dinner, Emile was ready for a nap.

"Do we need to cleanse your wounds, and change your bandages now, before you rest?" Marie Therese asked, rising from the table and taking him by the uninjured arm, as they walked up the stairs.

"Sometime today, but it can wait till after a nap," he assured her, and wondered what kind of nap they would have, or if she was just coming upstairs to check on the baby.

She hurried into their bedroom ahead of him, and bent over the crib.

"This is a good chance for you have a look at him, while he is peacefully sleeping. Then I'll get Mammy to help me wheel him into another room, so he won't wake you up, Emile. He will soon be up, and full of demands,... to be changed, to be fed, to be changed again, and then to be entertained. He much prefers to interact with people, and isn't very satisfied with just toys. After you have rested, and when he is all full of food and milk, that would be a good time for you to have your first real meeting."

Mammy appeared at the door, hesitating, and Marie Therese beckoned her in.

"Good te see yuh back, Massa Emile. I see yuh got some bandages, but from de looks a things, yuh oughta be good as new one a dese days. Now, ma young Missus wants me te help move our little prince outta hieh, so he don't wake yuh wid all hiz hollerin'," and Mammy took the crib by one end, and Marie Therese took the other. Emile came to help them, but Marie Therese frowned and beckoned him away.

"No, Emile, you mustn't. We can handle this by ourselves," so he merely held the door wide open as they trundled the crib out. His son had very dark hair, like his father and his grandfather, and long, dark eyelashes too. He had several fingers in his mouth, and sucked loudly on them, but never woke as he was being moved. Emile had to smile at the loud sucking noises, and wondered if his son would even realize he was in a different room when he woke up.

Marie Therese was back quickly, and bent to take his boots off, as he sat on the bed. She helped him with his shirt and jacket, and then stopped.

"Shall I leave you to rest, Emile?" she asked. "I have left Mammy in charge of our Pierre. She can even nurse him if needed. While you were gone, she and Jefferson also had a baby, so she is still nursing, and has enough for two, so she helps me out. Our son has a huge appetite!"

"If things are under control, then perhaps you might enjoy sharing a nap?" Emile inquired softly, leaving the decision up to her.

"If that won't disturb you, I will stay," she murmured, busying herself picking up baby clothes which were scattered about, and not looking directly at Emile.

"I would like you to stay," he finally said, unbuttoning his trousers, and slipping off the last of his clothes. Marie Therese took his clothing from him, and Emile thought she was trying to avoid seeing his nakedness. It both amused him, and irritated him. He was proud of his body, he was lean and well-muscled, even if he wasn't as tall as he wished he was. Nana had no reservations about looking at him nude, and in fact seemed to enjoy it. But then they had experienced a much longer relationship. Now he would have to try harder with his wife. He realized that before he had left for Mexico, he had been a dutiful husband, but he had done little to awaken her to the pleasures of marriage. Although he was tired, and his arm was throbbing, it was well past time to take care of her. Still, he didn't feel up to undressing her, so he said,

"Yes, join me, will you? With my wounds, I don't think I can help you undress yet, but I would like it if you would stay."

Hurriedly she took off all her clothes, and almost before he could get a good look at her, she was under the covers. He reached his good arm out, and drew her closer, so he could begin to feel her body, and fondle her with his hand. He raised himself up a little and kissed her, tenderly at first, then he probed her mouth with his tongue, and his kisses became more passionate. He was thrilled at her response, and his hand sought out her thighs, and moved between them. She broke from his kiss, letting out a small gasp, and turning her head from side to side. Her hands felt for his body, caressing his chest, and moving down his hips. She moaned softly, as his fingers moved between her legs, and he felt she was ready, so carefully he slid on top of her, bracing his injured arm on a pillow. They were joined, and he initiated the rhythm and she responded, taking them together to a faster pace. When he heard her cry out softly, that spurred on his own response. Their bodies quivered together, and pleasure so sweet, and so beautiful, coursed through them both. For a time, the pleasure dulled the ache in his arm.

"Does that almost make up for our long separation?" he asked quietly.

"Oh yes, Emile,..." came her softly whispered answer.

He kissed her lightly on her ear lobe, then started to move off of her.

"No, Emile, don't move," she said. "Stay there, please."

"I'm not too heavy?" he asked.

"Oh, no, and it's been so long since we were together like this. It feels wonderful."

Emile was encouraged by her responses, and realized that although what he felt for his little wife was not on the level with his deep, passionate commitment to Nana, he could feel a new and warmer relationship beginning to develop. If he could manage to keep both of them contented, he could enjoy both relationships. He was thankful that he had not had time for a better start to Nana's day, because as exhausted as he was, he wasn't sure if he could have performed so well at Marengo; but as he recovered, if he could keep a balance between his two relationships, he felt proud, and convinced that he could satisfy them both. He could see no other way, he was honor-bound, his commitment had to be to both women, and it should be fair to both.

After their nap, Marie Therese helped him dress, her hands caressing him fondly as she did so, her eyes rewarding him with their deep, green gaze of love. He felt passion begin to rise in him. Later, tonight,... he thought. Now it's time to meet my son.

"Mammy surely has seen to Pierre's needs, and he should be fed and contented. It would be a good time for his first visit with his Papa," Marie Therese said, smiling, as she took hold of his good hand, and helped him up from the bed.

"I can't guarantee he will behave himself, Emile, but are you ready for your first meeting with your son?" she asked, a bit anxiously, as they went to the next room beyond theirs, which had been fixed up as a nursery.

"While you were gone, I kept Pierre with me in our room. It was so much easier to get to him quickly, and nurse him, but now that you are back, our young man will have to settle for the nursery, so we can have a little privacy," she said, smiling demurely at Emile from under her long, dark eyelashes. He was both pleased and amused to see that when their eyes met, she blushed.

Although he had thought her attractive from the day he first met her, he was revising his opinion now. She was, in her own French Creole way, quite beautiful... petite, but with very nice, full breasts, probably augmented now through nursing, softly rounded hips, pretty legs, and tiny feet. Her face was exquisite, her long, dark eyelashes which she employed so effectively, her intriguing, deep green eyes seeming so full of promises, her short, curly, dark hair. He had noticed today, that when she grew warm, her hair formed tight little ringlets around her forehead, and he found that especially inviting, and looked forward to fingering them, even kissing them.

His father had picked well, and he would have to tell him that, at some point. At first he had been so frustrated and irritated at having to tend to another woman, particularly one he had not chosen nor courted nor wanted, and so he had been dutifully correct, and no more, resenting having to spend time with her, and take care of her wifely needs, when he wanted so desperately to be with Nana. He had expected to spend several more years with Nana, before being pushed into the arranged marriage he had to agree to. But the war had taken all that out of his hands, and, given his frustration over having to bed a wife, he knew he hadn't been fair to her.

But things seemed different now. Earlier he had not allowed himself to see her capacity to love, nor had he sensed her sensitivity,... both of which he saw so clearly now. Perhaps the war, and the pain and suffering he had just come through had changed him, and he was more perceptive now, and more willing to be caring. Confronting death so immediately had, he realized, given him a more profound capacity to live, and to love. And whether he had initially wanted her or not; as his wife, Marie Therese was now his responsibility. As her husband, he would have to meet her needs.

They entered the nursery, and found Mammy sitting in a rocking chair, singing softly to Pierre, and he was smiling contentedly from his place on her lap, his back firmly supported by her body. He reached out his little arms and crowed to his mother, and she came and took him up, giving him a kiss on his cheek.

"Our little prince, he be in fine fettle now, fed an' changed, an' in one a hiz best little suits. He's as ready as he'ze gonna be, for hiz first meetin' wid hiz Papa," Mammy said, getting up and smiling at little Pierre.

"Why not sit in the rocker, Emile? You will be more comfortable than if you try to hold him without supporting your wounded arm, and besides, he does love to be rocked," Marie Therese said, waiting to place Pierre in his father's arms.

"There you are, my darling," she said softly to her son, as she transferred him over to his father. "This is your Papa. Mama has told you a lot about your Papa, and here he is, safely home, and ready to meet you!"

Emile couldn't help noticing that his wife's voice also reached a higher tone, when she talked to their baby, and he smiled. He wondered if this was universal,... between women and their babies.

Pierre turned his little head, arching his neck, and looking up at the stranger who held him. Emile smiled and kissed his son on the forehead, and speeded up the rocking, just for good measure. "Can I have a toy he likes, something to entertain him with?" he asked, and was handed a stuffed, little clown doll, which he dangled in front of Pierre, making funny sounds, as if they came from the clown. He was immediately rewarded with a loud chortle from his son, and a swift dive to capture the clown,... so swift and sudden that he wasn't expecting it, and nearly lost his grip.

"Whoops!" Emile exclaimed, laughing. "Master Pierre, you nearly got away from me!"

After a little teasing, holding the clown doll just out of Pierre's reach, and continuing to make funny noises, Emile finally let Pierre grab the doll, and he watched him turn it this way and that, examining it. Next it went in the mouth, and all three adults laughed. Pierre let go of the clown from between the two baby teeth he already had, and laughed back. Noticing that Emile was tiring, Mammy reached out for Pierre.

"I'ze gonna change 'em, an' den I bring 'em downstairs te yuh. He likes te be on de rug in de family room. I gonna bring a few a hiz favorite toys too, so yuh kin keep 'em occupied down dere. Den I come an' get 'em back afta a while, so yuh can have yuhr supper in peace. He ain't too good yet in hiz highchair, gets restless, an' den he tries te slide out from undeh de tray. He'z real good at dat! He's gonna find hisself on de floor one a des days!"

Marie Therese slipped her hand into Emile's, and they went downstairs together.

His father came out from behind his newspaper.

"It's good to have you safely back, Emile, and in a week or two, I will count on you to again take over my business in the city. I haven't enjoyed all the trips I've had to make while you were gone, so I'll be glad to turn all that over to you, as soon as you feel well enough to take it on,... perhaps after a week or two of rest."

"Yes, Papa, that sounds good. I'll be glad to help with that," Emile answered quickly, trying to keep any excitement out of his voice. His father was going to continue to help provide him with excuses to go to New Orleans, that was clear, and Emile was relieved. He couldn't abandon Nana, Nanette and Lucien.

How strange, he thought, to have two sons born almost at the same time. As if to assure himself of that strange fact, he asked Marie Therese,

"So what exactly is Pierre's birthday?"

"Well, we all thought it was going to be December 17th, but it did take a little longer, so he was actually born on the morning of the 18th."

Emile nodded, and thought how strange it was, Lucien on December 8th and Pierre on December 18th. The closeness of the dates should help him remember both birthdays, he hoped. Other than twins, he wondered how many men had sons born that close together! Only under circumstances similar to his, he concluded, and smiled. Although he was sure that Marie Therese couldn't have guessed his thoughts, she smiled too, giving him a fond look. He said a silent little prayer, asking God to help him remember which one of his sons to call Lucien and which one to call Pierre. He knew it wouldn't be so disastrous if he were to call Lucien Pierre by mistake, since Nana knew he had another child at Marengo, but the reverse might have more serious consequences. The revelation of another relationship and other children might be devastating to this marriage. And it certainly would have been easier for him if both his baby sons had been given the same first name! Again he smiled at the thought.

He noticed his father was looking at him over the top of his newspaper. He had been sending money to Nana while Emile was with the army, and only yesterday he had seen the two of them on the street, with his little daughter holding his hand, and the baby carriage. Emile was amazed; this was the second smile he had seen from his father in less than one whole day! Sometimes over the years, there had been whole months between his father's rare smiles. He found himself wondering if his father had picked up something of what caused his smiles.

During his first week back at Marengo, Emile's wounds became less painful, only bothering him when he got too tired, and that tiredness would come upon him very suddenly, so it was difficult to time his rests before the pains began. His relationship with Marie Therese was deepening. They were both enjoying each other's company more and more, and Emile found himself looking forward to his nights with her. From a virgin with no previous knowledge of sexual relations, she was becoming more sensitive to his needs with every passing night, and becoming more receptive to any novelties he initiated. As his arm still gave him pain, they had to be more sexually inventive, and Emile was pleasantly surprised at how readily Marie Therese adapted to that. He realized he was lucky in both his women. No cold fishes, both alive and pulsating with desire. He felt almost guilty that he should have been so lucky.

As for this son, Pierre had evidently decided to admit his father into his little circle of acceptable adults, and they were able to spend more time playing together, especially when Emile got down on the carpet in the family room, and challenged Pierre with new toys to play with, new faces to make, new noises to imitate. Only his own mother worried him. She seemed to have aged during his absence, and seemed weak, and tired most of the time. He wondered what was wrong, and soon the answer came with terrible clarity. She took to her bed, and turned yellow, a high fever set in, and then the fatal, black vomiting began, and continued unabated, until within a week, she was dying of yellow fever.

Emile ordered that Pierre was not to be near his grandmère, and he felt guilty of depriving her of even the sight of her grandson, but the fever had taken such a hold on her, that she hardly seemed to notice even the comings and goings of the adults around her. Emile also wanted Marie Therese to stay away, but she firmly shook her head at such directions, and continued to help with the care of Madame Blanche.

The priest was called, and came to give the unconscious woman the last rites of the Church. Emile wasn't even sure if she realized that the priest was there, ministering to her. The vomiting had finally stopped, but no one saw that as a sign of improvement. Madame Blanche lay quiet at last, the thin fingers of one hand clasping her rosary, the other hand limply resting in Marie Therese's little hand.

Besides witnessing the terrible suffering of her mother-in-law, her death would be a blow to Marie Therese. It was Madame Blanche who had accepted her, first made her welcome, and finally, in her own withdrawn and distant way, come to love her. Marie Therese loyally waited with her until the hand in hers lost its warmth. Emile appeared at the door; carefully Marie Therese placed the cold hand with the other, the pale fingers intertwined in Madame's rosary, and then she came to meet Emile.

"Dieu merci, c'est fini," she said, her eyes shiny with tears, which were slowly finding their way down her cheeks. Emile nodded, and putting his arm around his wife, he drew her from the room. She had spent so much time with his mother, he knew she was exhausted, and he feared that perhaps she might also come down with the dreadful illness. He made sure that she was in bed very early that night after the death, and for several nights after, as well as joining him for afternoon naps. She was so exhausted, and shaken by grief; Emile realized it was not a time propitious for lovemaking, and most nights he just held her in his embrace until she fell asleep.

The funeral was held at Marengo, with the closed coffin that his mother had asked for. Her coffin remained overnight in the Grand Salon, with ivory tapers burning all around it, and a fresh collection of Marengo's flowers on top. Emile and his father, and some of the house servants carried the coffin slowly to the Marengo family cemetery near the alley of live oaks, and it was lowered into the open grave, as the priest intoned the words of burial. In one horrifying week his mother was gone. But at least he had managed to get home for a few days before she was stricken. And she was able to enjoy his presence before the fever took her away from them all, into a land of unconsciousness and finally of death.

Summers in New Orleans always brought with them the terrible threat of yellow fever, cholera too at times, and other illness such as smallpox, and a fatal form of dysentery. Then there were other devastating fevers that doctors had not yet found names for. Some believed they came with the ships into the port, but no one really knew; only that with summer, the illnesses increased, and their merciless grip on the population would only be loosened somewhat with the coming of cold weather.

The illness and death of his mother kept Emile longer at Marengo than he had planned, and he knew Nana must be wondering when she would see him again, so he was making plans with his father for a trip to the city, when Washington came to him late one morning.

"I jus' been te de city, Massa Emile, an' stopped at de house on Felicity Street. Miss Nana's Mama, she met me at de doorh, her face all covehed wid tears. All she tole me waz te tell yuh te come quick,... today."

"She didn't tell you exactly what was the matter, Washington?"

"No, Sir, she jus' couldn't eben speak, she cry so hard. I take yuh dere, raight away, if yuh be ready."

"Yes, just let me tell my father and my wife. You can pull the carriage up, and I'll be right out," Emile said, then he ran to the family salon to find his father.

"Papa, there seems to be some emergency. I have to go right away to the city, so will you please think up some business that will explain my absence for a few days. I will just tell Marie Therese I have to go, and I'm leaving the rest, any explanations, in your hands."

His father nodded his agreement.

Emile took the stairs two at a time, and found himself winded, too winded to explain very well, when he reached his bedroom, and found his wife there.

"Papa has some emergency business I must attend to in the city, and I'm just going to grab up a few things in case I have to stay overnight, then I must go. I'm sorry, but it can't be helped. Everything came up so fast. It may take a few days, but I'll be back as soon as possible."

Marie Therese looked up at him with a puzzled expression as he gave her a quick goodbye kiss, and then he was off, down the stairs in a rush. She looked out of the window and saw him vault into the open carriage door, and then Washington got the horses going faster than she had ever seen him do before, and in minutes the carriage had disappeared into the oak alley.

"What waz alla dat about?"

Marie Therese hadn't even realized that her Mammy had come in, and was standing behind her, watching the carriage leave.

"I don't exactly know. He said some emergency business he had to take care of, for his father, and that he might be gone a few days." Marie Therese turned to her Mammy with a puzzled but sad expression on her face. Her Mammy put her big arms around her, and just held her, saying nothing at first, then she said,

"Maybe dis be de end of dat business. I sureh hope so."

"What business, Mammy? Do you know what it is?" Marie Therese asked, her head still buried in her Mammy's ample bosom.

"I don' raightly know, baby, but it ain't good. An' it appears, dere ain't much we kin do about dat business, 'cept te hope it's oveh an' dun wid. Dat's all...." And Mammy pursed up her lips and wouldn't say anymore. "I gotta get our little man. As I cum in hieh, I heard him jus' startin' te pipe up," and with that she was gone.

That night Marie Therese couldn't fall asleep. She had grown used to Emile being beside her, so the bed seemed very empty, and her thoughts wouldn't leave her alone. She had heard rumors before her marriage that Emile had some sort of "fancy girl" in the city, and she remembered the interaction she had observed at the opera that night, when Emile had taken champagne to the young Creoles of color, and slowly kissed the hand of that beautiful woman. Their eyes had met then, and somehow she had come to believe that both of them played special roles in the life of Emile. Perhaps this emergency had something to do with all that. It might also explain what her Mammy had just said, and what she had not said. She wondered if perhaps someday Emile would be able to tell her the truth. She resolved not to bother him with questions, but just to wait for any explanations he might give her, and to accept them, even if she didn't entirely believe them. That was all she could do. He was her husband, and now that she knew him better, she didn't think he would leave her. And he had become much more caring since his return from the war. Then too, her little Pierre would, one day, inherit Marengo. If things didn't get any worse, she decided she would not leave. Her son's future might well depend on their remaining at Marengo.

She got her rosary, and sat down in the window seat. If a carriage came back, she would see it from there, as it came out of the oak alley, but even when night came, the moonlight only revealed an empty drive. She ran through her rosary several times, adding special prayers, and finally, somewhat quieted, she crawled up into the empty bed, hoping that God would hear her prayers, and answer them. She had asked only for the best for everyone, surely that couldn't be denied....

   *   *   *

Washington drove faster than Emile had ever known him to, except when he had driven them to the fire that night when he had rescued

Nana. He was afraid to think what could be the matter. When, at last, they pulled up to the little house, he just said,

"Wait until I see what's the matter," and he hurried up the steps to the door, and rang the bell insistently.

Mama de Lis met him. "Oh, thank de Lawd, yuh're hieh. I kin't do nothin' wid her! She jus' don' stop cryin'"

"What's happened?" Emile asked.

"It's our little man, he dun up an' died, so sudden-like. Mr. Armand came, an' he took us te de hospital, but eben dey couldn't do nothin' forh him.... He got a terrible fever, an' den he jus' close hiz little eyes, took one last, tiny breath, an' waz gone...."

"Oh, mon Dieu," Emile exclaimed and hit the stairs at a run. He found Nana lying in bed, hugging Lucien's lifeless body to her. Her face was lined with tears.

"Emile, he's gone, just gone, and we didn't even get him baptized.... I wanted to be sure you liked his name, and now it's too late. Surely God won't keep him from heaven for that, will he?" Nana reached for him, and he knelt beside the bed, holding her to him.

"No, God can't be that cruel.... He's a loving God, and He surely will have a place for another little angel, another cherub. Even if we are sad at losing him, he will be happier there, Nana." He felt her sobs shake her whole body, and his as well. For a long time he just held her, occasionally kissing her on her forehead, and the nape of her lovely neck. He stroked her back with his good hand.

"I am sorry I have been gone so long, but we lost my mother to yellow fever, and I couldn't leave. I'm thankful that I got home in time to have a few days with her before she succumbed to the fever. She suffered badly for most of a week, and then it was over. We just buried her, and I was discussing with my father what sort of business excuse might bring me to the city for a few days, when Washington came to tell me you needed me right away. If it hadn't been for my mother's illness, I'd have been with you sooner."

Emile got to his feet, and came around the bed to his side. He sat down and took the body of his son in his arms. His eyes brimmed over with tears. "I must have just missed him now," he said softly. "Such a short, little life.... But at least I got back from Mexico in time to see him kick, and laugh...." Emile sighed, looking down at the small body he held. "Now we must see about burying him. I will go make the arrangements, and be back as soon as I can."

"Will the priests let him lie in holy ground?" Nana asked anxiously. "I don't want him to be in that place where they put people who sinned when they took their own lives."

"I won't even mention that he wasn't baptized. Try to rest, chérie. I'll take care of everything. And remember, I love you, and always will. Don't blame yourself. Perhaps God only intended to share him with us for a short while,... but I'm thankful that I got back in time to know him a little." He gave Nana several kisses, and then went downstairs.

"I'm going to see about a casket, and burial," he said on his way out.

When he returned later, he brought with him a little casket, carved with rosebuds and leaves, and wrapping Lucien in the lacy white blanket intended for his christening, Emile placed him in the casket. Nana was consumed by a fresh flood of tears, and he stopped and held her until she quieted. Then he helped her dress, and accompanied by Madame de Lis, they took the little casket into the carriage, and rode to the cemetery. The priest met them at the entrance of the St. Louis Cemetery. Emile had already purchased a tomb there, big enough not only for Lucien's little casket, but for several adults as well.

They stood woodenly by the tomb, as the priest went through the burial service, and the little casket took its place inside the tomb. Emile had sent Washington to buy a floral wreath, and Emile and Nana placed it in front of the tomb, then he took Nana firmly by the arm, and led her away.

"I can't bear to leave him here," she sobbed. "It's like losing a big piece of my own heart. Why did we have to lose him, and so soon?"

When he had helped both ladies out of the carriage, back at the house, he turned to Washington.

"Tell my father there's been a death, and I won't be home for a while. Come for me, or for a message in three days, Washington."

The old man's eyes were brimming with tears.

"I'ze sorry, real sorry, Massa. You dun have a lot te bear in jus' dis one week, your mama, an' now de baby. I'ze verra sorry."

Emile welcomed the old man's sympathy, nodding sadly, and then he turned and escorted the ladies inside. Nana collapsed on the piano bench, the closest piece of furniture. As if she couldn't face the thought of music, Emile saw her close up the sheet music which was open on the piano, and firmly put the lid down over the keys. He poured a stiff drink for each of them, then he drew Nana up and sat with her on the sofa, putting his good arm around her.

"Would you like to take a short walk along the river a little later, or would you rather stay here?" he asked softly, gently kissing Nana's hand, and her cheek.

"Just stay here tonight,... tomorrow maybe a walk. Please hold me, Emile," she answered, and he did. Mama de Lis looked at him questioningly.

"I don't think any of us will feel much like eating, so perhaps some tea or soup for supper?" he suggested, and she nodded.

"I'm jus' gonna lie down forh a little while, den I come make soup or fix tea forh alla us," she said, disappearing into her room.

Finally Emile felt the tension draining from Nana's body. Gently he pulled her head down into his lap, and finally both of them fell asleep. When he woke up, several hours later, Nana's eyes were open, and she managed a wan, little smile up at him.

"Thank you, darling, for coming so quickly, and taking care of everything," she whispered. "And I'm so sorry to hear you lost your mother also. It's been a terrible week for you...."

"I guess part of why it's been so hard, is that both deaths were so sudden and unexpected. My mother just seemed very tired and pale when I first got home, and in a week she was gone. And Lucien seemed so lively, so healthy...."

There was a hesitant knock at the door, and Emile rose to answer it. He opened the door to find the three musicians on the porch, with their battered instrument cases.

"Gentlemen, I'm afraid this is not a good time. We lost our little son, and have just returned from burying him. The first thing Nana did on coming back to the house was to put away her music, and close the lid of the piano. I don't think she is ready for music today. Perhaps in a week or two.... I know that normally she enjoys your music sessions, but not today...."

Armand nodded sadly. "I'm so very sorry," he said, and the other two murmured their agreement, and they turned to leave. "Please give our sympathy to Miss Nana. We will stop by in a week or so, to see how she is," Armand added. His eyes met Emile's and instantly Emile became aware that this man was also in love with Nana. He felt no anger or jealousy, though perhaps he should, he reflected, since this man clearly was not only in love with her, but he could offer her marriage.... Emile couldn't even conceive of his own life without Nana, but perhaps marriage and a more normal family life would be better for her.... Still it just wasn't something he could even consider. Quickly he shoved it from his mind.

When he closed the door, Nana looked up at him questioningly,

"It was your musical group, and I told them perhaps next week would be better, that we had just buried our son, and music might be too much for you now."

She nodded, and rested her head against the back of the sofa. While he could see she had stopped crying, she looked totally limp.

"Shall I make some tea, or would you rather wait and have some soup with your Mama?" he asked.

"I think tea now, Emile. Shall I make it?"

"No, chérie, I think I can find my way around the kitchen. Let me make some and bring it to you."

Soon he was back with a tray full of cups and saucers, silver, sugar, some slices of lemon, and a pot of tea. She gave him a weak smile of appreciation.

"Can you stay with me, Emile?" she asked, not daring to ask for how long.

"I told Washington not to come back for three days, and then I would either go with him, or simply send a message home. So, yes, chérie, I will stay with you if that's what you want, tonight, and several more nights if you wish." He held the sugar bowl, and let her spoon out what she needed. "Lemon too?" he asked, and she nodded, so he squeezed a slice to free the juice into her tea, then dropped the rest in.

For a while they sat silently, drinking their tea. On the chance that she might eat when faced with food, he brought out a tin of biscuits too, and she did eat a few. He poured each of them some more tea, and added lemon as before. Rituals can be helpful in restoring a bit of normalcy, he realized, and when he squeezed more drops into her second cup of tea, he tried to entertain her by the intentionally clumsy way he did it, and was rewarded by a slight smile.

Nanette came into the room slowly, and climbed into her mother's lap. She put her thumb into her mouth, but finally she took it out, and asked,

"Where didja take Lucien? Te de hospital agin?"

Emile took one of her soft curls in his fingers, and stroked her head.

"God took him, to be one of his little angels," he said softly.

"So why didn't God take me too? I'd like te be an angel..." she answered.

"We don't always know what God plans for us, but your Mama and Papa, and your Grandmère would be very sad and lonely, if God wanted both of you at the same time," Nana said, and somehow that seemed satisfactory, and there were no more questions.

Grandmama de Lis came in and took Nanette by the hand. "Time forh bed, an' den I gonna tell yuh a good story about a little black bear who walked all oveh dis hieh state te find hiz mama an' papa bear." Nanette gave goodnight kisses to her Mama and Papa, and went willingly with her Grandmère.

Emile took away the tray, and then, taking Nana by the hand, he led her up the stairs. He tried to be as tender as possible, as he helped her undress, and into a silken negligée. Fortunately someone had removed the crib from the room, and he silently gave thanks for that. All the little toys, and baby clothes had also vanished, and the changing table was back to being simply a table. Perhaps Mama de Lis had done all that before she went to rest. If so, he would have to remember to thank her. The fewer visual reminders at this point, the better, and he realized that even thinking of all those things hurt, and he felt a great, painful emptiness in his heart. He could only imagine how much worse it must be for Nana, who had spent nearly every waking moment with their son.

When they were about to get in bed, he noticed the little indentation in the covers where Lucien had last been, and quickly he pulled the covers to make it disappear. He hadn't been quite quick enough, her dark eyes sadly took in what he was doing.

He wasn't quite sure if she wanted him to love her or not, so he waited for her to give a sign. She moved close to him, and her arms came around his shoulders. He wanted to be tender, but she flung herself on him, and urged him on. Soon there was no holding back, she slid on top of him, taking him in, with a moan. His arms reached for her, holding her tight, and moving to the rhythm she set.

"Come, Emile, give yourself to me, I need you so much," she sobbed, and he did, and for the first time all that day, they submerged their grief in a tide of love. And afterwards he held her to him, not with tension, but in calmness and tenderness, their bodies intertwined.

The way she had reacted, he wondered if she had hoped to conceive another child immediately, but he knew better than to ask. Time would tell. He briefly thought again of the look he had seen on Armand's face, but he knew it was much too soon to even allude to that matter. That too must come up at some future time. Right now she needed as much reassurance of his love as he could give her, and he regretted that he couldn't be with her all the time. This was much too sad a burden to bear in loneliness,... the loss of their beautiful child and so soon. Surely he was an angel, looking down on them now. He must be with God, it was impossible to believe otherwise. And surely God understood the dilemma of his two loves, and would not punish an innocent infant for the sins of his father.... How could he honorably have let go of his Nana when forced into a marriage he had not sought? He saw his obligations to her as just as sacred as those he had later promised in his legal marriage.

"Nana, I love you," he said, kissing her shoulder, her neck, and then her cheek. She was already half asleep, but her mouth curved into a slight smile for him, although her eyes were already closed. He kissed her eyelids, and the corners of her eyes, and was thankful to find they were dry. And the last thing before he fell asleep holding her, was a prayer he said silently for her, and for their son. He thanked God for allowing them to have him, even for such a short time, and prayed that He had indeed received him in Heaven, and let him play with all the other little infant angels there.

Emile woke first the next morning, and was able to wake Nana with a kiss. She clung to him, and they dozed, their bodies interlaced. Later he felt her stir, and he opened his eyes to hers. The sun hadn't broken through the clouds, and it seemed to be a pearl-gray day, which was probably better, more in tune with the first day after their loss. A brilliant day, a radiant sun would have been hard to bear.

"Today, if you like, we will take a stroll, go to the French Market, buy some nice fresh fruits and vegetables, and perhaps some seafood, and whatever else your little heart desires," he said, trying to be a bit playful, and getting a little smile as a reward.

"Yes, a nice walk, after breakfast, although I will give you time to read the paper first, and have all the coffee you need to get you started. Do I need to dress your wounds? I notice one bandage is entirely gone, and the other one, on your shoulder, is much smaller. Do they still pain you, dearest?"

"Not as much, and not as often. Only if I use that arm too much, or get too tired. Gradually things are getting better. Soon I'll even be able to pick you up!" he threatened in play, reaching under her buttocks and shoulders. She squealed, and smiled, and seemed ready to enjoy some play, and that made him feel very relieved. He knew there would still be many sad moments, but perhaps he would be able to help her through those more easily than he had expected.

He pulled his arms back, and dipped his face into the hollow of her breasts. She held his head, running her fingers through his hair, then pulling his head up, until her lips met his. Already this morning she wanted him, and he knew he wanted her.

"I think breakfast, the paper, and a walk might have to wait a little," he whispered, as he kissed her ear lobe, and lowered his body on hers. On a pearl-gray morning, they made love more slowly, more tenderly, and afterwards it seemed they were more at peace.

Twisting her fingers in his hair, she leaned on one elbow, and asked "So did you have another son?"

"Yes, but wonderful as Pierre is, he is not a consolation for the loss of our Lucien," he answered, his eyes sadly meeting hers. He hoped she would understand, and never resent the other son who still lived.

"Yes, thank you for saying that. You are right. And will you continue to come to me, Emile?"

"Nana, what happened yesterday in no way changes my feelings for you, except that I sorrow with you, deeply, but I love you as always, ma chérie, and hope you will continue to love me, and want me with you. Do you? Has anything between us changed?"

But then before she could answer, he kissed her, and said, "There is something I've been meaning to talk over with you. And please, just listen. I don't want any answer from you right away. I want you to listen, and just think this over.

"I am very aware that I am not the only man in love with you. Armand's eyes give him away, and of course, I understand, since I am also in love with you. What makes things difficult is that, as you know, I am not in a position to offer you marriage, but he is."

Nana shook her head, and wanted to interrupt.

"No, let me finish, please, darling. I love you as always. My life without you would be almost unbearable, but most of all I want what's best for you. Your mother knows from her own experience with plaçage, and she grieves to see you sad and lonely, when I can't be with you. I want you to talk everything over with her, and think about this. I don't want to give you up, but I will, if that will make you happier. You come first, and your long-range happiness. Please don't misunderstand. I am not trying to foist you off. I just want you to choose between what could be a happy, normal marriage with a loving, caring man, and children, or a continuation of the often lonely days you spend, waiting for me. Don't say anything now. Neither of us can stand any more pain in what has already been a terrible week. I just want you to realize that I am setting you free to reach whatever decision you feel is best for you and any children you may have, either with me, or with him. He is clearly a good man, and he is in love with you, although I don't have any idea how long he would wait for you. Also you do share your love of music, an important bond. I enjoy music, but both of you love it, and live for it, and making it together. He could take you to the symphony, and to the opera, and he could even sit with you there. For us, such situations only bring sadness, remember?"

Nana smiled tenderly, and traced the line of his lips gently with a finger.

"Emile, you are the one I love. I can't even consider anyone else, and I am willing to take the loneliness, the embarrassments we may face, just to be with you. Being with you, being loved by you, and having more children together,... that's what I want, only that. I have already known the sadness, the loneliness when you can't be here with me, and yet, when you come, when you smile at me, and when you love me,... nothing else matters at all.... Do you understand? There is no 'either - or' here for me. Just you, my darling, even if I have to wait alone between your visits."

Emile noticed that Nana's eyes were filling up, and he knew his were.

He leaned over her, and kissed her breasts, and then her lips.

"Thank you, ma chérie," he said, his heart too full to let him say any more.

Later he did say, "Remember, you may change your mind at some point. Don't ever be afraid to tell me. I love you, Nana, and I want what's best for you, no matter what."

He kissed her again, and then said,

"Shall we get dressed, and do you know somewhere where I can safely take you out for brunch? I have learned my lesson from our sad experience with the opera. Now I will take your suggestions, and your mother's, and even Washington's. He adores you too, you know?" Emile smiled when he saw her eyes twinkle, and her mouth curve into a mischievous smile.

"He is a lovely old man, and I appreciate his adoration, but he is not you, not even close! You have no competitors, Emile! And yes, my Mama will tell you she knows just the place for us to have brunch, and how to get there!" Instantly Nana was out of bed, and already searching in their armoire, deciding what to wear.

A little later, with directions from Mama de Lis, who declined Emile's offer to accompany them, they set out for brunch.

"Our places are not usually called restaurants, but eating places, coffee houses, or even just kitchens, but the food is usually very good, and so are the prices," Nana said, as they neared a place with a sign painted on the window proclaiming it "Madame Helene Toussaint's Eating House." A wonderful spicy smell greeted them as Emile opened the door for Nana. They were met by a smiling Madame Toussaint herself, and ushered to a quiet corner table. Emile seated Nana, noticing with pride how many males turned to look at her. He knew she was simply gorgeous, but it was pleasant to see that other men, of all shades, seemed to agree with him. He was also surprised to see how many couples of mixed colors were there. He didn't feel as conspicuous as he had expected, finding himself simply one of many. But none of the other Creoles were as splendid as his Nana, even though he was surrounded by Creole beauties.

The food turned out to be delicious; as good, Emile had to admit, as what was served in the city's top restaurants, and a good deal more reasonable in price. And best of all, they had found at least one place where they could celebrate together without fear of being embarrassed, and surely, Emile thought, this was not the only such place. Together they would find many more. Suddenly an emotional cloud had lifted. It had been so restrictive, not being able to take Nana places with him, or having to come into an establishment as if they were separate customers, or as if she was his slave. Surely Mama de Lis and Washington would be able to tell him of many more places where they would be welcome together. The thought was liberating, and he found himself smiling.

"What is it, Emile? You are grinning like a tomcat! Please tell me, what's so amusing?" Nana asked, smiling back at him.

"I was feeling so liberated! Why didn't you and your Mama tell me about places like this sooner? I didn't realize that evidently there are lots of places we can go to together. I've so wanted to take you places...."

"Perhaps Mama thought you weren't quite ready to hear her suggestions until now," Nana said, hoping he would understand.

"What an idiot I've been! So now, you must all help me to hear and understand better!" he said, laughing, and grabbing her hand, and holding on. "You are finally getting through to me, so there's still hope for change!"

Emile found everyone very welcoming, and it did make him wish that was more generally true. Why was the world he moved in so different, so unyielding? He talked for several minutes with Madame Helene as he settled up their bill, and assured her that they would be back. She reminded him that the law forbade her to sell wine, but if he wanted to bring a bottle in a bag next time he came, she would mysteriously find some wine glasses. Emile smiled and nodded. He realized that Madame Helene's was so conveniently located too, only a few short blocks from their little house.

"It's like entering another world, Nana, a much friendlier world. I'm so glad I finally listened to you and your Mama. The food, and the service were as good as anywhere, and the atmosphere was warm, and very accepting."

She nodded, smiling and trying to keep up with the long steps he was taking.

"Oh, I guess I need to slow down a bit. I'm sorry," he said, squeezing her hand in his. "After so much time in the military, it was unconscious, that longer stride. I certainly didn't mean to make you run! I apologize, my darling," he said. They laughed together, and shared a quick kiss, right there on the public street. "I love you, Nana, and more than ever," he said softly, and smiled at her reply, whispered into his ear as he leaned over her.

"Emile, mon chèr, I love you too,... so very, very much."

They got back to the house, and he went into the kitchen where he heard Mama de Lis bustling with pots and pans.

"I just want to apologize for not listening to you much earlier! We had a great brunch, everyone was so friendly, and I hope Nana will be ready to go back to Madame Toussaint's again very soon. Thank you for the recommendation."

Mama de Lis smiled broadly. "Dat's one fine place, eh? Lot cheaper dan some of de fancy white restaurants, food jus' as good or betteh, an' dere be lots morh places forh yuh te try, besides Madame Helene's, lots more fine places I kin tell yuh about!"

"Good, I'm ready to listen!" Emile said, and he turned and hugged her daughter.

And as they investigated further, Emile discovered to his surprise that almost anything they wanted, could be obtained from an establishment run by Creoles of color. There were furniture makers, mattress makers, shoemakers and leather workers, tailoring establishments, watchmakers and jewelers. There were clothing stores, confectioneries, coffee shops, eating establishments, dairies, blacksmith shops, rental stables, and pharmacies. In the arts, he already knew there were artists of all kinds, sculptors, painters, musicians, and writers, but now he learned of architects, builders, and iron and marble workers. The iron workers were responsible for most of the decorative iron work on houses and fences, while the marble workers created the finely designed tombs found in every New Orleans area cemetery. He learned of a dentist, several physicians, lawyers, lithographers, engravers, publishers, journalists, and of course, he had already been aware that there were some Creoles of color who owned thriving plantations, and he learned also that the cigar-making business in the city was almost entirely in the hands of free Creoles of color. He already had known that Creole builders, carpenters, masons, bricklayers, plasterers, woodworkers and painters had created many of the houses and other buildings of such faubourgs, as Marigny and Tremé, but now Emile found that there was an entire world of Creole professionals and artists, a world he had never suspected to be so broad, and inclusive. Madame de Lis, herself was very proud to earn her living as a modiste, much more than just a seamstress, one who designs and makes up fashionable clothing, even making hats as accessories to go with her dresses. She also told him that she was sure that the Legoaster brothers were among the wealthiest men in the city, holding whole blocks of valuable city property, and they also were Creoles of color.

Had it not been for Nana, and his desire to protect her from prejudice, he would probably never have discovered the extent of this rich, creative population which formed a special middle class in his own city, New Orleans. But he did remain embarrassed, over how long it had taken him to learn all this. Perhaps there were only limited areas in which the different worlds of their city overlapped. In his case, as with other white males, it had come only through his love relationship. The Quadroon Balls opened one area of overlap, as it had for him. Why then did it take so long to establish the trust needed before a white male could enter freely into the world of the free people of color? Was it a self-protectiveness by the Creoles themselves? Or was it that white males simply didn't pick up the hints and suggestions made to them, only coming into contact with individuals as they sought out people with special skills, or fell in love, as he had, across the strict boundary lines of color? Madame de Lis and Washington had both tried to reach him, and perhaps Nana too. Only now did he realize that, and how long it had taken him to really listen and to actually hear what they were trying to tell him.

He sat, ostensibly reading the newspaper, as he thought this through, and he put the paper down, and looked at Nana, who was quietly sewing, sitting in the other wing chair opposite him.

"Nana, I've been thinking, and I've suddenly realized what a large part of the population of this city I hadn't really been aware of, until just recently. Why, now I know that almost anything you and I need, can be obtained through the establishments and talents of your people. Why didn't you set me straight on this sooner? And from now on, I want you and your mother to be entirely honest about things. When I don't seem to follow what you are suggesting, please keep trying! I guess I grew up in a very narrow world, and you need to keep enlightening me. Don't ever be afraid to set me straight, please, ma chérie."

Nana smiled at him, and nodded. "I guess we were just embarrassed sometimes, and didn't know quite how to tell you about things, such as where we could go together, and where we couldn't. I think you understand that better now, and besides, Emile, my people will be glad to have your patronage. It won't make our two worlds come together, but we can build our own small bridges, you and I.... between two different worlds."

"We do already, my darling, just by our love for each other, and through any children we may yet have...." And then Emile realized that even without intending it, he had reintroduced their grief back. Lucien's beautiful little face again rose to dominate their thoughts, and he saw tears begin to well up in Nana's lovely eyes.

He got up, and knelt before her. "He is our very own special angel now. We lost him to heaven, but we will go on and have more children, you and I, Nana. Please don't grieve," and tenderly he kissed both her hands, and rested his head in her lap. "We will always have a special place in our hearts for Lucien. He will always remain a special child of our love, even if God has him now."

She nodded silently, and he took his handkerchief and wiped the corners of her eyes. "Be brave, chérie. God will give us another child. And, of course, we still have our darling little Nanette to cherish. And she will need us even more. She must be lonely, missing Lucien."

"You don't think we are being punished because our love is not blessed through the vows of marriage?" she asked timidly.

"No, I can't believe that,... ever. God would not let us create a child through our love, then kill that child to punish us. I can't believe in that kind of God, and neither should you." He continued to rest his head in her lap, embracing her hips with his arms. After a while he became conscious of the throbbing in his right arm. He got up, and held his left hand out to her.

"Suddenly I am terribly tired, and my wounds are throbbing. I guess I need to listen to that message, and go take a nap. Will you come with me? It might do you good too. I'll even promise to behave, if you do...."

Nana smiled at him, and put down her sewing, carefully sticking her needle into place. Then graceful as ever, she rose, took his hand, and followed him upstairs. True to his word, when they had both settled in bed, he simply stroked her back, and finally his hand stilled in place, and they slept.

Evidently the promise to behave didn't extend beyond the nap, since when Nana awoke, she found Emile watching her, as if he was just waiting for her to wake up.

"Have you been awake long?" she asked.

"No, just long enough to enjoy looking at you," he said, and he rolled to her, and embraced her, sealing off all further conversation with his lips.

Washington arrived as scheduled, only to be told to come back again in two more days. Emile couldn't bring himself to leave.

Armand stopped by, and it was Emile who met him at the door.

"I need to talk to you," Emile said, "but it should be privately, man to man, so can we sit down together on the front porch?" Armand nodded hesitantly,

"How is Nana today?" he asked.

"She is gradually recovering her balance," Emile replied. "He was our first son, such a special child, and gave us so much delight. It is very hard to give him back into God's hands so soon."

For a few moments they sat together on the steps in silence. Finally Emile spoke.

"Armand, I think you love Nana, perhaps almost as much as I do. I see it in your eyes when you look at her. And this presents some terrible choices for me. I cannot marry Nana, as you know, although I love her deeply. I can't even be with her as much as I would like. If you do love her, would you be willing to look after her when I can't be here? I already asked you to take her to the opera, the symphony, and other events, and you agreed. I can't even sit with her. I tried once to take her with me into our box at the opera, but that wasn't allowed, and it was very sad for both of us when we had to leave. And she needs more than just an escort to such events, important as they are. I want her to be happy, and I am aware that during the times I cannot be with her, she is not happy.

"I have already told her that I will abide by what she chooses. I feel very badly that I cannot offer her marriage, but you can. If you love her, as I do, will you give her some time to decide what direction to turn? It is too soon after the loss of our Lucien, she can't make any decisions now, but later perhaps. I have told her that I will free her to make whatever decision she thinks is best for her, and our little Nanette. I love Nana enough to understand if she chooses you, even though it will be very painful.

"Although I believe she knows how you feel about her, I think it's important for her to hear it from you, and I will not oppose that. Please understand, nothing has changed between Nana and me, except that I have come to better understand what her commitment to me deprives her of,... daily companionship, and a real marriage. If you have been hesitant to approach her, don't be. She needs to know, to have full knowledge of what her alternatives are. She does understand that inevitably there must be a limit on the length of time you will wait for her decision." Emile stopped and looked at Armand, then he smiled slightly as he added,

"You know you already have won the approval of the formidable Madame de Lis? She herself was caught in the plaçage system, and she well knows its pains and sorrows. She likes me, and has expressed gratitude for what I have done for her daughter, but she does see a better future for Nana with you, and she hasn't been hesitant in telling me so! I understand, she just wants what she thinks would be best for her beloved daughter."

Armand shook his head slowly, his fingers playing with a tuft of grass by the porch steps.

"Monsieur Emile, I don't know what to say, except that I greatly admire you for what you have just said. The thought of losing Nana has got to be very painful, but you are considering that, if it is better for her future happiness. You are right, I do love her, and want her to become my wife, but she will have to make that choice. Since you give me your permission, I will tell her of my feelings. Once I realized what you meant to her, I have respected that, and not spoken to her anymore about my love for her.

"And, Sir, I do understand, this will have to wait until she has worked through the grief of losing Lucien. If, before Nana marries me, you father another child with her, I am prepared give that child my name, if you will allow me, and to help raise the child as if it were my very own. And you are right about Madame de Lis. She has urged me to tell Nana how I feel, but only now, with your permission, do I feel I can do that, later, when the right occasion presents itself. Until then, I guess we can both look after her. I will continue to take her to all the events, and to thank you for making that possible for both of us; and when you can't be here, I will watch over her. Shall we leave things like that, until she is able to think about any other big decisions?"

"Exactly," Emile said, holding out his hand and shaking Armand's hand. He put his other hand on Armand's shoulder. "I'm glad we could talk things over. After all, we both want her happiness above all else.

Unfortunately I must leave in two days, so please come by, and do what you can to help her with her grief. I will leave some more money for theater and symphony tickets. She needs the distraction of going out, but stick with things which aren't sad, at least for a while! And you will know when she is ready to handle music again."

The two men got up together, looking at each other with new respect and understanding.

"I won't come in now, so please give her my condolences and greetings. I will stop by in a few days, and see if she would like to go to the theatre, but, as you say, nothing sad, of course," Armand said.

Emile went back inside the house. He knew that Nana was upstairs bathing and fixing her hair, so he took the opportunity to talk to her mother privately in the kitchen.

"You probably saw that Armand and I sat outside on the porch, and had a long talk," he began.

"Yes, I seen dat." Madame de Lis said, as she continued to roll out dough for biscuits, expertly scattering flour as she did.

"I know we all want to see Nana happy, and I have seen by his eyes, how much Armand feels for your daughter. I have encouraged him to see as much of her as he can, and take her out when I can't be here with her. I also freed him from any hesitation he may have felt, perhaps because of me, and told him he must let Nana know how he feels. Only she can reach a decision about her future, but first she needs to hear what he has to tell her. I know you appreciate what I have done for Nana, and you must know how much I love her, but I also realize that you know the pains and sadness of plaçage, from both your own experience, and your daughter's, and that you think a real marriage could bring her more happiness. Right now, Lucien's death still absorbs her, but there will come a day when she will be able to think more about the future. Armand may be able to offer her more than I can. I know that, and although it would be very painful for me, I love Nana and most of all, I want what is best and happiest for her. It's not that I want to end my relationship with her, not at all. I love her as much as ever, perhaps even more, as we grieve together over the loss of our son. But I also realize that I cannot be with her all the time, and perhaps she would eventually be happier if she had a man who could share all her days and nights.

"If, in the future, she chooses marriage and Armand, then let me tell you that I will leave her everything, the house, and all the rest. I just want you to know that now. It's too soon to try to explain all that to her now while she is grieving so. And if she does choose marriage and Armand, you must promise me that if any emergencies arise, in which I can help with love or money or anything, you will let me know. I will help, even if I have to do it without Nana knowing I am helping."

Emile smiled as Madame cut out her biscuits. He put one hand on her shoulder.

"So promise me, if I have to give way to marriage and Armand, that you will let me know if and when I can help in any way. I know you favor a real marriage, and you like that fine young Creole of color, but at least promise me that. You know I love your daughter, and I always will, no matter what she decides."

Madame straightened up, abandoning her biscuits for the moment.

"I promise. Yuh iz a fine man, Monsieur Emile. I 'preciates what yuh is sayin' very much, an' respect yuh forh dat. Thank yuh forh thinkin' about what's best forh ma Nana, an' lettin' her decide dat forh herself. Yuh already saved her life once, from dat fire, an' I know yuh means te do what's best fer her."

And for the first time Mama de Lis looked with real respect at Emile, and he could see her eyes were brimming with tears. He patted her shoulder, and said,

"Thank you for your promise. If she chooses Armand and marriage, you know I will never forget her, and will always be there to help in any way I can. Now I guess we've said everything that needs saying, and only time will bring about her decision.

"Unfortunately I have to return to Marengo the day after tomorrow, so I have told Armand to come around, and take care of you here. I will leave money with you for household expenses, and also to give Armand for opera, theater tickets, and dinners out, when she feels ready. You will look after all that, won't you? I will try to be back in a few days or a week. I hate to go, but I must...."

Emile handed her a wad of money, and then headed upstairs to check on Nana. He found her just getting out of the bath, and came over and wrapped her in a towel and in his arms.

"You still haven't agreed yet to let me come help you with your bath? Still shy?" he asked, laughing and kissing her.

"Yes, still shy," she answered, smiling and kissing him back.

He could feel all her curves deliciously through the towel, and she was warm still, from the warm bath water. He picked her up, and gently put her down on their bed. She reached for his shirt and unfastened it, and slid her hands down to unbutton his pants. When she had successfully freed him from clothing, she rolled over to him, out of the towel, and he took her, lovingly but sadly, remembering the agreements he had just made with Armand and her mother. Would this be their last time together, he wondered, before losing himself in the passion of the moment.

* * *

As Emile stepped out of the carriage at Marengo, he saw a curtain flicker closed in the window of the bedroom he shared with his wife, and realized she had seen him arrive home. What would he say to her, how would he explain his absence, and the nature of the emergency which had taken him to the city for several days? His emotions had been so intense; he hadn't had time to even consider what he would say to Marie Therese by way of explanation.

Before he could climb the four steps up to the porch of the Big House, she came rushing out the door to greet him. He bent over to receive her kiss and embrace, then slowly he straightened up, his face and body showing exhaustion.

"It doesn't look like you have been taking care of yourself," she said, watching him.

"That's true," he wearily agreed as they walked together into the house. Not seeing his father about, he headed for the stairs, his arm still around his wife's waist, and together they went up to their room.

"How's our little man?" he asked, a bit fearful that as worn out as he was, he might use the wrong name.

"He is just fine, beginning to crawl, so he's into just about everything. He crawled after one of the dogs, and tried to pull its tail, so now your father has banned all his hunting dogs from the house for a while, until his grandson learns better manners!"

This drew a slight smile from Emile, who threw his overnight bag down on a chair, and stretched out on their bed. Marie Therese took his boots off for him.

"Is there anything you want to tell me about the emergency you had to handle in the city?" she asked, watching his expression carefully.

"Not really, and not now anyway. I am exhausted. If you have things to do, that's fine, but if not, perhaps you would like to lie down with me. I just want to rest... nothing more," Emile answered, so, taking off her dress, Marie Therese joined him, putting her little arm over his chest, a gentle and caressing gesture.

"It's good to have you back," was all she said, and soon he was asleep. Marie Therese at last let her tears flow, the tears she had tried hard not to shed while her husband was still awake.

Emile awoke to see shadows closing around them, and realized it must be almost time for dinner. He did feel more rested, and was anxious to see his son. He looked over at Marie Therese, and found she too was awake.

"Is this a good time to pay a visit to Pierre?" he asked, and she nodded and smiled at him.

"He just woke up himself a little while ago, and Mammy will have fed him, and dressed him, so it's a good time."

She helped him dress, and together they went to visit their son. Emile smiled, and drew a smile and a chortle back, then he had to turn away. It was just too much, and his eyes filled up with tears. He sighed and ran a hand over his eyes, hoping to wipe his tears away unobtrusively. Mammy gave him a long look, as he turned away, and headed slowly for the stairs. Marie Therese stayed and took her son from Mammy's arms.

"What do you suppose that was all about?" she asked Mammy.

"De folks in de quarters, dey heard from Washington dat Massa Emile dun lost a chile, anudeh little boy, so be careful what yuh say raight now, forh he be sufferin' bad. Don't matter what we think about dat odeh woman of hiz; but losing a chile, dat's a powerful hurt...."

"Mammy, that is terrible! I can't begin to imagine how I would feel if suddenly something happened to our little Pierre. I'll be very careful. I won't ask him anything about where he's been, or what happened these last few days. Did you also hear how old the child was?"

"Dey say jus' a little oldeh dan our Pierre, maybe by a few weeks. An' I did hear dat Massa Emile got involved wid dat chile's mother years beforh hiz papa made him marry yuh."

For a few moments Marie Therese remained silent, fondling the child in her arms. Finally she said,

"I know Emile is a man of honor. He must feel he has obligations to her as well as to me, and his obligations to her seem to have begun years before his father arranged our marriage. I begin to understand. I used to resent her, and the time he spent with her, but now I just feel very sorry for her. Knowing all this will make it easier to endure his unexplained absences, especially now. It must have been terribly difficult to leave her in her sorrow over their baby. Thank you, Mammy, for telling me all this, and I hope you will tell me anything else you hear. I want to understand him better, and do whatever I can to help him. There was a time when I considered leaving him, but that's long ago. Somehow I will manage. I do love him, and I am sure she does too. It's a terrible dilemma for all three of us, perhaps especially for him...."

The next day, late in the morning, Marie Therese had settled in the window seat of their bedroom with *Godey's Lady's Book*, when Mammy knocked and came in.

"About some'in' important, ma Missy.... I hears dat beforh Madame died, she dun sent a slave woman into de city te train wid a fine hairdresser dere, so she could come back an' be yuhr lady's maid, since now I'm back to bein' a mammy agin. I don' much like dis, but what kin I say? Dere iz too much te do, bein' mammy te dis hieh young man of ours, an' bein' yuhr maid too. She be back now, an' if you want, I bring her te meet yuh, so yuh kin decide forh yuhrself, now dat yuh iz de mistress of dis hieh Marengo."

"Yes, Mammy, we can do that today. Mistress of Marengo,... you know since we lost Madame Blanche, I really hadn't even considered that. Goodness, there's so much I need to learn. Perhaps I can help distract Emile by letting him show me what I could take over now."

An hour later, after Massa Pierre had consumed a good lunch, and played with what was left, Mammy took him up, washed the remains of his lunch off him, and put him down for his afternoon nap. She settled in the rocker near his crib, and pretending not to watch his efforts to catch her attention, and resume play, she began softly to sing to him, and finally he settled down and fell asleep. Mammy waited for a while, continuing to rock, so the creak of the chair went on as before, until she knew he was sound asleep, then she carefully got up and tiptoed out, closing the door very quietly behind her.

A few minutes later she brought Hetty to meet her Young Missus.

"Dis hieh be Hetty, back from de city, an' ready te be yuhr maid, M'am," Mammy said, and from behind her bulk, a slight mulatto emerged.

"Welcome Hetty. I do badly need a good maid, now that Mammy is so busy with our little Pierre. Mammy can explain your duties better than I can, to look after me, help me dress, look after my clothes and this room, bring up our coffee in the morning, to set and light a fire in the fireplace on cold mornings, and of course, to fix my hair. Most days I don't expect you to do much with it, but especially when we go out, once our mourning period for Madame Blanche ends, then I'll count on you to find some special ways to fix it. And also, usually I like to have my daily bath in the late afternoon, before I dress for our evening meal or to go out, so will you plan on bringing up the hot water for that, afternoons, around four? I will tell you if sometimes I want to change the bath to morning. I think that's all I need to say; Mammy will tell you all the details you need to know. And this afternoon, I will expect you to start with the bath, and then help me dress and do my hair for the first time. Is there anything you would like to ask me now?"

"Yes'm," came Hetty's response, as she looked her mistress up and down. "Duz I or duz Mammy git first choice of dos clothes yuh don't want no morh? I'ze jus' about de raight size, an' could walk straight outa dis room in dem...."

"Well, Mammy has been with me, she will tell you, since I first opened my eyes, so she has always taken any clothing I no longer wear, and chosen what she wanted, and then handed out the rest. You haven't even started work as my maid, so I think you should understand that Mammy will continue to get my clothing, and she will decide what to give you. It will be up to her, of course. Perhaps later, after you have faithfully served me for some time, we may consider some changes in this.... I think that's all for now."

Marie Therese could see Mammy's face behind her new little maid, and she could see first some surprise, then anger, and finally, as she finished speaking, Mammy gave her a wide grin, before grabbing Hetty's shoulder, and spinning her around to leave the room. It didn't appear that the two of them were off to a good start, and Marie Therese smiled as they left, knowing she would hear a good deal more about this from her Mammy. Mammy had never been one to mince words, and that wasn't about to change, she knew. She wondered whether Hetty realized what a formidable rival she had, and what sort of limits she should recognize, in order to survive as maid to the Missus. Regardless of her skills, she could easily find herself back in the cane fields, almost before she realized what was happening to her. Surely Hetty wasn't enough of a fool to dismiss the influence someone like Mammy would have over the decisions of her mistress, especially after being with her so very long.... Or was she? This power struggle ought to be interesting to watch, she thought and found herself smiling.

After the two women left, Emile joined her.

"So did the interview go well, and is Mammy content to let you have a new maid?" he asked, smiling slightly. "Mammy is very much the boss around here, and what she doesn't approve of, won't last long. Even I know that I have to walk with care, and that she would give her life to protect and defend you. Even just a slight she might *imagine* I'd given to you, could get me in some serious trouble!"

"Well, I guess Hetty is merely on tolerance at this point. I told her what I expected would be her duties, and said that Mammy would fill in the details for her, then I asked if she had any questions, and she had the effrontery to ask if she would get first choice of whatever clothing I cast off, or whether Mammy would."

"That's one nervy little chit! Did Mammy hear that?" Emile asked, laughing.

"Oh yes, Mammy was standing behind her, and I wish you could have seen the various expressions on her face! I almost laughed out loud, and, of course, I told Hetty that Mammy had been with me since I first opened my eyes, and had always been given my clothes, and would continue to be, and that Mammy would decide who would get what. She didn't seem very pleased with that, so I did add that since she hadn't even begun her job, I wouldn't change things now, but perhaps in the future I might reconsider. I guess she'll have to be satisfied with that. Are you up here to take a nap, Emile, or just to hear the latest?" Marie Therese smiled fondly at him, hoping she would be invited to stay for the nap.

"Yes, I am still exhausted, so a nap is in order. You are welcome to stay and nap too."

"Then I will," she answered, reaching to take off his cravat, and his jacket, and helping him out of his boots, and other clothing. She chose to respect his grief and exhaustion, and made no moves to arouse him, deciding that later would be better, and he seemed willing to go along with that. He stretched out full-length on the bed, and turned his face into his pillow. Marie Therese wondered if that was to hide tears from her. When she settled beside him, he did throw his arm over her shoulders. As she drifted off to sleep beside him, she couldn't help feeling a wave of sad sympathy for him. She knew what he was going through was very difficult, especially since he felt unable to talk about it. She also felt better about the other woman who shared in his love, now that she realized that her arranged marriage had come about much later than the other relationship. Emile was a man of honor, he would feel obliged to protect and care for both the women he loved. She understood the situation much better, and felt she could live with it and with him, as his wife.

When Emile awoke, he looked over and found Marie Therese was already awake. He raised up on his elbow, leaned over her and gave her a gentle kiss on her cheek. She turned her deep green eyes on him, and waited to see what he would say. To her surprise he finally said,

"Although I still can't talk much about it, I have just experienced a terrible loss,...a death I am finding very difficult to deal with.... I just want you to realize that it isn't something you have done which saddens me.... I couldn't bear to have you upset too. It isn't about you."

"Mammy hears things in the servants' quarters, and she told me that almost everyone there feels very sorry for you, and that they say you have lost a child...."

"That's true,... a little boy, and my heart is breaking over it. Just be patient with me, that's all I ask. I fell in love with his mother years ago, long before our marriage. I feel I still have an obligation to her, and we are not even able to help each other get through this terrible loss together. Soon I must go back to the city for a few more days. I hope you will understand.... I can't leave her to face this terrible loss all by herself.

"Perhaps it helps you to know that when the war slipped up on us, my father insisted on an arranged marriage, so that if anything happened to me, there might perhaps already be an heir for Marengo on the way, before I left. I was in no position to deny that, although I did feel that my father seemed to care more for Marengo than he did for me. And here I am, with obligations of honor to two women, obligations I feel I must fulfill...."

"Emile, I am glad you can tell me all this, but I already know you as a man I respect as well as love. You are a man of honor, and I understand that you must do what you feel is best. I will probably always be upset when you spend nights in the city, away from me, but I do understand your dilemma.

"There is one thing I've wondered about.... Does your father understand and help provide the excuses for why you go to the city? It has sometimes seemed so to me."

"Yes, and that must be difficult for you to accept. I think partly he feels that since he forced me into an arranged marriage much earlier than expected, he has to help me deal with the situation he got me into. And sometimes I wonder myself, if maybe at some point, when he was young, perhaps he had a similar relationship. I have no proof of that, but

I have wondered. And I don't believe he thinks less of you, because of all this. He admires you, especially after the way you cared so devotedly for my Mama during her last days. So try not to hold any of this against him...."

"Oh, Emile, I won't. But there is one more thing I need to ask you. Now that your Mama is gone, surely there are things that I can help with here at Marengo? I realize that the operation of this place is so well-oiled, that it could probably operate all on its own, with just you and an overseer, but there must be things concerning the house, the slaves, the entertaining we will do, once our period of mourning ends, things like all that, which I could take over. I just need you to help me see where I can be of more use. While your Mama was still able, I tried to do what I could whenever she asked, but she seldom asked me to do anything. But now you must show me how I can take over some of the responsibilities of this place. Will you? And if I have more to do, I won't have as much time to brood when you are gone, and I will feel more a part of your wonderful Marengo."

"Of course. Tomorrow before I leave for the city, as I must, I will take you on a tour, and we'll look at all the operations my Mama oversaw, and that you could take over. Will that take care of things, chérie? I do thank you for asking, and wanting to do this. And I greatly appreciate also your sweet understanding and sympathy in this terrible loss I am enduring. I know the entire situation is difficult for you, and not in any way, one of your own making. I never want to lie to you, and I have hated having to give excuses for my absences. They were true, but not the entire truth. I didn't want to hurt you, and I felt the truth would be an awful shock to you.

"It may not make it any easier for you when I must go, but at least you know that you are in no way at fault, and that the relationship predates our marriage.... Perhaps too, you can understand that I feel honor-bound to two women, and I believe it must remain that way...."

*   *   *

And true to his word, the next morning after breakfast, Emile took his wife everywhere; to the sewing and laundry rooms on the back wings of the Big House, under the covered walkway to the kitchen, where she finally met all the people who worked there under Emile's valet and now chief cook, Tom. Then they visited the smoke house, stopped at the chicken coops and by the fields where the cattle were grazing, and visited the little store, where he showed her the various things they had to sell to their people: Everything from pots and pans, to ribbons, bolts of fine fabrics, clothing, shoes, toys, tobacco, and various preserved, pickled and dried foodstuffs. She noticed that there were no guns, no ammunition, and no knives for sale, and nothing alcoholic.

"If someone wants other merchandise, and has the credit here at the store to afford it, we will take orders for them," Emile assured her. "We do a big business in this little store, especially right before Christmas. As you probably are aware, we let our people earn extra money by taking on extra chores, either in the field, or for the women in sewing, knitting, and even in making quilts from the scraps left after our women cut out clothing. Helping with the preserves my Mother made, or even in the flower gardens, these are all ways they have to make some extra money. Sometimes we need more hands for a party at the Big House. Although that is work expected from the house servants, we do give them bonuses if the hours are longer than expected, and we bring others up from the quarters to help, and pay them for their extra work.

"And as you see, we do not sell any weapons or alcohol; that combination is just too dangerous. The only time alcohol is permitted, is when we provide it at Christmas, New Year's and at the Sugar House Party at the end of grinding season. We know that some of them make their own stuff, in stills hidden in the swamps, but we usually can't find it, and as long as they don't show up for work rip-roaring drunk, we try to ignore it. Those who abuse alcohol, we try to deal with on an individual basis, denying visiting off the plantation, or Sundays at Congo Square, or requiring extra hours of work from them."

Next they made their way to the hospital and clinic.

"Mama has run this for our people, and I guess it has actually been a part of Marengo long before that. Doctor Rideau comes each week, and more often, if needed,... if we have some sort of epidemic, such as flu or measles or whooping cough. Several of the women from the quarters work here whenever there are patients. You can supervise here, and then there are the communal kitchen and dining hall for our people, and the nursery. Each of these usually falls under the supervision of the mistress of the Big House. You won't have to go there every day, but just to visit occasionally, unless problems arise to bring you there more often. My drivers and our overseer are really responsible for the quarters. They ring the bell for getting up, being on the way to work, and for dinner and finally a bell, which tells everyone that they must be in their own quarters for the night. You may want to visit the quarters from time to time, especially to look after the old people, and the children in the nursery. My Mama also visited all our new mothers and their babies. We provide a package of baby things for each of them, and my Mama always liked to personally deliver those gifts."

"I'd like to take on those visits, and to present the baby things myself. Are there some new babies now, born since your mother's illness? I should begin with them, shouldn't I?"

"I'll find out, and let you know. If I can find that out this morning, you could bring Mammy with you, or that new maid of yours, and start on those visits today, while I must go to the city. I'm sure you know what I must do there, but I also do have a legitimate errand to perform for my Papa. We had a blacksmith run off recently, probably because my father punished his wife for fighting by putting her in the stocks for a day and a night. Well, she was released the next afternoon, and by the following morning they were missing, the blacksmith, his wife, and an older boy. I heard that they left two little ones here with relatives. The slave patrol is on the alert and is looking for them, but they haven't been found, and are probably far away by now. In the meantime we do need a new blacksmith badly, not just for banding the sugar barrels, but also for shoeing our mules and horses. That can't wait. And often there are emergency metal repairs to be made on the grinder and rollers, and other parts of our sugar processing equipment. We need a person handy with metal right here day and night during grinding season.

"Since the blacksmith's wife was a field hand, my father has suggested, depending on how much I have to pay for a blacksmith, that any money left be spent on one or two more field hands. So I have to do something I really loathe, go to the slave auction. At least I won't have to supervise their trip here, with my gun in hand. We will send a wagon for them. That will allow me to spend some time in the city, as I must."

So later that same day, Marie Therese, taking Mammy with her, made her first visits to the nursery, and then to the new mothers and their babies, after she gave Emile a kiss, and sadly waved him off on his trip to the city. She was thankful that he felt he could confide in her, and that he had told her as much as he did, but even understanding didn't make it much easier to see him leave, and know where he would spend the night.

*   *   *

When Emile reached the city, he had Washington stop first at the little house on Felicity Street. It was early still, and he didn't expect Nana to even be up and dressed. He knocked at the door, and was met by Madame de Lis.

"Is Nana up yet?" he asked, hoping that he could run up and wake her.

"'Course not. She still be a'layin' in de bed. Yuh wanna go up an' wake her?"

Emile smiled and nodded, then hurried up the stairs. Nana was just opening her eyes.

"Oh sorry. I must have made too much noise on the stairs, but I was in a hurry. I wanted to wake you with a kiss or two or three...." Emile said, and he sat down next to her on the bed, and began to kiss her.

"What a very nice way to wake up!...." Nana murmured, responding by wrapping her arms around him. "Are you staying, and do you want to climb in bed with me?" she continued, offering him a sultry, inviting smile.

"That's very tempting, ma chère, but I have some errands I must do this morning; however I was planning on coming back here tonight, and for several more nights, if that meets with your approval. Does it? Will you give me a personal invitation to return tonight?"

"But of course, my dear, all the nights you can manage!" she answered, smiling with delight. "But what brings you to town so early in the morning, and can I come with you while you do your errands?"

"When you hear what I must do, I doubt you'll want to accompany me. I have to go to the slave auction for my father. I know you wouldn't like that, would you?"

"No, Emile, that is one place you will have to go to all by yourself. I hate everything having to do with slavery, as you know. But you will come back to me here, afterwards?"

"Yes, I will be back, ma chère. It might take me a couple hours or so, but at least you can begin to plan where you would like to go for a midday meal, and then for an afternoon together. Let me have a couple more kisses, and then I must go. I promise I'll be back just as soon as I can." And with that he collected his kisses. At the bedroom door he turned, and smiled.

"Those kisses will have to nourish me through the next few hours, but then I'll have to come back for more! It's your kisses that keep me alive, and give me energy!" he said, and he grinned and blew her a few more kisses, before turning and hurrying down the stairs.

He peeked in the kitchen. "I'll be back in a few hours," he said, "and then I will probably take Nana out to lunch, so think up a good place for us to go!" Mama de Lis grunted her assent.

The front door closed, and through the dining room window she saw the carriage leaving.

Nana came bounding down the stairs. She was wrapped in Emile's heavy, blue bathrobe, and her hair was flying wildly around her.

"He's coming back! He's coming back!" she sang out, dancing around the dining room table, and then around her mother.

"But forh jus' how long?" her mother grumbled, giving her daughter a restrained smile.

"A couple nights, at least," came the answer, but the dancing stopped, and Nana gave her mother a reproachful look. "Don't spoil things, Mama," she said, as her mother poured her out a cup of coffee, and set down a plate of cornmeal muffins before her daughter.

"He dun tole me he be back soon, an' he wants te take yuh out te eat. He eben 'membered te ask me where it be good te go, so let's talk dat oveh raight now," and she sat down with her daughter to talk over the possibilities.

"Oh, and Mama, when Washington comes back with him, will you give him a note for Armand, and tell him where the cigar factory is, so he can deliver my message? I have to let Armand know that I can't go with him to the opera tonight, and if we reach him at work, he won't need to stop here, and it may be early enough for him to find someone else to go with him."

"Yeah, dat's good, but don' yuh go makin' it too easy forh dat nice Creole man te find someun else,..." her mother warned, only to receive in return a sigh and a roll of the eyes.

*   *   *

Emile had Washington pull over in front of the high wooden fence that enclosed a couple of buildings opposite the St. Charles Hotel. He jumped out and went to the entry and knocked. After a while Emile heard a rattling of chains, and then a key was inserted in the high gate, and it opened just a little, on a chain. From inside, a tall, gaunt, elderly Negro looked warily out at him.

"I need to buy some slaves," Emile said. "Especially a blacksmith, if you have one."

"All our slaves, dey be on the auction block oveh at de St. Charles Hotel dis mornin'. Yuh kin go oveh dere an' see what we got. I think we got a blacksmith dere."

Emile thanked the man, and after asking Washington to stay with the carriage, he sprinted across the street and into the St. Charles Hotel. There in the rotunda, up on a high platform, were about thirty men, all dressed in dark blue suits, wearing black hats, and carrying a pair of shiny, new black shoes in their hands. There were a dozen or so women, several of them, with small children clinging to their hands and skirts. The women wore neat, clean calico gowns, nearly all of the same print, had white kerchiefs over their hair, and carried new shoes. The children were also dressed in what looked like new, identical clothing, but had no shoes. The skin of all those on the platform was well-greased, to give them a healthy glow, and they were all briskly marching about, at the shouted orders of the auction manager. None of the adult males appeared to be over the age of twenty-five or six, and most of the women were younger, between the ages of about seventeen to twenty-four, as close as Emile could guess.

Emile went up to get a closer look, and to find the manager of the auction. It was Theophilus Freeman, a slender, yellowy mulatto whom Emile had dealt with before on other sales.

"I'm Emile de Marigny from Marengo, and I need a blacksmith, and depending on how much I have to pay you for him, perhaps a couple of field hands as well."

"Yes, sir, I 'members yuh. I do haf jus' one blacksmith, an' I'll give 'em te yuh forh $1,800.00. Dat be a raight good price forh a fine blacksmith wid experience. Must yuhr field hands all be male? Reason I ask, iz dat de blacksmith has a wife, an' she look like she be strong wid de hoe. Biggest of de women, she be de one on de far right end of alla de women. Dis hieh lot iz a choice lot, they be healthy an' young, an' seasoned te dis hieh hot climate too, since dey be mostly from South Carolina."

Freeman shouted for the parade to stop. Then he resumed his remarks to Emile.

"Den if yuh take 'em, since dey be husband an' wife, I throw in one child a deres forh yuh forh only $35.00. It be de girl hangin' on her mother, see, jus' a pinch of a little thing, too small to do much but weedin' or feedin' chickens now, but lookin' at her ma, maybe dat little chit dere grow up big an' stron' like her, make a good field hand an' a damn good breeder one day.... Whatja say?"

Emile was silent, looking over the family. "That child by law must go with her mother, if I buy the mother," he reminded the trader. "You know that she's too young to be sold separately, under the law."

"Yeah, dat's right, so I make yuh a good deal, take de parents, an' de chile be yuhrs for only $35.00. How 'bout dat?"

"How old are you?" Emile called out to the blacksmith.

"Close as I kin reckon, Sir, I be 24, an' ma wife hieh, she be 22."

"You all been sick much?" Emile asked.

"No, Sir, jus' one winteh, when almost ebrybody on de plantation got sick, dat's all."

"How many children have you given birth to, and did they all live?" Emile asked the wife.

"I'ze a good breeder, Sir. I had four chillum, but one a dem died as a baby, when we all had de feveh dat winter he tole yuh about. The rest, dey all born healthy an' strong...."

"So, whatja think? Yuh ready te make a deal on alla dem?" Freeman asked Emile.

"I'd like to see their backs, and talk to them first. And also to that strong, tall fellow second from the left among the men. Can you have someone bring them back over to the pen so I can see them up close, and talk to them?"

"Sure, we kin do dat raight now. I bring dem myself," and tucking his whip tight under his arm, he beckoned out the slaves Emile had asked for, and tied them together for the walk across the street. Then Emile noticed that Freeman not only got his whip out again, but had a pistol stuck in a holster on his belt.

"Can't take no chances, 'specially wid such valuable merchandise," Freeman said, as he and Emile walked behind the group. Emile did not hear any coughing, or wheezing as the slaves walked ahead of them, and he saw no signs of limping. In fact the adults all walked with good, strong strides. He would have to check their backs for any signs of heavy whipping, which could indicate past behavior problems.

Again the man inside the fence labored to unlock the gate, and then pushed it all the way open for them to enter. Freeman led them to a small room across a heavily pebbled yard, and when they were all inside, he locked the door and stuck the key in his pocket.

"Thar yuh be. Yuh got questions te ask?" he said, looking over at Emile.

Emile nodded, and walked over to the blacksmith first. "Where are you from, and how long have you been a blacksmith?" he asked.

"Me an' ma wife hieh, we waz born an' raised in South Carolina. Our owner he got hisself in too much debt, an' hadda sell off most alla hiz slaves, an' den we waz all marched south on a coffle line. Sir, I been a blacksmith for oveh six years, waz trained in dat by ma fahdeh. He be a smith beforh me, an' till he died, we worked togetheh. If yuh take ma wife an' little girl too, I promise we be good workers forh yuh, an' we won't cause yuh no trouble. Ma wife, she'll cry herself to death if our little girl be separated from us.... We already had two chillum sold away from us. Jus' take all three of us, Sir, please."

"I'm considering that," Emile said, looking the man straight in the eyes. "But first I need to see your backs; you and your wife both, just to check that you haven't caused so much trouble that you got lots of whipping."

"Yuh wanna see dem stripped down? Or jus' de woman stripped down?" Freeman asked.

Emile inwardly cringed, although he knew that stripping slaves down, especially the women, was a common practice when a sale was being considered.

"No, I just want to see their backs," he answered.

"He wants te see only yuhr backs," Freeman ordered.

For the two men that meant just pulling their shirts loose from their pants and flipping the backs up, but for the woman, it meant letting down the entire top of her dress. She did so, but grabbed the front of her dress and held it up over her breasts. Her eyes looked down at the ground, and Emile could see she was trembling. He felt sorry for her, and quickly ran his fingers over their backs, detecting no whip scars on the blacksmith, and only a few on the woman.

"You two, that's all," Emile said softly, pointing to the blacksmith and his wife. The entire process was very embarrassing to him but he knew if he got them to Marengo, and his Papa found their backs too scarred, he would be bringing them back to the city the very next day. Turning to the wife, he said,

"I saw some recent whip scars on your back. What were you whipped for?"

"Sir, I had doz two oder chillum, an' I fought te try te keep dem from bein' sold away from us, but dey waz sold, an' I could hear dem callin' te us as de traders took dem away in de wagons, eben when der voices were faint an' far off in de distance. Ma fightin' did us no good, not forh dem, not forh me. Dat's de story, de true story, Sir. Dey waz both too young te be sold away from der family, but both of 'em waz big forh der age, so dey waz taken. Likely we neveh see 'em agin, neveh eben know where dey's going....

"I swear te yuh, Sir, I'ze neveh been no troublemaker beforh dat, an' if yuh buy dis one las' chile wid both a us, we be thankin' yuh an' doin' de best work we kin do. I'ze a good weaver, an' spinner, an' I kin do fieldwork too." She raised imploring eyes to Emile. "I kin eben run a plow team, if yuh ain't got enuf men te do dat. Poleezze, Sir, kin't yuh buy us all three, an' keep us togetheh?"

"I'm considering doing just that, if Freeman here can give me a decent price for you all."

Then Emile examined the back of the last male. He had a number of scars, but all of them appeared to be old ones.

"Your scars don't look recent, but I'd still like to know how you got them," Emile said.

"Yes, Sir, I tell yuh.... Awhile back I hadda work on a ferry, Sir, an' de owner, he say I waz too slow, but de current a de ribbeh, it run hard, an' I waz real sick wid a feveh. I couldna pull any harder aginst dat current. Ma hands were all cut up from pullin' but I did de best I could do, bein' sick. I dunna have any morh fevehs afta dat, 'cept when alla us got down wid de feveh dat one winter. But dat be how I got alla doz scars, ebry one a dem. Ma boss, he tried to whip me to git me to pull harder, but eben wid de whippin', I couldn't do no betteh.

"An', Sir, I come from de same plantation dat des odeh folks come from, we be cousins, Abraham an' me. We played togetheh as chillum. So I be a good worker for yuh, if yuh buy us togetheh. We'z all been close a long time."

He showed Emile the many scars on his fingers and the palms of his hands.

"See, der be morh scars from pullin' dat ferry. Des scars dey don't hurt me no morh, an' I kin work as good as any odeh man."

The honest look in his eyes convinced Emile that the man was telling him the truth.

Emile knew that some of the stories were made up by the slaves themselves, and others taught to them by the slave traders, but some of them did tell the truth, and he believed all three of these. Besides, it looked as if this group might turn out to be a good buy. They wanted to be kept together, and seemed willing to do good work if they were, so he turned to bargaining with the trader, and they settled up for $4,000. including the little girl. Emile felt he got a fair price, not low but fair. Then he arranged for the group to be picked up the next afternoon by a wagon sent from Marengo. Finally he paid up, and watched as the group were all tagged for Marengo, and placed back in the slave pen, rather than returned to the auction.

As he left the slave pen, he heard the blacksmith call out, "Than' yuh, Massa, forh buyin' us all togetheh. We sure do 'preciate dat, an' we promise yuh, we be good workers forh yuh."

Emile turned back, nodded and waved to the heads he could see at the little barred window.

"My folks'll be coming for you all tomorrow, and bring you to our Marengo," he said, wondering if any of the other slaves would tell them how lucky they were, that Marengo was a good place to go to, and that if they did their work well, there was little reason to fear the whip, and that things would be even better when he became their master. So many slaves brought to the Deep South from other states, were often threatened for years with the fate of being walked south on a coffle line, and sold to work on sugar plantations. They were told that would be a fate as bad as if they were sent straight to hell. Now they would learn that the threats they had heard for so many years, were not always true, and soon they would see for themselves - that they wouldn't be true at Marengo.

The worst part of his day was over now, and Emile could look forward to a few days and nights with Nana. When they drove up to the little house, Madame de Lis hurried out to meet them, waving a piece of paper in her hands.

"Nana asked if Washington could leave dis note off forh her, beforh he goes home te Marengo. It's te Armand. He waz gonna use some a dat money yuh left te take her te de opera tonight, an' 'course she rader stay wid yuh. She jus' wanted te let Armand know early on, so maybe he could git somebody else te go wid 'em."

"That's fine," Emile said, smiling and handing the note up to Washington.

"Will you deliver this first, and then go home to Marengo. Be sure to tell my father that I got us a new blacksmith, and a couple of field hands, and will you be sure a wagon is sent for them tomorrow to that pen opposite the St. Charles? They are all tagged and paid for, so everything should go smoothly. As for me, I plan to stay tonight and two more nights here. If you will, come back for me the next morning after that. All right?"

Washington gave Emile a nod, and started off. "Yes, Sir, I be back fer yuh in three days."

Emile went inside, and found Nana waiting for him, with a kiss.

"Well, have you and your Mama conferred on where you would like me to take you for luncheon?" he asked, putting his arms around her waist, and exchanging more kisses. "You know, if Madame de Lis would like to come too, she is also invited," he added, looking over at Nana's Mama, who had just emerged from the kitchen.

"No, Sir, I stay hieh. I got things te do, lotsa sewin' te do forh ma white ladies. Lotsa dances an' soirées alla comin' up fast. But we did decide dat yuh an' Nana should go try Madame Rose Nicaud's new café. She used te sell de best New Orleans coffee in de French Market, but now she dun gone in de restaurant business. Nana knows 'xactly where her place iz; it's not far from hieh. Little Miss Nanette an' I, we stay hieh, an' keep ourselves verra busy!"

So they set out, walking hand in hand. Emile looked at Nana with love and pride. She was beautifully dressed in a pale green dress, with a matching little hat trimmed with green and gold feathers, and a parasol of green, with gold and orange flowers painted on it.

"Did you and your mama make up that dress and hat? And who painted the parasol so beautifully?" he asked.

"Yes, we made the dress. It's a new pattern from France, and Mama made it up first in a light blue for one of her ladies, and then we did it in green for me. I made the matching hat, and painted the parasol too. Do you like it all?" Nana asked, stopping and turning around, then flouncing her parasol at him playfully.

"Yes, the outfit is gorgeous, and so is the lady who wears it, even if she is armed and dangerous with that parasol!" Emile replied, smiling and kissing her hand.

Soon they were seated at Madame Nicaud's and before their meal arrived, Nana asked "So how did your errand go, the one you had to take care of for your father?"

"Very well, I think. They had just one blacksmith, and we did need one right away. I was able to arrange to buy not only the blacksmith, but his wife and little girl, keeping the family together. It was sad. Their owner in South Carolina had apparently had to sell most of his slaves to avoid bankruptcy, and when the blacksmith and his family were sold, apparently two older children were bought separately, breaking up the family. The mother had been whipped when she fought to prevent it, and both parents begged me to buy their last child, a little girl, along with them, which I did. Perhaps if I had gotten there a few days earlier, I might have been able to buy the entire family, older children as well, but I did the best I could, and they seemed very grateful. In return they promised me that they would do their best work. I also bought a young man as a field worker, a cousin of theirs, who also came from the same plantation, and all of them seemed happy with that too.

"Most slaves brought this far south for sale, are told that conditions here, especially on sugar plantations are very bad, and that they will be treated cruelly, so I hope they'll be surprised at how good things will be for them at Marengo. We only sell those who are troublemakers or refuse to do their work, and they will have clothing, shoes, and medical care when they need it, and reasonably good food. It's hard work, but there are days off, and plenty of chances to make money, if they want to take on extra tasks. I think my Papa is too strict, and he has let our overseers put people in the stocks, but when I am master at Marengo, one of the first things I plan to do is take down the stocks. I do find myself wondering if it is possible to free one's slaves, and still run a sugar plantation profitably. I plan to read up and see if anyone has done that successfully. I know that using free Irish and German immigrants hasn't worked out. They have brought ruin to some plantations by waiting till grinding season is well underway, then refusing to work unless the employer gave them unreasonably high wages."

"Well, at least you did manage to keep a family together. I'm glad to hear that," Nana said, smiling at him as their meals were being placed before them.

After an excellent meal, they walked back to the house. On the way Nana looked up at Emile, and said "You know, my dear, God has answered my prayer, and we are expecting another child, in about seven months. I wanted you to be the first to hear, even my Mama hasn't yet noticed."

Emile bent over and embraced and kissed her. "That is wonderful news, indeed. Have you had a chance yet to check with Marie Laveau as to whether it's a girl or a boy?"

"Oh, stop teasing me, Emile! I may yet go and consult her, but just for fun. I know you don't have much faith in her predictions, but that little bag she made up for you to carry through the war, maybe it did help protect you from being killed, who knows?"

"I can't quarrel with that. I did return alive! But how much that was due to the little bag with a blue ribbon on it? I don't know. I do know that I never went anywhere without it, because I was sure you would question me when I returned. And just to satisfy you, I really did keep it in my vest pocket the entire time. Satisfied? Of course, Marie Therese insisted on putting a little gold cross around my neck, so both of you were trying hard to preserve my miserable hide!"

"A little gold cross" she murmured. "Now why didn't I think of that? That's nice. Do you still carry the little bag, and wear the cross?"

"Oh, indeed I do! I know what's best for me, and I have to please you both," Emile replied, laughing, and relieved that Nana was again able to be light-hearted, and seemed to be emerging from the worst of her grief over Lucien. Perhaps a girl would be a blessing, since she wouldn't be such a reminder of Lucien as a little boy would be. He decided to pray for a little girl.

The next few days and nights they spent happily together, but as the day dawned on which Emile had agreed to return to Marengo, he noticed a rising level of tension in Nana, and that her mother watched her more carefully than usual, noting the change in mood. Washington was not to come until after supper, so Emile took Nana for a long walk through the French Market, buying things for her, and then they strolled along the levée, admiring the ships docked there, and enjoying beignets and coffee. Finally he knew it was time to head back to Felicity Street, that Washington would soon be arriving for him.

Supper was some of Madame de Lis' delectable fried catfish with all the trimmings, but the three of them ate silently, so silently that Emile could tell without looking when the carriage drew up outside. Much as he wanted to stay longer, he couldn't, and he knew the departure would be best if it was quick. He thanked Madame for the fine meal, then rose and gave Nana several quick kisses. She rose and accompanied him to the door, apparently intending to walk with him to the carriage.

"Please Nana, let's make our good-byes inside and quickly. It will be less painful for both of us. I love you, ma chérie, more than I can ever tell you with words. I will be back as soon as I can, you know that. In the meantime, let Armand take you to the opera, the symphony, and the theater. I have provided the funds for just that, and I don't want to think of you sitting here alone...."

His last embrace was longer than he had planned, but when he heard a little sob from her, he broke free. "It's best to be quick about this," he said, and then he was gone. Nana stood at the window, holding the curtains back, looking out and hoping for a last blown kiss or a wave, but all she saw was the carriage pulling away. She broke into sobs. Her mother came to her and held her in her arms.

"See, dis be de part a plaçage dat I don't like te see yuh go truh," she finally said. Nana nodded silently, and started up the stairs. She didn't want to talk about it, but she didn't want to throw herself on that empty bed either. She did finally settle on the bed, drawing Emile's pillow to her for comfort.

*   *   *

As the carriage turned into Marengo, Emile sensed that something just wasn't right. It was already dark, but he could smell something acrid in the light breeze which came to him as he climbed out of the carriage. Smoke! He ran up the front steps of the Big House, and inside. The smell was even stronger. He dashed through the dining salon, following the smell and noticing more smoke as well. In the family parlor he saw his father, his head down on his desk, and there was a fire flaming up in the carpet, and curling up the legs of the desk.

"Papa, what has happened?" he cried, but he got no answer. And when he touched his father's hand where it lay palm down on the desk, it was cold. It took both of his hands to lift up his father's head.

"Oh, mon Dieu!" he cried. There was a pool of blood where his head had rested on the desk, and then Emile saw a dagger plunged deep in his father's throat. Blood was still seeping slowly out of the wound, and Emile knew just from looking, that he was too late to save his father's life. He gasped in horror. His father was gone, but he could still save his Marengo. The flames were beginning to spread from the carpet, already twisting up the legs of the desk. He knew that once such a big wooden house caught fire, there would be no hope of saving it, especially since the nearest, and very ineffectual fire department was in New Orleans. Quickly he grabbed another smaller carpet and began beating out the fire. As he did so, he shouted for help, and to call everyone down from the upstairs.

Marie Therese, followed by Mammy carrying Pierre, appeared in the doorway.

"Get outside!" he shouted at them, "And Mammy, call some of the men up here to help me. Tell them to bring water and brooms. I think we can put this fire out before it spreads." Then he went back to beating the carpet. He could see he was making progress, the fire was nearly out, but it could smolder and burst back into flames at any time. Several men arrived, with buckets of water which they threw on the flames; others came with brooms and helped beat out the last of the flames.

Finally Emile was able to turn his attention back to his father. He had known from the first touch of his hand that he was gone. He called for some fresh towels to staunch the bleeding, and sent for a coffin from the carpenter's shop. Fortunately there was one there that was long enough for a tall man like his father. Carefully they eased his body into the coffin, and carried it into the Grand Salon, where the body would stay until a grave could be dug in the family cemetery, and a priest could come to conduct the burial service.

Marie Therese came back inside, holding a sleeping Pierre in her arms.

"How strange," she said in a hushed voice. "We had just gone to bed upstairs, and we heard nothing,... absolutely nothing. Who would have done such a thing?... Kill your father, set a fire to cover it up, and kill all of us in the Big House?"

"All I can think of is that bunch who ran away recently. The wife was a troublemaker, and after Papa ordered her into the stocks, she probably wanted to get even. I figured they were long gone from here, since no one had seen them about, and the slave patrols hadn't caught them. I can't think of any others who might have done this.... I'll send right away to the Landrys, since Jacques is the head of the patrol this month, and perhaps they can put on some extra patrols, and catch them if they're still around here."

Quickly Emile gave out orders, and two of his drivers set off on horseback to notify the patrol, while others were placed on guard around the plantation for the rest of the night.

"The children of the blacksmith, the two little ones they left behind when they ran off, are they still here? Will someone run to the quarters and see, and report back to me," Emile shouted. And in a few minutes the word came back that the two children had also disappeared.

"Well, that seems to support my theory that the parents were here, and may well have been responsible for all this," Emile said, turning to Marie Therese.

"Thank God, you and our little Pierre are all right," he said softly, embracing her, burying his face in the curls of their sleeping son's head, and then giving him a kiss.

The fire was completely out, the carpet area wet with water, so no further flames would burst out, and guards had been posted all around the plantation. Emile took his wife by the arm, smiling wearily down at Pierre. Amazingly, providentially, he had slept through the entire episode, and would bear no scars from seeing his dead Grandpapa, or the fire. When they reached the foot of the stairs, Emile said,

"Now you and Mammy and Pierre go back to bed. I must stay up, and see that our guards are vigilant. I will also plan out guard duty assignments for this next week. Maybe in a few days we will have word that the culprits are caught, and we can relax some of our precautions. In the meantime, we can't dismiss the possibility that they may have hidden in the swamp nearby, and are waiting to see this house go up in flames. By now they may realize that we were able to stop the fire. They could return and try to start another fire, so we can't let down our guard."

He gave Marie Therese a kiss on her cheek, and watched her as she climbed the stairs. He heard their bedroom door close, and then he headed back to the family parlor. Someone had already cleaned up his father's blood, for which he was profoundly grateful. Even the desk chair had been cleaned, and he sank onto it. He turned, suddenly realizing that perhaps the safe might have been burglarized, and breathed a sigh of relief on seeing it was still intact and still locked. He made a mental note to hang a large picture over the safe opening in the wall, so it would be less noticeable. Perhaps it would be even better to have a second safe, hidden somewhere else in the house, and of course, to put more of their cash and valuables in their New Orleans bank.

"Almighty God, what a lot of money would also have gone up in smoke if the room had really caught fire!" he whispered to himself. "Apparently this was not a burglary, but it was a murder, and an attempt to cover it up with a fire." Aloud he added, "Papa, I will live always with the regret that I didn't get home in time to save you, but at least I was able to save everyone else, and our home...."

He shook his head sadly, rubbing his sooty hands through his hair before he had given any thought to the soot on them. Strange how only today I was thinking of what I would change when I became master, and here I am, master, but not at all in the way I would have liked it to happen. I had hoped my father would be here for many more years. He has been remarkably healthy all his life, and if the family tradition of longevity had held, he should have lived many more years. Both parents gone so quickly! Although he had longed for the day to come when he would take over, and could do so many things differently, he now felt uncertain and unready for his new role as master of Marengo. At the moment he realized that the most immediate task was to draw up the duty assignments for guards for the next few days, and he pulled open the desk drawer to get out some paper, only to draw back in horror. His father's blood had seeped down into the front of the drawer, and pooled there. He steeled himself and rummaged in the back of the drawer, and at last found a few sheets of paper which were clean, and began to make out his list.

"I wonder what the new slaves I just bought, thought of all this?" he muttered. "I hope some old hands in the quarters have told them that nothing like this has ever happened here before. And to think how confidently I assured them that they would like it here, and feel safe! And that Marengo is a good place to be...." he said, and laughed a dry, ironic laugh. Then he found he was answering himself. "It *has* been a good place, one without any serious trouble, until tonight, and *it will be that way again, very soon*." Staring at his father's blood in the drawer, he vowed,

"I will see that it's like that again, Papa, *I swear*. Marengo will survive even if I couldn't prevent your death, I promise."

He sighed, and started to work on guard assignments. He set up a sentry system for a week. He would add more days to it later if the runaways weren't caught. He began to think about that. If they were caught, they could be shot resisting capture, which might be the solution. If they were dragged out of the swamps alive, and hauled into the city for judgment, he knew what the outcome would be, death by hanging for the two adults. That wasn't usual for women, but this woman had a long history of fights and other rebellious behavior, as well as probably being a participant in his father's murder and the fire. It was unlikely that she would see any mercy in sentencing. Emile tried to remember how old their oldest son was, somewhere around 15 or 16, he thought. The boy would probably serve a prison term, how long he didn't know, but he did know that when and if he finished that term, he would have him sold. There could not be a return to Marengo for that boy, he concluded.

Again he realized how fortunate it was that he had returned to Marengo that evening. He knew it would be late when he reached home, and he had hesitated, thinking about spending one more night with Nana. Usually he would have done just that, but somehow he felt a strong urge to return home. Had he not come back in time to stop the fire, he might have lost another son, and Marie Therese, as well as the Big House, the house of all his memories.... Still he regretted he hadn't come back earlier.... Perhaps he might have been able to save his father's life. He knew this would haunt him for a long time, perhaps for the rest of his life....

News of the murder and the fire would undoubtedly be in the *Times Picayune* in the next day or two, so he should send off messages to the factor who handled the plantation's business affairs in the city, and to their insurance agent to come and appraise the damages. He wasn't sure if his father's life had been insured. That would also have to be looked into, and he should send a note to Nana, to let her know he was alive, only a bit scorched at the hairline, and on his hands. He brushed a hand across his eyebrows, and found they were scorched stiff and falling out as he touched them. He smiled wanly at the vision of how he must look. No, not a note. He would have to go to the city, so he would make it a point to stop and see her.

He looked out the back window, and saw that the sky was already turning a lighter gray, and that a couple of shadowy figures were slowly arriving at the kitchen. Soon he would be able to get some coffee. The side door to the parlor opened, and Tom's head appeared.

"Massa Emile, yuh still up? Yuh been in dere all night? I guess yuh'd like me te bring yuh some fresh-made coffee? I knows dis isn't 'xactly de way yuh wanted te get te be de real Massa hieh, but now yuh iz, an' we all gonna be mighty proud of yuh as our new Massa."

Emile was a bit surprised to notice that already he had been addressed as the real master, and it sounded especially good coming from Tom, who had been his valet for years, and had recently returned from a year in France, spent learning French cuisine. Although he had agreed to take charge of Marengo's kitchen on his return from France, he insisted on also staying on as Emile's valet. Their relationship had been and probably would always be a very good one, and Emile knew that Tom exercised great influence not only in the kitchen of the Big House, but in the quarters as well.

"Coffee sounds very good, Tom. But before you go make it, tell me what you think of everything that's happened here in the last twelve hours or so. Can you think of anyone, other than the recent runaways, who might have been angry enough to kill my father?"

"No, Sir. Dey be de likely ones, an' I hope dey be long gone from around hieh. I dun like te worry 'bout dem hidin' out in de swamps, an' still bein' a danger te us an' te dis fine place."

"If they're still around, the slave patrols have probably been increased, and they'll be caught. I will have to sell the boy, if he survives whatever prison term he is given. I can't let him come back to Marengo after this...."

"No, Sir. I guess he be young enuff te escape de noose dat hiz parents sureh te get, an' I kin see how yuh don't want him back 'round hieh. It be real sad dat yuh dun lost yuhr papa so soon afta yuhr mama died. I'ze verra sorry 'bout dat, Massa ."

"Thank you, Tom. I still can't believe he's gone, or that now I have to take over here. I'm counting on you and lots of our people to help me out. Papa let our last overseer go, so I guess I have to begin by hiring a new one. After you bring me some coffee, could you send word to all our drivers to come see me here right away, before work begins this morning? And in memory of my father, you can tell them to let our people out of the fields early today, by noon. And tomorrow, when we bury Papa, that will be a whole day off for our people, in his memory."

"Yes, Sir. I git de message out jus' as soon as I bring yuh dat coffee."

Although Marie Therese usually had her breakfast in bed, and didn't emerge downstairs until at least mid-morning, spending time with Pierre, helping to nurse and bathe him; this morning she came down to share breakfast with Emile.

She was dressed in a pretty, light muslin dress, with a high-waisted broad green sash. Emile looked up from his newspaper as she came into the dining salon, and had a smile for her.

"You look very pretty, chérie, your green sash matches your eyes perfectly,... but isn't this a bit early for you?" he asked, and reached an arm around her waist, as she bent over to give him a morning kiss.

"Yes, but I thought you could do with some company. Usually you and your Papa had breakfast together, and I felt sure it would be lonely for you without him."

Suddenly she noticed his eyebrows, and ran her fingers over them. A small shower of hair fell into her hand. She smiled at him,

"I guess your eyebrows will grow back soon enough! Other than being covered with soot, and losing your eyebrows, I don't see any other effects, Dieu merci! I do regret that your eyelashes are still longer than mine!" She smiled teasingly at him, then she thought to distract him with news of their son's morning.

"Our little Pierre is in fine fettle this morning, I nursed him, and now Mammy is trying to avoid being covered with his cereal. He just loves to fill up his cheeks like a chipmunk, then spit it out, all over the person trying to feed him. He knows he shouldn't, but he loves doing it all the same. Full of mischief already at this age,... makes me wonder what we have to look forward to as he gets older. He could be a real holy terror!"

Emile looked up and smiled slightly, relieved to be distracted.

"I imagine many little boys and girls enjoy covering adults with their food, especially the foods they don't like. We probably did that too, when we were his age!"

"You could be right, my dear. Especially since the foods infants don't like are usually the very soupy, mashed ones, like spinach, or green peas!.... Perfect ammunition!

"But changing the subject, what must you do today, now that all of a sudden, you are in charge? And what can I do to help? I will see that your father is prepared better than we were able to do last night. We will wash him, put him in some better clothes, and have him ready for burial. Will you set some men to digging a grave for him, wherever you would like it to be in the family plot, and will you send a man to arrange for his funeral with our priest?"

"Yes, I'll have some men out there digging, and will send for a priest. Papa should be laid to rest next to my Mama, and we left space there,... I just didn't think we'd be putting him there so very soon.... I think in view of Papa's condition, we should have a closed coffin, as we did for Mama, and just a short, private ceremony at graveside. I don't think he would have wanted a large funeral, say, at the Cathedral,... just a quiet ceremony here. If one of the local priests can come, we should be able to have it late tomorrow afternoon.

"Today I must go to the city to interview for a new overseer. Remember, Papa threw the last one off the property just a week ago, and I really do need the help of an experienced overseer as soon as I can find one. If I can hire one today, I might be able to bring him back with me from the city either tonight or tomorrow, so I won't know exactly when I will be back. I have ordered that work will stop in the fields by noon today, in Papa's memory. I plan to let our people also have a day off tomorrow, the day of the funeral, except, of course, for guard duty during the night. We must continue that. I have a schedule all set up for guard duty around the plantation for the next week. I will see that the drivers all have copies of that, so they will be able to supervise it, if I have to stay in the city tonight. I don't think you need worry about anything. Jefferson, Mammy's husband, is one of our best drivers, and he will make sure everything is done properly. While I'm gone, he should report to you. With the sentries posted, everyone should be well-protected, and, in fact, if another attack is planned, just the number of sentries standing watch may be enough to discourage it.

"I plan also to take some of the paper money in the safe and deposit it in our accounts in the city. Papa kept too much money on hand here, and during the night I suddenly thought about how serious it would have been if the safe had been broken into, and all that money stolen. There's probably at least a year's worth of profits stacked in there in neat piles,... much too much. Another matter I need to deal with is insurance. I know Papa had insurance on the house and plantation, and we might get some financial help in the repairs we need to make after the fire. Whether he had any life insurance, I really don't remember him ever telling me, but our factor will know. And I plan to give orders to have the stocks taken down the day after the funeral. I do believe that woman's stint in the stocks may have been what set off their plans for revenge against Papa. Besides, I have never favored using stocks as a form of punishment; I want our people to see the removal of the stocks as symbolic of better times, which I hope to begin right away. What do you think, chérie?"

"Yes, Emile, I agree entirely. Taking down those awful stocks is an excellent beginning, along with a day and a half holiday. Do you want our kitchen staff to work with the ladies in the communal kitchen and prepare a nice meal as well? I guess it's customary to do that with births and funerals, and we didn't do it, when Pierre was born, so perhaps now is a good time to celebrate his birth as well as to commemorate your Papa's death. If you approve, I'll go right away and discuss this with the staff, so we can have a nice dinner prepared for tomorrow evening, after the burial. Then you can explain what we are commemorating, and tell them about your decision on the stocks."

"Yes, I do agree with your plans for a dinner. We need to start things out here on the best possible footing, and a nice banquet and the removal of the stocks should help. Since we aren't in grinding season, could you have some of our people tidy up the Sugar House so we can use it for the feast? If so, then you might want to line up some of our own musicians to play, and we can have dancing after the dinner. I think that sounds good."

Suddenly Emile had an idea which he found irresistible. This might be the chance he had always dreamed of, to let Nana see his beautiful Marengo. It would only require having that old piano moved from the Chapel to the Sugar House, and he could have her come as part of the orchestra he would bring from the city,... Armand's group. Very casually he said,

"I may even bring a couple more musicians back here with me tomorrow night, and pay them to participate. I can't be sure I can find any on such short notice, but I'll try. Anyhow go ahead and line up our own banjo and guitar players, and a few to man the drums, and on the chance that I can round up some more musicians, have that old piano moved to the Sugar House from the Chapel, just in case. I think the Sugar House would be the best place, since there is more room for dancing there than in the dining hall in the quarters, and everybody on the plantation can fit in better, including us. We should certainly make an appearance, eat there, and maybe dance a little. If Master Pierre is awake and in good form, we might bring him along for a while, but have Mammy bring him back here if he gets to fussing.... How does all that sound to you, chérie?"

"That sounds excellent. I will get to it right away. And you do promise to be back in time? I don't think I can handle a Sugar House party all on my own...."

"Yes, I'll be back, never fear. If I haven't finished up everything I need to take care of in the city, I can go back there another day." Emile was silently delighted at that thought. He really didn't need his Papa coming up with excuses for him to go to the city. Now that he was in charge, he could easily manage that. He looked at his wife, and saw that she might also have come to the same conclusion. Her expression was quite restrained, and somewhat sad. He rose from the table, and bent over her for another kiss. Their lips met, tenderly, and for a moment or two, she clung to him.

"I'm so sorry about your Papa. This has been a horrible year for you; and Emile, I want to do all I can to help."

"Thank you, ma chère. You will already be doing so much today and tomorrow to help. I don't know how I would have handled all this without you. Now I must hurry off. It just might be tomorrow sometime before I can get back,... but I will be back here in plenty of time for the funeral, and to help with everything at the Sugar House."

She heard his footsteps on the stairs as he went up to collect a few things and throw them into his overnight bag, so she decided to go up too.

"Have you everything you need?" she asked as she entered their bedroom, and saw him methodically looking about to see if he had forgotten anything.

"I think so," he said, and she came to him and raised her face for kisses. Then he hurried down the stairs, and as she looked out of the window, she saw the carriage start out for the oak alley. She realized he had to go, and yet she had to wipe a few tears away. She was thankful that she had enough to do to keep her too busy to worry during the day, but at night,... that would be another matter....

*   *   *

On reaching the city, Washington knew without asking, and directed the horses to Felicity Street. Before the carriage had even completely drawn to a stop, Emile was out and charging up the porch steps.

He found Madame cutting out a dress pattern on the dining room table.

"She ain't outeh de bed yet," she muttered, and Emile headed for the stairs. This time he went up very quietly, and got his chance to wake up Nana with his kisses. He lay down beside her, and just held her to him. This was the comfort he needed, and momentarily he was afraid he might even cry. Everything had been so terrible, and had happened so unexpectedly, so fast. The image of his father, head down in his own blood, filled his mind.

"I love you, Nana," he murmured, kissing her long throat, and then her lips, as she woke in his arms.

Then he propped himself up on one elbow, and held her close.

"So much has happened since I left you yesterday, I hardly know where to begin. When I got home last night, I smelled smoke. I ran into our family parlor, and there I found my father, head down on his desk. I touched his hand, and it was cold. I called him, and got no answer. I felt for a pulse in his neck, and there was none. I lifted his head up, and found a knife in his neck, and a great pool of blood. If only I had gotten home just an hour or so earlier, he might still be alive! I guess I'll always wonder if I could have made the difference, an hour or so earlier. There was a fire already started near his desk, in a carpet, and after shouting to everyone upstairs to come down and go outside, I called for men to help. And after something of a battle, we managed to stop the fire by beating on it with brooms, and pouring buckets of water on it. Only then was I able to thank God that no one else in the Big House was hurt or killed. We could have lost the house and everyone in it....

"Marie Therese, Pierre, and Pierre's Mammy had all gone upstairs, perhaps an hour or an hour and a half earlier, and none of them heard a thing. We found the back window to the family parlor open, so perhaps whoever did this, climbed in there, and immediately killed my father. The safe behind him was untouched. No money or valuables were missing. It appeared to be a revenge killing. I think I told you how our blacksmith, his wife and oldest boy had run away a few days ago. The wife had been involved in a fight in the quarters, not her first by any means, and my father had ordered her put in the stocks for a day and a half. Soon after she was released, they all took off into the swamps. They are most likely responsible for my father's death, and for setting the fire to try to conceal what happened."

"How dreadful!" Nana said softly. "First your mama, then our Lucien, and now your papa, and in such a short time.... I am so sorry, chèr. Have the runaways been caught?"

"Not yet, but the slave patrol has been increased, and are looking for them. Until I hear they have been captured, I have increased security around Marengo. Every male will stand watch. We will bury my father late tomorrow, and then provide a feast for our people in his memory. Since all of us want music as part of the celebration of his life and death, we will have that tomorrow night, and some dancing also in the Sugar House. I have to stop to see our factor, and if possible, hire a new overseer, since my father let ours go a week ago, then I would like to see Armand, and see if I can hire his musicians to come and help provide the music."

"I'm sure he will be glad to do that for you, Emile. Washington knows how to find him at the cigar factory where he works."

"And Nana, this is our chance, to show you my Marengo. I am having an old piano moved from our Chapel to the Sugar House, and you can come with Armand, as a part of his group. I do so want you to see my Marengo.... Will you agree to come?"

"Oh, Emile, much as I would like to see your beautiful home, it will be very difficult, to see you with your wife, and your little son, so soon after we've lost our Lucien,... and not to be able to even have a kiss from you. I don't think I can do that...." Nana looked at him, her dark eyes wide open, imploring him, and he could see they were filling up with tears.

"Oh, please, ma chérie. I do so want you to see Marengo,..." Emile said, trying to kiss away her tears. "If it proves too much for you, I will have a carriage ready to bring you home whenever you want.... At least promise me you'll try to come."

"If it means so much to you, Emile, I will try, but won't your wife recognize me from that night at the opera? And what will she do? Will she greet me, or will she refuse to acknowledge me? And how will she treat you later, if she does recognize me?"

"She may not even recognize you, and if she does, I think I know Marie Therese well enough to say that she will be entirely gracious to you. I couldn't hide my grief over our loss of Lucien. I had to tell her, to explain why I was so very sad, to let her know that my sadness was not something she had caused. You have nothing to fear from her; even if she recognizes you, she is not the type to make a scene. In fact, since Pierre's about the same age as Lucien was, she has a great deal of sympathy for you.

"I have been honest with her, and told her I had a relationship with someone long before she came on the scene, and that I have obligations to that lady. She isn't happy with the situation, but she did respect the fact that as an honorable man, I must look after you and our little girl.... So Nana, please will you come? It might be the only chance I'll have to show you my Marengo...."

"I will try, since it means so much to you, Emile, but at the last minute, I may not be able to go through with it, so please, if that happens, do understand. Your wife has everything I never can share with you. It will be very, very difficult,... very painful."

"Yes, I'll understand, chérie. Now, I have to go for a little while. I have a number of things I need to discuss with my father's factor for the estate, and then I am going to try to hire a new overseer, and, of course, to see Armand, and see if he and his group can come. If he can, chère, he will be there to comfort and help you...." Pierre shared several long kisses with her.

"I can't begin to tell you how much I'd like to just slip into bed with you right now," he said, smiling and running his hands down her body. "But, Nana, I will be back just as soon as I can. I'll make you a promise on that, and I will spend tonight with you."

"You aren't worried about another attack tonight?" Nana asked anxiously.

"No, I've arranged for sentries all around the place, and the slave patrol will also be coming by during the night. It's possible that they have already caught those responsible."

"It's a terrible crime, but I hate to see them all hanged, especially a young boy. Can you intervene and do anything to at least save his life?"

"Yes, I plan to see what I can do for the boy. I won't bring him back to Marengo, but after whatever prison term he'll be given, I will see that he is sold to a good master, if I can. His parents,... I fear I can do nothing for them. If they are caught, they will surely be condemned to hang. Perhaps they have already fled north, or are in a cimarron camp, hidden away with other lawbreakers deep in the swamps. It's possible they never will be caught. I do worry, if that's the case, that we may have to spend a lifetime watching out for any return they might make to Marengo. Although I don't like to see anyone hanged, their crime is a terrible one, and it would be a great relief not to have to continue to worry about any more acts of violence they might try.... In any case they don't know anything about you, chérie, so there's no need for you to worry about being a target. Just stay away from Congo Square where they will be hanged, if condemned to death. Now, give me another kiss to carry me through till I can return later today, and spend the night with you," Emile said, stealing three more kisses before leaving.

He left the money with his factor to be deposited to Marengo's bank deposits, and immediately felt better. His factor told him of a new arrival from Cuba, a man who was seeking a job as an overseer, a solid man with a family. A message was sent to him, and pleased with the man after meeting with him, Emile arranged that José Garcia would arrive the next day at Marengo, and the overseer's house would be made ready for him and his family. Emile also learned that his father had carried life insurance, and the factor promised to look into that, and also to arrange to send an agent to Marengo to check on the property insurance and what would be available to help repair the damages from the fire.

Last of all he stopped to see Armand. The warehouse was a very large one, and fragrant with the odor of tobacco. Soon the manager produced Armand, and together they walked outside to talk. When Emile told him of the death of his father, and his plans to provide time off, and a feast and music for Marengo's people, he quickly volunteered to help. He tried to brush off Emile's offer to pay the group, but Emile was insistent.

"Please accept my offer to pay you; and Armand, I would also ask another favor of you. Just as I have arranged for you to take Nana to the opera, symphony and theater, I hope you will bring her with your group to Marengo. I have arranged for a piano to be moved into the Sugar House, for her to play. She is reluctant, but it may be the only chance I will have to show her my beautiful Marengo, so I believe she will come, and play the piano with your group. Can I ask you to look after her?"

"Monsieur Emile, won't your wife be there, and won't that be difficult for Nana, and perhaps also for your wife, if she realizes what role Nana plays in your life? It does seem risky to me." Armand gave Emile an anxious look as he waited for an answer.

"My wife knows I have another love, and have obligations to that love from long before our arranged marriage. I have explained that I feel honor-bound to both of them, and she seems to understand. When we lost Lucien, I couldn't keep my sorrow hidden, so I told her what had happened, and since she has a son with me, and he is about the same age, she has a great deal of sympathy for the mother who has lost her son. I know my wife well enough to firmly believe that she will be entirely gracious to Nana. There will be no scene. And I would like Nana to see my beautiful Marengo."

"If you insist, Monsieur, and if Nana agrees, I will bring her, and protect her. I still think it will be too hard, too painful for both women, and I would advise against it. Could you not just drive Nana through Marengo some moonlit night? Wouldn't that work out better, and be less painful?"

"It might, but I would much prefer to have her come with you tomorrow night. Can I count on you and your group to come and play, and on you to look after Nana?"

"Yes, you can," Armand answered, and they took leave of each other. When Armand returned to the table where his friends were working, he told them of the engagement to play at Marengo the next evening, and they became excited about that. When he also told them that Nana would be coming with them, and accompanying them on the piano, they all fell silent. They all knew what role Nana played in Emile's life, and evidently felt much the same doubts about her coming, as did Armand.

With his errands all taken care of, Emile returned to spend the night with Nana. In his pocket he carried a box he had claimed from the safe at Marengo, something he planned to give Nana, - a beautiful, elaborate necklace of many pendant, jet black ovals, matching jet earrings, and a little gold ring with a cluster of jet stones, shaped like the petals of a flower. When they had finished supper, he drew her to a sofa in the living room, and put the little box in her hands.

Nana opened up the box, and took out the necklace.

"It's perfectly beautiful Emile. But shouldn't it go to your wife?" Nana asked.

"No, my darling, I want you to have it." And Emile helped fasten the necklace around her neck, and then he took the ring, and kissing the palm of her hand, he turned her hand over, and placed the ring on her finger. Nana put on the earrings, and he kissed them into place, as he did whenever he gave her earrings.

"I was emptying out the safe last night, and I found these, and I knew I had to give them to you. I think the set has found its rightful, beautiful home," he said, kissing her above and below the necklace, and even further down into the hollow between her breasts.

"These pieces have been in the family a long time. My mother used to wear them when she wore a black evening gown. When I found them last night, I knew just where I wanted to see them, and now they are there. I hope you like them, do you, chérie?"

"Emile, they are fit for a queen. They are very beautiful. But are you sure you want me to have them?"

"Yes, they are for you, ma chérie. And already I love seeing them on you," he replied. "With your dark hair, and your beautiful, long neck, the necklace is absolutely perfect!"

Before they went to bed, they stopped to say goodnight to their little Nanette. Emile read her a story and then, closing the book, he bent over and gave her a kiss. Nana tucked the bedcovers around her, and leaned down to give her a kiss.

Nanette looked up at them both. "Papa, why is it dat yuh can't be hieh wid us alla de time like de papas of ma friends?"

For a moment Emile was silent, then looking sadly at Nana, he said, "It's my work, ma petite; it keeps me away."

"But can't yuh do somethin' else, so yuh kin be wid us alla time?"

"It's not that easy, chérie," Nana answered her daughter. "And no more questions now, it's time for you to go to sleep."

After they closed the door, and were in their own room, Emile looked at Nana, and all he could manage to say was "Ma chère, I am so sorry that can't be, and I wish I could make it right.... Can you forgive me, and do you suppose someday Nanette will understand how much I do love you both?"

"I know that, Emile, and someday I will be able to explain it to her. Nanette will always love you as her father."

*   *   *

A light rain and mist swathed Marengo as the men bore Monsieur Louis' coffin to the burial grounds where his own Madame Blanche, his grandpère, his great grandpère and their wives were buried. Marie Therese and Emile followed the coffin, and behind them came all the house servants, and a number of their other people. All stood silently with their heads bowed as the priest read the burial service, and bestowed a final blessing on all of them. The coffin was slowly lowered, and the earth closed over it. Emile looked sadly at Marie Therese, and sighed. While his father had been a somewhat cold and unresponsive man, he had always been a towering presence. Little had occurred at Marengo that he had not had a hand in. He had known the finances of the plantation down to the very last pennies. He had been the autocrat of both the plantation and his family. Suddenly there seemed to be an enormous vacancy,... a vacancy Emile wondered if he could ever fill. He pursed his lips, and took Marie Therese by the arm, leading her away from the grave,... back to the Big House, and to their new roles.

It was customary with both black people, and with French Creoles of New Orleans to celebrate a life ended, with food and music; and so it would be for Master Louis. Lights blazed from the Sugar House, tables inside were covered with food, and already the musicians were beginning to tune up, as Emile and Marie Therese arrived, with Mammy just behind them, carrying a benevolently smiling Pierre. A crowd soon gathered to admire and touch him. With him, everyone knew that the future of Marengo should be secure, at least for another generation.

Tom presided over the food, and when he saw Emile arrive, he came to seat the family, and to present them with plates of food. As soon as they were served, everyone else crowded around to get their food, women in their best dresses and tignons, children dancing around in their Sunday best. Within a short time, the musicians were ready to begin. Emile put up his hand for silence, then he said,

"Luckily I was able to arrange for some of these musicians to come from New Orleans, to join in with our own Marengo musicians on this special occasion. Their leader, Armand Saint Pierre, has performed for a number of events in the city where I have been present, and I thought they would add to our music here tonight. I don't plan to do this often, bring extra musicians from the city, perhaps not again until we are ready to hold a ball here for our Pierre, all grown up into his teens! But they are glad to help us celebrate my father's life and accomplishments here, and the birth of our little Pierre," Emile said, smiling. Then he sat down and the music began.

Marie Therese had only taken a few bites of her dinner, but suddenly she pushed her plate away, and took Pierre into her lap, so Mammy could enjoy her dinner unencumbered by Pierre's fingers reaching for what she was eating. She had noticed that the band leader was the young Creole of color she had seen before at the opera, and she was sure she recognized the beautiful young Creole at the piano. Could Emile have arranged this, she wondered? Why? It is embarrassing, even painful for both of us, she thought. She knew that at some point in the evening courtesy required that she would have to greet the members of the orchestra, and that seemed to mean that it would be unavoidable for her to meet face-to-face with Emile's other woman. Emile, seated at her side, was still busy eating, and hadn't yet noticed her sudden loss of interest in food, or the glances she had thrown in the direction of the orchestra.

Finally he finished up and turned to her. "Do you want me to hold Pierre for you so you can finish your dinner?" he asked, holding out his hands for his son.

"No, I'm not hungry any more. Why, on earth, did you do this?" she asked him in an undertone, so no one else would hear.

"What exactly do you mean?" Emile asked.

"Invite her here tonight. I do think that is going too far."

"She plays with the orchestra. It would seem odd if I invited everyone else in it, but not Nana," he answered calmly. "You have said you bear her no ill-feelings, and in fact, that you sympathize with her in the loss of our baby. Perhaps you can tell her that. I do plan to introduce you to all the members of the orchestra."

For a few moments Marie Therese didn't answer. She was seriously considering whether she should leave, taking Mammy and Pierre with her. To most everyone it would seem that she was simply going to the Big House to put him to bed. Almost nobody would give a second thought to her departure. But then she wasn't sure she should leave. No, she decided; she had to stay, and had to greet the woman as graciously as possible. Any bad blood or resentment between them would only complicate things for all three of them. After all, only she and Emile, and perhaps her Mammy, would know what was actually going on. For most everyone else, the beauty playing the piano was merely a member of the orchestra, and probably married to one of them. Marie Therese swallowed hard. The burial had been difficult, and now this! It was a day she knew she would remember for a very long time, although she doubted she would say any more about it to Emile. Still, she wondered what had possessed him to arrange this meeting? Was it just that he wanted her to see his Marengo, or was there more to it? Was this a test for both women? And how could he not realize what a painful test it would be for both of them?

Soon the open area cleared for dancing was filled with people, and Emile asked her to dance. Slowly she rose, and handed Pierre over to Mammy, then followed Emile out onto the dance floor. It was impossible to relax in his arms, she still resented the test he was putting her through. She found she couldn't meet his eyes. Mercifully, soon they would be able to leave.

She noticed that the pianist was keeping her eyes fixed on the score in front of her. Surely this must be even harder for her, Marie Therese thought, and again she wondered what in the world had possessed Emile to do this, to place both of them in such a difficult, painful position.

At last, as the music ended, he said softly,

"It isn't just that I wanted her to see my Marengo, although I did want that. But there is another reason for the two of you to meet, and I will explain it all when that moment arrives. Since the orchestra members are about to take a break, let me introduce you to them," and Emile's hand gripped her arm very firmly, and he propelled her across the floor to the orchestra. It was clear to Marie Therese that he wasn't going to let her escape whatever he had planned.

"Marie Therese, I'd like you to meet Armand Saint Pierre and his orchestra. They are all fine musicians, and I will ask Armand to introduce you to each one of them, since unfortunately, I don't remember all of their names," Emile said.

Armand bowed to her, and drew each of his musicians up and introduced them to her. Finally he drew Nana forward.

"This young lady plays the piano with us, and her name is Nana de Lis. She is not only beautiful, but she is a fine musician," Armand said, staying right beside Nana, as the two women looked at each other and smiled politely.

"I understand you recently lost a child. Please accept my prayers and deepest sympathy. Only now that I have a child, do I have any idea of how painful such a loss must be," Marie Therese said, taking Nana's hand in hers, and holding it.

"Thank you, Madame. It is true, nothing could be worse than the loss of a child, and it was a terrible shock. He had always been such a healthy child; but in just two days he sickened with a very high fever and then he was gone. Armand helped me get him to the hospital, but even they couldn't do anything to save him...." Nana's eyes were already brimming with tears, as always when she remembered her beautiful Lucien.

Emile stood on the other side of the two women from Armand. He took both of them by their hands.

"It's true that I wanted you to see my Marengo," he said, turning to Nana, "but that isn't all. Now that my father is gone, and I am master here, if anything were to happen to me, I want both of you to know that I hold my wife responsible not only for the running of this plantation until our son, Pierre, is of age to take over, but that the financial obligations I bear for Nana and any children she and I have, will continue to be recognized even if I should die. Now I ask that Marie Therese will promise me, in your presence, Nana, that she will see that you receive the support I have always promised you, no matter what."

Emile turned to Marie Therese "Will you promise that now? I want Armand and Nana both to hear you make that promise."

Looking straight into Nana's beautiful, dark brown eyes, Marie Therese, still holding her hand, said quietly and firmly, "Yes, Emile, I promise to uphold your pledge of financial support. I respect your promise to Nana, and to any children she may have with you. Is that enough to satisfy you?"

"Yes, entirely. This is the real reason I wanted the two of you to at least meet face-to-face once, so that this pledge could be made, and you would each know about it. That's all."

Nana was trembling. "Thank you both," she said very softly, and then she fainted, collapsing into Armand's arms.

"This has been too much for her, Emile. We must get her outside in the fresh air," Marie Therese said, and quickly Armand carried Nana outside. Another orchestra member brought a chair out, and carefully they lowered Nana onto it. Her eyes fluttered open, and they were full of tears.

"Please take me home," she begged Armand. He looked at Emile, "May I borrow your coach?" he asked, and Emile nodded. Together they carried Nana to the coach. Armand climbed in, and Emile helped him lift Nana inside.

"I'm sorry, chérie, to put you through this. I hope you understand that now that Marie Therese has met you, and made that pledge in your presence, I can be assured that your needs will not be forgotten, if tomorrow night or in the future, those who murdered my father, or perhaps others, come to Marengo and cause my death."

Emile wasn't sure if Nana was conscious enough to hear him, but he also knew that the pledge once given, would be kept, and that gave him a great sense of relief. It was one thing to know there was another woman in his life, but quite another to have met her, and seen what a fine person she was. He knew that Marie Therese would fulfill his promises to Nana, now that she had met her and seen that she wasn't just some common woman of the streets, but a wonderful, soft-natured, sensitive and caring woman, to whom he had been committed long before their own marriage.

Inside the coach, Nana regained consciousness enough to say "Armand, please,... take me home.... This has been too much,... much too much...."

His arms came around her, and her head sank down on his chest. When they reached the house on Felicity Street, he carried her inside, and gently laid her on one of the living room sofas. Madame de Lis bustled in,

"Dat waz a bad idea, dat it waz," she muttered, and she got a wet cloth to place on Nana's forehead.

"Not entirely," Armand said. "Emile wanted the two of his women to meet, so he could get his wife to promise, face-to-face with Nana, that if anything happened to him, that she would continue his financial support for Nana and any children he might have with Nana. After his father's death the other night, this has apparently been very much on his mind. It wasn't easy for any of the three of them, but now that I understand what Emile had in mind, I agree with him; it was necessary, though painful to all. And the excuse that Nana played with the orchestra provided an explanation for why she was there. No one but those immediately involved would suspect anything. It was harsh, but I'm sure the face-to-face meeting and the pledge will lay Emile's fears to rest, and that he knows he can trust his wife in this, should anything happen to him. And it was certainly better than just bringing Nana to the Big House. Although Emile didn't think there would be any scene, having lots of people around, may well have helped to prevent that."

"Well, thank yuh forh bringin' her home," Madame de Lis said to Armand. After she saw him out, she helped her daughter upstairs and settled her for the night as she had done so many times when she was a child.

"Dere you be, ma baby. An' don let dis fine young Creole git away from yuh. Dis hieh plaçage,... it iz jus' plain too hurtful. Armand wan's te marry yuh, an' dat be betteh forh botha yuh. So dream yuhrself a dream about dat now, Nana, so yuh wake up in de mornin' knowin' it's de truth. Don' wait too long, baby, or yuh could lose your best chance te be happy...."

Tears were the only answer Nana gave her mother.

Back at Marengo, the music continued to blare from the Sugar House, even though the orchestra members from the city had finally all gone home. The banjos and the drums continued on into the night. Mammy had finally taken a fussy Pierre off to bed, shaking her head and muttering to herself over the goings-on.

Emile finally wished everybody at the Sugar House goodnight, and escorted Marie Therese slowly back over the lawn, through the moonlight, to the Big House.

"You asked a great deal from Nana. It was too much for her, Emile. I would have gladly made that promise to you any time, without having to inflict such pain on her," Marie Therese said curtly. "You could have just put it in writing, and I would have signed it. That would have been all that was needed, rather than tonight's painful drama."

"I knew that, but I wanted her to hear it directly from you, and for Armand to be a witness. With my father's death, I realized I could also be murdered, and I wanted this matter settled. I also felt it was valuable for you to see Nana, and realize that she is a lovely person, and not just dismiss her as some woman of the streets."

"I knew anyone you fell in love with, even as a very young man, had to be a special person, Emile. You didn't have to prove that to me. I feel very badly that she suffered so much this evening. It must have been very difficult for her to have to meet me, your wife, and our little Pierre, and to see everything you and I share here, and know she could never be a part of it all."

"You are making me regret arranging this meeting here. But shocked by my father's death, I suddenly realized my own mortality, and I wanted the matter settled this way, with both of you. Marie Therese, I trust your word more than I trust what lawyers might do to my will."

Slowly they made their way upstairs, and began to undress. Neither of them seemed to want closeness. Emile undressed on his side of the bed, and Marie Therese on her side. Finally they both crawled into bed, but curled up facing away from each other, leaving a lot of space, like an invisible wall between them.

"I am going to pray for her every day, your Nana," Marie Therese said softly. "She has not had an easy time of it."

"Thank you, ma chère, for your prayers. Someday I will tell her about them."

Simple goodnights were exchanged, and both of them fell asleep, emotionally exhausted.

Emile's last thoughts were of Nana, and he hoped that with all the pain and suffering she had experienced that evening, at least she would understand why he thought the meeting was so important. He knew it would be difficult for all of them, but he hadn't realized how difficult, especially for his Nana. Silently he sent her his love, his prayers, and his regrets for whatever pain he had inflicted on her. Plaçage, he now realized, was a system which asked far too much of the placée. He had entered into the relationship full of love, but only now did he realize how much sorrow and pain it had brought to his beloved.

*   *   *

When Nana finally awoke, she realized that though the pain had lessened somewhat, she was still despondent. She began to think that no matter how great the love, somehow it was not enough to overcome the pain. She put on her robe, ran her fingers through her long hair, and slowly went downstairs.

Her Mama had already fed Nanette, who was outside playing in the yard. Nana could hear the sounds of happy play, squeals and songs, and laughter. It made her own sadness seem even deeper.

Her mother brought her a cup of coffee, and some corn bread.

"I 'spect yuh jus' ain't real hungry dis mornin'," she said, and was careful to say no more.

Nana took a sip of coffee, made a wry face, and added two spoonfuls of sugar, a little cream, and stirred it. She took another sip, then with shaking hands, she struggled to put her cup down on its saucer. It took both hands, but finally she succeeded.

"Mama, I don't think I can go on like this,..." she said softly, and the tears began to trace a path down her cheeks.

"I know, truly I do," her mother answered, forbearing to say how she had warned her many times of the pain of plaçage, from her own experience.

"I can hardly bear having to tell Emile, but I must do it. A letter just won't be enough. I fainted last night, it was so very painful. Surely Emile must have realized that,... even his wife did, I know. The whole reason for the meeting was to have her promise that if anything happened to Emile, she would continue supporting me and any children Emile and I have. I guess his father's sudden death preyed on his mind, and he wanted this settled, but, Mama, meeting her was much harder than I ever thought. Seeing her there, holding *their little boy*, and with Emile beside her, and that beautiful place, and all their people,... it was too much. After that, I know I can't continue on this way, living all my days in anticipation of the short time he can spare for me. I know he loves me, and I do love him, but I can't go on like this.... I want a life with a man who can be with me every day, through the sad times and the special ones, not like this. Perhaps I'm not strong enough to handle so much on my own, and it is such a lonely, sad life so much of the time. If Armand still means what he told me, then I have to reconsider, but first of all I must tell Emile. I owe him that, and so much more."

"He'ze been verra good te yuh, baby, but yuh'ze raight. Dis iz a hard life, dis way, jus' waitin' forh 'em. I'ze glad yuh's willin' te see it, beforh it makes yuh sick. When he be hieh next, do yuh know? It be betteh te have dat little talk soon, an' put alla dis sadness an' pain behind yuh,... de sooner, de betteh, chile."

"I don't know when he'll be coming, we never got a chance to talk alone. I suppose if he doesn't come this week, he will send Washington, so I'll write a note for Washington to take to him, asking him to come as soon as he can. I need to end this pain. I can hardly stand it any more...."

"An' Armand, whatja gonna tell 'em, an' when?"

"I will tell him the truth, that I am breaking out of my relationship with Emile, but that Emile must always have the right to see our daughter, and later, the child I am carrying, which is his, but that the rest must end, if I am to live.... Then if Armand can accept that, it'll be up to him if he still wants to marry me."

"Dat sounds good. Armand's likely te be round hieh today or tomorrow. Can yuh tell 'em den, whatja mean te do?"

"Yes, I can't wait any longer." Nana said, looking at her Mama, and noticing that she too had a trail of tears running down her cheeks. She smiled weakly at her mother, and took her napkin to gently brush away her mother's tears, and then her own. Nana was moved by her mother's tears. Usually her Mama took pride in hiding her emotions.... But now she saw that the suffering was her mother's, as well as her own....

Nana pushed the corn bread away, and went upstairs to dress. When she came down, she placed an envelope on top of the piano.

"Here's my note for Emile, on the piano, in case Washington comes, Mama."

"I hear yuh, chile, an' I'll see dat Washington gits it."

Later that evening Armand came by, without the rest of the musicians. Madame de Lis let him in, then made herself scarce, after giving him a specially encouraging look.

Nana came downstairs to meet him, and he kissed her hand.

"I hope you have recovered from last night," he said softly, studying her expression carefully for any clues it might give him.

"Not entirely. When I woke up this morning, I realized how painful and sad my life had become, and I knew that somehow things had to change. I would like to be able to tell Emile my decision face-to-face, but I don't know when he will be here, and I don't think I should keep you waiting another day, Armand.

"I have decided I must end my relationship with Emile. He has been wonderful, loving and caring, and so generous, but for me, things have gotten more and more painful. Seeing him at his Marengo, surrounded by his people, and with his wife and their little son,... that just made the contrast so clear. I can never expect to play more of a role in his life, and with his increased responsibilities as master of Marengo, I will see less and less of him. I know I just can't go on this way. If I do, I will get sick from the pain and sorrow of this life. So I'll tell him I must end things. I do feel he should have every opportunity to see his children, and for that, things must remain friendly, but that's all. It will be difficult, but that's how I think it must be. He can provide financial support for his children, but I will no longer allow him to continue to be my protector,... my lover. That has to be my decision...."

Armand nodded silently, and drew her over beside him on the sofa. Then, taking her hands in his, he spoke quietly,

"I feel sorry for Emile. I know he loves you, Nana, very much, but you are right. This has become just too painful for you. Sometimes I have had trouble watching, realizing how you felt. And you know, I'm sure, that I have been waiting for you, that truly I love you; although until you reached this decision, I tried not to tell you that very often. Now I can tell you, and yes, I love you deeply, Nana, and I want you to marry me. Today would not be too soon!"

Armand smiled as he took Nana in his arms. "I've waited a very long time to hear you say yes. Can you say that now?" he asked, kissing her below her ear, and then on her cheek as he waited for her answer.

"Yes, Armand, yes, I will marry you. I feel free now to love you, but you must promise you will not oppose Emile's right to see his children. That may be difficult, but it must be...."

"I agree to that. While certainly I've been jealous of him, I admit that, still I have been able to remain friends with him, and I think it can stay that way. The question is really can he be satisfied with just being a good friend with you? I hope so, for the children's sake."

"I do think I must tell him all this, at least before we marry, so can you agree to wait till that's accomplished, Armand?"

"As long as I've waited, a few more days won't matter! Of course, I long to be your husband, and the sooner the better, but I do agree, it wouldn't be right to face Emile with a *fait accompli*."

"My Mama already knows that I must break off with Emile, and she's been your loyal supporter for a long time, so we need to tell her our news." Nana said, and she smiled for the first time that day.

Armand burst out laughing. "I know, I know! She has never made an effort to hide her support!" And then he added, "Let's see if she can pick up a musical clue," and he sat down at the piano, and began to play a wedding march, one heard often in the St. Louis Cathedral. "Surely she will recognize this!" he said, leaning back over his shoulder and smiling at Nana, as he played loudly and emphatically.

"What's dat I hears yuh playin'?" came the question as Mama de Lis exited her kitchen and came into the parlor. She looked at Nana and then at Armand, and her face lit up, her eyes twinkled, and a broad smile appeared. Then she hurried over to hug first Nana, and then Armand. "Iz I raight? Doz dis mean a weddin'? Iz I gonna have a real son-in-lawh raight soon?"

"Yes," Nana said, laughing. "Armand has asked me, and I have said yes!"

"I think this deserves a celebration!" Armand announced, and he uncorked a bottle of champagne and poured three glasses full, remembering a bit sadly that the champagne was another gift of Emile's. He chose not to remind anyone else, and they clinked their glasses together and drank to the future, and all it now meant.

        *   *   *

A few days later, Washington pulled the coach up outside, and came to the door himself.

"Massa Emile dun tole me te stop an' see if dere's anythin' yuh'all need."

Madame met him,

"No, Washington, nothin', but Nana has dis note forh him, so kin yuh take it te 'em?"

"Sureh, I'll do dat. An' dere's nothin' else I kin do forh yuh'all?"

"Not today," Madame de Lis said, smiling from ear to ear, as she waved him off.

And the very next afternoon, the coach arrived again, and this time Monsieur Emile came to the door.

"Is Nana here?" he asked, and Madame de Lis nodded, and let him in.

"She be down hieh directly," she said, returning to the kitchen. Emile settled himself on the sofa and waited. Soon he could hear Nana's light footsteps on the stairs, and he got up to greet her with kisses. Then he invited her to sit with him on the sofa, and was a bit surprised when she took a wing chair instead. Perhaps she is still upset over her visit to Marengo, he thought to himself, then he began,

"I'm very sorry that the visit the other night was so painful for you. I hope you understand why I thought it was so important. I wanted you and Armand to witness the promise Marie Therese made.... And for all of us to hear her promise you financial support."

"Emile, the visit was much more painful than I expected.... To see you in your own setting, at your beautiful Marengo, surrounded by your people, and with your wife and little son beside you.... It shattered me, and it made me realize again, that I can never be a part of that life of yours, and that our life together was such a contrast. I have lived just for the time you could spend with me, the rest of the days of my life didn't really count, they were hollow days of sadness and pain. I realized that night that I just couldn't go on this way, that the pain and sadness have become too much, so I have to ask you to let me go, to allow me to end this relationship before it kills me. I will give back everything you have so generously given me, and I will promise that you can always come to see our children, Nanette and the new little one I now carry, but I would ask that you come as a father, and as a friend,... nothing more. I have loved you, and I still love you, Emile, but the pain has come to outweigh the love. I can't bear it anymore. Please understand...." Nana twisted her hands together tightly in her lap. She couldn't bring herself to look at him, or she knew sobs would overwhelm her.

There was a long silence, then Emile sighed deeply and began to speak.

"I guess I've seen this coming, and I can understand how the other evening may have affected you. I never meant to bring you sorrow or pain, Nana, and I regret that very much. I do love you, and probably always will, but if you ask for release, I must give it to you. I guess I am a lucky man, to have had your love for so long.... I will always remember,..." he said, smiling sadly at her, a smile she looked up briefly and saw. It almost broke her heart.

"I want you to keep everything I have given you,... this house is yours, everything,... and I want to continue to provide money to support our children, and you too, if you will allow. I am already desolate at the thought of losing you, but I will honor your freedom, and ask only to see our children from time to time. I will always want to see you, to be sure that you are all right, and to help you if it's needed, but you shall have your freedom.... The sadness, the pain,... they will be mine now, that I know. I love you, but I must bring myself to do as you wish, so I will just say au revoir, Nana...."

Slowly he got up, and came over to her. He knelt before her, and kissed both her hands, first on the palms and then on top. Then silently he rose to his feet, and let himself out the door, closing it quietly behind him.

The tears came streaming down Nana's face, and she couldn't stop the sobs.

Her mother came running from the kitchen. "So it be oveh?" she asked, and Nana nodded mutely, unable to say a word. Then she got up, and slowly went upstairs, still sobbing. It was late afternoon, but she didn't come down again that night, and her mother wisely left her alone.

The next day nothing was said about what had happened. It was a tacitly agreed upon truce of silence. Nana would always treasure Emile and her time with him, and she would have risen up in anger if anyone had said anything the least bit negative about him. Her mother knew her well, so they talked only of Nanette, played with her, and worked on the pile of sewing her Mama had waiting for her, orders she had to fill for her customers.

Armand showed the tact he was known for, and stayed away for several days, but finally he arrived one evening, bearing a bouquet of lilies for Nana, and accompanied by his musician friends. They opened up their instrument cases, and settled in to an evening of music, picking pieces to play which were not sad or brooding. Little Nanette came down in her nightgown and everyone joined her for cookies, then she had goodnight kisses for them all, and taking her grandmère's hand she went nicely off to bed. Soon after, the musicians packed up their instruments and got ready to leave. The last to leave was Armand. He said nothing but "Goodnight," and kissed Nana on her cheek. He knew somehow that Nana had been able to meet with Emile, and win her freedom, but he also knew that it was too soon for him to ask, or to share plans with her regarding their future. He was content to wait until she was ready.

The next day there came a big box of yellow roses, and nestled in with them was a note:

> With my love always,
> Emile

Nana took the roses and held them up to smell them. The tears started again, and as she reached for her handkerchief to staunch them, her hand met a thorn. It drew blood. The tears continued to flow. She was helpless to stop them. And the trail of blood wound down into the palm he had so recently kissed. Their goodbye was more terrible than she had expected,... the blood drawn and the tears.... Had Emile walked in at that moment, she would have flung herself into his arms, and everything she had said, would have been forgotten. He would have stayed the night, and many more.... How could she deny her love for him? It would always be a part of her, she knew, and from her own sad, lonely days, she knew what he must be feeling, and she breathed a prayer for him.

"Please, Lord, let it not be as painful for him as it has been for me...."

A few days later, Madame de Lis noticed that her daughter was still appearing for breakfast with red, swollen eyes.

"Yuh still havin' trouble wid de breakup, baby? It gonna git betteh afta a while," she said consolingly, bringing Nana a cup of coffee.

"I want to go see Marie Laveau today, Mama. Maybe she'll be able to help me see my way through all this, and tell me something hopeful about my future."

"Dat's good. Yuh want me te come wid yuh?" her Mama asked.

"No, you have so much sewing to do. I can go on my own."

And pushing her coffee cup aside, Nana went upstairs to dress. She looked into the armoire. Tears came again; his clothes were all still there. She stroked the sleeve of his evening jacket, and sobbed. Then she remembered, he had worn it the night they were refused entry into the box at the opera. That's how it would always be, she reminded herself, and wiping away her tears, she pulled out the silvery blue dress she had worn the first time she went out with Emile, and once she was dressed, she put on the matching hat, with its little veil. Somehow it seemed fitting, perhaps because it was what she wore when everything began, that she would wear it again now, when everything was ending. Sadly she surveyed herself in the mirror, before she went downstairs.

"I'm going now, Mama," she said, hearing her mother bustling about in the kitchen. Her Mama peeked out at her.

"Oh, yuh ain't worn dat in a long time, an' baby, it looks so fine! Here be some blueberry muffins yuh kin take te Marie. Gotta take her a little somethin'."

When Nana reached the house on Saint Ann Street, she knocked timidly on the door. Marie Laveau herself opened it.

"I see yuh're back hieh, Mademoiselle Nana. Yuh have grown tired a de pain? Let me see what I kin see ahead forh yuh. Come on in."

Nana walked in, and was escorted to the back room, where the white tablecloth lay across the floor, covered with candles and flowers. She didn't see the box with the snake, and was glad of that. She shivered, just thinking about it.

"I brought you some muffins from my mother, Madame. Blueberry. I hope you like them," Nana said, handing over the basket of muffins.

"Thank yuh, chile. Now let's see what I kin find out forh yuh. Yuh won't mind if I takes a little clippin' of yuhr hair, will yuh?"

"No, M'am, if it will help."

Marie Laveau took a short strand from behind Nana's ear, and she wrapped it around her fingers, then she drew two flickering candles towards her and Nana.

"Yuh break up wid 'em, an' yuh wonderin' if dat waz raight. Dere's anudeh man, a nice, young Creole like yuhrself. Marry 'em. He will make yuh happy agin. A woman kin't live forh a love which comes only once in a while. Dat bring so much pain an' sorrow, ain't dat raight? Yuh knows all about dis now, don'tja, chère? An' yuh know dat waz de sad path yuhr mamma, yuhr grandmère, an' maybe yuhr great grandmère walked. Dat plaçage, it mighta seemed like de only way back den, eben if it tore 'em all apart. But yuh, chile, yuh kin haf a betteh life. Yuh got de chance te make a change from dat long chain a sufferin', ain't yuh?...."

Nana was so close to tears that all she could do was mutely nod.

"Don' yuh cry no morh forh what'z oveh. Say yes te dat fine young man who'z been justa waitin' forh de chance te marry yuh. And do dis raight away, as soon as yuh kin, beforh yuh kin talk yuhrself back into plaçage. Dat odeh man, your Frenchie, he been mighty good te yuh, generous too, but it be bad forh yuh. Don' turn back now, yuh know better dan te do dat. Goin' back, dat be temptin'. I know yuh love dat man still, but goin' back kin only bring yuh sickness, an' once yuh take te de bed, yuh ain't never gonna git up from dat bed. Eben wid ma magic, I won't be able te heal yuh den. So turn yuhr pretty face forhward, dat's what I tell yuh, an' do it *raight now....*"

Marie Laveau got up from her kneeling position beside Nana, and pinched out the candle flames. Nana fumbled in her pocket, and placed some coins in Laveau's hand.

Marie Laveau put a hand on Nana's arm. "Yuh an' I know, yuh iz pregnant agin, but dun let dat hold yuh te yuhr Frenchie. Best fer yuh, te give 'em up raight now....Yuhr new man, he be so glad te have yuh hisself, he don' mind dat yuh be pregnant, an' he'ze gonna treat dis chile jus' like it's hiz verra own, yuh'll see...."

"Thank you, Madame. You have helped me make up my mind," Nana replied. The two women stood looking long into each other's dark eyes. At last the voodooienne dropped her hand from Nana's arm, and nodding, she led her to the door.

"Yuh kin break dat chain of unhappy love. Plaçage, dat haz always been jus' one step up from slavery, a slavery a de heart, de feelin's. Find what makes yuh really happier," she said, as she saw Nana out. As the door closed behind her, Nana suddenly realized she had been so overcome that she forgot to ask if her baby was a boy or a girl. But she couldn't bring herself to go back inside to ask.

Outside she stopped on the doorstep, and breathed a big sigh. Perhaps she could go through with this sad break after all, and find happiness again, this time with Armand. He was just waiting on her decision, she knew. She walked through the little garden, and opened the front gate. No sooner had she stepped out onto the banquette, than

a strong pair of arms seized her. Her attacker was behind her, and she
hadn't even seen him, or gotten a look at him.

"Eh bien,... hieh's dat pretty little lady I met out dere by de lake, on
St. John's Eve. Honey, did Marie tell yuh I was jus' awaitin' hieh 'specially
for yuh? An' dat I gotta one terrible need forh yuh? I neveh could put
yuh outta ma mind.... An' hieh yuh are, Madame Laveau dun put yuh
raight back in ma arms agin.... What powerful voodoo magic dat woman
kin work!"

With a sinking heart, Nana recognized the voice. She had again
fallen into the grip of Dr. John, and already his tall, hard body was
pressing against hers. She knew that alone, she wasn't strong enough
to get away from him, and taking a quick look up and down both sides
of the street, she saw that there was no one in sight to help her. He
picked her up, laughing with a glee she found ominous, and he carried
her a short block to another fenced-in little house. She tried to struggle
free, but he held her so tightly, it was painful. She became resigned, and
began to cry. Was this God's way of punishing her for her sinful life?
Surely not! And how would she be able to escape from this vicious man,
she wondered, continuing to struggle, although she knew it was futile.
She saw her pretty little hat fly off, as she struggled. It fluttered down
onto the banquette. Perhaps someone would see it, and rescue her, she
prayed.

"Hieh we be, pretty thing, at mah own house. I'm takin' yuh home
wid me, like I planned te do, so long ago" he said, between breaths. He
appeared winded from carrying her, and he put her down inside the
fence, but kept a painfully tight grip on her arm. He kicked open the
door to his house, and shoved her in. It was dark, and very smelly, with a
dirt floor, and only a rough-hewn table and a couple of chairs. He kicked
open another door, and thrust her ahead of him into a small bedroom.
There he forced her down on a chair, and bound her wrists behind the
chair, and tied her ankles tightly to the chair legs. The smell in the room
was overwhelming,... dank human perspiration mixed with the stink of
stale beer, and cabbage, and other meals eaten long ago. Her long hair
hung in tangles over her face, clinging to her mouth. Her tears ran freely
down her cheeks, and into her hair. There was absolutely nothing she
could do but pray, and that she would do.... Had her life been so sinful

that this was to be her fate; that she would become Dr. John's whore? Oh, please God.... Better to die....

"Dere, yuh jus' wait hieh, till I'ze ready te give yuh a treat lateh tonight," he said, laughing gleefully again, and he slammed and locked the door behind him as he left.

Nana looked all around. There was a very small, high window, and it had bars on it. There seemed no way to escape. There was only a thin pallet on a wooden bed frame, and the sheets were yellowed and smelly. She wrinkled up her nose, and shivered. The best she could do was pray he got drunk and forgot about her; and that before he had a chance to harm her, someone would realize she was missing and come to her rescue.

What could she do, Nana wondered. It would take a day or more to get a message to Emile, but in spite of everything, she knew he would still come to her rescue. Perhaps her mother would be able to reach Armand, and he and his friends could find her. She realized that besides praying, there really wasn't much she could do, and finally she dozed off, only waking when it must have already been late at night. No one apparently saw fit to feed her or even bring her some water. Her throat was parched dry, and her lips had already begun to crack. But maybe one of her prayers had been answered, that Dr. John might have gotten drunk and passed out, forgetting all about her. Again she slept fitfully, miserably uncomfortable, her muscles stiff and sore. And in the fetid darkness, she murmured,

"God, do you mean to take me now? If not, then, please, let someone come.... Send someone to find me, or let me die.... Perhaps I'm not fit for heaven, but this is just too much to bear...."

*　　　　　　*　　　　　　*

As the afternoon continued on, and Nana still had not returned home, Madame de Lis became alarmed, and decided it was time she paid a visit to Marie Laveau herself. She washed the flour off her hands, and changed her dress, and set out. When she knocked at the door, Marie Laveau opened it.

"Ma daughter, Nana, waz comin' te see yuh dis mornin' but she ain't neveh come home. Can yeh help me find her?" Madame de Lis' eyes were filled with tears, and a look of alarm.

"Dat don't sound good. Come in, an' let's see if we kin figure dis out," Marie Laveau said, drawing Madame de Lis into her inner room. There they knelt down together in front of the white tablecloth spread on the floor, and Marie Laveau drew a cloth bundle from her skirt pocket. In it was a small crystal globe. She put it down before her, and muttered an incantation. The gray haze in the globe began to swirl, and then a clear spot opened up. Madame de Lis leaned forward, trying to see what was in the globe, but she couldn't make out anything. After a few moments of silence Marie Laveau spoke,

"I see an ole shack, an' dere's a faint light comin' from one of de windows. Seems like yuhr daughteh is in dere, but she kin't git out. Outside, somewhere near, dere's somet'in' blue. Looks like it kin lead us te her." Madame stopped for a moment, and frowned.

" Dr. John waz te come see me dis mornin' an' we all know how he likes dem pretty girls. Dat could be hiz shack in mah globe. He only lives down de street a little way from hieh, so git yuh some strong men to go check."

Madame Marie Laveau stood up and walked Madame de Lis out to the street, and pointed out Dr. John's house. "Yuhr daughteh be dere, I'ze as sure a dat as I'ze sure a ma own name."

"Thank you, Madame. Now I gotta hurry an' git me some help," Madame de Lis said, thrusting a few coins into the voodooienne's hand.

Madame de Lis hurried off to find Armand. She knew where he lived, and by this time he should be home from work, unless he had gone out to play with an orchestra. She prayed hard that she would find him at home, and as she neared his house, she saw him sitting on the front porch with some of his musician friends.

"Armand, alla yuh, please help, " she cried out, and Armand ran to meet her.

"Nana went te see Marie Laveau dis mornin' an' she ain't neveh come home. I jus' went te see Laveau, an' she say dat she thinks Dr. John took her. She say Dr. John waz s'posed te come te see her dis mornin', an' she be afraid he met up wid Nana jus' as she waz comin' out. Armand, do yuh 'member how he tried te carry her off once beforh, an' yuh helped her git away from him? Can yuh an' some of yuhr friends come help rescue her? I kin show yuh where hiz house iz. An' Laveau, she's sureh our Nana be dere.... We need te do somethin' an' mighty quick!"

Armand shouted to his friends, "I need your help. Nana is missin' and her Mama here knows where she could be. It's Dr. John again, remember he tried to kidnap her that St. John's Eve, and I rescued her then? Come on, we've got no time to lose...."

Immediately they were up, and following Armand and Madame de Lis down the street. Just outside Dr. John's fenced-in yard, Madame de Lis picked up Nana's little blue hat.

"Dis hieh be Nana's hat. She an' I, we made it, so a course I recognize it! An' Madame Laveau, she said somet'in blue would show us de way! She be raight!"

They found the gate unlatched, and the front door gave to Armand's gentle push. Inside they saw Dr. John sprawled on the floor, apparently passed out drunk, and two sets of dark eyes followed them from a corner of the room. It was two women, in rags, huddled together. One of them got up, and taking a key from the table beside a spilled glass of brandy, she handed it to Armand, and silently pointed to the door to another room. Quietly Armand tried the key, and it worked. Madame de Lis grabbed up a knife up from the table, and followed him.

As they opened the door, they heard little creatures squeal and scuttle away into the corners of the room and under the bed. Madame de Lis sniffed in disgust, but then, as her eyes grew accustomed to the darkness, she saw her beloved Nana tied to a chair.

Nana's head drooped, her hair concealing her face. It was hard to tell if she was conscious or not.

"Baby, we'z hieh te git yuh out," her Mama whispered, kissing the back of her daughter's neck.

"Oh, praise be, God heard my prayer,..." Nana whispered, and sighed, as she turned her tear-stained face up to them.

Quickly Armand cut the ropes which bound her hands and ankles, gently he took her in his arms, and very quietly they made their way out of the house, and outside the gate to the street.

There Armand set Nana down on her feet, and embraced her with great tenderness.

"Are you all right? I'll kill him if he hurt you, Nana! Do you think you can walk, if we hold onto you? We need to get you away from this place as fast as we can."

"Yes, Armand, hold onto me, and let's hurry. He must have gotten drunk, and forgotten about me. That's what I was praying for, and that you would come. I think I can walk, if you and Mama hold onto me. I'm very stiff from being tied up in the same position for so long,... ever since this morning.... And very thirsty too."

Soon they had Nana home. Mama de Lis poured out a brandy, and handed it to Nana.

"Drink dis, baby, an' den I put yuh safe in de bed," she said, hugging her daughter.

"Are yuh hungry, sugah?" Mama de Lis asked, after Nana finished her brandy.

"No, just some water, please, that's all, then bed," came the soft response.

"I think a couple of us should stay here tonight, in case that rascal comes to and decides to hunt for you," Armand suggested.

"Armand, I appreciate everything, the rescue so quickly, and now your offer to stay here tonight. Please do, I'll just feel so much safer, knowing you are here," Nana replied.

Armand helped Nana upstairs, and into the bedroom he had never seen before. Gently he placed her on the bed. It was a big, luxurious bed, and he felt strange, as he thought about who had probably bought the bed, and shared it with Nana so many times. Nana slumped down on the pillows and just looked at him. She knew she owed him a great debt of gratitude, for rescuing her, but she hoped he wouldn't want to collect the debt just yet. Emotionally she was totally exhausted. She felt utterly defenseless, lying there, just waiting....

"No," he said decisively, as if he read her mind. "I want to wait until we are married. You have had more than enough for today. Sleep well, chérie. Marcel and I will be downstairs all night, and no one will get past us. You and I will have time to start our relationship off right, and this just isn't the right time." He bent over her, and kissed her once, gently, on the cheek.

"Thank you," she whispered, and he could see the tears forming in her eyes. He too was overcome, and he took her hand and kissed it.

When Armand came downstairs, Madame de Lis smiled at him, as if understanding something of what had happened upstairs.

"I told Nana that Marcel and I would stay here, downstairs, and see that no one bothers her tonight," he explained, taking a place on one of the sofas. Marcel nodded in agreement, and taking off his shoes and jacket, he settled down on the other sofa.

"Dat's good. Den I be goin' up te help her git ready forh bed," Mama de Lis said, and she went on upstairs.

"You dun want Armand up hieh wid yuh tonight?" she asked, as she helped Nana out of her clothes and into her nightgown.

"I would have gladly had him snuggle in with me, but I wasn't up to more than that. And before I could say anything, he said no, that he wanted to wait till we were married."

"Gotta admire 'em forh dat.... Woulda been real easy te jus' slip in wid yuh tonight. Dat's one good man, so baby, don' let 'em get away from yuh, hear?"

Nana simply nodded. She didn't have any energy left to contest anything.

Mama took some ointment, and rubbed it onto Nana's wrists and ankles, where the ropes had rubbed her skin raw, and then gave her a kiss, and shared a hug with her.

"Thank de Lawd, an' Armand, forh lookin' afta yuh!" she said softly to her daughter, and then she went back downstairs.

She saw Armand curled up on the sofa, and she smiled at him. "Yuh'ze one good man," she said, "an' I has te thank de Lawd an' yuh an' yuhr friends forh savin' ma baby."

Armand looked up at her, and said,

"Tomorrow, or as soon as I think she feels ready to hear it, I will ask her again to marry me, and if she says yes, then I will go to the Cathedral and make all the arrangements."

"I know she'ze gonna say yes te dat!" Mama de Lis answered. "Dis hieh iz what I been prayin' forh a long, long time. I knows Massa Emile's a good man, but she grieve so bad when he weren't wid her, an' dat waz mosta de time.... It waz so hard on her, an' finally she tole 'em she couldn't go on dat way no morh. I thank de Lawd she ain't already taken sick from alla de pain an' loneliness."

The next morning, after a breakfast of blueberry pancakes prepared by Mama de Lis, Armand took Nana by the arm, and they walked out onto the front porch, and sat down there together.

"Have you recovered from your bad experience yesterday, Nana?" Armand asked.

"Pretty much. I still don't want to go anywhere near St. Ann Street. In fact I really don't want to leave this house yet for a day or two. Do you understand? That man is so very strong, and he remembered me from that night out by the lake! Can you believe that, Armand? I wonder if I'll ever get over my fear of him?"

"It should die down after a while, I guess. But do you feel ready to think about a different future? A future we could share, Nana?"

Nana turned to him, and smiled, waiting for what he would say.

"Then, Nana, will you consent to marry me?" Armand asked, looking deeply into her lovely, dark eyes as he waited for an answer. "I want to love you, and be with you to protect you, I want to make music with you, and have you as my wife. Please, chérie, can you tell me now? "

"Yes, Armand, I will marry you," she replied, and leaned into his kiss.

"I promise to love and protect you every day of my life, Nana" he said, when the kiss ended, "and with your permission, I will go to the Cathedral to see when the bans can be announced, and we can be married. Do you think you can hide away safely in your house, with your Mama, while I am gone? It won't take long, and I have already waited a long time for this...."

His arms came around her, and this time his kiss was much longer, and more passionate. Then he helped her to her feet.

"It's time we tell your Mama," he said, and holding hands, they went into the house.

"Madame de Lis," Armand called out, and she came bustling downstairs to meet them.

"I have again asked your daughter to marry me, and she has consented. Now I am off to the Cathedral to find out the earliest that we can have the ceremony. While I am gone, will you keep my future wife safe here? Keep your rolling pin handy just in case you get a surprise visit from that old monster. I won't be gone very long."

"Yes, I protect her, but not wid my rollin' pin! I wack 'em wid ma biggest skillet if he shows hisself hier, " Madame de Lis promised.

When Armand had left, Mama de Lis gave her daughter a long hug.

"I know dis be jus' raight forh yuh, baby. He's not gonna leave yuhr side, an' togetheh yuh be happy. Maybe haf some morh chillum, an' hafva papa raight hieh wid 'em. It be good forh our little Nanette too. She already loves Armand, an' she needs a full-time papa. He be dat forh her too, an' any oder chillum you haf...."

"I'm back!" Armand announced a short while later, and with a big embrace and kiss for Nana. "The bans have to be read for three Sundays, and then we can be married. I guess I can survive that long!"

Nana smiled at his enthusiasm, but she also wondered if during that time Emile would stop by, at least to see his daughter. She wanted to be able to tell him about the wedding before it happened.

And as if he had picked up a message from her, two weeks later she saw the familiar carriage pull up, and Emile jump out. Nana met him at the door. "Come in," she said, accepting his kiss of her hand, and another on her cheek.

"Nanette will be so glad to see you," she added. "She is outside playing, but before I call her, I have something I must tell you."

Emile cocked his head, and waited, wondering if she could possibly have changed her mind, and wanted to let him back into her life.

"Emile, this is very difficult,..." she began. "Dr. John kidnapped me, and I thought terrible things were going to happen to me. I had been to see Marie Laveau, hoping that she could help give me a glimpse into my future, and what I should do. Well, as I came back out to the street, there was Dr. John, apparently on his way in to see Marie Laveau, and he grabbed me and carried me off to his disgusting, filthy little house. He tied me up in a bedroom, all alone, and I prayed he'd get drunk and forget all about me,... then perhaps the next day, I could somehow escape. Well, my prayer was answered, he passed out drunk.

"In the meantime Mama became worried, and went to Madame Laveau, who remembered that Dr. John was supposed to come see her, and she felt sure that he had carried me off. Mama hurried to Armand's house, and he and his friends came and rescued me. Last night Armand and Marcel slept here on the sofas in the living room, just in case Dr. John found out where I lived and came after me.

"This morning, when I had recovered somewhat from that terrible experience, Armand asked me again if I would marry him, and I have agreed. I do love you too, Emile, but I can't go on living alone so much of the time, just waiting for you to come and be with me. Armand has agreed to any visits you want to make to see Nanette, and this new baby, and he assures me that he will treat all the children I have as if they were his own. He also agrees with me that you'll always be welcome here, as a friend, Emile, and as a father. And should you want this house back, I will give it back to you, and everything else you have given me. You have always been so very generous, and generous with your love too, as much as was possible under the circumstances; but I've come to realize, I need more, I need a husband who can be with me days and nights....

"Being kidnapped, and knowing that I couldn't reach you easily, made me more aware of the difficulties of my life. Do you understand, Emile? If it's any comfort for you to know,... I will always love you."

Emile reached for her hand, and held it, as he replied.

"I'm so sorry to hear of your frightening experience, and I understand your helplessness in not being able to reach me quickly enough to help you. If there is to be another man in your life, I can accept Armand. I know he has loved you for a long time, and that he will look after you. It's true, I could only be with you from time to time, and I know that's been painful for you. For that I'm truly sorry. All I can say now, is that I wish you every happiness. I want you to promise that if there is anything I can do, please call on me. I do want to visit our Nanette, but I know that for a while, you and Armand will need time alone together, and for a while, coming here will be too painful for me as well. Everything I have given you is yours. I wouldn't want it any other way, and we shall remain friends, I hope, and I know, I will always love you, Nana...."

As Emile kissed Nana's hand, and turned to leave, Armand arrived.

"I offer my congratulations to the lucky man," Emile said, "I know you will love Nana and care for her. I will occasionally stop by to see Nanette, but not at first; and as I have just told Nana, if I can help you both in any way, please don't hesitate to get in touch with me. This house and its contents, I have assured Nana, are all hers. Now, on my way out, I'll stop to see Nanette."

Nana was on the verge of tears as Emile let himself out. From the window she saw him squat down, and take Nanette on his knee and talk to her, then he kissed her, and smiled at her little wave goodbye, and he was gone. She turned into Armand's arms.

"This is so difficult," she sobbed. "Please, just hold me."

He did, and after a little while, he picked her up, carried her over to the sofa, and put her down. She rested her head against his shoulder. Finally her sobs became less frequent, then stopped, and she fell asleep. Armand sighed deeply, knowing that this had been her definitive break out of plaçage, the system which, though it had provided her with some economic security, had all but crippled her emotionally. He looked forward to building an enduring relationship with her, one which would give her love every day and every night, as long as they lived.

*   *   *

Emile felt drained of all emotion, as he rode back to Marengo. He realized that this would be best for Nana. The pain she had endured for so long, when he couldn't be with her, that pain would live with him now, and perhaps as long as he lived. He already felt as if an iron band was constricting his heart. He tried shifting his position, but the pain still bound him. Visual memories of Nana flooded his mind, and he knew that he had to force them away. Finally the carriage entered the oak alley, and just the sight of the trees, Marengo's grand sentries, eased his pain a little. Washington pulled up right in front of the Big House, and slowly Emile climbed out. Every muscle, every nerve in his body seemed to be exhausted by grief. He saw no one in the downstairs rooms, so slowly he climbed the stairs, using his hand on the railing, to help himself up. He opened the door to the bedroom, and found Marie Therese there, sitting on the bed.

"I'm just waiting for my new girl, Hetty, to arrive with the last of the water for my bath," she explained as she rose and came to give him a kiss. Then she noticed his expression.

"What's the matter, Emile? Are you sick? Do you need to lie down?"

Her expression became anxious, a little frown drew her eyebrows closer together, and she studied his face for any clues it might yield. His whole body seemed to slump as he walked into their room and just stood there. His face seemed gaunt and gray.

"Just exhausted," he replied. "It's been a very painful day, but I think I did the right thing. Nana has been so despondent, especially since that night when she was here with the orchestra, so I have freed her from plaçage, and although I have promised to continue support, I have come to realize that as little time as I can be with her, she would be far happier if she were free to marry. Remember Armand, the violinist and leader of that orchestra which came out here? He has been in love with Nana for a long time, and I believe it would be best for her to accept his proposal of marriage. The life she has led, since you and I married, has been very painful and lonely. This will be much better for her...."

"No wonder you look so exhausted. This must be very difficult for you, Emile. I know you have cared deeply for each other for a long time. And don't you have a little daughter with her?"

"Yes, and I must continue to see Nanette whenever I can. She knows I am her Papa, and she is sad when I can't see her very often. And there is another child on the way, one conceived right after the death of Lucien. I am that child's father too. Nana had a difficult time giving birth to our other two, so I worry about how she will do this time. A complete break is not possible; I must continue to see our children, but with Nana, it will be terribly hard to be just a friend, and no more than that...."

He sat down wearily on the bed, and Marie Therese moved over closer to him, and wrapped her arm around his waist. A knock came at the door, and before either of them could answer, Hetty appeared, hauling up a large container of bath water.

"Hieh yuh be,... Missus,... de last a de watah. If yuh be ready,... I pour it in raight now," Hetty said, panting a bit between words, from the effort of carrying the water up the stairs.

"Yes, go ahead and pour it in," Marie Therese said, as she began to unbutton her clothing.

"I can help you with that," Emile said, and slowly he began unbuttoning the bodice of his wife's dress, starting from her neck, while she unbuttoned from below her waist, their fingers finally meeting on the same button. He managed a slight smile, which she answered with a smile, and a sense of promise seemed to linger in her dark green eyes.

"Thank you, Emile. Now while I bathe, why don't you stretch out on the bed, and rest? You look so very tired."

"Yes, I will," he said, stretching out and and covering his eyes with one hand. Marie Therese disappeared behind a screen, and he saw her clothing being draped over the screen, and then he settled down to rest. Even the thought of his little wife, nude behind the screen, and so near, didn't rouse him from his exhaustion. Just as he was drifting off to sleep, he heard a splash of water as his wife settled into her bath. But then she screamed, a scream of horror and fear. He shot straight up.

"Help, Emile," she cried out, trying to get to her feet, and slipping back into the water. He rushed to help her, and lifted her wet, nude body from the water, and wrapped her in a towel.

"Whatever happened?" he asked, holding her and adjusting the towel around her.

"Spiders!... Two big brown spiders, brown recluse spiders. They came out from under a washcloth on the side of the tub, and oh, Emile, they swam so fast, and right toward me! I think I slapped them both off me. I didn't feel them bite me, but their bite is so dangerous...."

"First, we need to be sure they aren't still on you," he said, and pulled the towel away from her, and inspected her carefully, his hands touching her everywhere.

"No spiders visible.... Nice body though!" he said, smiling slightly, a hand at last resting possessively on her hip.

"Now let me see if any spiders are still alive in the tub," and he went over to check. "Yes, there are two of them," and she heard him slap several times with a towel.

"Yes, brown recluse!" he said. "Usually they live in damp woodpiles, and decaying vegetation, so how did they end up in your bathwater?" he asked, then evidently a thought occurred to him, and he stepped outside into the upstairs hallway, and yelled,

"Mammy, will you come here right away!" and she came bustling out of Pierre's nursery.

"What's de mattah, Massa?" she asked.

"Poisonous spiders in Madame's bath water, brown recluse.... Go find that Hetty, and bring her to me immediately!" Emile ordered.

"I get her raight dis verra minute!" Mammy replied, her big face stiffening with anger.

" I aim to find out the truth, so get her here fast!" Then Emile returned to his wife. "Are you all right?" he asked again. "Do you suppose that silly fool of a maid put those spiders in your bath? Maybe she thought she'd get all your clothing and a lot faster!"

"Do you really think she would do that intentionally, Emile?" Marie Therese looked up at him anxiously.

"Well, one spider might be accidental, but two?..." he answered. " I'd better check and see if there are any more of them," he muttered, heading back to the tub.

One washcloth was floating in the water, but another one was dry, and still draped over the edge of the tub. Emile lifted the dry washcloth, and found another spider clinging to the underside of it. Quickly he threw the washcloth on the floor, and stomped the spider to death.

"Sacrebleu! I just found another recluse," he said, turning to his wife. "This no longer looks like an accident to me! One might have been an accident, but three very poisonous spiders, all concealed in your washcloths? No.... I wonder how this idea came to her? She must be crazy!"

There was a loud knock on their door, and almost before either of them could say "Entrez," Mammy marched in, her strong arms wrapped around Hetty. She marched her right to the tub, and with both her arms on Hetty's back, she began to push Hetty's head down into the water.

"Yuh see dem spiders in dat watah? Yuh eider gonna git bit by dem, an' die, or yuh gonna drown, unless yuh tell us jus' 'xactly how dis happened," Mammy said, pushing Hetty's head down into the water again. The room was full of the sounds of sputtering and choking.

"Dey bite yuh an' kill yuh, or yuh drown! Which it be, or iz yuh gonna talk 'bout how alla dis happened?" Mammy shouted loudly, and began to plunge Hetty's head under again.

"I talk! I talk!" Hetty wailed, coughing and starting to cry. Evidently she hadn't noticed that the spiders were no longer moving, although drowning was still certainly a distinct possibility.

"So, start talking," Emile said, rolling up his sleeves, and standing intimidatingly over Hetty. "This wasn't a simple accident; we know that, so you better tell us the whole story!"

"But she dun tole me te use three spiders, dat it would work den...." Hetty whimpered.

"Who tole yuh dat, yuh little debil?" Mammy shouted.

"De woman I larned hairdressin' from," Hetty answered, between sobs. "She tole me... dat it work fast... if I use three, an' she gave me de spiders, de raight ones...."

"Who gave them to you?" Emile thundered, raising his arm and threatening to hit Hetty.

"Don' hit me, Massa. It were Marie Laveau. She taught me hairdressin'. She be verra good at dat, but she taught me a lotta odeh things too, about voodoo an' gris-gris.... "

"I guess so, you little witch! I shoulda drown yuh," Mammy said loudly.

"Why did you do this?" Marie Therese, still wrapped only in her towel, spoke up, her voice still a bit shaky from shock.

"Cause yuh got eberythin'.... Yuh'z pretty, yuh got de rich massa, an' lotsa jewels. I know 'cause I look at 'em when I help yuh put 'em on. An' yuh got alla doz pretty clothes, an' pretty white skin. I ain't got any a dat...." Hetty lapsed into sobs again. "None a dat...."

"Dis hieh girl, she gotta go te jail. She ain't good enuff te keep, eben if yuh send her out te work in de cane fields. I wouldn't eben trust her wid one of doz cane knives eitheh!" Mammy said, keeping a tight grip on Hetty. "Stupid! Yuh'da had it good workin' hieh, forh dese fine people, but no, yuh gotta mess up yuhr life real good, an' now yuh gonna hang forh dis, or if de judge haf mercy on yuh, he gonna jus' lock yuh up with all dos odeh crazy people!"

Emile had his arm wrapped around Marie Therese, who was very pale, and still shivering from shock. He looked angrily at Hetty, sobbing and cringing in Mammy's tight grasp.

"What she tried to do, that was attempted murder, first degree murder, planned out ahead of time, and intentional," he said. "Tomorrow we have to send her off to jail, and later I'll have to go and testify. Tonight she confessed in front of all of us that she intended to murder her mistress. A court will have to decide if she hangs, or is locked up in an insane asylum for the rest of her life. And for tonight, Mammy, will you and Jefferson guard her, so she doesn't slip away into the swamps, or try to hurt someone else?"

"Yeah, I take verra good care of her myself tonight, an' we send her off in de mornin'," Mammy said, dragging Hetty out of the room. But before she closed the door, Mammy looked back at her little mistress, and love and caring shone in her eyes.

"Yuh be all raight, ma sugah? Dis witch hieh ain't neveh gonna git near yuh agin. An' tonight, if she makes one step toward tryin' to run away, I git her good, an' mah Jefferson, he take hiz whip to 'er. After we finish wid her, dere won't be alotta her left to sit in de jail and wait forh de hangin'!"

"Yes, Mammy, I'm all right. No bites, just frightened!" Marie Therese smiled as she answered. She had finally curled up on the bed, exhausted and still wrapped in her big bath towel.

When the door closed, Emile came to sit beside her, and gave her a long, tender kiss. "I guess you had a close call, chérie. Do you still want a bath, after all this? If so, I will personally go and get fresh water for you."

"No, my taste for another try at a bath tonight has completely gone!"

"I rather thought you'd say that!" Emile answered, laughing at her. "So may I assist you out of your present garb, and into bed?"

"Yes, if you like, Emile," and she welcomed his embrace and more kisses.

"Do you remember the best birthday or Christmas present you ever got as a child?" he murmured in her ear.

"Uh hummm, yes...."

"Well, for me, taking your towel off you now, is just like that. So here goes with the wrappings," he said softly, as he loosened the towel, and drew his nude little wife into his arms.

"After all those spiders, you need a lot of comforting, and I can take charge of that," he murmured, turning the light way down, and pulling off his own clothes in a rush.

"From somewhere, I frankly don't know where, I have just gotten a whole new rush of energy.... Enough to take care of you," Emile said, as he began with kisses.

The next morning, as soon as the overseer had everyone at their assigned jobs, they lifted the still-bound Hetty into a wagon, and she left Marengo for good, headed for a very unpromising future.

Mammy stood on the front steps of the Big House, her arms akimbo, her face dark with a ferocious scowl, and that was the last face that Hetty saw, before the wagon disappeared through the shadows of the oak alley.

"Good riddance!" Mammy muttered. " She nearly took de life of my darlin' little Missus.... Dat Hetty dun belong te de debil hisself, an' soon he probly gonna haf her back, in dat burnin' place a hiz! An' dat's 'xactly where she belongs, dat little witch!"

*　　　　　　　　　*　　　　　　　　　*

When the bans had been read for the required three Sundays, it was time for a wedding. Although originally both Nana and Armand had wanted to have it at the St. Louis Cathedral, where Nana and her mother had always gone, and they wanted kindly old Père Antoine to perform the ceremony; they discovered that the Cathedral was booked so far in advance that they might have to wait as long as a year, and they also learned that Père Antoine was not well enough to celebrate a wedding, restricted by his poor health to saying his required priestly Masses in his own bed. So, instead, the wedding would be at Armand's family church, St. Augustine, one of the oldest churches in America attended by free Creoles of color, French Creoles, and even slaves.

Neither Nana nor Armand wanted a big wedding, so only their closest friends were invited, Armand's musician friends, Nana's special girlfriends, and the extended families on both sides. The musicians insisted that they should play for the wedding, and they augmented their group with one more member, who would play the church organ.

Nana's mother would, of course, make her daughter's wedding apparel, and a little peach-colored dress for her granddaughter, who would be flower girl.

One day while Armand and Nana were out, Emile came for a short visit with Nanette. When he came in, he found Madame de Lis working on a beautiful, ivory satin dress, and immediately he knew.... Madame de Lis looked up, trying to gauge how he was reacting, and his sad expression made her feel genuinely sorry for him. Perhaps he would always love her daughter, she thought.

"I won't attend the wedding, but if there's anything I can do, anything I can help with, please let me know," he said, and she saw his dark eyes were full of sadness.

"Well, matter a fact, dere is one thing. Creole libres like us, we not supposed te ride around in carriages forh hire, an' a course, we ain't got one,..." she began.

"Is it for this Sunday, that the carriage is needed?" he asked.

"Yeah, forh three o'clock, afta alla de Masses are done."

"I'll send Washington in, to be here in plenty of time, and he will wait to bring them back from the church," Emile said, standing just inside the doorway. "Is there anything else I can help out with? How about some food to be delivered here for a reception afterwards? How many should I tell Antoine's to plan for?"

"I guess about thirty-five."

"And for about four o'clock?"

"Yes, dat's mighty generous a yuh, Sir. Thank you." Mama de Lis said, as he started out the door. She shook her head, wondering whether and exactly how she would tell Nana about this.

When Sunday came, it was a dazzling day, just fit for a wedding. Fall had brought with it a breeze with a little coolness to it, and long, feathery white clouds were moving, like schooners with great white sails, across a deep blue sky.

Mama de Lis helped her daughter into her ivory wedding dress, then set little rosebuds into her hair, and pinned on the veil. Both of them looked into the long, oval mirror, and smiled at each other, although both of them were having a difficult time holding back the tears which brimmed in their eyes,... tears,... but for different reasons.

"Dis hieh iz de happiest day of ma life, seein' my beloved chile in her weddin' dress, an' gettin' married te such a good, kind man,... a man of her own kind, a man who be wid her, an' love her day an' night,..." Mama de Lis said, taking the back of one plump, brown hand to wipe the tears from her eyes.

Nana looked at her mother, and her eyes were also brimming with tears.

"I guess this is the right thing I'm doing, Mama.... It's what Armand wants, and I do love him. And it will be good for Nanette too, but I can't help feeling pain for Emile. He is so good, so generous.... I've loved him so long, and I guess part of my heart will always belong to him.... I think I am doing the right thing, marrying Armand, but still it will be hard for me to make those vows, and then to ride home in Emile's carriage...."

"Yuh mustna think bout dat, baby. Yuh doin' raight, an' life be betteh forh yuh, forh Armand, an' forh our little Nanette too. Jus' as yuh needs a full-time husband, she needs a full-time papa, yuh know."

For a last few moments mother and daughter stood looking at each other in the mirror. Nana swallowed hard, unable to speak, and just nodded to her mother. Then, with a sigh, she picked up her skirt, and with Mama holding up the train of her dress, they slowly went down the stairs. There Nanette waited for them, jumping from one foot to the other in excitement, her hair up for the first time and decorated with little rosebuds, and wearing her new, little peach-colored dress -

her first long dress, and her first long, lacy petticoat. She wore white silk stockings - her first stockings, and little white shoes with straps that buttoned. She was even allowed to wear some tiny pearl earrings in her newly pierced ears.

"I thought I tole you to jus' sit dere, quiet-like, in dat chair!" Mama de Lis said brusquely to her granddaughter.

"Yuh did, Gran'mama. Yuh did say dat, an' I heared yuh, but I got jus' plain too excited te stay dere in de chair. I jus' hada jump up an' down, but dat's all!" Nanette said quickly, continuing to jump around, until her grandmother took her by the hand, and led her out of the house.

The carriage waited just outside, and soon Nana was settled in it, and her mother and Nanette. Washington clicked to the horses, and they were off. At the church, everyone was gathered in the front rows, and Armand waited in the front aisle of the nave, with his friend Marcel, his best man. The orchestra valiantly struck up with a wedding march. First, smiling brightly, and very energetically scattering rose petals from a little basket on her arm, came Nanette, all but skipping down the aisle. Armand had to smile. Just as Nanette reached the first row of pews, her Grandmama's strong arm shot out and captured her, pulling her into the pew with her, before she could head off into any sort of mischief. Then came his Nana, an ivory vision, caught in a long shaft of golden sunlight, her gown glimmering, her bouquet of ivory lilies cascading down into the sun's rays, her dark hair piled up, with only a few long strands curling by her cheeks, her face a soft, luminous vision under the wedding veil. She came closer, and only then did Armand realize that he had been holding his breath. Finally this was really happening, he thought, as he allowed himself a deep breath. He could see Nana's dark eyes were focused directly on him, as she held the arm of her mother's brother, Ambrose, who escorted her, and who would give her away.

Armand gave her a smile full of love and encouragement, and soon her hand was in his, their fingers firmly interlocked, and the priest was before them, leading them through their vows. Marcel handed over the little gold ring to be blessed, and then the priest handed it to Armand, and he put it on Nana's finger. As he pushed it into place, his eyes met hers, and he was overcome with joy. The dream he had cherished for so long, was at last coming true. Gently he lifted her veil, and gave her a tender kiss, the first kiss of their married life. Then he took her hand, and proudly escorted her down the aisle. As they exited the church, he took a deep breath, filling his lungs with fresh air. Gently he pulled Nana to one side of the door, where they waited to greet all their friends and family.

"You are my beloved wife now, Nana, and I will love and protect you as long as I live," Armand said softly, and tenderly he kissed her on the cheek. She turned to him, and gave him a look of love.

"This must be right, because I do love you, and I know you love me, and my little Nanette," she replied, and then they were surrounded by well-wishers, all congratulating them and wishing them happiness and good luck.

The priest came out last, and putting a hand on Nanette's little head, he gave her a special blessing, and for that she was able to stand still, and just smile sweetly.

Madame de Lis, who then managed to corral Nanette in her arms, set her in the carriage, and with Marcel's help, made her own way up into the carriage. Then Armand helped his bride in, carefully arranging her voluminous skirt, and then fitting himself in around the stiff ivory folds.

For just a moment, he saw sadness in Nana's eyes. He knew the loan of the carriage was making her remember Emile. He thought it wise to say nothing; instead he simply leaned to her, and kissed her on the cheek. She turned into his kiss, their lips met, and his arms went around her. The road surface was uneven, and it made for an interesting kiss. Armand and Nana both burst out laughing, and Nanette joined in.

"You're funny, Papa Armand! Please don't break mama's teeth jus' tryin' te kiss her!"

"That's the first bumpy kiss I've ever had, but to protect our teeth, I guess we'll have to wait till later for any more!" Armand responded, chuckling.

At last he had banished that sad look from Nana's eyes, and made her smile.

At the house, they noticed that a great spread of hors d'oevres covered the dining room table, with more boxes still unopened in the kitchen. Two uniformed waiters were there, busily opening champagne bottles. They handed the first two glasses to Armand and Nana.

"To you, ma chère, with hopes that I can make you very happy, and very secure," Armand said softly, touching his glass to hers before they took their first sips.

Nanette and her grandmère burst into the house, followed by the rest of their guests.

"What's dat stuff yuh're drinkin' an' kin I have some too?" Nanette asked, jumping up and down in front of Armand and her mother.

"It's a grown-up drink, but you can have just a taste from my glass," Nana said, bending down and holding the glass for her daughter.

"Ouuh! Dat's too sour!" Nanette said, making a wry face. "An' it went up my nose too!"

The guests laughed at Nanette's reaction to the champagne, but were happy to accept their own glasses of it.

"Well I won't turn down a glass of that sour stuff," Marcel said, taking a glass of champagne in one hand, and slapping Armand on the back with the other. Gustily he kissed Nana on both cheeks, then shouted over the noise of conversation,

"Congratulations to our good friends, Nana and Armand, an' may they have many years of happiness!"

"Yes, many years!" Everyone agreed and drank to that.

Grandmère hurriedly fixed a plate of little sandwich bites and petit fours for Nanette, which easily distracted her from the ugly champagne, and after the orchestra members had downed some champagne and sampled the hors d'oeuvres, they took out their instruments and tuned up. Marcel tapped his bow on his music stand to get everyone's attention.

"This is the first waltz, and we want our newlyweds to begin the dancing," he announced, and smiling at each other, the bride and groom began to dance. Soon other couples joined them.

Grandmère led a sleepy Nanette off to bed, and gradually the rest of the guests began to say their goodnights, and drift off into the moonlight. Finally the newlyweds were alone. Nana collapsed on a sofa, kicking off her slippers, and Armand took off his jacket, and joined her.

"You know, I have a confession I need to make to you now," he began very soberly.

Nana gave him a puzzled look, and kissed him on the cheek. "And what is that?" she asked. "Surely you don't have to go play in the French Opéra Orchestra tonight?" she exclaimed, smiling. "I certainly hope you got someone to take your place for tonight!"

Momentarily she got a laugh from him, but soon his sober look returned.

"No, nothing like that, but it is an important confession.... Nana, you need to know, what happens next is all new to me. You'll have to be patient with me. I have waited for marriage...."

"That's beautiful, Armand," she said softly. "I will show you how to love, if you will let me...."

"Yes, please. That's what I need, Nana."

"So, are you ready for your first lesson in love and marriage?" she asked.

"Yes, I am full of love for you, Nana, but completely unsure of how to express it, and to bring you love, but that's just what I want to do, so, chérie, help me.... Show me what to do," and he stood before her, holding out his hand.

Nana got up from the sofa, slipping her shoes back on, and taking his hand she led him upstairs.

"The first thing you need to know, and I think you already know this; I won't be able to get out of this gown, unless you undo the buttons down the back," she said, sitting down on the edge of the bed, and kicking off her slippers again. She looked back up at him, teasingly, "So that's your first task,... and a good place to begin!" she said.

"But before that, there's something I need," he replied, and he knelt down in front of Nana, and drawing her face down to him with both his hands, he kissed her. She responded, pressing her tongue against his lips until he opened them, and let her explore his mouth. He came up gasping.

"Now I guess I'm ready to face all those buttons," he exclaimed with a smile of appreciation for the kiss, and he sat down behind her, so he could reach the buttons down the back of her gown.

"Mon Dieu, there's such a long parade of them!" he exclaimed, kissing the nape of her neck. Then slowly he unbuttoned, kissing her back as he proceeded lower and lower. Finally all the buttons were undone, all the way down to her hips.

He lifted the gown loosely forward, dropping it down to her waist in front. His fingers loosened her chemise, and slipped open the buttons at the waist of her petticoats. Then he came around, and sat down in front of her.

"You are so beautiful," he said softly, his fingers gently touching her on her breasts.

Her fingers undid his shirt buttons and drew his shirt from him. His eyes closed as he felt her caress his chest. She stood up, and all her clothing slipped to the floor, except her white silk stockings.

"Yes, Armand, you are doing very well," Nana said softly, looking at him, and giving him a sultry smile, as she stood before him.

For a moment he just admired her, standing there, just looking at him, and with nothing on but her silk stockings, held up with rosebud ornamented garters. He stood up beside her, and folded her into his arms, overwhelmed by the feeling of her soft skin against him, her breasts pressing into his chest. Then he took off the rest of his own clothing, helped by her fingers at his waist, loosening his trousers. He took her by the hand, and led her to the opened bed. She lay down there and silently waited for him, her dark eyes full of love.

He took off her stockings, and kissed her feet and her ankles. She reached up for him, and drew him down on her.

"I'm not too heavy for you?" he asked softly.

"No, it feels wonderful," she responded. "But now, do you want my help?"

"Yes, darling, please...."

"You have done perfectly so far," she said, smiling up at him. "Now might be a good time for me to remind you that women need much more touching, much more caressing, much more kissing,..." and before she could say anything else, his mouth was on hers, and his tongue exploring.

"Kissing where?" he asked, raising up a little and looking at her.

"Anywhere,... everywhere," she whispered, closing her eyes as he
· began to follow her advice. "Oh, yes, Armand,... like that, just like that,"

she murmured as he kissed her breasts, and his fingers tenderly explored her hips, and her thighs, with kisses following.

"Oh, this is wonderful, you are so beautiful,..." he said, as his hands worked up her thighs, and curved around her buttocks. His fingers found the curls between her thighs, and hesitated there, softly fingering.

"Yes," she encouraged him, "yes, please...."

She knew he was fully aroused, from the feel of his body pressing close.

"Will I hurt you?" he asked softly.

"No, but let me help you now," she said, and suddenly her arms were around his hips, and she slid on top of him, driving him into her, and initiating a movement he was impelled to follow. He felt her close around him, and the warmth and moistness he encountered, caused a wave of emotion to form in him, rising high and still higher into a crest of intense pleasure, until suddenly she held him absolutely still, and the wave began to break over them both in a giant tide of feeling. She moaned as his fingers gently reached up and caressed her breasts. She began to move again, and his body responded, and together they rode a tide of passion to its peak, both of them crying out as they clung together on the crest of the wave, riding it until its last, soft ebbing. As their bodies relaxed together, he was unable to speak, only to tenderly press a kiss on her ear lobe.

"Oh mon Dieu. Thank you, ma chérie," he finally whispered. "You've brought me to the greatest pleasure I have ever known, and to think, we have only just begun, we have a whole life of love ahead...."

The next morning, Nana awoke to find Armand already awake, his hand at her waist, his eyes open, full of love and tenderness as he looked at her.

"How wonderful,... to wake up and find you here beside me," he said softly, his fingers stroking her waist and down along her hips. She realized from a quick glance at the firming of his jaw, the passion suddenly visible in his eyes, that he wanted her, and that this time he was ready to take command, and she let him. She turned over on her back, and waited to see what he would do. His hands and lips worked over her body without hurrying, just tasting and arousing. With the pressure of her fingers, she guided him, tightening her grip on his shoulders to let him know when she was ready. And then suddenly he was on top of her. His eyes checked hers, and evidently he understood what her fingers and eyes were telling him, and this time he initiated their action, thrusting and withdrawing, until they were both experiencing an agony of pleasure. This time there was no doubt who was in command, as he drove into her again and again, until she murmured,

"Oh, please, now, Armand, please," and together they trembled on the very edge of the world, until suddenly it was as if they rode out together into a path of stars, meteors flaring all around them, and finally they drifted back,... gradually,... down to earth.

Later, after they slept a while together, she looked over and saw he was awake.

"See, it didn't take you long to learn, now did it?" she said, smiling at him.

"Was it good for you, ma chère?" he asked. "I am such a beginner, I have to ask.... Surely it was,... but you must tell me the truth, and help me learn what's best for you."

"Oh, yes, Armand, it was very, very good," she said, leaning over and planting a kiss on his shoulder.

"And to think that once, when I was an altar boy, I thought of becoming a priest!" he murmured, and a satiated smile curved on his lips. "Now there is no hope at all of a celibate existence! That ended last night! God will simply have to settle on letting me be a married man, married to you, my Nana....

"From yesterday to today, I have learned what love really can be. Thank you, chérie, for being so patient and helping teach such a beginner. I can't tell you how afraid I was, of not being able to please you, to love you as I wanted to. You have given me the confidence to love you.

"But starting today, I have another role to learn also, how to be a father to Nanette, and later, to the child within you," he said, his palm smoothing down softly on the firm, little paunch she was developing. "Somehow I think the role of father might be easier to learn, and if I make mistakes, they can be corrected through experience. Loving children is, after all, not nearly as complicated as loving an adult, this wonderful woman who is my bride...."

Every night and every day Armand worked on mastering the two new roles of his life, learning quickly, and being helped by Nana's gentle suggestions. Although he still had to be gone some nights, when he played in the orchestra of the French Opéra House, and for the Quadroon Balls, there were no longer absences than those, and for Nana, that seemed to make all the difference. She no longer waited for a lover who often couldn't be with her for weeks, and Nanette, although still remembering her other Papa Emile, was happy to have Papa Armand around to hug and kiss her, and play with her everyday.

For Emile this was a difficult time. He consciously made an effort to stay away from the little house on Felicity Street. Occasionally he sent Washington in with money, and the carriage, in case it was needed for running errands, and sometimes he provided tickets to special performances, or sent dinners from Antoine's to the house. And he never failed to send money for anything needed for Nanette.

He stayed away, and wondered which he would find harder, staying away for long stretches of time, or going, and seeing Nana in her new relationship. He wanted desperately to know if she was happy, and in his heart, he sadly realized that it must be true. He would always miss her, and he knew he would always love her. And without her, there was a great empty place in his heart, a place which seemed to ache with a terrible hunger he could not satisfy.

His relationship with Marie Therese had continued to develop. She was much happier since his frequent overnight visits to the city seemed to have come to an end. He had explained why, but she realized that the less said about things, the better. Sometimes when they were together, she saw a sad look in his eyes, and she knew he still remembered, he still hurt. How long would it take for that sadness and pain to go away, she wondered, and she did all she could, to try and provide love and caring. She knew he hadn't been to see Nana for nearly four months, and she knew that soon he would feel it was time to visit his little daughter. How would that go, she wondered. Would he be able to enter that house as a father and just a friend? Marie Therese hoped that with the coming of their own next child in a month, he would be able to satisfy some of his need to be a father - at Marengo, although she knew he would not forsake his little daughter in the city, nor did she want him to.

One morning as they sat having breakfast together, Mammy having already come to release Pierre from his highchair, and take him out for a walk while it was still a pleasant, cool morning, Emile finished up, and settled in to read the paper, as he sipped the last of his coffee. A page or two into the paper, he suddenly exclaimed,

"Oh, mon Dieu!"

"What is it, Emile? Was there a sudden drop in the price of sugar?" Marie Therese asked.

"No, not that, but there was a dreadful fire at the cigar factory in the city, the walls collapsed in, and a lot of people were injured and killed. I must go to the city today."

"I'm sorry to hear of the deaths and injuries, but how does that relate to us?" Marie Therese asked.

"Armand worked there in the daytime. You remember, don't you, he had that little orchestra, and he married Nana de Lis some months ago?"

Immediately she knew what was at stake.

Emile threw the newspaper aside, and hurriedly drank the last of his coffee.

"I must leave immediately," he said, and within less than a quarter of an hour, the carriage was waiting at the front door.

"We have to hurry, Washington, to the little house on Felicity," Emile said.

"Somet'in' wrong dere?" Washington asked anxiously.

"I won't know until we get there," Emile replied as he vaulted into the carriage.

Again Marie Therese found herself standing by the window, and watching her husband leave, as she had done so many times before. Her heart was heavy. What would this event mean? In Nana's life, in her own life, and in Emile's life? She took her rosary out of her pocket, and resolved to pray for all of them.

Washington lost no time, and when they pulled up before the little house on Felicity Street, Emile jumped out before the carriage had stopped moving.

He knocked at the door, and was let in by Madame de Lis. He noticed that the curtains were all still drawn closed, and things seemed out of place, dishes on the table with the remains of a meal still on them.

"What has happened? I saw from the paper that there was a fire at the cigar factory. Is Armand all right?" Emile asked.

"Don't 'xactly know if he be all raight. He be in de hospital, an' Nana be dere wid 'em. He got out all raight, but den he saw hiz friend Marcel waz still missin' so he dashes back into de factory te git Marcel. He finds 'em, but as he's draggin' Marcel out, some walls come down, an' alotta dem people inside, dey be burned pretty bad, an' some eben died, raight den an' dere."

"He's in Charity Hospital?"

Madame de Lis nodded. "Don't know if he gonna make it, or not,..." she said sadly.

"I'm going to the hospital to see if there's anything I can do," Emile said, and hurried out to the carriage.

"Take me to Charity Hospital," he ordered Washington.

As he strode into the hospital, Emile couldn't help remembering how, years ago, he and his friend John had brought Nana to the same hospital, also from a fire. He had carried that beautiful young woman out of the fire in his arms, and from that moment on, his life had never been the same....

Quickly he found out the room where Armand was, and he hurried upstairs, and down the long hall. He looked in the room, and immediately his eyes and those of Nana met. Hers, he saw, were full of worry, and she looked exhausted.

He went to stand behind her, and looked down at Armand.

"How is he?" he asked.

"He's still unconscious, and he has some bad burns, especially on his hands and chest. And you know how important his hands are, as a musician,..." Nana responded sadly.

"What have they done for him so far?"

"Tried to get some broth and water into him, and given him laudanum for pain. He talks sometimes, but I can't understand most of what he says, or tell whether it makes much sense. I just wish he would open his eyes, and look at me. He hasn't opened them since they found him, unconscious, and with Marcel, also unconscious, right beside him."

"The fire was yesterday morning?" Emile asked.

"Yes. His friend, André Boisblanc came to tell me. He escaped the fire, and ran to tell me, and then Marcel's family. I came here right away, and have stayed with him ever since they put him in this room. Marcel is right next door, and he is badly hurt too, and like Armand, it's his hands.... I don't know if either of them will ever play in an orchestra again,... and that would be a terrible blow."

"Well, before we worry about that, let's pray they both live through this. Let me go and talk to the doctors, and see what they can tell us," Emile said, and difficult as it was to touch her, he put his hand down on Nana's shoulder, to try to comfort and steady her. Her hand rose to meet his, and he trembled at her touch, and realized how vulnerable he still was. Nothing had changed. He was still as deeply in love with her as ever....

"Thank you, Emile for coming to help," Nana said, as he moved away and hurried out the door. The last thing he saw was her beautiful face wet with tears, her hand resting on the sheet, below which Armand's chest was still moving, as he breathed.

Emile found one of the doctors and asked about both Armand and Marcel.

"It's difficult to tell their condition. Both have been unconscious ever since they arrived here early yesterday morning. We don't know how much smoke they inhaled, and that's a key question. Their burns will heal, but I understand both of them are musicians, so again, it's hard to say if their fingers and hands will heal enough to let them continue as musicians. Did I hear rightly, both of them played stringed instruments?"

"Yes, that's right, Marcel played the cello, and Armand played the violin, and also conducted. How long do you think it might be before we will know if they will revive?"

"Sometimes unconsciousness can last quite a while, even weeks, or more. Sometimes even years. Of course, the longer they are in such a state, the less hope there is for their recovery. We know so little about the brain...."

"Well, thank you, doctor, even if that wasn't very encouraging. I am a friend of both men, and if there is anything I can do, any funds I can supply for medicines or treatment, please let me know." Emile scribbled his name on a piece of paper, and also gave the name and address of his factor.

"Although I live outside the city, if you contact our plantation's factor, he will get any messages to me. Please call on me for anything I can do, or any funds I can provide. Treat them, and don't spare any expense. I promise to cover all of it for both men."

"Thank you, Monsieur. I will keep in touch with you in any event. These men will, I hope, be able to give you their thanks themselves one day soon," the doctor said, tucking Emile's note in the pocket of his white coat.

Emile returned to Armand's room.

"So what did you find out?" Nana asked anxiously, and the pain in her beautiful dark eyes resounded all through him. He stood at a distance, hoping that would help, but he yearned to even just put his hand in hers,...just to touch her.

"Only that there is hope. The sooner they snap out of unconsciousness, the better the situation will be. The doctor thinks the burns will heal, what they don't know is how much smoke they inhaled. You may remember from long ago, when that was true for you...."

Emile summoned up his courage as he spoke to her.

"But now we need to look after you, Nana. I'm sure you have been here since yesterday morning sometime, and probably not eaten. I have Washington outside, with the carriage, waiting to take you home to eat and rest. I will stay here with Armand, and I hope you will go and let your mother fix you something to eat, and then you should lie down and rest for a few hours. And also drink some fluids. Have you had any water, tea, or soup since you've been here?"

"Just one glass of water, when the nurse came to try and get some into Armand, she made me drink a glass."

"That's not enough. Now I promise I will stay right here with Armand, if you promise to go home for a bit. If there is any change in his condition, I will send for you right away. I know he'd much rather open his eyes and see you, but he will also understand when I tell him I sent you home to eat and rest. He may well be aware you have been here with him. He'll understand. Anyhow, I will take the blame for sending you away for a while, so go,... go right now." Emile smiled as he helped her to her feet, and gently pushed her out of the room. He watched as she went down the hall. Twice she turned, and hesitated, as if she was about to return, but when she saw him watching her, she smiled slightly, and continued on. Emile breathed a sigh of relief. She had to be at least in the eighth month of her pregnancy, and this whole experience so emotionally exhausting for her.... He worried, as he watched her round the corner to the stairs. She was as beautiful as ever, he thought, and sighed softly. And would he ever get over the pain of their separation, he wondered.

He returned to sit beside Armand. He studied his breathing, and watched the beat of his pulse in his neck. He seemed to be breathing normally. Perhaps he could hear if I talk to him, Emile thought. Would that help to bring him around?

"Armand, it's Emile here beside you. Nana has been here all the time, but I sent her home to get some rest and food. I will be here until she returns...."

A flicker of a change of expression seemed to pass over Armand's face. Emile decided to try talking some more, perhaps talking to him every few hours.... He kept an eye on his watch, and when an hour had passed, he began to talk again, saying about the same thing he had said before. Again he thought Armand's expression changed momentarily, but that was all. Still Emile found even that encouraging, and he resolved to try again in another hour or two.

A nurse came in, and checked Armand's pulse and heartbeat. "He's still with us," she said. "It's important to get some fluids into him if we can. I will try a little, and then if he swallows that, perhaps you could give him a little more. Not too much at one time though, we don't want him to choke." She smiled at Emile, and dribbled a little water from a cup into the side of Armand's mouth. He swallowed.

"That's good!" the nurse encouraged him. "Monsieur Armand, we want you to take some water, and when you can swallow the water, then we will give you some broth."

To Emile she said, "That's the first time I've seen him swallow any water. Will you keep trying to give him some from time to time? I will bring some broth in a little while. Maybe we can get a little nourishment into him, if he will swallow the broth.

"Did his wife leave? Poor thing has been here with him ever since he arrived, and as far along as her pregnancy is, this hasn't been easy on her."

"No, it hasn't. I'm a friend of theirs, and I sent her home in my carriage, with the instructions to eat and get some rest. I promised I'd stay here until she comes back."

After the nurse left, Emile tried a little more water at the corner of Armand's mouth, and again he swallowed.

"Good, Armand. We are trying to get some water into you, and then later some broth, now that you seem to be swallowing. Keep it up! This is Emile talking to you. Nana has been here with you for so long, I made her go home for food and a rest. She will be back in a little while." Emile knew what just might reach his friend, but it would be difficult for him to say it. Finally he gritted his teeth momentarily, and then he spoke, carefully trying to curb his own emotion.

"So how does marriage agree with you? Marriage to Nana...."

There had been a little flicker of an expression when Emile had earlier mentioned Nana's name, but when Emile mentioned marriage, and repeated Nana's name, he was astonished to see Armand's eyes open.

"Hey, man, that's good. Now keep those eyes open. Do you know me?"

Armand looked at Emile for a while, then he spoke haltingly,

"Yes, Emile,... I know you... for a good man...."

"Thank you, Armand. Today I'd even accept curses from you, just keep those eyes open and in focus, and keep talking! Now I want to give you some more water." And with that Emile raised Armand's head a little, and held the cup of water up to his mouth.

This time Armand actually drank from the cup, finishing up all the water.

"I'm so thirsty," he said softly.

"Good! Let me holler down the hall for a nurse, and we'll get you more water, and something more nourishing, perhaps some broth," Emile said, and he went to the door, and beckoned for a nurse. The same nurse who had just left them, returned. She saw Armand's eyes were open, and she smiled.

"So, had enough sleep?" she teased him. "If you'll stay awake long enough for us to get some broth into you, then perhaps next time we feed you, you can ask for something more substantial."

"Steak?" Armand asked, with a slight smile.

"Yes, Sir, filet mignon, if you can stay alert for it!" came her reply. "Now excuse me while I get you some broth. We'll start with the easy stuff first!"

In a few minutes she was back, and began feeding Armand spoonfuls of broth. Emile saw a good chance, while the nurse was with Armand, of sending off a message to Nana telling her that things were improving, so he said,

"While you are here, nurse, I'd like to send a message to Armand's wife, to let her know that he is conscious again, and is taking some broth. I am going to suggest she stay at home and get some more rest before she comes back.... That things are under control here, and that I will stay until she returns."

The nurse nodded to Emile.

"Yes, I'm sure she will be glad to know of the change in her husband's condition, and I'll stay right here with him until you return."

So Emile hurried to the front lobby of the hospital, and hired a boy to take a message to the Felicity Street house. He bought a cup of coffee from a woman hawking coffee outside the hospital door, and then returned to Armand's room. Emile pulled up a chair and sat down beside Armand's bed. He leaned over closer, and said,

"I sent a message to let Nana know that you are alert, although I do hope she will stay at home and rest for a while. I assured her I will stay with you, until she returns."

Armand nodded, and after taking some broth which the nurse brought, and some drops of laudanum for his pain, he closed his eyes. Emile wasn't sure if he was sleeping, or unconscious again.

Six days passed, with Emile and Nana taking turns at Armand's bedside. Each day he was alert for longer and longer periods, and finally he was released to go home. His burns were healing, but his hands still had to be dressed with ointment, and wrapped up in bandages. Although Armand said nothing about it, both Nana and Emile saw him studying his bandaged hands, and they knew he must be wondering if he would ever be able to play his violin again. They brought him home in Emile's carriage, and at his request, settled him on a sofa downstairs for a while. Nana came from the kitchen with a bowl of her mother's gumbo, and fed it to him.

"That's the best food I've had since I left this house!" Armand told his mother-in-law with a smile. "You can bring me some more of that later!" And she did.

Twice a day Nana carefully unwound his bandages, gently applied ointment to each of his fingers, and covered them with fresh bandages. Gradually he began very carefully to try to move his fingers, to see what sort of dexterity might be coming back.

"It's the scar tissue," he grumbled, flexing his fingers slowly.

"That must still be painful,..." Nana said, watching anxiously.

A week after he helped bring Armand home from the hospital, Emile stopped at the office of his factor, Alex Montegut. After Creole embraces, and some talk about plantation business, Emile said,

"I have a proposition to make to you, Alex. There's a friend of mine, a fine man, a free Creole of color. He was injured in that recent fire in the cigar factory. The factory burned down, and he has no job now. He is also a fine musician, but there is some concern that the burns he suffered on his hands, when he went back into the building to help rescue a friend, may keep him from ever playing his violin again. I want to help him get back on his feet, and to do so without his knowledge, so I am proposing that you hire him as an assistant, and I will set up a fund with you to pay his salary. He will have a job, and you will have an assistant at no cost to you. My conditions are that I don't want him to know about our financial agreement, or feel beholden to me. No one must learn about our agreement. Is that clear?"

"Yes, Emile, that's very generous of you, and there is no way I can possibly refuse. When can he start?"

"Thanks, Alex. I hoped you'd find that an offer you just couldn't pass up!" Emile said, smiling and slapping Alex on the shoulder. "I'll let you know exactly when he can start work, probably sometime this next week. And remember, there is to be no word about my role in all this...."

After leaving his factor's office, Emile stopped by the house on Felicity Street. Madame de Lis let him in. He sat down, and watched as Armand worked his fingers. Sitting on the piano bench, he stretched to see if he could reach an octave, but made a wry face when he reached as far as he could, over the keys, and was still short of an octave.

"I used to be able to reach that easily," he muttered sadly to himself, then he turned, and saw Emile had come in and was watching him.

"Oh, Emile, I didn't even hear you come in. Comment ça va?" Armand said, getting up to greet him, then motioning him to again sit down.

"Bien, merci, et vous?"

"Fine, but a little discouraged. I was hoping that by now my fingers would have loosened up more, and I could begin to play the piano and my violin again. Progress is very slow."

Armand turned around on the piano bench, and faced Emile. His expression was sad, and he continued to flex his fingers slightly.

"Well, at least you don't have those bandages any more, so your hands must be getting better," Emile said, trying to be encouraging.

"You know, Armand, you may have to find something else to do, since making cigars may be too difficult for your hands at first. I was talking to my factor this morning, and he mentioned that he was looking for someone he could train as an assistant. I told him about you, and he is willing to take you on. He will pay you better than the factory did, and he needs the help. It could be a permanent position for you, with good pay. In a week or so, you can start with him, if you are feeling up to it."

"That is good news. Thanks Emile. I do need to support all of us here," Armand said, his face lighting up.

"Yes, I stopped to see him about plantation business, and he complained about how difficult it has been to find a competent assistant, so I mentioned you to Alex. He asked me to tell you to just come by his office when you are ready to start. Here, I brought you his business card, with his address on it. He suggested that perhaps for the first few days, you could work only half a day, but when you are stronger, he says he could use you five days a week, full-time. I didn't plan to stay for much of a visit, but while I'm here, I'll spend a few minutes with Nanette. I saw her out in the yard, so let me say my goodbyes for now, and I'll be stopping outside with my daughter. Is Nana feeling well, as well as can be expected at this stage?"

"She seems to need more rest these days, so I encouraged her to go upstairs and lie down for a while. Would you like me to call her?"

"No, just give her my best regards; don't wake her up, Armand. And let me know if there is anything I can do to help all of you."

"Emile, you have been more than generous. I learned that you picked up all my hospital and doctor bills and Marcel's also. We are both slowly recovering. Thank you for all your help."

Emile bowed slightly, and let himself out. Armand could hear Nanette's happy greeting, and their voices for a while, then he heard the wheels of the carriage, as Emile left.

Gradually, as Armand continued to improve, Emile was able to reduce the number of his visits to one every two weeks. He was carefully keeping an eye on Marie Therese who was expecting their next child at any time, and on Nana, who was expecting also in the very near future. In the early days after Armand's accident, Emile had watched over Nana especially carefully, seeing that she went home from the hospital for rest and food regularly each day, and remaining with Armand during her absences. He knew that if he didn't promise to stay with Armand, she wouldn't leave the hospital.

At Marengo, Marie Therese at first worried that Armand might not live, and that Emile would then return to his relationship with Nana, and she begged Emile to keep her informed about Armand's progress. Emile did not, however, mention Nana's pregnancy to her. Again, he was finding it strange that his women were both expecting at almost the same time.

     *   *   *

One morning Emile got up in a hurry, and was preparing to leave for the city, when Marie Therese said,

"From the way I felt during the night, and how I feel now, I think we may have a new little de Marigny today or tonight."

Emile, searching out his clothes for the day, and beginning to dress, stopped in the middle of buttoning his shirt, and went over to sit down next to his wife on their bed.

"Do you really think so?" he asked, and when she nodded, he added,

"I was planning to go to the city, and check on Armand, but now I think I'd better stay here today, with you. Shall I call Mammy to you?" he asked, as Marie Therese slowly and deliberately finished buttoning up his shirt for him.

"Yes, after she has given Pierre his breakfast, perhaps she could come. The pains began during the night, but they are still fairly far apart, so nothing is likely to happen right away. And thank you, Emile, I would like it if you would stay with me today."

Privately Marie Therese thought how hurt she would be if he left her alone, and went on to the city. She knew it would be difficult for her to forgive him, if he spent the day with Nana in the city, while she was suffering through the birth of their child.

He nodded, and slipped into his boots. "I'll stay home today, and right now I'll go let Mammy know," he said, "and I'll bring you up some coffee. Shall I bring toast, eggs, anything else for you?"

"Perhaps a muffin or toast with marmalade, and coffee,... that's all I want...."

A short while later, Mammy stuck her face around the door.

"I'm puttin' Annie in charge of Pierre today, so I kin come an' be wid yuh, sugah. Soon as I git Annie, an' tell her wha' needs te be done wid our little boy, I be back directly."

Emile stayed with Marie Therese, settling for just toast and coffee with her. He could see that her face was very flushed, and occasionally she would gasp as a pain hit her. Finally she simply put down the piece of toast she had started to eat, and pushed her breakfast tray away.

"This one seems to be in a hurry," she said, smiling faintly at Emile.

"That's good news," he replied. "I'd like to see you get through this misery as quickly as possible. I hate to see you suffer...."

Marie Therese groaned softly. "Please help me get up and walk around. I can't stay still any longer." So Emile helped her find her slippers, and lifted her out of bed and into his arms. "I wish I could just hold you, and make it better," he said. "It's times like these that make a man feel guilty...." He held her, and kissed her.

"Please put me down, Emile, I have to walk.... This is not a time when being held in anyone's arms helps! And why should you feel guilty?" She knew why, but she just wanted to hear him say it, especially now, with the pains coming faster and faster.

"Because I got to participate in the lovely event when we created this baby, but now you get all the misery and pain. It doesn't seem quite fair, does it? God should have arranged things a bit differently."

Marie Therese laughed, as she walked slowly about the room, holding onto her husband for dear life.

"I appreciate... your sentiments, Emile,... but I doubt... that God is going... to change things!" she said, breathing hard between words. Little beads of perspiration were breaking out on her forehead, and finally she stopped walking entirely. She held her breath, her hands flew to her stomach, and even through her cotton nightgown, Emile could see the force of a big contraction expand her abdomen further, and hold it taut.

"Shouldn't you get back in bed?" he asked anxiously, and when she silently nodded, her dark green eyes full of pain, he simply picked her up, and gently returned her to their bed.

Mammy bustled in, bringing an armful of towels, and a pitcher of hot water.

"Dere we be, an' it looks like we ain't gonna wait verra long forh dis one," she said, taking a look at Marie Therese's expression, and noticing how hard she was breathing.

"Let me git you morh comfortable, baby," she said, and her strong arms came around her little mistress, quickly padding the bed down under her mistress's body with a pile of towels, and then easing her back down.

Then Mammy stood up, and surveyed her mistress carefully.

"There we be. Now God, jus' let dat chile come raight along. We'z all ready," she said, and holding her mistress's little wrist in her own large hand, she took her pulse.

"Master Emile, you kin go now dat I'm hieh. I call you when it's time,…" Mammy said. Emile came up and soothed his wife with kisses on her forehead.

"Do you want me to stay right up here with you?" he asked softly.

"No, Emile, this could go on all day. You don't need to stay. Your part in all this is long over!" she said, giving him a slightly teasing look. But already as he hastened to the door, he noticed that the teasing look and smile had vanished, and a hard contraction gripped his little wife. He uttered a silent prayer that all would go well, and he made his escape from the room. He carried another cup of coffee into the family parlor, and settled down at the big desk, preparing to work on the account ledger for the plantation, but as he sipped his first swallow of coffee, he heard a piercing scream from upstairs.

"Oh, mon Dieu, don't let this last much longer," he prayed. Silence set in, and he began to flip the pages of the ledger, but he wasn't seeing anything before him, the neatly inked figures were making no sense. Another scream brought him to his feet, and he began to pace, his coffee cup in his hand, taking sips now and again, almost without realizing it. Another heart-rending scream, and then he heard Mammy give a joyful shout.

"Surely that's it," Emile said to himself, hoping and praying he was right, and a few minutes later Mammy called out to him from upstairs,

"Come on up, Massa Emile, an' see yuhr new son!" and he rushed up the stairs two at a time.

"At least this one was prompt," Marie Therese whispered. She lay back in the bed, her hair all tangled and wet with perspiration, her color paler than usual.

Mammy was washing up the baby, then wrapping him in a towel, she handed him over to his father.

"Least dis one hieh ain't born screamin' hiz head off, like Massa Pierre. Dis one, he be nice an' calm, an' he's got pink cheeks, not red all oveh like hiz big brodeh waz. Looks like hiz hair gonna be lighter too, maybe dis hieh be a blond boy," Mammy said, her big fingers smoothing down the baby's fine hair.

"Whatja picked out forh a name forh dis hieh boy?" she asked.

"May I present Philippe Louis de Marigny!" his father said, smiling broadly and holding his son high in the air. "And Sir Philippe, over there, that's your Mama, and you owe her a great debt of thanks for all she's been through in the last nine months, and especially today!"

Marie Therese had to laugh, Emile was being ridiculous, but she loved it when he was.

"Now dat little bugger needs te eat, so we get 'em started," Mammy said in a business-like tone, and she took the baby from Emile, and put him at Marie Therese's breast.

"Lawd's sake, he caught on mighty quick!" Mammy said with admiration. "None of hiz big brodeh's fussiness! An' afta he's full up, I take 'em forh a nap in de nursery, so hiz poorh motheh kin git some rest. I bet you ain't got much sleep last night," she said, looking over at Marie Therese, who nodded her agreement.

"Well, we gonna baby you a lot des comin' days," she promised, taking a cool, wet cloth, and gently wiping down her mistress's face.

When the baby had finished, and fallen asleep at the breast, Mammy took him away to the nursery, and Emile came and sat down on the bed next to his wife.

"I've been praying it would be quick this time, and I guess it was. Thank you, ma chérie, for another beautiful son. If my papa were here for this, he might even have managed a broad smile for the occasion! The future of our beloved Marengo seems to be well-secured now with an heir and a spare! Now perhaps we can afford to actually have a daughter! I would love to greet a baby daughter next time!"

Marie Therese rolled her eyes at him. "Don't even talk about a next time! I'd love a baby daughter too, but not for a while, Emile! Please, no orders for another baby just yet! And don't you already have a little daughter? That's what I heard...."

"Yes, I do, and she is delightful, but I surely would love another daughter, and I can assure you, you would love that too...."

He kissed her cheeks, her forehead, and finally her lips, and then he tiptoed out, leaving his little wife for a well-deserved rest.

*   *   *

Two weeks later Emile was finally able to make that overdue trip to the city.

When he arrived at the little house on Felicity Street, Madame de Lis opened the door for him.

"Armand's gone to work dis mornin' but Nana ain't feelin' too good, an' she stay'd up dere in de bed," Madame said.

"Do you think she would mind if I went upstairs to see her?" Emile asked.

"Dis waz yuhr house, dat bed waz yuhr bed, an' what's happenin' up dere, dat be yuhr business," Mama de Lis said rather abruptly and coolly.

Emile didn't waste any time, but hurried upstairs. He knew the baby was due any day, and he felt sure that was what was at stake,...their baby.

Nana lay limp in the bed, looking very small and fragile in the big bed.

Emile came to her side of the bed, and kissed her forehead, and then he knelt down beside the bed, and took her hand in his.

"Is this what I think it is?" he asked. "Is it just starting?"

"Yes, it's our baby, but it's not just starting. I've been having contractions ever since yesterday morning. I am so ready to have this over,..." she replied softly and plaintively. Then she let out a long moan.

"Shall I call your mother?" Emile asked, and got a quick nod in reply.

"Madame, your daughter wants you upstairs," he called down to Mama de Lis and in a few minutes he heard her slow, heavy footsteps on the stairs. She was carrying a pitcher of water, and an armload of towels.

"Shall I bring up some more water?" Emile asked, hoping he could somehow be helpful. Another baby about to be born, made him feel even more guilt, and anguish over the suffering of his two women.

"Yes, go heat some morh water on de stove, an' bring it up hieh," Mama de Lis ordered, and he was only too glad to have something useful to do, and something which would take him away from the suffering, from that face he loved, which was now showing so much pain. He hurried downstairs, and put some large pots of water on the stove to heat.

"Mama...!" He heard the painful cry, and it made him shiver.

More cries followed, and moans. The water was ready, but he wasn't really ready to return upstairs. He left the other pots on the stove, turned down low, and took the largest one, and slowly started up the stairs. When he started into the room, he saw Nana turning and twisting on the bed, and heard her cry out, "Oh, mon Dieu...." Her cry was followed by sobbing, and gasping for breath, and then a series of long, high screams.

"Please, God, let this be over!" he said, and after putting the pot of water down, he began pacing.

Another series of piercing, high screams, followed by sobs. Then it seemed as if Nana was gasping for breath, as if she might not even live to see their baby....

"Oh my God, you can't take her too," Emile whispered to himself, watching Nana grow pale and seem to fail before his very eyes.

"Honey chile, it's all raight, it be nearly oveh," her mother said, trying to calm her daughter. "Jus' a couple morh good pushes, an' den yuh kin rest."

And after another two long hours of misery, the child was born, covered in blood, and slithering into the world... dead. Madame took the baby into a towel, and moved away from the bed. Emile saw the look on her face, and knew the worst, but couldn't bring himself to say anything.

"Is it a boy or a girl? What's the matter?" Nana gasped, trying to pull herself up so she could see her baby. "Show me," she cried. "I need to see my baby!"

"It waz a boy, but Nana, ma chile, he's dead," Mama de Lis said sadly. "Born dead."

"Dead? No that can't be! Let me see, let me hold him," Nana begged.

Her mother came to her, and put the baby in her arms.

"Oh God, I am so sorry, Nana," Emile said, and he came over to the bed to console her.

"No, don't touch me!" she screamed, clutching the baby, and trying to move herself away from the edge of the bed. And then the tears began, and she cried until she was exhausted, and no more sobs would come.

Emile felt totally helpless, and in despair. He tried once more to go to her, and at least kiss her hand, but he saw a terrible anger flare up in her dark eyes, and he knew he could do nothing to help. She wouldn't let him near her, or near their dead son. She held the baby to her breast, and tried to make him nurse. "Here, my baby, this is what you need," she said softly, nudging his mouth to her nipple.

"He won't nurse, Mama. What can we do?" she cried out. Her mother went over to comfort her.

"Nana, ma baby, he iz dead. Leave 'em be now. Let me take 'em an' dress 'em forh hiz funeral." And she took the baby from her daughter, and silently began to dress him. There was not a sound, not a single baby's cry, and the little body moved loosely as Mama de Lis tried to dress it. The baby was limp and lifeless in her hands.

Emile turned to Madame de Lis, and quietly, sadly said,

"Call for me whenever you think I can be of help. I will go ahead and make all the arrangements for a coffin and a burial for late tomorrow, and if Nana is unable to handle it, I will take the body to be buried. I am so very sorry,..." and he looked once more at Nana, who quickly turned away from him and buried her face in her pillow.

"Oh, Nana, let me help and comfort you. I am so sorry this has happened," he said, and he watched for a sign, just any sign that she heard him, and wanted him to console her. Her face remained buried in the pillows, and there was no answer except her weeping, so he went down the stairs, and let himself out of the house. Her sobs followed him, and he cringed with sadness and guilt. Was their relationship, outside of the bonds of the church, the reason for the loss of both their sons? He couldn't believe that God would be so vengeful, but somehow he couldn't overcome his feelings of guilt. He had experienced great joy in their love. How could it be considered so sinful, and did they deserve such a terrible punishment?

To Washington he said, "We have to go for another coffin, and to arrange another burial. My son was born, but he is dead." And woodenly he shrugged his shoulders, and climbed in the carriage, tears flowing down his face. Again he had lost a son and gained a son at almost the same time. What was God trying to tell him, he wondered.

Was a plaçage relationship, even if it was based totally on love, such a sinful thing, and was this their punishment? Surely not. Why should innocents suffer, innocents born of our love? If he was to continue to believe in the existence of a loving God, he couldn't believe that. But then he remembered that the God of the early Israelites had been a God of Judgment, an awesome, autocratic God who gave out the Law on stone tablets, with no deviations allowed. And for sins against His Law, He delivered swift punishments... then. Was that still the Truth?

What kind of God was he to believe in, or was there simply no God at all, merely a universe set in motion, and continuing on its own, erratic way, with no meaning in any events,... accidents, births, deaths, wars? What could he believe in? He prayed for an answer, but none came. There was no answer at all,... only a sad and dreadful silence.

When he got back to Marengo, and went upstairs to see his wife, he found her nursing their baby son, and it was too awful a contrast. He slipped into an armchair, and let the tears fall. Marie Therese looked over at him, over the curly head of their newborn, and waited for his explanation.

"Nana gave birth today, but our son is dead. How can such a thing happen again? She is very angry at me, as if she thinks I am responsible for the sins which led to this. I wonder if she will ever forgive me? Perhaps she is right, and this is the punishment for the sin of plaçage...."

Emile stopped speaking, but the tears continued to trace their way down his cheeks.

Marie Therese said nothing, and let him continue to face his grief. Finally the tears stopped, and his dark eyes, full of sadness, briefly turned to her.

"I have made all the arrangements, ordered another little coffin, and arranged with a priest for the burial tomorrow afternoon," he said haltingly, and then he could say no more. "I must go and see it through," he finally added, his head turned away from her.

"I am so sorry, Emile, but as to blame, surely no one can be blamed for this. Sometimes we cannot know what causes such tragedies; we must just grieve and then accept them as simply being beyond our grasp. Right now the little one's death is too close, but perhaps someday you will be able to accept it, and know that you and Nana are not to blame."

He stayed in the chair, his head thrown back as if in total despair. Marie Therese longed to go and comfort him, but she knew he would have to suffer through this crisis alone. He might let her hold him, and console him, but there was little she could do or say that would help. Perhaps later, but not now....

       *   *   *

At least Nana was able to accept comforting from Armand. She didn't have to tell him anything when he arrived home that night from work. He came upstairs, and saw her holding the dead infant.

"Oh, mon Dieu, no," he said, and he came to her and held her in his arms, not saying anything more. Finally she let him take the baby away from her. He wrapped him in a little blanket, and placed him in the coffin which had been delivered earlier that afternoon.

"Emile has arranged burial for tomorrow afternoon," she said. "I don't think I can go, Armand. I can't bear it, another son taken so soon,... like Lucien. I do believe God is punishing me and Emile. We were never married. But how can God punish our little innocents? I could understand it better if He gave us both terrible, fatal illnesses, but to punish those little innocents?.... And I don't think I can face Emile over another little casket, at another child's burial...."

"I will go for you, chérie. You should stay here," Armand suggested, and she nodded her agreement, thankful for his willingness to help. He embraced her, and left her to rest, carrying the little coffin downstairs. He realized that the sight of it, would only mean more floods of tears. Could Nana be right, he wondered. Was plaçage such a serious sin in the eyes of God?

That next afternoon he saw Emile's carriage pull up, so he lifted up the little coffin, and bore it out. After it was safely stowed in the carriage, Armand climbed in. He put his arm on Emile's shoulder, and quietly said,

"I'm sorry, very sorry. I will come with you and help see this through. Nana is too distressed to come, and I promised her I would come in her place. She is still in bed, and running a high fever, and her emotions have overwhelmed her. She is convinced this death, like Lucien's, is because of her sins, and nothing we say, seems to have any influence on her."

Emile nodded, and finally spoke, his voice thick and heavy with sorrow.

"I saw her at the time of the birth. I just happened to come on that day, and I realized when our baby was born dead, that she saw it as punishment for sin, and that she came to believe that it was our plaçage relationship which had angered God. Our punishment, she feels, is the loss of both our sons. I can't see a loving God exacting that kind of vengeance, and perhaps someday, she will see things differently.

"I will continue to help out from a distance, but Armand, it is you alone who can help her through this. Call on me any time, for anything I can do to help, but I won't be coming to the house for quite a while, even though I want to see Nana very much, and to offer comfort, if she would only let me. I will always love her, but I know that my presence now is very hard for her to bear, so I will stay away. Perhaps you can tell me when things seem better, so I can see Nanette?"

"I will bring Nanette with me to your factor's office if you let me know when you will be in to see him. You need to be able to see your little daughter, and that, or meeting for a walk along the levée, might be best for a while. I'll see to it, and I know it will make our little girl happy, having those chances to be with you."

"Thank you, Armand. I know I can count on you to care for Nana, and our little girl. I will plan some visits with my factor, and send you word through him."

Together Emile and Armand carried the little coffin into the St. Louis Cemetery, and laid it in the tomb with the coffin of his little brother Lucien. The sight of the two small coffins was more than Emile could bear, his eyes overflowed, and Armand put a hand on his shoulder, as they listened to the priest read the last rites, and consign the second little brother to the tomb.

Even at Marengo, as he watched his two sons grow, the contrast was almost too much for Emile to bear. He said nothing about it, but his continued sadness was all the evidence Marie Therese needed to sense his suffering. She tried to be as loving and caring as she could, in her relationship with Emile, and to accept him as he was, and not to expect too much from him. He seemed to need to seal off all his emotions for a while, and she understood that. Recovery from the death of two children would take a long time; she would just have to be gentle with him, until he was able to smile again. She couldn't even imagine how it must feel to have suffered two such devastating losses, and she would look at her healthy, happy little sons, and wonder if she could have survived their loss, and would she still have been able to believe in God....

*   *   *

Armand's new job with Alexander Montegut, factor for Marengo and several other plantations, was going well. He liked the social side of the job, and was quickly learning the business side. He continued to flex his fingers daily, and made sure to spread the salve on them every day after work. He was a little afraid to try playing his violin yet, but he had confidence that someday he would be able to play again. He did finger out simple pieces on Nana's piano, once she was able to bear the sound of music again, and he would take Nanette out for a walk, or to the office some mornings with him, and Nana would agree, and wave them off. She must have understood the purpose of those excursions, since surely

Nanette must have told her that they met her other Papa, but Nana made no move to join them on their excursions, she did not inquire about them, nor did she ask for them to stop.

Occasionally, when Armand was alone with Madame de Lis, they would share their impressions. Neither of them had heard Nana speak of Emile since the burial of the baby. In fact, when Armand returned from the St. Louis Cemetery, she hadn't asked him about the burial, and he decided that anything he could share with her, should wait until she asked.

Armand's friend Marcel, for whom he had chanced his own life in going back into the burning factory to rescue him, had completely recovered, except for a few scars from his burns on his face and his arms. He was once again playing his cello, and when Armand felt that Nana was finally able to enjoy music again, he encouraged his friends to come to their house for more musical evenings as they had done in the past. He would participate a little, by joining Nana on the piano bench, and adding in chords and minor embellishments in a second, improvised, simple piano part. Sometimes he would even try to tease Nana by tapping out notes inside of her fast-moving hands. This usually ended up discordantly, but at least with laughter. Gradually she was beginning to revive emotionally, and as she did, she also craved his love, and embarked on a new round of teaching him more about physical love.

Armand felt some hesitancy when Nana initiated love-making. He was fearful of what another pregnancy might mean, particularly if it brought a child who would only have to join its half-brothers in the marble tomb at the St. Louis Cemetery. He wondered if it wouldn't be better if he and Nana had no children, and if she should go and see Marie Laveau, and procure one of the voodoo queen's special concoctions which was supposed to prevent conception. He never mentioned such thoughts to Nana though, fearing that even the mention of such an idea might set back the recovery he saw occurring in her.

For Emile, it was difficult not to visit the little house on Felicity Street. He enjoyed the regular, weekly visits with Nanette, that Armand made possible, and he chose not to ask if Nana knew about them. He threw himself into longer and longer days of work at Marengo, keeping the ledgers himself, ordering supplies, personally overseeing the work in the fields and in the sugar house, and going for long rides alone, or with his overseer.

Marie Therese, accompanied by Mammy, had resumed her visits to the quarters. She brought layettes to the new mothers, and checked on their health, and the health of their babies. She stopped in at the nursery at least every week, and regularly checked on the quantity and variety of the meals in the communal kitchen. She and Emile also set aside hours each day to enjoy playing with their two little sons, and almost as soon as Marie Therese had finished nursing Philippe, she told Emile that she was pregnant again. As her little waist expanded, they joked that this would be the daughter they both wanted, and indeed it was. Their daughter Christina was born, more easily even than Philippe; and she, like Pierre, soon showed the dark hair, and dark eyes of their father, and both parents were sure she would grow into a real French Creole beauty, with fair skin, dark eyes, and dark hair. And two years after Christina's birth, Emilie Marie was born, red-headed, and feisty from her first breath.

Several years passed, with Emile continuing to see his Nanette fairly regularly, but he avoided all contact with Nana, until one day Washington returned from delivering money to the Felicity Street house, and he knocked respectfully at the family parlor. From his eyes, Emile realized that perhaps this was a message he should step into the hall to receive alone, rather than simply have Washington come into the family room where he and Marie Therese were playing with their children. So he slipped out into the hall.

"Massa, dere's been some kinda serious trouble at yuhr house in de city, an' Madame de Lis, she asks if you could come in,... maybe tomorrow," Washington reported, nervously turning his hat round and round in his hands.

"Do you know what the problem is?" Emile asked.

"No, Sir, she dinna tell me 'xactly what, but from her look, I 'spect it be serious," came the answer.

"All right, will you get the carriage ready, and take me into the city tomorrow? We can leave about ten o'clock, after I meet with José Garcia, about plantation business."

"Yes, Sir. I git ebrythin' ready forh ten."

The next morning, when they arrived at Felicity Street, Madame de Lis let Emile in. She shook her head, and gave him a long, sober look.

"She be upstairs. And dis time it be real bad, but she'll tell yuh. *She wanted* me te send forh yuh dis time. Massa Emile, you be de only one who kin reach her. She eben turn herself away from me, her verra own mama.... An' she neveh, eveh dun dat beforh."

Emile slowly climbed the stairs. He knocked on the side of the door frame, and receiving no answer, he walked into the bedroom. Nana was on the bed, curled up tight, and he could hear her sobs.

He walked over to the bed, sat down beside her, and began to gently stroke the slender back which was turned to him.

"What is it, chérie? Can you tell me, and can I do anything to help? You know I'm always ready to help you, whenever you need it,... that I will always love you, Nana...." He leaned over and kissed the nape of her neck, his fingers caressing her long, dark locks.

"He's gone, Emile, gone, and he only just got to know what love can be,..." she sobbed.

"Gone?" he asked, wondering what could have happened, and between sobs, she told him.

"Marcel, André, and Armand were coming home late two nights ago, after playing with the Opéra Orchestra.... Some men attacked them in the dark.... Marcel got away, but they hurt André and Armand, and dragged them off.... Marcel watched, and he saw them taken aboard a ship, the *Phantom*. Marcel brought the police there very early the next morning, but the ship was already pulling out. They were too late,... there was nothing they could do.... Once that ship untied, police jurisdiction over it ended. They clearly saw André and Armand being made to work on deck, and when the ship started to move downriver, Armand dove into the river. André did too.... Their heads only came up once, and then nobody saw them again. Marcel told us that the police would try to hold the ship when it stopped at Pilot Town, but Armand, and André,... nobody's seen them since. They're gone, I just know it!

"He drowned trying to get back here, I'm sure of it. Maybe he thought he would never be able to return, that he'd be made to work on ships for the rest of his life. So he took the only chance left to him, to turn to the river, and hope he could make it to shore. Emile, that man only just learned about love,... he told me he never had a woman before he married me.... And now I'm sure the river took him. He'll never make it back alive. Oh Lord, why did he have to die so soon?"

Although Emile knew that very few who fell prey to the currents of the Mississippi got out alive, he still hoped to comfort Nana. There was at least a grain of hope....

"Perhaps Armand did manage to make the shore, and will be turning up here any day," he said, continuing to stroke Nana's long hair.

"I'll pray that's true," she said. "Perhaps God will grant me a miracle this time...."

"We will all pray for that," Emile answered. "Do you want me to check along the river and see if anyone saw one or two men reach shore?"

"Yes, please, Emile, and if you hear or see anything, will you come and tell me?"

"Of course, if I learn anything, I'll come tell you right away. If not, I will pay some men, dockworkers and sailors in port, to keep watch, and report to my factor, then I will bring you whatever news there is. Keep calm, chérie, perhaps he will return. We will all remember both of them in our prayers."

Emile took Nana's hand and kissed it. "I'd like to stay and try to comfort you, but I think it would be best if I go and make inquiries along the river. It may take a day or two before I can bring you any news, but in the meantime, perhaps Armand will walk up the steps of this house, and back to you."

At the bottom of the stairs, Mama de Lis met him, twisting a dishcloth in her hands.

"Do yuh think dere be any hope?" she sadly asked.

"Not much really, but until bodies are found, one can always go on hoping, and perhaps for now, that's best. I'm going to pay some dockworkers and sailors to bring any news to my factor, and then I will come and share the news with you. I'm also going to hire some men to check along the river banks. I'll be back in a few days."

"Thank yuh, Massa Emile. Yuh always such a good, kind man."

As Emile walked to his carriage, he wondered how it would all turn out. He knew there was almost no hope of Armand surviving the river and returning alive, but as long as no body emerged, perhaps the delay could help Nana adjust, and let her hopes down slowly.

If Armand didn't return, would she allow him back into her life, he wondered. He knew he still loved her, and wanted to protect her and care for her, and for his Nanette. He knew it was much too soon to present any such ideas to Nana, but perhaps some day....

He spent liberally along the levée and docks, giving out his factor's address to all those to whom he gave money. And then he hired a few to search along both banks of the river. He hoped no bodies would be found. That would be much easier on Nana, than another burial so soon after the loss of their baby son. Finally he ordered Washington to take him home. He had done all he could do.

As the carriage turned out of the oak alley and headed towards the Big House, he could see Marie Therese seated on the porch swing, with several little figures beside her, and their littlest daughter, Emilie in her lap. Mammy appeared in the doorway, and hustled the children in for their supper, taking Emilie in her arms, and Marie Therese came to meet him with an embrace and kiss.

"Did it turn out to be serious?" she asked, anxiety etching lines in her forehead as she looked up at him.

"Yes, very. It's likely that my friend Armand is dead. He and a few others were headed home night before last, after playing in the French Opéra Orchestra, when some roughs beat them up, and hauled André and Armand off. Marcel escaped, and watched what happened. It seems the two of them were knocked unconscious, and impressed aboard a ship in the harbor. The next morning Marcel brought the police to the docks, but the ship was already turning in the channel, to head to the Gulf. They saw Armand and André put to work on deck, but the ship was already out of the jurisdiction of the city police. Armand must have realized that, and probably thought he would never see New Orleans again, so he dove overboard. André followed him. Their heads came up once, but after that no one saw either of them. I'm afraid they didn't survive the current, but I have paid men on the docks to watch, and sent some others searching along the river banks. I am praying that no bodies are found. I wonder if Nana could survive another burial so soon. While it's painful to continue to wonder if they might have survived and will show up, that's easier to bear than finding their bodies. It's terrible, and Nana is an emotional wreck. I asked if anyone found out anything, they should report to my factor, and then I will try to break the news to Nana. I did promise to come back in a week, no matter whether I have news for her or not. She is simply distraught. Someone has to help.... I hope you understand."

Marie Therese could see the tears welling up in Emile's eyes.

"Of course you must do what you can to help. It's very sad, and so soon after the loss of the baby too. God has given Nana such heavy burdens to bear. I will keep all this in my prayers, including you, Emile. It won't be easy, especially if you must tell her of Armand's death, and have to arrange for his burial. I am so sorry...." She put her arm around him, and together they went into the house.

*   *   *

The news when it came was not good. Two badly decomposed bodies had been found along the river's bank, not far from the harbor, and one was André's and the other was Armand's, as identified by their clothing, the content of their wallets and the religious metals on chains around their necks. Emile decided to go ahead and arrange for both burials, and only after that was done to bring the news to Nana.

Fellow musicians from the French Opéra Orchestra and members of Armand's own orchestra carried the two coffins into the St. Louis Cemetery, while other Orchestra members played a somber musical accompaniment. As the music played, Emile looked out over the marble city of the dead, the large ornate tombs, the stone angel statues, their wings unfurled, their hands prayerful, the obelisks pointing defiantly or prayerfully at the sky. The celebration of death, he thought, was appropriate to this city where the fevers ride in on the tides, with foreign ships, to take so many lives; where so many wives die in giving birth or from milk fever later, and so many infants do not see their third birthday, even if they manage to survive birth. He prayed silently for all of them, his own and others.... He stood isolated, behind the small group of mourners and André's family. The priest committed his body to the tomb, and then they moved on, to the burial of Armand. His elderly parents, both with canes in hand, were bowed over with the loss of their only child. They didn't ask him about Nana, or why she wasn't present. Emile assumed that they were too overcome with grief to even think of that.

When both burials were over, Emile fished in his pocket, and brought out the two chains with their St. Christopher medals, and handed one to André's mother, and then asked Armand's parents if he might save Armand's medal to give to his wife, and mutely, with tear-filled eyes, they nodded their agreement.

Emile simply told them that Nana was too distraught to come, and they seemed to understand.

Later Emile knocked, then let himself into the little house on Felicity Street. Madame came to greet him, and when she saw his expression, she took Nanette by the hand, and said softly to her,

"Sugah, let's you an' me go forh a nice walk. Massa Emile, we be back in a little while," and they went out together.

"Nana, are you upstairs? May I come up?" he called out.

"Yes, Emile," she answered, ducking her face out around the lintel, and looking at his face as he climbed the stairs. He tried to keep his expression neutral, and he stopped at the top of the stairs, and kissed her hand. She led him in, and sat down on their sofa, and he joined her. There were few moments in life which he had found as difficult and as sad as these.

"I'm afraid I don't have any good news," Emile began, and he took her hand, and placed Armand's Saint Christopher's medal in her palm.

"This is all?" she said, beginning to sob.

"Both bodies were found, and I went ahead and arranged both burials. I didn't want you to have to go through that. It's all done now, and time to pray for their souls. There is no more hope that either of them will turn up alive. Perhaps a clean break like this is better than living for ten or fifteen years always wondering if he will return. I'm very sorry, Nana, to have to bring you this news. My heart is breaking for you, chérie. Please let me do whatever I can to help. I will see that you and your mother, and our Nanette will always be provided for financially, and I will do whatever else you ask me to do, chérie. All you have to do is ask.... I think you know that."

She turned to him, and buried her head against his shoulder. "I don't seem to have any strength left,... " she said, with a little sob. "And I think I have cried almost all my tears out.... I'm not even thirty, but I think I've shed all the tears allotted to me for a whole lifetime...."

He held her in his arms, and she allowed him to stay with her that night and the next; just to hold her, he sought nothing more.

*   *   *

That summer brought the worst attack of yellow fever that New Orleans had ever known. Nearly every house bore a black wreath on its door, and all night long the death wagons moved through the streets, picking up the bodies, and the grave diggers worked day and night, unable to keep up with the deadly harvest.

A very few of Marengo's people fell sick. It seemed that gradually slaves had perhaps acquired immunity from "yellow jack." But among those stricken, was Emile's Marie Therese. Mammy and Annie took turns nursing her, and Dr. Rideau came nearly every day. Emile hardly left her bedside, except when others made him go and try to eat. What sleep he got was taken in the big armchair beside the bed.

As women usually do if they are pregnant when they fall ill with yellow fever, Marie Therese, after weeks of high fevers and long periods of unconsciousness, finally lost the baby she was carrying. It was a little son, to be called Bernard, after another early de Marigny ancestor. She nearly made it to the end of the pregnancy, and with Dr. Rideau present to help, she was delivered of a living child, whether she knew it or not. Bernard cried fretfully for a short while, and then was gone. The next morning, Emile saw to it that another little grave was dug, and this son was laid to rest. The other children were told that Bernard had gone to heaven, and was an angel, and they saw the brown earth of the grave in the de Marigny family cemetery, and picked handfuls of flowers from the garden to lay there.

As for seeing their mother, the children weren't allowed in the room, for fear they might also come down with the terrible disease, and she lingered on, near death. Finally one morning, she opened her eyes and looked at Emile over in his armchair.

"I've been on the very edge of life and death,..." she said, and Emile nodded.

"Do you want me to come back?" she asked tremulously. "I've not been sure...."

"But of course, chérie. I've prayed for that every day that you've been sick. Please, Marie Therese, I love you, and I need you...."

"Merci, Emile. I have waited a long time to hear you say that.... Oh, tu pauvre," she whispered, then feeling her stomach was very small, she asked, "Did I lose him, our little one?"

Emile nodded sadly, "Yes, he was born alive, but lived only a short time. Don't blame yourself, ma chère. Perhaps, even without your being ill, we would have lost him. Surely our little Bernard is with God, in a better place...." She nodded.

"Yes, in a better place," she repeated softly. "I had thought to join him, but if you need me...."

Her great green eyes rested on him, as if she begged him for his answer,... for another confirmation of his love.

"I do, ma chère, I do need you,... very much, and so do our children," he replied softly, and took up her hand and kissed it. "Please, you must believe me.... And forgive me. I should have told you a very long time ago that I love you."

During her illness her rosary had lain untouched on her bedside table, but now her hand reached out for it, and Emile saw her work it through her pale fingers, until she ran out of strength. He left it in her fingers as she slipped back into unconsciousness. But the next morning she was alert again, and Emile was sure that she had reached a turning point, that he wouldn't lose her after all. Her eyes were clear again; her mind seemed focused. Was hearing him finally tell her that he loved her, the key to her recovery, he wondered? And guilt overcame him. Was that long overdue acknowledgement what now reinforced in her the will to live? He recalled how swiftly his mother had been lost to the same dreadful disease. Had the increasing coldness of his parents' relationship mattered, and been a factor in her loss of the battle to live? Would a kiss on her burning forehead, or a simple confession of love by his father have made a difference, have helped her to also win her struggle against the implacable disease?

He had become more confident that Marie Therese would live, but would she ever recover, he wondered. A life spent in bed as an invalid would not be a life she would want to live, but if that was God's plan for her, he knew she would acquiesce, and live it courageously.

"The rest of our children?" she inquired.

"They are well, and anxious to visit you, when you feel strong enough," Emile answered. "Would you like to see them all briefly today, ma chère? If so I will shepherd them in, and stay to see they don't exhaust you."

"Oh yes, Emile, today, please, just a short visit. They must have grown and changed so much, and I wasn't able to see any of it,..." she said sadly.

"It's a miracle you are still with us. The death toll this year is the worst ever. Almost no one who has been taken ill with the disease has lived, but you have, my dearest, and we will take very good care of you until you have fully recovered."

"And your family in the city, Emile, have they come through this safely?" she asked.

"Yes and thank you for asking about them. They have survived, sadly a little cousin was lost, but no one else."

"Have you been able to see them?"

"I haven't wanted to leave this room, so no, I haven't been able to get to the city. I have only sent Washington to see what might be needed, and take care of it. In a week or two, as I see you getting better, I should go myself, but not yet."

Over the next years Marie Therese remained bedridden, and subject to sudden high fevers, and terrible bouts of weakness. She determinedly tried to walk but it took two people just to support her, and even then she was unable to manage more than a few steps. Gradually Emile realized that she was becoming resigned to life as an invalid.

He did return to sleeping beside her, but she remained too weak to chance any resumption of marital relations. Many times she would look over at him, and with tears in her eyes, she would say "I'm so sorry, Emile. As a wife I am not much use to you. Perhaps one day...."

But both of them, although they wouldn't confide in each other, thought the likelihood of that happening, and of further recovery improbable.

Emile's visits to the city did resume as Marie Therese returned to consciousness, and her condition more or less stabilized. During the long illness of Marie Therese, Nana had had time to adjust to Armand's death, and gradually she began to be more and more aware, and more and more thankful for the continuing care and protection Emile provided. And with time, she felt a renewal of her feelings for him. He never pushed, just let her come around to him gradually, on her own terms. She no longer seemed to blame him for the deaths of their sons, and the bitter anger she had once shown toward him, seemed to have vanished. First she became more cordial, but gradually that too changed.

"Emile, will you forgive me? I was wrong to blame you for so much," she said sadly one night, and put her hand imploringly on his shoulder. Quickly he covered her fingers with his own.

"Of course, chérie, I forgive you.... Can you forgive me too?" he asked.

"*What must I forgive you for?* You have been a constant source of support for me,... through everything, and you were unselfish enough to let me go, even to let me marry Armand," she answered, her big, dark eyes turning to meet his gaze.

"Regrettably, there have been so many times when I couldn't be here with you, when you needed me...."

"But we knew that would happen, right from the beginning, and I can't blame you for that. I know you must divide your life. Can you find time in your life again, for me?" she asked softly, afraid to look directly at him.

"Long ago I made a commitment to you, my Nana. When you asked me for your freedom so you could marry Armand, I gave it to you freely. I have always wanted the best for you; your happiness, chérie, has been my goal, no matter what that meant for me. I tried to stay away, to give you and Armand a chance, and he brought Nanette to see me, so I didn't have to come to this house. But, as I told Armand and your mother, I wanted them to call on me, whenever I could be of help. If you couldn't be mine, if you chose, as you did, another course, I have tried to be a protective shadow behind you, always,... as I promised long ago."

"But I don't want you to be a shadow anymore, Emile. I need you with me, please.... I'm not sure I am strong enough to face life without you.... Will you come to me when you can?"

He drew her to him, and held her, kissing her hands, her neck, and finally her lips.

"You are asking me back into your life? You truly mean that?"

"Yes, Emile, please come back to me," she said, almost afraid to look at his face, his eyes.

Emile picked up her hand, and kissed both sides of it, and he said, "Then I will come...."

"Carry me upstairs like you used to do,..." she murmured, raising her face to his kisses, and he did. Gently he lowered her onto the big bed, and stood back, waiting. Her arms stretched out to him, imploringly, and he could no longer hold back. Slowly they undressed each other, their hands almost reticent after so long. He drew the satin sheet up over them.

"Do you still want me?" she whispered, her dark eyes questioning.

"Ma chérie, I have always wanted you," he answered softly, and his lips and hands were gentle on her body. "I have always loved you, but I have also tried to give you whatever space you asked for."

"Take me back into your life, Emile,... take me,..." she answered softly, and their bodies met, their senses shattering in the resurgence of their love.

In the morning, Emile woke to find her eyes studying him. He took her in his arms, and once again their bodies met in the first light of a new day.

Later as they lay side by side, with full sunlight blazing into the room, she asked,

"How is Marie Therese? She has been sick, hasn't she? Is she better now?"

"Yes, I thought we would lose her to yellow fever, but miraculously she seems to be recovering now, but very slowly. She may never walk again. She seems resigned to a life as an invalid. She did ask me to tell you that she was praying for you, and for Armand's soul."

"She is kind, Emile. Tell her that her prayers have helped me through the worst, and I thank her. And I have prayed for her, and I will now pray for her full recovery. But do you think she will be willing to share you with me?"

"Yes, I believe she understands that I must honor my long relationship with you. Can the two of you agree to share me?" Emile's tone was light, but it was clear that, in spite of the tone, he was totally serious in what he asked.

Nana turned the full force of her big, dark eyes on him, and after a brief silence, she said,

"It's taken us a long time, but I think we respect each other now, Marie Therese and I. We have both been supportive of each other through the worst of times. We have learned that we cannot deny each other's existence. At first, I think we both hated each other, and sometimes even you, Emile.... But now, for your sake, Emile, we must co-exist, each in our own space, willing to share you. And I think we have at last learned to do that. If you belong to us both, then we must share you. Clearly it is a matter of the heart."

Emile leaned over, and kissed Nana tenderly, gently.

"It's never been easy, has it? But still, often I feel that I have had the very best of two worlds, two different worlds, and with two such loving women...."

Glossary

This is a brief explanation of some of the French words and expressions used in this book which are not self-explanatory:

A bientôt - So long, goodbye for now.

Beignet - A fritter, or French equivalent to a doughnut, but much better. Come to New Orleans and try some! They are fried, then liberally sprinkled with powdered sugar.

Bonne chance - Good luck.

Brioche - A breakfast roll.

Creole - There are multiple meanings to this word. Originally it was used to distinguish people of French and/or Spanish descent, born in the colony based on New Orleans, as distinct from those born in Europe.

Later in Louisiana, it has been used to distinguish individuals born here, and of French or Spanish cultural background, and language, for example, French Creoles.

It was also applied to individuals who were the children of mixed marriages, which would include individuals with ancestors who were African Negroes, and whites, and even including some Native American ancestry.

The term Creoles of color, or referred to as gens de couleur or gens de couleur libre (meaning free) appears frequently in history and literature. Some of these Creoles of color came to Louisiana from Saint Domingue (Haiti now) already freed by their owners, others were born here, of mixed parentage, such as in a plaçage relationship.

Use of the term Creole predates the arrival of immigrants from Saint Domingue, and intimate relationships across racial lines seem to have characterized New Orleans almost from its very beginning, even if marriage in such cases was illegal.

Both in the past and the present there is widespread disagreement over the proper use of this term. Some sources refer to Creoles of color as "Gumbo People," since the dish gumbo contains a variety of ingredients.

French Creoles, and those who maintain their ancestry was entirely French and/or Spanish, have asserted that the term Creole could only be correctly applied to those who claimed a pure white heritage. This view was especially prevalent right before, and after the Civil War, and there are some who still maintain that interpretation of the term today. An attempt was also made to distinguish French Creoles from others claiming to be Creoles, by the use of the term "ancienne population," but it proved too cumbersome.

Comment ça va? - How are you? How do things go?

Croissant - A crescent-shaped roll, such as a dinner roll.

Double entendre - Having a double meaning, lending to more than one interpretation, with one meaning risqué or sexual.

Fait accompli - Something already done or accomplished, and frequently irreversible.

Faubourg - A sector or subdivision of a city, such as Faubourg Marigny or Faurbourg Tremé in New Orleans, and also used to describe sectors in French cities.

Garçonnière - Bachelors' quarters, usually for older sons, and often these were in a tower or two towers separate from the main house.

Gens de couleur libre - Free people of color. Creoles of color.

Gris-gris - (sometimes also gri-gri, or gree-gree) This term refers to the items of magic, or charms, usually obtained from a voodooienne, such as the famous Marie Laveau, and were concocted of a wide variety of ingredients, insects, pieces of human or animal hair, various herbs, bone fragments, and other atrocious ingredients.

The purpose was usually to bring good fortune, or to win or keep someone's love, or to jinx or bring bad luck to someone, such as a rival in love.

Plaçage - (or in speaking of a woman in a plaçage relationship - placée) This term described the intimate relationship, in which usually a Creole woman of color became the mistress of a white man, most frequently of a French Creole.

The relationship was usually based on a verbal agreement, in which the man became known as the "protector" of his placée. He usually provided her with living quarters, furnishings, took over most if not all of her bills, and agreed to support any children produced through the relationship.

If the man was not married, he might live with the placée, or elsewhere, and if married, he would usually be a frequent visitor. The relationship could last only until the man tired of it, entered a legal marriage, or it could last for the lifetime of the individuals involved, even if the man did marry. In the past, several generations of women from a family would be expected to enter such relationships, be groomed for plaçage, and presented often to white men at the famous Quadroon Balls, or the more elitist Cordon Bleu Balls. The mother or aunts of the young woman would act as chaperones, and usually participated in the oral negotiations which set up the relationship.

Men of color were not permitted to dance with the young women at these balls, although they often performed in the orchestra, or may have served as waiters, etc.

If the "protector" was married, the two women often knew of each other, and sometimes even connived together against the man in their lives. While both the woman involved and her children might be slaves, (since the condition of the children legally followed that of the mother,) the "protector" sometimes did free them, or if they were slaves of another, might buy them and set them free. This was frequently a condition insisted on in the initial negotiations of the plaçage relationship. But many of the women, like Nana, were free Creoles of color.

The male offspring of these relationships were often financially assisted by the father who provided money for training for a profession, and sometimes even for stays in France, where there was considerably more tolerance towards matters of race and color. Some even remained in France, taking French wives. In Louisiana the marriage of a Creole of color and a white was illegal until quite recently, even if the appearance of the Creole of color was entirely white. Some, especially males who could pass as white (passé blanc) left the state, and broke off their family ties, entering the white population in other cities and states. Birth certificates issued by the state of Louisiana, until fairly recently, identified an individual by race, thus making it legally impossible for individuals to marry across racial lines.

Some recent sources point out that not only was plaçage a way that a woman of color could gain some degree of financial security for herself and her offspring, but that plaçage was almost necessary, since the demographics from the earliest days of New Orleans, show that white men greatly outnumbered white women, and at first, there may have been a distinct prejudice about marrying the women sent out from France, since many of them had been prostitutes, or "inmates of asylums and houses of correction," and were described by men as "ugly, ignorant, irascible, and promiscuous." *

Recently some doubt has also been cast on the so-called "casket girls" who were thought to have come from more respectable backgrounds, since there is little if any historical documentation about these girls, and the Ursuline nuns, who were thought to have chaperoned them until their marriages were arranged, have denied "having had anything to do with such girls."[**]

Later demographic figures show that white males continued to outnumber white females, and colored females continued to greatly outnumber colored males, so it becomes easy to understand why plaçage relationships developed. There were simply not enough white women, or Creole men to go around.

Parrain - Godfather. A godmother is called a marraine.

S'il vous plaît - If you please.

Tignon - A scarf or piece of material wound around the head turban-style. The tignon was required by law for Creole women of color, in place of hats. It was intended to set them apart from white ladies, and was considered demeaning. In an effort to make them more distinctive and attractive, bright colored materials were used, and often gold pins or chains, and even gems were placed on such tignons. Their arrangement could also be quite distinctive, as was true of the tignons worn by the voodooienne Marie Laveau, whose tignons often were arranged to rise up into four to seven points.

[*] Dormon, James H. "Louisiana's 'Creoles of Color': Ethnicity, Marginality, and Identity,"
    Social Science Quarterly 73, No. 3, 1992. Pp. 615-623.

[**] Rankin, David C. "The Forgotten People: Free People of Color in New Orleans, 1850-1870."
    Dissertation, University of Chicago, 1976.

Gehman, Mary. "Women and New Orleans." New Orleans, La., Margaret Media, 1988.

About the Author

Mary Culver began writing short stories and poetry as a child, and continued on during high school, adding newspaper articles on a variety of subjects, first as a contributing reporter, then as the editor of the school paper.

Her intention, on entering Bryn Mawr College was to enroll in a major in English emphasizing creative writing, but she drifted into Russian Language and Literature, and Political Science, getting a degree in the combined major at the University of Michigan. She continued on, getting an M.A. in Russian Studies and Political Science, and took the equivalent of another degree in Journalism.

In 1956 she married Professor Andrei A. Lobanov-Rostovsky, then Chairman of the Russian Studies Program at Michigan, and continued on with her work in Journalism, and Russian Studies, with the idea of writing articles jointly with her husband on Russian affairs, and possibly writing a book together.

With the birth of their two children, she put aside her academic career, although she continued to write, especially children's stories, poetry and an as yet unpublished historical novel set in the Middle Ages.

In 1969 she married Captain William R. Culver, and gained three more stepchildren, daughters of her husband. They moved to Louisiana, and Mary continued her teaching and her education, getting a M.Ed. from Tulane University in education and psychology.

Her teaching career spans the period from 1954-2005, and includes teaching both on the college level and the high school level, and in such subjects as Russian language, Russian history, American Government, World History, Contemporary Issues, and Psychology.

Upon retiring in the spring of 2005, after more than fifty years of teaching, she has returned to her first love - writing, and is presently completing a series of historical novels dealing with a French Creole family in the period from the1840's thru the 1890's. Hurricane Katrina led her to want to commemorate New Orleans, and assist in its recovery, so her historical novels are entitled "Before the Storm," "Caught in the Storm," "End of the Storm, and the Journey Home," "Recovery," and "Prodigal from Marengo." Her intent was to compare the impact of the Civil War on a family to that of Katrina, and to dedicate the series to New Orleans now, and its recovery. A first historical romance, preceding the historical series, is this book, "Matters of the Heart - A Creole Love Story." For readers who wish to follow the characters introduced in this book, their stories do continue on in the additional books of the series.

In addition to her writing, Mary is a devotee of Siamese cats, having shared her home with many over the years. She is also a lover of classical music, ornithology, and is an avid reader.